Frank Coates was born in Melbourne and for many years worked as a telecommunications engineer in Australia and overseas. In 1989 he was appointed as UN technical specialist in Nairobi, Kenya. For nearly four years he travelled extensively throughout Africa, during which time he met and married a Tanzanian woman of the Nyamwezi tribe. He also began research into the political and cultural history of East Africa which was to form the setting for *Tears of the Maasai*, his first novel. Frank is now divorced and currently lives in Sydney.

TEARS
OF THE
MAASAI

FRANK COATES

HarperCollins*Publishers*

HarperCollins

First published in Australia in 2004
by HarperCollins*Publishers* Pty Limited
ABN 36 009 913 517
A member of the HarperCollins*Publishers* (Australia) Pty Limited Group
www.harpercollins.com.au

HarperCollins*Publishers*
25 Ryde Road, Pymble, Sydney, NSW 2073, Australia
31 View Road, Glenfield, Auckland 10, New Zealand
77–85 Fulham Palace Road, London, W6 8JB, United Kingdom
2 Bloor Street East, 20th floor, Toronto, Ontario M4W 1A8, Canada
10 East 53rd Street, New York NY 10022, USA

National Library of Australia Cataloguing-in-Publication data:

Coates, Frank.
   Tears of the Maasai.
   ISBN 0 7322 7920 8.
   1. Maasai (African people) – Kenya – Fiction. I. Title.
A823.4

Cover and internal design by Gayna Murphy, HarperCollins Design Studio
Cover image: Getty
Author photograph by Stephen Oxenbury
Maps and genealogy chart by Margaret Hastie, Ikon Graphics
Typeset in Sabon 11/14 by HarperCollins Design Studio
Printed and bound in Australia by Griffin Press on 70gsm Bulky Book Ivory

5 4 3 2 1   04 05 06 07

In memory of Bernd Torzewski —
a man of Africa

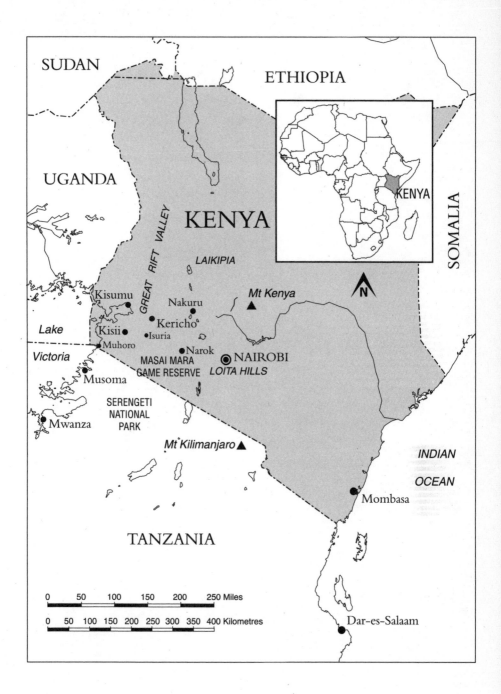

SUDAN

ETHIOPIA

UGANDA

KENYA

GREAT RIFT VALLEY

LAIKIPIA

Mt Kenya ▲

N

SOMALIA

Kisumu

Nakuru

Kericho

Kisii ● Isuria

Lake

Muhoro

Narok

◉ NAIROBI

Victoria

MASAI MARA
GAME RESERVE   LOITA HILLS

Musoma

SERENGETI
NATIONAL
PARK

● Mwanza

Mt Kilimanjaro ▲

INDIAN

OCEAN

● Mombasa

TANZANIA

● Dar-es-Salaam

| 0 | 50 | 100 | 150 | 200 | 250 Miles |

| 0 | 50 | 100 | 150 | 200 | 250 | 300 | 350 | 400 Kilometres |

KENYA

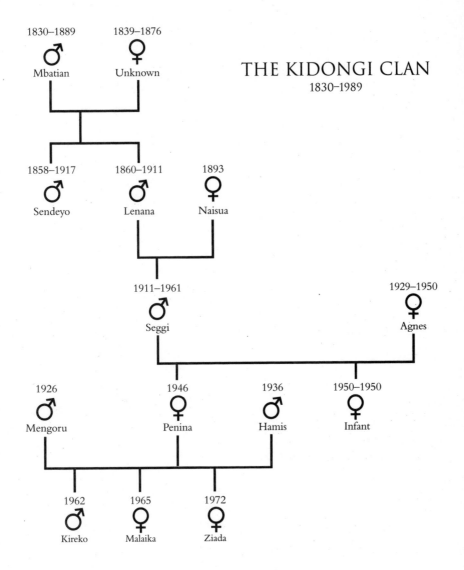

THE KIDONGI CLAN
1830–1989

PROLOGUE

They came from the north, from the basin of the Nile River from which they took their name: Nilotes. Tall. Ebony black. They were a people of great resilience; the men as tough as a leather thong. The women, elegant and graceful. Beautiful.

They had tilled the soils of their valley for three millennia. Food was plentiful and the people were happy. For all of this time life was good, so good they needed little governance. When disagreement loomed, the elders would talk.

In Eden there was no sin.

On the lower reaches of the basin, where the mighty river's black soil was replenished by her seasonal floods, the bounty continued year upon year, decade after decade. But elsewhere, on the slopes and the plateau above the basin, there were many who did not flourish. The land began to lose its strength. It teased them by repaying years of drought-ridden hard work with a single year of plenty. It cheated the people, forcing them to turn to the sheep and goats that ever more became their salvation in the bad seasons.

Over generations the people of the plateau grew increasingly restless. The animals demanded more and more pasture as the land failed to nourish them. It was these people, the pastoral Nilotes, who heeded the territorial imperative and, more than a thousand years ago, began to drift southward.

They came for the land. But others had arrived before them — people from east of the Congo whom they met near the great lake, later called Victoria. These Bantu people were organised and aggressive. They supported great armies on the wealth of their agriculture. The pastoral people had few skills in the art of war and were no match for the power of the Bantu. It would be several centuries before their dead were avenged.

Against the shield of Bantu power, the Nilotes's southward thrust was deflected into the path of another migration. The meeting of these tribes would soon shake the continent and shape the next ten centuries of Africa's history.

The Ethiopian highlands to the east of the Nile were the traditional home of the Cushites, people with brown skin, straight noses and high cheekbones — features more of the Mediterranean than of Africa. Why they moved to the moist forests of East Africa, leaving their grand terraced farmlands behind, is unknown. When the Nilotes drifted in from the west, they engulfed their fine-featured neighbours, not by war but by marriage.

The stories from these ancient times tell of the first child born to the first marriage. His name was Maasinta and he grew into a fine young man. Tall like his father, the Nilote, with long strong muscles, as tight as bowstrings on his slender frame, but with the elegant fine-boned face and the gentle, slightly almond-shaped eyes of his Cushite mother. His Maa language and his shining black skin were of the Nile, as was his demeanour. Some would see it as aloof, even arrogant, but it was not so. Maasinta's bearing reflected the pride he felt in being the son of such fine parents.

One day, when Maasinta was searching for food, a voice like thunder came to him from the cloudless sky.

'Maasinta!' It was the voice of the beginner of the earth, the *ngai*, the god of his Cushite family. 'You must make a large enclosure between the holy mountain of Ol Doinyo Sabak and the silver peaks of Kilima N'jaro. Build a house at its centre and await my word.'

Maasinta went and did as he was told and waited for *Ngai*'s further instructions.

When *Ngai* returned he said to Maasinta: 'Tomorrow, very early in the morning, I want you to go and stand by your house, for I will give you a gift called cattle. The animals are strange but have no fear. Above all, you must be silent until you have received all the cattle you want.'

Very early next morning, Maasinta did as he was commanded. Soon he heard the sound of thunder and God released a long leather thong from heaven to earth. Cattle descended down this thong into the enclosure. The surface of the earth shook so vigorously that Maasinta's house almost fell over. He was gripped with fear, but did not make any movement or sound. But while the cattle were still descending, the Dorobo, who was a neighbour of Maasinta, woke from his sleep. Upon seeing the countless cattle coming down the thong, he cried, 'Ai! Ai! Ai!'

On hearing this, God took back the thong and the cattle stopped descending. God said to Maasinta, thinking he was the one who had cried out, 'So these cattle are sufficient? Very well, that is all you will receive. Treat them well, as they are your life. Cherish them as I do you, for they are the last gift you will receive from me.'

This is how the Maasai came to own all the cattle on the earth. It is also the reason the Maasai despise the Dorobo. For Maasinta was angry with his neighbour for causing *Ngai*'s gift to be cut short. He cursed him, saying, 'Dorobo, you are the one who cut God's thong. May you remain poor as you have always been. May the milk of my cattle be poison on your lips.' To this day the Dorobo remain hunters of the forest and are never given food by the Maasai.

The cattle grew and flourished, as did the Maasai, because, as *Ngai* had promised, cattle were their strength.

From cattle the Maasai were fed, clothed and housed. Cattle were their bride price and the measure of a man's status in society. Food came from milk mixed with blood taken from the living animal. Hides were used for mattresses, sandals, utilities and accessories. The dung was a major building material. Even the cattle's urine could be used for medicine and cleaning. In the mother-tongue, over a hundred Maa words were available to describe the beasts.

As Maasinta's descendants ventured into the Great Rift Valley, the first print of a white foot appeared in the sands on the island of Mombasa. By then the Maasai's cattle had spread across the savannah in great numbers. The rumours of that strange pale tribe at the furthest edges of their grazing land concerned them not at all.

The Maasai feared no one for they had developed a deadly war machine in the centuries since their earlier expulsion by the fierce Bantu people. A tight formation of warriors, or phalanx, formed a mobile fortress, ideally suited to the savannah. And Maasai weaponry — a short sword and long- shafted spear — ensured its protection so long as the formation remained intact.

The Maasai custom of dividing the generations into age-sets was inherited from Maasinta's Cushite mother. It provided the vital glue that held the phalanx together during attack. Men within an age-set were brothers in every way but blood. The age-sets progressed from boyhood to warriorhood to elderhood together. Each step tightened the bond that was key to the success of the military technique. And it was the military machine that had enabled the Maasai to expand the land needed for their beloved cattle.

The Maasai were reluctant to change the old ways. The customs from Maasinta's times had seen them grow in strength and wealth so they found no need for formal leadership. The warriors, or *moran*, had their age-set leaders to coordinate military campaigns. The elders provided wisdom and moral leadership, whilst a few exceptional individuals, the *laibon*, provided spiritual guidance.

One such gifted individual was Mbatian ole Supet. His reputation as a medicine man and prophet earned him the title of the Great *Laibon*. He lived at the dawn of the white man's entry into central Africa, at a time when the Maasai were perhaps at the peak of their formidable strength.

But Mbatian was tormented by terrible visions. He called the Maasai elders together and said to them, 'I am about to die. I see a large black rhino cutting a line across the land. There are pink men on his back. I see the end of my children and of the land. Do not move from your land, for if you do you will die of

4

a terrible unknown disease, your cattle will perish, you will fight with a powerful enemy and you will be beaten.'

If this brief history conveys an impression of a sweeping migration, coming like a storm, wild and full of quick destruction and plunder, it has misled. The Maasai's progress was a drift rather than a drive. They trod softly rather than thundered. But the demands of their cattle were paramount and all who resisted perished. The destruction of their enemies was total; their progress like the flow of molten rock from an ancient volcano: slow, deadly, irresistible. They pushed all before them until the Maasai territory stretched from the Indian Ocean to the great lakes, from the snows of Kilimanjaro to the edges of the Sudanese wastelands.

The Great *Laibon* was succeeded by his son, Lenana, who promised his people that by giving some of their best land to the white man, they would appease the invaders and avoid further tragedy.

He was wrong.

PART 1

THE BLACK RHINO

CHAPTER 1

PEABODY'S GUIDE TO EAST AFRICA (5ᵀᴴ ED):
The tourist in East Africa is encouraged to explore its rich array of tribal cultures, many of which have interesting oral histories.

The Maasai for instance, have a story of an ancestor called Mbatian, the Great Laibon, who dreamed of a black rhino and strange, dangerous men who rode upon its back.

In 1896, seven years after Mbatian's death, the black rhino came. It was filled with fire, panting and bellowing plumes of smoke as it rolled on iron rails into the heart of Maasailand. It carried the new enemy as predicted. And in its wake came the rinderpest, which decimated the Maasai herds, and the smallpox, which inflicted a most horrible death on every second man, woman and child.

1892

The forest at the foot of the mountain brooded. As Lenana entered its shaded mansion, green walls closed around him. The enveloping tree canopy concealed the bright morning sky and he felt his mood deepen as the jungle darkened. His thin leather sandals pressed soundless footprints on the moss-covered ground. His path climbed slowly, passing first beneath the heavy understorey of bamboo and then between massive sycamores and fig trees. Before long his knees were aching and his breath came in painful bursts. He rested a moment and the silence of the forest enveloped him like a cloak. Not a wind-rustle or a bird disturbed the vine-covered branches above him.

Climbing on, he was soon amid the broken rock formations at the brow of the mountain and then at the rocky summit with its tussock grasses and dwarf lobelias.

The forest's dark mood had followed him from its verdant footings to the rocky crown. It was fitting, for Lenana was greatly troubled and Donyo Lumuya, the mountain birthplace of his ancestor, knew it and brooded with him.

He found the sweep of petrified lava that formed a shallow cave and sat cross-legged at its mouth. The sun rose behind the ancient mountain, striking long shadows across the Great Rift Valley that sprawled before him to the west.

His mind drifted into that quiet place where his dreams and his magic dwelt. He hummed his welcoming song to Ol-le-Mweiya, the First One. Mweiya would know if he had truly lost his power. He would know why he, Lenana, had failed to see the signs of the coming deaths. And why so many of his people had died, and continued to die. He rubbed his fingers together to warm them and ease the ache. Mweiya would know.

Even little Interekai, his second-born girl-child of his third wife, was ill and he, the *laibon*, was again helpless. *Why?*

The friendly mist gathered in his mind as he softly hummed his song. With bony elbows resting on bony knees, his head slowly slumped forward to fall lightly on his folded arms. The mist coloured to warm green then deepened to orange, blue and violet — the sign that a spirit approached. But his dream colours disappeared. Lenana frowned, willing the colours of the sun to return and bring Mweiya as always. But the mist remained a shifting cold grey.

A figure suddenly emerged. It was not Mweiya, but yet was familiar.

'Sendeyo!' Lenana said.

'Brother. You are surprised to see me?'

'How did you come here, Sendeyo? I did not summon you. Now be gone. I am awaiting Mweiya.'

'But it was he who sent me to you, brother.'

'Lies, as always. And now you would shame yourself before the First One.'

'Not so, brother. You want answers to the misfortunes of your people, do you not? I have been sent because I have what you seek.'

Lenana tried to read his brother's eyes. 'Speak then.'

Sendeyo smiled, enjoying his moment. 'Brother, the pestilence and your people's suffering come from your own *enkang*, your own village.' He paused to savour the bewilderment on his brother's face. 'It was your deeds that brought it upon your family and your people.'

When Lenana made no response he continued. 'When you stole succession by your trickery —'

'Our father Mbatian gave me the stones!'

'I am the older son. The succession was mine by right.' Sendeyo's image quivered in the flickering light.

'But I am the *laibon*,' Lenana insisted with a wry smile.

'It was your trickery that won you your succession.'

'And you are a thief, Sendeyo! You stole Mbatian's sacred stones to practise black magic. For that crime I banished you.'

'Yes, you banished me and my clan ... No matter, I have the stones and I have learned how to use their powers.' His laughter was an evil sound echoing in the swirling mists of Lenana's vision. 'You are witness to my success with their magic, brother.'

'What do you mean?'

'This death that takes your loved ones and defies your miserable efforts to defeat it was spawned in your *enkang*. Spawned by your trickery!' The mist billowed around Sendeyo in great clouds. 'I am the instrument of your punishment. I have placed this curse upon you and your clan. Hah! If you are truly the *laibon* why can you not see the thorn of your torment and pluck it out?' Sendeyo laughed again.

Lenana clenched and unclenched his aching fingers. 'Enough of your vile prattle. If you have come to gloat at our suffering, enjoy it and be gone. Leave me in peace.'

'No, brother, I have come not to gloat but to inform. Since you are unable to find the cause of this suffering, I have come to inform you.'

'Why?'

'Ah, because it will please me for you to know.'

'Tell me then,' Lenana hissed through tight lips.

'Oh come, Lenana. You must know it. Think. Or has your feeble mind deserted you? Here, I will help you. Answer me this: when did your people first suffer the illness of the fever, the sores that leak water and pus?'

The mist revealed a vision of his pitiful people, their bloated bodies lying in their own filth. The terrible disease came out of the southern savannah, carrying a swift but ignominious death.

'And when did the cattle plague begin? You must remember the deaths of your own cattle, my brother.'

Lenana did remember. The herds had drowned in their own mucus. Their bodies had blackened the land from horizon to horizon. Famine had followed. Then warfare between the clans over the few remaining cattle.

It was too much for Lenana. He couldn't think. When was it? The drought had followed the disease. But when did it start? Was it during the dry season after his father's death? Yes! That was it. The year that little Interekai had her naming ceremony.

'That was the beginning. Now, before I reveal it, know this: you have paid dearly for your trickery but there is more to pay.' Sendeyo's image wavered in the mist. 'My curse will not just follow you to your grave, it will haunt all your clan. All the Aiser will suffer. This is your fate, brother, and the destiny of all the Aiser *laibons* that succeed you.'

Sendeyo began to chant:

'Oh, you *laibon* of the Aiser,
Oh, you *laibon* of the Aiser,
Enjoy your sons as they come,
Enjoy your sons while you can.
But hearken on the birth of a daughter.
Let the first of your daughters be your warning,
For the second girl-child will unleash the demon,

The demon of death in your *enkang*.
The second-born daughter unleashes the demon,
The demon of death in your *enkang*,
And many Maasai will die I forewarn.
Oh, many, many Maasai will die.'

Sendeyo's image began to melt away. 'I go now, so curse me if you wish, Lenana. You can do no worse than what has already been done to me.'

'There is no need to curse you, Sendeyo, for the same evil that drove you to this slaughter is stalking you like a wounded lion. And it will kill you just as surely.'

The cold mist slowly lightened to warmer pinks and yellows and the image of Lenana's younger daughter replaced Sendeyo. She looked at her father with sad, sunken eyes.

'Interekai! My daughter, what brings you here?' He had been close to his second daughter ever since her difficult birth. He had tried to strengthen her, but she remained frail. 'Come to me, little one.'

She raised her tiny hand to him. The mist's colour was fading. Her image dissolved and the cold grey returned.

Lenana awoke with a start. He painfully unfolded his long thin legs and struggled to his feet. *I must go to the* enkang! He hurried to the path.

Oh, you laibon *of the Aiser* ...

Sendeyo's words hounded him as he plunged through the tall forest.

Let the first of your daughters be your warning ...

He pushed through the rough bamboo stands. They slashed at him, tore and scratched his body.

For the second girl-child will unleash the demon ...

Now clear of the forest he ran through the tall grass. The *enkang* with its lazy smoke and sleepy goats was in sight. Heavy gasps burst from his chest.

The demon of death in your enkang ...

Through the pounding that filled his head a terrible sound came faint and forlorn across the dry, brittle grass. Maybe it was a trick of the wind. He held his rasping breath to hear it again. Nothing. He hurried on. Between gasps he kept his ears alert for its return. All quiet.

He held a long breath, listened, then exhaled with a rush. It was there, then gone again.

And many Maasai will die, I forewarn ...

On the low rise above the *enkang* he filled his chest with the warm smell of good pasture. He held it inside until the sound came again. It chilled the dry air. He knew this sound. He knew what waited for him at the *enkang*.

A long wailing lament drifted from the hut where a woman emerged carrying a small body. Hands flapped on dangling brown arms. Thin legs swung limply as the sobbing woman pressed her face to the dead child's breast. Two women followed, their voices rising in a discordant dirge as others also came to the woman. His third wife. A growing chorus of grief filled the valley.

Lenana raised his face to the sky and the wind. He prayed for forgiveness, but knew he would take the agony of guilt to his grave. Knew the self-pity that now washed over him would disgust him when his grief was finally resolved. Tears rolled down his cheeks. His cry, like that of a wounded beast, rose into the clear blue sky of *Ngai*'s heaven.

Oh, many, many Maasai will die.

CHAPTER 2

PEABODY'S GUIDE TO EAST AFRICA (5TH ED):
The energetic tourist in Kenya might like to join a Hash House Harriers run to break the monotony of shopping and safaris.

Often described as 'the drinking club with a running problem', the Hash meets late every Monday afternoon. Two 'hares' set a paper trail to guide the pack along a run of five or so miles.

'You're the new guy.'

'Yeah.'

'Soil and stuff, right? I'm Hoffman. Telecommunications. They call me Bear.' He was big. Although his shirt was clean and pressed, he looked untidy. It was as if his body had rejected the clothing.

'G'day. Jack Morgan. Rural Development.' They shook hands.

'You've been here, what ... two weeks?'

'About that.'

'They've given you a shit office, man. That sun's gonna fry your ass around four every day.'

'It'll do.'

'At least you've got a view.' The big man stepped to the window and looked into the distance. 'Ngong Hills.'

Jack didn't respond. He'd often sat in silent contemplation of those brooding grey forms on the western horizon.

'Where you from?' Bear returned to the other side of Jack's desk and flopped into the high-backed vinyl chair.

Jack stood and took a step to his filing cabinet, where he slipped in a pile of papers and removed another. 'Sydney,' he said when he had returned to his seat.

'An Aussie? Good.'

Jack looked up from his papers but the American did not elaborate.

'What they gonna have you doin' here, Jack?' He leaned back, pulled a leg over his knee and, with his fingers intertwined, placed his hands purposefully on top of his balding head.

'Don't know yet.'

'No?' Bear raised his eyebrows and pushed his brow forward. The collision of wrinkles made deep furrows on his forehead.

'Not exactly.'

Bear waited.

The silence intensified. Jack relented. 'They said rural aid, Kenya and Tanzania.'

'Not bad.' He nodded his approval. 'Not bad. Just keep away from those Somalis. A real bunch of bad-asses.'

Jack continued to look busy, rearranging files on his desk.

'I'm telecommunications.'

'So you said.' He slipped a file into his desk drawer then opened another.

'Yep,' Bear said, nodding. 'Telecommunications. Mostly radio. You know, rural VHF. A bit of HF. Satellite's starting to come into places like Zimbabwe. But mainly spectrum management and administration. I've got me a project in Tanzania that . . .'

Jack didn't understand a thing he said, but nodded now and then. It gave him time to compose himself. He was uncomfortable with people prying into his life, especially now. But Bear Hoffman was incorrigible. When he showed no sign of letting up, Jack interrupted. 'I give up!' he said, slamming his pencil on the desk.

'Huh?'

'I can't understand a bloody word you're saying. Then again, who cares? I'm busy and all this is probably none of my business, so ...'

'Hasn't Bhatra told you?' Bear picked up a letter opener and began to clean his fingernails. 'I'm gonna be working with you on one of his so-called integrated development projects. The latest thing. According to him.'

'Is that so?' D K L Bhatra was Jack's boss. Their boss. Head of the Kenyan office of the United Nations Integrated Development Programme. Bhatra had met Jack when he arrived at Nairobi airport, jetlagged and hungover. A career public servant was Jack's impression. They had hardly spoken since. 'In that case, you'd better cut the bullshit and tell me what you really do.'

'Well, what I really do is get the basic network infrastructure to the village level for rural development work.'

Jack frowned at him. 'Make it easy for me, will you?'

'Telephones. Faxes. Simple stuff. I get in, get it done. So you guys, the health guys and everybody, can get it all on.'

'Hmmm. Get in and get it done, eh?'

'That's it. I'm your man.'

Jack picked up his pencil again and studied the man sitting opposite. He had a square head with wispy greying hair whose loose ends tended to take flight at the faintest motion. There was hardly a gap between the granite-like head and the shoulders that filled the crumpled shirt. On his thick forearms a reddish mat did not quite conceal a mass of freckles. His casual, frank conversation was a refreshing contrast to the general run of UN hacks Jack had met in the last few days. They all seemed to be clones of Bhatra, not one of which, he suspected, would ever admit to a mistake. They had endless reasons why things could not be done. That's been tried before. Didn't work. Bureaucrats. At least this 'Bear' had some enthusiasm. He looked at the ratty strip of beard running from ear to ear along the man's chin; it made him look as if he was wearing a World War II German helmet and chin strap.

'So is it Grizzly Bear or Polar Bear, or what?'

'Man, I can be grizzly and I can be cool. I can be any of them guys, depending on my mood. The black babes like me best when I'm Honey Bear.'

Jack smiled in spite of himself. 'Now I know you're bullshitting me.'

'Hah!' Bear laughed and slapped his knee. 'Aussie, I guess you're okay.' He continued to chuckle. 'Family with you?'

'Don't give up, do you?'

Bear put on a pained expression, shrugged and raised his palms upwards. 'Hey! We're all brothers in the UN, aren't we?'

Jack shook his head in disbelief. It was impossible to offend him.

'You're single,' Bear continued. 'Could pick it a mile off. Single UN man number five — that's you. Forget the other single guys. Bunch of assholes. So tell me, Jack, what do you do for activities?'

'Activities?'

'You know, sports an' stuff.'

'Sport? Who can play sport in this climate?'

'Been getting out after the office? A bar? Anything?'

'No.'

'You run?'

'You mean jogging? You're kidding.'

'We gotta get you out and about. Why don't you come to the Hash tonight?'

'What's the Hash?'

'The Hash House Harriers. It's a drinking club with a running problem. You do drink, don't you?'

'Yeah.'

'You got sneakers?'

'Yeah, but —'

'Great. Five o'clock start. Cross-country run, 'bout four, five miles. Have a few beers. How about it?'

'Nah ...' Jack ran a hand along his jaw.

'C'mon. You need to get amongst it. Meet people.' He made a rolling motion with his hands. 'Get things movin'. You're in Africa, man. Get into it.'

Jack looked at him. 'Shit! Okay.'

'You'll love it!' He stood. 'Okay, gotta go. See you 'bout four-thirty. Ciao, Jack!'

Jack felt a little foolish as the big man left his office. He hadn't yet beaten the hunted feeling when people, mostly strangers or new acquaintances, asked innocuous questions about his background. He still had a way to go to overcome it. Perhaps he was expecting too much from the short time since he'd left Sydney. Leaving had been a wrench, but he'd had to do it.

'I'm flying to Africa,' he had told his family. Fleeing to Africa was their opinion. They were right. But for the wrong reasons. They couldn't understand because they didn't know. Nobody could know. Not his parents. Not Liz. Certainly not Liz.

It was fear that drove him. Fear — the ultimate force. When self-preservation was at stake, logic could be an expensive luxury. And if the fear was not reason enough, an escape from the self-loathing that hung about him like gaoler's chains was another.

His mother couldn't understand why he didn't simply face Liz and sort it out. He couldn't say it had nothing to do with Liz; it did, but not as she imagined.

His father was annoyed. Jack supposed it was because his son showed none of the discipline he had tried to instil in him almost from birth. Discipline and order were worth fighting for, he would often say. And fight his father did — with the council over repairs to the footpath, with the neighbour's dog for crapping on the nature strip. He'd fight paspalum for daring to invade his pristine quarter-acre of lawns. Plans for the future. An ordered life. These were qualities expected of a son whose father had lived through the Depression. Fought the bloody Japs in bloody New Guinea. And had scrimped and saved to get his son a decent bloody education.

'If y' know yourself and where y' wanna be,' he'd say to Jack, 'you're halfway there. It's like havin' a flamin' road map of y' life. Y' never get lost. Always get where you're goin'.'

Jack wondered about his road map. Where had it been when he really needed it? Why couldn't he see he was going off the rails back there in Honolulu? Why couldn't O'Hara have stopped it before it reached the point of madness on that last night?

JACK SLIPPED ON THE TRAIL made muddy by a hundred earlier feet, clutched at a thick vine hanging in his path and brought it down with him in a graceless slump to the grassy verge. On hands and knees he rasped for breath after desperate breath, while the edges of his vision blurred into a pink cloud. It seemed ages since he last caught sight of Bear jogging effortlessly out in front and hours since the last hold where the Hashers regrouped.

The jungle closed around him and his throat constricted as if there wasn't enough air in all of Africa to fill his lungs.

With an effort that he felt may be his last, he pulled himself to his feet, but his leg muscles refused to respond. They were rubber.

'On, on!' an encouraging female voice shouted as it jogged by. Jack moaned and forced himself forward. The girl, a slip of a thing with legs like a gazelle, ducked under a branch and was gone.

Jack plodded in her wake and stumbled into a clearing. A clearing with cars — familiar cars. He could see Bear's Land Rover. He was back at the Sigona Golf Club car park where the run had begun, about twenty kilometres out of Nairobi, high on the shoulder of the escarpment that, a few kilometres further on, plunged nearly two thousand feet into the Great Rift Valley. And there, not fifty metres away, leaning against a 44-gallon drum, beer in hand, was Bear, with barely a sign of sweat. He saluted Jack with his bottle.

Jack would have loved to salvage some dignity with a spirited finish. Even a hint of a spring in his step would be satisfying, but the best he could muster was a stumbling lurch that petered out well before he reached Bear, who had been joined by another runner.

The big man fished a Tusker from the ice. 'Here you go, buddy,' he said, shoving the dripping bottle in Jack's face. Jack slumped forward, taking his weight on his arms braced against his knees. His head hung from taut shoulders for a long moment. When he straightened, he threw his head back and filled his chest, the muscles along his ribs etched into the sweat-soaked tee-shirt. 'Whew!' he gasped.

Bear said, 'Lars, Jack. Jack, Lars,' then jabbed the beer at him again. 'Here you go.'

Jack put a hand to the Tusker, but had to dash to the edge of the car park where he dry-retched into a bush.

Lars and Bear sipped their beers in silence until Jack's heaving shoulders became still.

'Altitude,' said Bear.

Lars took a thoughtful swig. 'Yah. Altitude.'

'That's it, Jack. More big breaths, buddy,' Bear called. 'You'll be fine.'

Jack straightened slowly. Holding his midriff, he turned back to them, eyes streaming. 'Shit!' He accepted the beer and took a tentative sip, then a larger mouthful.

'The altitude'll do it every time,' said Bear, nodding wisely.

'Altitude, huh?' Jack said, blinking away tears.

'Yep. It's a killer. The city's about five and a half thousand feet. Out here in Sigona we'd be, well, let me see, I'd say, six and a half. What ya think, Lars?'

'Yah. Maybe seven thousand.'

'And you don't have to be runnin',' Bear continued. 'Last month a guy from the Swedish Embassy bought it going up Kilimanjaro.'

'German,' said Lars.

'Huh?'

'German Embassy. He wasn't a Swede.'

'Are you sure?'

'Yah, of course.'

'Wait a minute, wait a minute,' Jack said. 'Are you telling me someone actually died of climbing a mountain?'

'Not even climbing,' Bear said. 'Kilimanjaro's just an easy walk. The tourists take four days to walk up, one day to come down.'

'Except for the German,' Lars said soberly. 'He died on day three.'

'What have you organised for afters?' Bear asked Lars, finally letting the dead guy be German. 'I think Jack's about ready to party.'

Jack winced. It was an effort to lift the beer; sweat trickled into the dark stubble on his jaw and his hair stuck to his forehead in wet strands.

'We didn't organise anything out here,' Lars said.

'Not to worry, I'm kinda —'

'Too difficult,' Lars continued. 'But when all this is gone,' — he indicated the beer, cold sausages and peanuts — 'we'll go to Buff's. As usual, yah?'

'Yeah. Great.' Bear noticed Jack's raised eyebrows. 'It's in Milimani Road. Better seen than described, eh, Lars?'

'Yah.'

As evening lengthened into night, the Hashers, many now in tracksuits against the cool night air, began to disperse. The die-hards stayed on until the 44-gallon drum of beer contained only melted ice. Bear and Jack offered to help empty it and clean up, but Lars waved them away. 'Nah, me and Muni are okay. You guys get out of here. See you at Buff's.'

Bear threw the old Land Rover down the winding dark roads, playing between brake and clutch pedals. Jack tried to remain detached by keeping his mind on the lights of the city and suburbs below. Bear kept up a constant chatter, explaining that Buff's was populated by what he called 'semi-working girls', meaning those who were out for a good time and a bit of income on the side, and enthusiastic amateurs. 'Picking the difference,' he said, turning to Jack for several alarming moments as the car plummeted through a forest in total darkness, 'is a skill needing great imagination and cunning.' He slapped Jack on the thigh. 'Hah! Just stick with me, Jack, my boy.' He regained control of the vehicle in time to take a sliding right-angle turn. 'Just stick with old Bear.'

When Jack finally spotted the sign, *Buffalo Bill's Wild West Saloon and Eating House*, he allowed himself a sigh of relief. It was a few hundred metres up the narrow street before they could find a parking space. Bear handed a teenage boy a handful of coins to guard the car. 'It's an insurance policy,' he explained. 'I give them some coins and they don't break off my mirrors.'

Halfway down the hill towards the hotel, Jack realised he had left his wallet in the car. 'Don't worry about it,' Bear said. 'I'll spot you for tonight.'

Music wafted up Milimani Road, becoming louder as they approached the pub. After Bear's description, it surprised Jack to find the place was set in a well-tended garden. Floodlights illuminated the trees and surrounds. It was strangely familiar.

They walked through the garden gate and it hit him. This was Honolulu again! The paved patio. The stark, banded trunks of palm trees. The hibiscus bushes. He stopped at the stone steps leading to the terrace.

'What's up?' Bear was already on the patio.

Jack felt cold. Even the music was the same. Thumping guitars, harsh driving lyrics. 'She Drives Me Crazy'.

'Hey, Jack! You okay?'

He stared at Bear. What could he say? Moments passed. Bear's brow furrowed. Before he could speak again, Jack said, 'My wallet!'

'I told you, don't worry. I got it covered.'

'No. The street kids. I'd better get it.'

Bear shrugged and tossed him the keys. 'Whatever. I'll order the beers.'

Jack turned and hurried down the path to the reassuring anonymity of the dark street.

THE BOY THEY'D PAID TO guard the car was nowhere in sight. Jack opened the passenger side door and retrieved his wallet. This end section of the road was quiet and dimly lit. He decided to stay for a while. The panic attacks had become less frequent, but when they hit, he had to respond or risk falling apart. He wiped a hand across his brow.

Fear had stalked him with the relentless determination of a starving man-eater in the days, weeks, following his return from Honolulu. He had trouble concentrating, his every waking moment spent tracing and retracing the details of the last night on the beach in Hawaii.

23

He made no effort to rationalise his responsibility in the affair. He knew the woman had danger in her. He could have walked away at any time. But he was fascinated by her raw sexuality. The way she took the active role, the initiator, in their sexual adventures.

He was not a particularly reckless person, but on this occasion, when every molecule within him screamed a warning, he allowed himself to suspend all prudence. She drove him onward. He could have stopped. He *should* have tried to divert their rush into that last reckless moment when she trapped him into being her accomplice.

Liz was the innocent victim of his sin. He couldn't stand the thought of the pain it would cause her if she found out. He could see her now: a swish of golden shoulder-length hair; a sad smile. She knew something was wrong but thought it was in their relationship. Maybe even her fault.

'Jack, what's happened? What have I done?'

'You've done nothing, Liz, I swear it.'

'Then what?'

He didn't want to lie to her. He still cared for her. In a fashion, he still loved her. But now it was different — everything was different. 'Liz ... I'm ... I'm not ... Let me work it through. Okay?'

'Jack.' She held his eyes until he felt he couldn't bear it a moment longer. 'I want it to be like it was.'

He might have overcome the guilt by confessing all to Liz. It would have taken time to gather the courage, but he felt in his heart that she would forgive him. But that was no longer the issue. No matter how much he wanted it to be otherwise, his psyche had undergone an irreversible change. Honolulu had put a blowtorch to his Teflon coating. Beneath it was a person he didn't recognise.

His old self wanted to reach out to Liz, to console her, to beg forgiveness and return their lives to normality if possible. But for those six days in Honolulu he had experienced an intensity of emotion he had previously thought himself incapable of. He could see his life in the past — an average upbringing, suburban normality — and in the future: marrying Liz, raising a mortgage, rearing kids.

Now that could never be enough.

Living with Liz became increasingly claustrophobic. Their apartment closed in around him. Its innocence was an affront; its charm an obscenity in a world now fatally flawed. When his love for Liz went missing, a black despair took its place.

Soon it became more than he could bear. On these occasions he would quietly leave the house and take a walk down Lagoon Street to the five kilometres of sand leading to Long Reef. On the headland, with a roaring southerly whipping hair about his face, he would stare down at the surf crashing over massive sandstone boulders and dare himself to jump, while another part of him conjured visions of his bloodied body in the tangled seaweed on the rock shelf below.

Something had to be done. Anything.

The job vacancy caught his eye. It was common practice for UN positions to be circulated through all sister administrations. Africa. In all of his frantic attempts at emotional escape, he had never imagined leaving Australia. He put his name on the application and gave it no further thought.

Three weeks later, the position was his. He later learned he was the only applicant.

A month before the UN finally gave him a departure date, Jack moved out of their apartment. When Liz saw him off with the last of his belongings, she had a sad, resigned smile that didn't quite reach those honest grey eyes of hers. He'd hesitated, then lightly kissed her on the lips. Sometime later that night, as his disembodied mind hovered in the dim recesses of sleep, it had occurred to him that Liz hadn't seemed surprised. She had been expecting him to fall out of love all along.

THE HEADLIGHTS OF AN APPROACHING car lit the interior of Bear's Land Rover. Jack found himself staring at the empty panel in his wallet where Liz's photo had once been. He shoved it in his pocket and slammed the door, angry for having allowed himself to fall into spineless self-pity.

He walked briskly to Buffalo Bill's and vaulted the steps to the stone terrace. The drinking area was open to the cool night air on three sides. A stuffed and mouldy grizzly bear stood in frozen rage next to the jukebox. Coloured lanterns bobbed in the mild breeze, while a posse of equally colourful black women glided among the customers, serving or cadging drinks.

Bear and Lars were at the bar with a few other Hashers, predominantly male. Most were still wearing sweaty shorts and sneakers. Nobody in Buff's seemed to mind.

Bear pulled away from the bar and joined Jack near one of the sawn-off tree trunks that served as a table. 'Where'll you be stayin' when your stuff arrives?' he said as he handed Jack his beer.

Jack took a mouthful. 'Nairobi Hill. In the Jacaranda 'til then.'

'I'm in Westlands. Go right by you every morning. I can pick you up.'

'Well, thanks, but I've got a driver to get me around until my car arrives.'

'Ondieki?'

'Yeah, that's him.'

'Ondieki is an unreliable son of a bitch. And drives that Land Rover like it's a turtle. Man! Really pisses me off. Best I pick you up.'

An argument in Swahili erupted from the back of the bar, where four men in business shirts and a couple of girls were playing pool.

'That sounds like too much trouble. I'll be okay with Ondieki.'

'No trouble at all. Hey! We're all brothers in the UN, right?'

'If you say so.'

'Damn right!'

Lars joined them with three young women; one was a Hasher, still in her running gear. Her dark skin gleamed under the lanterns. Jack guessed all three were in their early twenties. 'Hey, guys! This is Flo,' Lars said, putting his hand on the shoulder of the girl in shorts. 'And this is Jo and Bo.'

The three women laughed.

Bear said, 'Hi, ladies. I'm Bear and this is my new buddy, Jack.'

'Hello, Jack,' Flo said with a smile. 'I saw you on the Hash tonight.'

Jack winced. 'Really?'

She didn't seem to notice his discomfort. 'And this is Josie and Benice.'

'Be Nice?' asked Bear with a look of incredulity. 'Is that how you pronounce it?'

'Yes,' said Benice, her breasts straining against the thin cotton of her tee-shirt. 'Hi, Jack. You're new here.' She held out her hand.

'Yes,' said Jack. 'I guess I'm new everywhere.'

'Would you like to buy me a drink?'

Her white jeans curved snugly over rounded thighs and buttocks. 'That would be ... um ... nice,' he said.

'I'll get them,' said Lars and headed to the bar. Minutes later he was back with six whiskies and six Tuskers. '*Skol!*'

The two men drained their whiskies. Jack followed suit. The beer chaser helped to kill the thirst he still felt from the run.

Benice moved close and patted his buttocks. She smiled. 'Nice shorts.'

He was dizzy with fatigue. And the worst of it, he thought with a sigh, is that it's only Monday!

AROUND 2 A.M. JACK AND BENICE tumbled into a taxi outside Buffalo Bill's, giggling in a tangle of arms and legs. 'Jacaranda Hotel,' Jack said to the driver.

'Hey, Benice,' he continued, a frown crossing his brow, 'I gotta tell you, I'm drunk. I think it must be the attitude. No, I mean the *altitude*. It can kill you. You know that?'

'What are you talking about, honey?'

'There was this Swedish guy from the German Embassy, walking along. Next minute, he's dead. Swear to God.'

'Really?' Her hand was on his thigh.

Jack pulled her face to his and kissed her.

CHAPTER 3

PEABODY'S GUIDE TO EAST AFRICA (5ᵀᴴ ED):
The Ugandan Railway cut through the heart of
Maasailand. Later, the British forced the tribe to accept a
resettlement agreement that dispossessed them of most of
their homeland along the railway's route.

1899

Naisua ran to the crest of the ridge and stopped. She sucked
on her little finger, buried to the second knuckle in her mouth.
It was true. The iron snake crawled from the distant grey hills
to the valley floor below. Men swarmed like *siafu* ants along
its length.

Her mother and the other women moved off down the hill.
They chatted and laughed together as they had since leaving
the *enkang* that morning. But Naisua didn't move. She didn't
like the look of the snake, and she had never seen such strange
men as those that surrounded it.

THE CHIEF ENGINEER GALLOPED TO the railhead, reined in the
mare and dismounted before she had quite stopped. He strode
to the jemadar and swung him about. 'Gupta! Where the hell
are those keys?'

The short Hindu was taken by surprise, not because
Railhead Engineer Colvan had shouted at him rudely — that

was not unusual — but because he thought Mr Colvan had gone to the supply depot at N'erobi.

'Sahib?' was all he could manage.

'The keys, dammit, man! They're still back at mile 327. How the hell are you going to lay a mile today without them?'

'The keys, sahib? Yes, I am getting them presently. When the men have finished their *chah* I am sending them. I am thinking I have plenty of them, Mr Colvan.' His head wobbled like a balloon on a stick.

'Those lazy bastards will take hours to bring them up. You'll be out of them by noon.'

Ravi Gupta had been foreman, a plate-laying jemadar since they bridged the Tsavo, but the young Railhead Engineer was slow to recognise ability. Even slower to praise it.

'Sahib, but I have keys enough for thirty lengths here, and there are enough for twenty more lengths up ahead.'

Colvan hid his surprise by rubbing the black stubble on his chin. It wouldn't be the first time that a wily old coolie had tried to put one over the young engineer. Gupta had a look of wide-eyed innocence.

'You have fifty boxes of keys?' Colvan asked. 'The quartermaster has you down for thirty.' No wonder stock goes missing, he thought.

'Sahib, maybe the quartermaster has forgotten the twenty boxes I was forward ordering. You know, the last time the hand trolley was breaking down we were losing a full day's work.' Gupta bobbed his head to emphasise it. 'So now I am forward ordering.' He smiled, a little more confident of his ground.

'Forgotten it or never knew about it. Either way, they're not damn well booked out.' No wonder the bloody superintendent was up in arms. Stock disappearing every mile of the track. If it wasn't stolen by the Maasai, it was the coolies giving gifts to their women. 'I'll have a word with him about this.'

'I am thinking all will be well, sahib.'

'Humph.'

'Perhaps Mr Colvan would like some *chah*?'

Colvan checked his time piece. 'Yes, Gupta, I will.' The ride to the pestilential depot at N'erobi could wait until the afternoon.

Gupta brought Colvan a pannikin mug of strong black tea. He took it without a word and carried it to a sleeper pile where he settled himself with a sigh. He reached for his pipe before remembering he had finished the last of his tobacco days ago. Colvan surveyed the landscape over the rim of the mug. It was a grim sight. In all the years of his childhood, travelling the world with his father, an engineer who spent his life building things in godforsaken places, he had never seen such desolation.

When he'd joined the Uganda Railway Commission in '96, they were just twenty-three miles from the coast. The land was tinder dry even then. As the line moved slowly up the thorn bush escarpment, any relief that a coastal shower might offer was lost. The dry spell on the Mombasa coast became a drought inland. Now the rains of two more wet seasons had failed. Hundreds of rotting carcasses confirmed that something terrible was happening. Even the dry-country trees were shedding their remaining leaves. There was famine from Voi to Lake Victoria. It was damned impossible to trade for provisions anywhere along the line. The already unmanageable locomotive traffic to and from the coast was further overloaded by food transports needed for the five thousand coolies strung over the entire breadth of the East Africa Protectorate.

Laughter drifted to him from the ridge to the north. The Maasai women were coming down to the railhead again. He shook his head in wonder. How can they laugh? The missionary fellow had told him that half of the Maasai had died in the last few years.

'Smallpox, Mr Colvan. Yes, indeed. The Maasai have no resistance to it. Died in their thousands, they did. Why, our people at Machakos tell of whole villages gone. Just gone! The dead abandoned to the hyenas. And rinderpest took most of their herds.'

It was seldom that Colvan received a visitor, especially a white man. Even though he didn't much care for the missionary's boring stories, his description of the drought and disease explained the devastation he witnessed from day to day.

'God's wrath has been visited upon the Maasai, I vouch. It's their wickedness, you know.'

The missionary was an excitable type. Spittle frothed at the corner of his mouth as he went on. 'Their sins, their nakedness and their taking of many wives. Fornication! Almighty God's hand has been at work in Maasailand, I say. It's been a dreadful decade for the Maasai. Simply dreadful. May God have mercy on their poor black souls. Yes, indeed.'

Colvan sighed again and tipped the remainder of his tea into the dust as he walked back to his horse. He swung easily into the saddle, tossed the mug to the kitchen hand and reined the mare about. He kicked her flanks and she cantered across the tracks behind a freight wagon.

The horse baulked instinctively but the Maasai girl was under the mare before he could rein her in. An unholy screech went up from a Maasai woman nearby.

He dismounted and swooped the girl up in his arms. 'Ai-ai-ai,' the woman wailed. He ignored her and, brushing through the gathering circle of women, carried the little girl to the sleeper pile. She had no sign of injury save for a cut on her forehead, probably caused by the surcingle strap as the mare chested her to the ground.

Most of the women were wailing now. Some were tearing at their bald scalps, making long pale scratches.

Colvan cupped the girl's cheeks in one hand and moved her head gently from side to side. Her eyelids fluttered; when opened, the eyes studied Colvan impassively, giving him the notion she might be concussed. But as he removed his hand from her cheek, the child revealed a smile made more charming by the customary missing two front teeth. Her face was healthy, if thin, and her eyes were bright and curious.

'There you are, nutmeg. You're all right, I think.' He sat her up but the women continued their wailing with vigour.

'Gupta!' he shouted, but Gupta was already at his side. 'Ah! There you are. Get the cook. Give this woman some *posho* to be off with.'

'Of course, sahib.'

'And give some to the others too.'

'Yes, sahib.'

Colvan stood, thrust his hands deep into his pockets and was about to leave when he noticed the girl watching him. Under his scrutiny, her little finger crept shyly to the corner of her mouth where it disappeared to the second knuckle. He fumbled in his pockets and felt the train whistle he used to gather the men. A solid object was in the other. Concealing his hands by turning his back to the girl, he looked at the whistle then the crystal prism he used as a paperweight. He must have put it in his pocket in his haste that morning. His fingers around the prism, he brought his closed hand to her face. She looked at the hand and then into his blue eyes.

His uncurling fingers allowed a rainbow of colours to flash in her face. The women gasped and some shrank away, but the little girl beamed at him. She removed her finger from her mouth and, looking to him for reassurance, inched her hand towards the prism.

Colours usually seen only in the rare rainbows of the grass rains radiated from her small fist. She turned it and turned it and the prism poured out its hidden treasures. She could not take her eyes from it.

By the time she was satisfied she had found all possible colours, the pink man had gone.

1911

A mad wind swept down Mount Kenya's tortured northern ridges. It ripped the snow from exposed crags, sending flurries streaming across the ice blue sky. From far below on the plains of Laikipia, the mountain looked to be wearing a wind-blown white cotton banner.

Naisua carried the calabash into the hut and fastened the cowhide door tight against the wind that blew with more than a hint of the distant snow. Her stomach churned in the oppressive air of the hut. She waited for the damp kindling to catch, her fingers playing idly with her new beaded necklace. Her three sister-wives had been shocked at her bold innovation, arguing at length for her to return to the traditional iron. *It is not fitting.*

Especially for a wife of the laibon. But Lenana was amused by her whim.

She experimented with colours and ways to thread the beads so they lay flat around her slender neck, like the old iron circles did. The earrings were more important. They were the symbol of her married status, so she wouldn't replace them until she had the design just right. But she could imagine the gossip in the *enkang* when she finally donned the new earrings.

Some of the older women were not so gracious. Their disapproval of Naisua and her ways was obvious. They would shake their shaved heads and tut-tut her.

'Odd' was a word often used to describe the young fourth wife of the *laibon*. It had begun as a child, when she had insisted on keeping the railwayman's sun-stone — an exotic dangerous thing not to be trusted in the hands of one so young. *It must be the knock from the horse that gave her such silly notions*, they would say. Even some of her friends teased her, calling her 'horse girl'. She didn't mind the names. She imagined herself as a young filly — sleek, quick and proud. In time the taunting stopped, but family members would occasionally recall the childhood nicknames to tease her.

The fire flared and she stacked dried cow dung around it. When the milk boiled she poured it onto the millet and, fighting another wave of nausea, carried the wooden bowl outside. The chill wind tugged at her garments as she climbed the hill outside the *enkang*. It was good to be in the fresh morning air.

Lenana sat in a circle of elders under the baobab tree. They looked like a nest of toothless cobras with their dark red cloaks drawn up over their heads against the wind and their shining black eyes.

Her husband nodded as she approached with his porridge, a hint of a smile on his thin cracked lips. He looked tired. She turned to go but, as he sometimes did these days, his subtle gesture made it known that she should stay. She curled her long legs under her and sat a little to the rear of him. She risked a glance around the circle of old men, then lowered her eyes. It was not good to look proud. The eyes that caught hers held more than a touch of annoyance, perhaps jealousy, at the privilege shown to her, a mere woman.

'Lenana,' an elder stood to speak, 'when the Maasai moved from Naivasha and Nakuru, you told us that the British had promised our remaining land would stay in our possession for as long as the Maasai exist as a people. You said the governor promised this. For as long as the Maasai exist as a people.'

'Yes, my brother. It was promised.'

'But now you tell us that they seek a new resettlement agreement?'

Lenana sighed. 'They say it is to our benefit. All our clans will be united on one piece of land.'

'The British promise this?'

'Yes, Governor Sir Percy Girouard.'

'Yes, the British. The same British who signed the first resettlement ...' He let his voice trail off. 'It is time to conclude my remarks, Lenana, for now I see the sun is already rising and the women will have food to quiet our bellies.'

Naisua could feel the eyes upon her.

'You have listened to our words through the long night,' the elder continued. 'What do you make of it? Should we bow to this new demand of the British to resettle us? Resettle us in the poor grazing land to the south, as our brother from Machakos has counselled? Or should we only agree if Mount Kinangop is preserved for our sacred ceremonies? Or perhaps, as our brother from Baringo has argued, we should seek not only land but many, many cattle?' He allowed the options to hang in the air as his eyes swept the circle. 'Or, as I and my brothers from the Loita Hills have argued, should we fight? Should we unleash our warriors upon the British? For we are strong again, brothers. We are stronger now than at any time since the years of the smallpox. Our herds are many. We can sustain a long war. We can again make the Rift Valley thunder with the war chant of the *moran*. We can push the British and the Kikuyu thieves off our land and beyond the mountains.' He paused again. When he continued, his voice was brittle. 'Brothers, let British blood fertilise our land for the cattle.'

Some old heads nodded as the speaker took his seat. Others

remained bowed, fixed on the stony ground at the circle's centre. Eventually all eyes turned to Lenana. He sat, a frail figure hunched against the Laikipia winds. Naisua resisted an urge to put a hand on his shoulder.

'All elders have now been heard. I thank you all for your long journeys and for your wise counsel,' Lenana said at last. 'I will seek guidance from the spirits before I give the British my answer.'

One by one the old men left the conference circle. Naisua watched them go. Some nodded to Lenana. Others looked away.

Naisua followed Lenana into their hut. 'I have kept some boiled milk for you, it will take the morning chill from your bones.'

'My bones. You are always fussing about my bones.'

'Well, I must, because you do not take care of yourself.'

'Listen to you now. You're barely more than a girl yourself and you give orders to the *laibon* as if he were a child.'

'I am seventeen years!' She poured the milk into a bowl.

'Oh! Now this Maasai girl counts years like an English woman.'

'It is modern. Mr Mackecknie showed me the numbers.'

'Ah, the missionary. At least your English lessons are useful.'

'And I am no longer a girl. Am I not your wife?'

'So you are, little filly. So you are. I am teasing you as usual.'

'And is it not my duty to look after you? Your milk.'

'Ai-ai-ai.' He took the milk and sat on the edge of the bed platform sipping it. 'I don't know how to care for my people these days,' he said sadly.

Naisua knelt on the cowhide at the bedside. 'Husband, you are always caring for us. Using your great medicine. And all Maasailand knows of your magic. Only last week, that *morani* gored by the buffalo — your great skills saved his life.'

'A child's game. Even you, filly, with the trifle I have taught you, could have cured him. No, what I mean is that my vision of our people's path grows dim.'

'Now you speak of the British again.' She placed her hand on his as it lay on his knee.

'Yes. If I were just a medicine man, life would be simple. But the Commissioner wants a Paramount Chief to speak for all the Maasai. What do we know of Paramount Chiefs? It is not our way. But the British say we must have a Paramount Chief to decide these matters of resettlement. They trouble me.'

'I know. It makes you ill with worry. But you are the *laibon*. When you make your decision, it will be the right one.'

'The elders from the west talk of —'

'The elders talk and talk but they do not understand.'

'Naisua, recall the story of the monkey who thought his brothers dim-witted because they made nothing but silly chatter. Are you perhaps not a similar monkey hearing naught but monkey chatter?'

'I might hear chatter, but I see other things. Yes, I do. I see that the governor must have this land so that the white farmers can come. Unless he fills the land with farmers, the railway men will not be rewarded. Without crops the iron snake cannot be fed. He will not be satisfied until it is given. Or taken.'

'You are correct, little filly. The issue is land. The elders from the west talk of war. And if we were to lose? They think only in terms of battles and glory. The Maasai, the *moran*, are not concerned about death in combat, but it is the land. The land is important. If we lost it ... I will not risk it. We will make peace in exchange for land. I must trust Sir Percy.'

'Yes, I could see it in your face at the circle. And hear it in your voice. I know you will do well for your people.'

'Ah, Naisua, I wish I had your faith. But you will come to the meetings with me. You will hear what Sir Percy has to say.'

'I am happy to sit with the *laibon*. But already the elders grow annoyed at my presence at the circles. This will start them talking again.'

'As you say, they talk and talk. But I want you at my side. You must prepare. You have a destiny to fulfil, little filly.'

'A destiny?'

'Naisua, listen carefully. My prayers to find the answer to Sendeyo's curse have not been heard. But Mweiya has sent me a vision. You will be a *laibon* in our clan.'

She sat back on her heels, her eyes wide as she searched his face for an understanding.

'Yes, Naisua, it is possible. You have a gift, a talent for medicines and for healing. Now I will teach you my magic and how to use it to guide the family. You will protect the women, the innocents, who will suffer most from the curse.'

'But surely your son — our son — will be your student?' Her hand dropped to her belly.

'Can I hope for a son? Four wives, each with a daughter. Now I cannot share their beds in case they produce another daughter and bring the curse upon us again.' He looked into Naisua's eyes. 'You are my last chance to bear a successor, little filly.'

'It *will* be a boy. And you will teach him the ways of the *laibon*.'

'There may not be time.'

'Why?'

'I have had other visions.'

'It frightens me when you speak so.'

'There is no need for fear.' He placed a hand gently upon her shoulder. 'Naisua, you will have a long life, and with the years will come wisdom, the wisdom to guide many generations of the Kidongi family. You will take my gift of magic and fight the curse until another *laibon*, a Great *Laibon*, arises to take your place.'

CHAPTER 4

PEABODY'S GUIDE TO EAST AFRICA (5TH ED):
Do not show your teeth to a monkey. (Maasai proverb
meaning: keep your secrets to yourself.)

Tuesday. Early. The unmistakable blast from a Land Rover
woke him.

His mouth felt like the bottom of a parrot's cage. He
remembered being very drunk, playing pool badly, and Benice
and the girls hovering with the demeanour of feeding sharks.

He swung his head to the empty pillow beside him and let
his breath escape in a long slow sigh. He wanted no more
complications. He wanted no more sex with mysterious ladies
of the night.

THE HOTEL LOBBY WAS STUFFY as the delegates milled about
before dispersing to the bar or one of the end-of-day
functions arranged by the conference organisers. Jack carried
his beer to the garden patio, which seemed deserted. The
palm trees and hibiscus bushes were lit from below. A cool
breeze drifted across the pool and from somewhere down the
beach drifted the latest hit by the British group Fine Young
Cannibals.

'Boring conference?' She held the martini glass an inch from
her lips. They were red.

'Huh? Oh, not really. Just been a long day.' Her breezy summer skirt matched the Honolulu evening. 'I haven't seen you at the conference,' he said, wishing he hadn't let his eyes drop to her legs.

'I'm not attending.'

'Then how . . .'

She ran her eyes, nervous cat's eyes, around the terrace then let them settle again on Jack; they held him with the same guileless, appraising expression that had slightly unsettled him at the outset. 'Let's just say I know the look.' She took a sip of the martini, camouflaging her smile.

'Are we all so predictable?' He smiled too.

'Ninety-nine per cent. Occasionally there's someone with the ability to surprise. Someone . . . interesting.'

'How do you know if you've found the one per cent?'

'Intuition. I just know.' There was a tiny chip at the corner of one of her otherwise perfect white teeth. Her tongue flicked forward to cover it. The action was somehow erotic.

'You seem to have great powers of observation,' he said.

'I do.'

'What else do you know?'

She studied him, running her eyes slowly up and down his body. He felt himself suck in his stomach, although he had nothing to hide.

'Hmm . . . not married. But a steady girlfriend . . . A professional man. Thirty-something. Thirty-two. Engineer. No. Something to do with soil. Soil conservation.'

He laughed. Notice boards with the daily agenda for the conference on soil conservation were everywhere. 'Brilliant!'

'Elementary.' She grinned, her pink tongue flicking again to conceal the chipped tooth. A cat licking cream from its lips. 'Another drink?'

'Oh! I'll get it. What would you like?'

'I asked you. Another beer?'

'Okay.'

Her name was O'Hara. That's all he could get from her. It might have been her surname or given name, she wouldn't say. In fact he knew very little of her, as she either changed the subject when it drifted onto personal topics or implied he should mind his own business.

They seldom had a real conversation after that first evening on the garden patio. She seemed to be at ease with the silence. Jack eventually gave up, becoming inured to the discomfort of gaps in the small talk. When he let himself ponder the life she concealed, he assumed she was married, perhaps unhappily so, her husband with some kind of sexual dysfunction. Maybe they had an agreement to take separate holidays; he to go fishing in the mountains, while she discreetly unleashed the sexual energy accumulated throughout the year.

It was always sex between them. When they weren't doing it, they were talking about doing it. Or she was getting him ready to do it again, tirelessly, patiently working him to arousal.

Her tongue, her mouth, could drive him to a climax that frightened him with its intensity. Her vagina held him like a warm velvet glove.

In the beginning they would meet in her room after the final conference session of the day. Then, a couple of times they met for lunch: oysters and Bollinger, again in her room. Sex would consume the remainder of the hour. His afternoon conference sessions were hell, trying to keep alert, or at least awake.

She was careful about being seen with him in public. That was how he got the impression she was married. They never returned to the patio where they'd met. She could not be coaxed to a restaurant, no matter how secluded. Their only outing was to a dimly lit nightclub on the far side of the city. Her preference was that he not contact her — she would make all arrangements. But if he did, it must never be from his room.

She called it The Game, and each part of The Game, she explained, must build on the equation: risk and consequence. She began by encouraging him into having sex in increasingly public places. Once, on his return to the meeting venue from a toilet break, she whisked him into a storage room and went down on him against the frosted glass door. At the nightclub, he entered her from behind on the crowded dance floor as a cloud of artificial smoke swirled around them.

She believed the combination of risk and consequence was a great aphrodisiac. 'All the really erotic acts involve danger,' she told him the night following their rendezvous in the linen closet. 'Long before civilisation tamed the sex act, primitive man took risks to plant his sperm. Some of that instinct survives. It's why people like to fuck in the back seat of cars. Outdoors. In public places ... Or in linen closets.' She spoke as if reciting a favourite thesis. 'There's a risk involved — the risk of being discovered. And a cost. In the case of the linen closet, it's embarrassment. Nothing to compare to having your brains scrambled by a caveman's club. But it excites.' Her eyes were wide and she appeared short of breath, almost panting. 'Risk times cost equals great sex. Raising either heightens the sensation,' she said, flicking her tongue over her chipped tooth. 'Getting caught in an elevator is not much more embarrassing than getting caught in the back seat of a car, but the risk of being caught, of someone calling the elevator, is greater. So is the climax.'

The following night O'Hara pressed him to make love to her on her balcony. Held only by his strong grip on her hips, she leaned backwards over the rail, writhing and pulsating fourteen storeys above the poolside patio.

Later she said, 'Now you know what I'm talking about, don't you? You felt it. Your orgasm was incredible. You loved every minute of it.'

'There was no way I was going to drop you.'

'Maybe not. Small risk. But the danger was there all right. Like, if you slipped, why ... I'd be dead!' Her eyes were wild and she began to laugh.

He should have known right then that there was something very wrong about the whole thing. Continuing to play The Game after that night proved her theory: he was hooked.

He impatiently filled his days while waiting for the next powerful erotic punch. Only his departure at the end of the week would put an end to it. But he could not stop until it was over. As the week progressed, the excitement, the incredible sensations, built inexorably. Each meeting was another higher mountain of sexual adventure to climb.

O'Hara must have known what the sexual summit contained. She would have planned it as well as she had planned every other part of The Game.

But the thought that would haunt him for ever was: how could he have been so self-centred, so selfish, to have absolutely no awareness of where they were headed?

How could he have missed the madness she had planned?

CHAPTER 5

PEABODY'S GUIDE TO EAST AFRICA (5 TH ED):
Eating in Nairobi is an incomparable experience.

Recommended is the open-air Toona Tree (behind the International Casino). Try genuine Italian pizza and pasta in the lower branches of the enormous toona tree that invades the upper floor. Diners are protected from the elements by a magnificent makuti roof which soars above them. The crab and lobster dishes are exceptional. Simpler meals are available if the budget is tight.

If you are a meat-eater, you must try the aptly named Carnivore (Langata Road). Explore the subtle chicken and fish taste of crocodile or the elegance of an impala steak. Later on, join the crowd in Carnivore's unique African discotheque.

Jack had his head in his hands, staring at the papers on his desk. It was bad enough the administration felt obliged to issue all file documents in the three official languages of the UN, making the English versions hard to locate; it was quite another thing to make sense of them when you did.

He was coming to grips with the UNDP's structure but there was a plethora of Kenyan government departments too, the titles of which gave no clue to their field of responsibility —

the exception being the Department of Regional Development which seemed to be involved in everything.

Then there were the non-government organisations, NGOs, that made regular appearances in the correspondence. The big one seemed to be AmericAid, funded by some billionaire in Idaho.

Even people's surnames were a challenge. 'Ng'ang'a,' he mumbled, testing his progress in handling the double consonant. 'Mbuuri.'

He shook his head. Turning the page in the AmericAid file he tried another. 'Kidongi.' That was a little easier. 'Maa-like-ah Kee-dong-ee,' he mouthed then flipped to an earlier page. Malaika Kidongi was his contact in AmericAid. At least he had some knowledge of that project. It was one in the so-called Integrated Development Programme and a hot item. Jack had been spending most of his time on this one project since arriving over a month ago, and it was not going well.

Apart from the respective bureaucracies, which made doing anything more difficult than necessary, his contact at the Department of Regional Development was giving him a hard time about the project's transport requirements.

Jack had learned that all aid projects' local transport needs had to be provided by the local provincial governments. By convention, these were first coordinated through Regional Development. For some reason, in the case of his Integrated Development project in the far west of the country, it hadn't happened.

Bear's voice came from the doorway. 'What's this I hear about the boss's pet project coming unstuck?'

Jack lifted his head from his stack of papers. 'What did you hear?'

'What story do you want? The one about someone at Regional Development sitting on it or the locals being difficult?'

'The one about the public servant at Regional Development I have, thanks. Guy named Onditi. I'm going over there to sort him out later this week. What's going on out west?'

'Only they don't care jackshit about the Integrated

Development Programme and the UN *mzungus* should just go find some other lab rat to test it on.'

'Where do you get all this stuff?'

'Connections.'

'What does your *connection* tell you about the locals?'

'The usual.'

'Jesus!' Jack threw his pencil on the desk. 'What's in it for me — right?'

'You got it. My guess is there's someone out there who wants a little *consideration*.'

'Like what?'

'Who knows? But it'll cost us.'

'Oh, right! The UN's going to bribe someone so we can give them aid.'

'Tea money, buddy. Nobody does bribes. Tea money.'

'That's bullshit.'

'Sure it is. Now why don't you tell ol' Mr Bhatra that? He'd love to hear your views.'

'Even Bhatra wouldn't agree to a bribe.'

'Bhatra has promised his left testicle to this Integrated Development Programme. He's promoting it in New York and Geneva. And just between you and me, he thinks it's his ticket to a Deputy Secretary position.'

'Are you saying he'd agree to pay the tea money to get it through?'

'Hell, no! He wouldn't dirty his hands with petty graft. But it's possible that a little help might find its way to the coffee co-op, or something similar, which by a strange coincidence happens to be run by the same Big Man out there. You know the stuff.'

'It's still a bloody bribe!'

'Jack! Don't be ridiculous.' Bear's tone dripped sarcasm. 'Bhatra is a senior member of the UN management team. He can't authorise a bribe! And besides, it's not his job.'

Jack leaned forward. 'What do you mean, not *his* job?'

'I mean, good buddy, he probably reckons it's yours!'

• • •

'MR MORGAN! DO COME IN.' Bhatra stood and swept his arm expansively to indicate the whole office. He looked like he was about to go to a wedding. His suit, the jacket of which he never removed even in the office, had a marvellous steely sheen to it, a blend of silk and cotton made popular by Singaporean tailors for tropical climates. Jack was glad he had rolled down his shirtsleeves on the way over.

'Sit, please sit, Mr Morgan.' Bhatra indicated a brown leather visitor's chair.

Jack sat at the mahogany desk opposite the mahogany nameplate: *Director, Aid Projects. D K L Bhatra*. He had no idea what the initials stood for, nor, as far as he could determine, did anyone else. Most people called him Mr Bhatra. It was a form of address that sat uncomfortably with Jack, who was more accustomed to being on first-name terms with his boss. Bhatra's fellow directors used the less formal 'Bhatra'. To Jack, the use of the surname alone was a little unfriendly. Although it made him ill at ease, he overcame the dilemma by avoiding any form of address. Overall, Bhatra made him uncomfortable with his nonexistent given name, his strict adherence to protocol and his polite formality. He guessed it must be an Australian thing and made a note to reach a more comfortable working arrangement with his boss.

Bhatra lowered himself into his high-backed chair and said, 'Now then. You are settling in well.' It was more of a statement than a question.

Jack thought he expected a response and said, 'Yes, thank you.'

'Excellent! Excellent! And your personal effects? Still not here, I suspect.'

Jack shook his head with a polite smile.

'Ho! Ho! The UN is a wonderful organisation but these things tend to take some time. Yes?'

'Seems so.'

'You know, for the life of me I don't know why.' His brow knotted in concentration. 'It seems there are always complications down there on the Mombasa wharves. Yes, complications. Why, even I had to wait two months! Ho, ho.'

Jack wished he would get on with it. The delay to the arrival of his gear was a sore point in which, he instinctively knew, Bhatra had not the faintest interest.

'All in good time, I'm sure,' Bhatra concluded.

Jack's fingers drummed on his knee. He nodded and tried another smile.

'Mr Morgan.' The smile melted. In its place was a look of sympathetic concern. Bhatra adjusted his gold cufflinks to sit tidily under his steel-grey sleeves. Leaning forward, he placed his clasped hands carefully on the polished mahogany. 'There appear to be some logistical difficulties with your area of the Integrated Development project, I understand.'

'Well, it's not so much logistics. The Regional Development Council have been, ah, less than enthusiastic.'

'Yes, I understand. I understand.' He fiddled with his gold watch, just visible below a crisp white shirt cuff. 'In using the term logistics, I'm of course referring to the grass roots involvement in the process. You know, Mr Morgan, in my experience, the grass roots are always the challenge for the UN. Oh, I can go along to the Minister and we'll have a cup of tea and between us we will agree concepts, policies. But the grass roots ...' He raised a finger. 'That is the challenge. The local administrators.' He seemed to seek a response from Jack. When none was offered, he continued. 'Our field operatives, people such as yourself, Mr Morgan, are the minders, the gardeners if you will, of the grass roots.' His voice became a stage whisper. 'And the key is creative solutions.'

Jack folded his arms and sat back in his chair, eyebrows raised. 'Creative solutions.'

'Exactly.' Bhatra's smile was regaining its verve. 'Some of our best operatives,' he made it sound like a CIA activity, 'achieve the UN's most challenging objectives by means of good field research. By coming up with a proposal that meets the objectives of the mission as well as satisfying the appropriate individuals' personal motivators.'

'Personal motivators?'

'Yes. The local customs may seem strange at first, but we at the UNDP should be cognisant of the imperfections in individuals ... Perhaps a carefully planned inducement might win such an individual's cooperation in ... '

Jack nodded. 'Why don't we just call it a bribe?'

The smile evaporated. 'Mr Morgan, I do not countenance bribery. It's against the law in Kenya. And it's certainly against UN principles and procedures.' His tone had lost some of its congeniality. He collected himself and continued in a more friendly voice. 'Mr Morgan, Jack, there are many ways of doing business the world over. In the US, for example, it's a network, a network born within fraternities or other connections made in college. In my own country, India, it's by gaining the good graces of influential businessmen sympathetic to the cause, or perhaps a family friend. In Australia ... well, I think you get my point.'

He sat back and, placing his elbows on the armrests with forearms raised, tapped his fingertips together. The gold watch slipped under his cuff and out of sight. 'I hope we understand each other, Mr Morgan.'

Jack ran a finger along his jaw. Bear had warned him about Bhatra. A smooth bureaucrat with a Machiavellian streak, he was part of the so-called subcontinental Mafia. His clique controlled Human Affairs in Geneva. Bhatra had been known to shunt troublesome staff — or operatives, in his words — to hardship posts for the remainder of their contract if they didn't conform.

Jack stood, carefully slid the large leather chair back into place and said, 'I believe we understand each other perfectly, Bhatra.'

JAMES ONDITI WAS ANNOYED. HE took another sip of the over-brewed tea; it needed sweetening. Despite his best efforts during his year in the Department of Regional Development, the stupid girl bringing the tea had again forgotten at least one of his four spoonfuls of sweetened condensed milk. He would make sure she knew about it next time he saw her.

He slammed the cup on its saucer, splashing three brown stains onto the pile of papers before him. Planting his palms on the desk, he stood, pushed back on his chair and sent it rolling across the vinyl-covered floor. It crashed into the desk two metres behind him, but he stormed off, ignoring the looks from his fellow office-workers.

The papers he needed on the extension of the Langata development were nowhere to be found. The Luo in Central Registry had sent him the wrong ones. You would think she would have more sense. Even Kikuyu would be an improvement; at least they understood business. But Luos, with their slow drawl and even slower wit, were hopeless.

Maasai are just as bad, he thought, recalling the girl at AmericAid. She annoyed him because she refused his attentions, and it annoyed him further that getting her into bed had become so important. He was usually quite successful at such things. Snobbish Maasai bitch. *Haki ya Mungu!* Her with her *mzungu* ways. Just because she worked for an American company didn't make her so special. Thinks she's too good for a Kalenjin. Well, he thought, I will settle that score one of these days.

The Luo files clerk could not be found. He stood fuming at the vacant desk, not noticing the receptionist a few paces away, clasping and unclasping her hands. When he turned to her she took an involuntary step backwards before blurting out, 'Mr Onditi!' Her lip went white as she bit it.

'Yes?'

'Mr Onditi,' she stumbled on in a breathless rush, 'there's a gentleman here from the UN. He says he has an appointment with you at ten o'clock.'

He gave her a sullen stare.

'A *mzungu*. From the UN office at the Kenyatta Centre.'

'Where is he?' he snapped, now even more annoyed. He had almost forgotten the meeting.

'At reception. Should I send him to conference room two?' She appeared on the point of tears.

'Tell him to wait at the door.' He needed to refresh his memory on the case. The meeting was too important to rush.

He marched down the corridor to his office, rolling his fist into his palm. The *wazungu* at the UN were becoming difficult. By stumbling around the Narok District on one of their little projects, they threatened to upset the little smuggling operation he was assisting his Uncle Nicholas to develop out there.

At his desk he unlocked his drawer and rummaged for his personal papers. Then he collected the official file, locked his drawer and headed out the door again.

It was already difficult enough. That other *mzungu*, Richard Leakey, had armed his rangers and given orders to shoot poachers on sight. He had been far too ambitious since the President had appointed him Director of the National Parks and Wildlife Service. This latest plan by the UNDP would make it too easy for Leakey to extend his operations outside the parks. He had made no secret of the fact he wanted to widen his search for ivory and rhino horn poachers.

Onditi's Uncle Nicholas, the Minister for Lands, had pulled some strings to get his nephew into Regional Development, where he was to keep an eye on the department's activities in the area where their smuggling operation was centred. And he had made it clear that if Onditi couldn't handle everything in the Isuria area, he would choose another of his many nephews who could.

Onditi savagely pushed open the door to the stairwell, startling another office-worker who glared. He ignored him and continued down the stairs. His uncle didn't understand the problems he was having with their contact in Isuria — some party hack with an overblown opinion of his abilities and his importance. But his Uncle Nicholas had chosen him, for some inexplicable reason, and Onditi had no choice but to work with him. If he was going to be successful in this new business he had to keep the Big Man in Isuria happy. To make matters worse, the hack wanted him to find his long-lost daughter, a runaway he had a score to settle with. Strange man — he had made it clear that if bedding her was necessary, it was not an issue that would concern him.

Onditi rounded the corner to the conference room door.

'Jack Morgan, UNDP,' the *mzungu* said, extending his hand.

He took it and was surprised at its grip. 'Onditi,' he said and showed the man into the meeting room.

He was younger than he had expected. What would he be? Thirty-five? Maybe less. Onditi always found it difficult to guess their age. Whatever it was, he was younger than the other UN people he had met during his time in Regional Development. Pasty white men with *unga* in their veins. For all he knew, they had the same maize flour in their *mapumbu* too. But this one had a little iron in him. It glinted in his eyes and behind the brief smile he gave as they shook hands.

'Please, take a seat.' Onditi indicated the one nearest the door then strode purposefully to the other end of the long table. He took a deep breath, trying to compose himself as he fumbled with his papers. The white man at the far end of the table flipped casually through his.

'Thanks for your time, Mr Onditi. Can I get straight to the point?'

Typical *mzungu* rudeness, Onditi thought. Not waiting for an invitation to begin. His anger began to rise again.

'We wrote to your department on the eighteenth of last month ...' He then reviewed all the boring details of their project. 'In summary, the UN will handle the agricultural side of things, AmericAid will do health. But we need help with transport.'

'And you think the NPWS can help,' Onditi said, folding his arms.

'Richard Leakey has kindly offered National Parks' assistance.'

Onditi was careful to take the edge off his voice when he said, 'Professor Leakey is a very generous man.' He didn't wait for a response. 'Tell me, Mr ah ...' He glanced at the business card. '...Mr Morgan, why is the UN troubling itself with this coordination work? Normal practice is that Regional Development makes all the detailed arrangements.'

'Let's just say that we are investing a lot of effort in the Isuria sub-region. Our intention is to ensure that the benefits reach the intended recipients ...'

The muscle in Onditi's jaw tightened.

'...in the most efficient manner possible,' Morgan finished with a faint smile. 'Neither the UN nor AmericAid has any spare transport.'

AmericAid, thought Onditi. Another mzungu organisation sticking their noses where they don't belong. It reminded him again of the Maasai girl.

The white man continued: 'The paperwork is in order. Routine stuff, except for the NPWS part. Is there a problem in getting this through your department?'

'Problem? Why would there be a problem?'

'Well, it's taking so much time. I would have thought three weeks was enough to push it past your Minister.'

Onditi placed the papers on the table before him. 'This is Kenya, Mr Morgan. We don't push *anything* at our Minister. You British seem to think we are still a colony. We do things in the African way now. And if it takes time — well, your little project will have to wait.'

'Yeah. Right. I'll give you a call in a few days.'

Onditi's smile was icy as he stood to indicate the door. 'You may call when you feel you must, Mr Morgan. But I wouldn't — how do you say — get my hopes up if I were you.' He placed his knuckles on the conference table and leaned forward.

The white man rose slowly to his feet and slid his papers into his briefcase. He was half a head taller than Onditi but about thirty pounds lighter. 'Sure.' He wore the same flinty smile as when he'd entered. 'Let's say Thursday then.'

Onditi's face was a thunderstorm about to strike.

The *mzungu* turned at the door. 'Australian,' he said, the handle in his grasp.

Onditi's raised eyebrows momentarily lightened his scowl. 'What?'

'Australian. Not British.' The door closed.

CHAPTER 6

PEABODY'S GUIDE TO EAST AFRICA (5TH ED):
A couplet written by the British poet Hilaire Belloc was
popular among the troops of Imperial Britain:
'Whatever happens, we have got
The Maxim gun, and they have not.'

1911

It couldn't be called a breeze, perhaps a shift in the air, but it
moved the dust curtain aside to reveal the twenty members of
the King's African Rifles. They marched proudly if not
proficiently. Their khaki shorts and shirts matched their dusty
black legs. Black tassels bobbed on their scarlet tarbooshes as
they followed the three mounted white men.

Governor Sir Percy Girouard's *askaris* were purely ceremonial.
It was just as well, for if they were intended as a show of force, it
would have been pitiful in the face of Lenana's honour guard.
Hundreds of warriors, resplendent in full battle regalia of spears,
stabbing swords and colourful shields, lined the last half mile of
the track to the *laibon*'s *enkang*.

The *moran*'s ochred hair matched their red *shukas*, which
barely covered their loins. The red and white ochre painted on
their muscular thighs rippled as the warriors stamped their
feet and chanted a song of respect and welcome to their fellow
men-at-arms. With shoulders thrust forward in a shunting

motion, they released grunts from deep in their chests. In the off beat, the thud of a thousand clubs against tough cowhide shields thundered into the surrounding hills. '*Hhuunh-huh!*' Thud. '*Hhuunh-huh!*' Thud.

The Maasai women formed a second line behind the *moran*. Wearing brightly coloured garments and bearing handfuls of dry grass, the Maasai symbol of peace, they sang a contralto harmony to the men's bass.

Sir Percy, in the official khaki dress jacket and braided cap of the Protectorate, rode at the head of the escort, his chin thrust forward on heavy jowls and his belly bouncing in counterpoint to the stride of his brown mare. Immediately to his rear rode his assistant, Charles Fothergill, an unimaginative man, content to spend the remaining days of his public service career in the shadow of his superior.

A man wearing a grey felt hat, its wide brim turned down front and back, with dark wavy hair to his broad shoulders, rode beside the governor. The deep bronze of his face and the pale lines etched at the corners of his mouth and eyes, more likely caused by laughter than age, told of a man who had seen a lot of the sun. He was not in uniform, but with his confident seat on the big black stallion he had the look of a man accustomed to giving orders. The stallion skittered nervously amongst the throng and the rider dropped his head low over the reins, murmuring to the animal and patting its neck.

As the party approached the village, the women's singing grew stronger and the *moran* raised their voices to match them, vigorously beating their shields.

An elder awaited them at the gate of the *enkang*. He was dressed simply and without ornamentation. Tall, thin, gaunt even, there was something about him that conveyed dignity and pride.

The rider on the stallion noticed the beautiful young woman standing with the old man. He had never seen coloured beads on a Maasai. As he studied them, and her, their eyes met.

The elder raised his hand and the singing and shield-thumping stopped. The sudden silence assailed the ears.

'*Habari*, Sir Percy Girouard. How is your news?' It was the customary African greeting.

'*Mzuri*, Lenana. Good,' said the governor, managing a dignified dismount until his boot became caught in the stirrup. There were several anxious seconds until he freed it, then with an embarrassed cough he extended his hand to Lenana. 'I am pleased to see you again, Lenana. You look well,' he boomed.

Lenana smiled wanly.

'When did we last see you, Lenana? Was it the Nairobi Show?'

'Yes, Governor. Nairobi.'

The governor continued in the loud voice he used on those not fluent in the English language. 'Yes, I think it was. Jolly fine event that, what? The cattle judging again, I think? Yes, of course. You've been doing it for … how many years has it been?'

Lenana looked puzzled.

The tanned man stepped forward with a few words in Maa. Lenana replied and the man said, 'The *laibon* has been judging cattle at the Nairobi Show for six years, Governor.'

'Thank you, Colvan. Since 1905, eh? My, my.' Turning to Lenana, he shouted, 'Jolly good, Lenana. Jolly good.'

Lenana nodded and with a gesture led the governor's small party to the shade of a large fig tree. Sir Percy declined an offer of milk and called to his assistant to bring the water bottle. Colvan accepted the milk gourd and, as he raised it, caught the Maasai girl watching him. She dropped her eyes.

'So, Lenana, your cattle are well? Good, good. Colvan, I will do this in English. Perhaps you can add the odd Maasai word here and there to help Lenana?'

Colvan spoke quietly to Lenana and the old man nodded slowly. 'Thank you, Governor,' he said in a voice without emotion.

Colvan studied the old man. The *laibon* of all the Maasai was not as he had expected. The image he held was of a man of stature and strong physical presence. The old man before him had neither. Even his dignity deserted him when he sat. He became a shrunken bundle, wrapped in a navy greatcoat. Colvan had heard about the coat. It had been a gift from the

East Africa Protectorate when the medicine man was given the title of Paramount Chief. The coat, plus six pounds, thirteen shillings and fourpence a year.

Sir Percy droned on and Colvan translated. It was an easy task once the florid language was reduced to bare facts. Lenana seemed resigned to the role of witness rather than participant. His gaze focused on a point somewhere over Sir Percy's shoulder. In the crook of his arm he held an old iron poker, the temporary replacement for the *laibon*'s iron club, lost by a clerical officer of the Protectorate some years earlier. Colvan had a glimpse of the person behind the vacant, rheumy eyes and tried to imagine how this proud old man managed to hide his indignation.

It appeared the girl was following the governor's words intently, her forehead creasing in concentration as Sir Percy lapsed into flowery hyperbole. Colvan wondered how she had learned English.

'To specific clauses of the resettlement agreement then,' the governor began.

'Second resettlement,' Colvan blurted.

'What?' Sir Percy frowned. He disliked his gubernatorial utterances being interrupted by trivia.

'It's the second agreement, Governor. The first was terminated by us.'

'Yes ... Well, as I was saying, Lenana, you have agreed on the general terms of the second resettlement agreement in preliminary discussions with my assistant, Mr Fothergill, here.'

Fothergill beamed.

'In those discussions you raised some specific issues. I can confirm that His Majesty's East Africa Protectorate agrees with retaining Mount Kinangop as Maasai land for the purposes of the *eunoto* ceremony to be held each seven years.' Sir Percy swept the small crowd with a look of smug satisfaction. 'However, as for the request for government resources to assist in the movement of cattle and sheep, et cetera,' his face clouded into a schoolmasterly scowl, 'we have given this very careful consideration but unfortunately we cannot agree. Out of the question. No resources for that. However, Mr Colvan, here,' he swept his arm in Colvan's direction, 'will act as liaison officer to ensure that your relocation is carried out in the most expeditious manner possible.'

Colvan's translation was lengthy, including some thoughts of his own on the Maasai's options for appeal. Lenana turned to him, perhaps seeing him for the first time.

Governor Girouard continued. 'So it remains for the Paramount Chief to sign the Memorandum of Understanding. Fothergill, the papers if you please.'

Lenana remained expressionless as he made his mark. Sir Percy pumped his hand and moved on to the other elders. Colvan hesitated before he stepped forward to grasp Lenana's long cold fingers. The old man would not make eye contact nor did he make any acknowledgment of Colvan.

Colvan had wanted to say something, but couldn't compose the words. *I am sorry that I am a part of this travesty. And I am angry, because we have not only taken your land but also your dignity.* Instead he stood awkwardly as Lenana shrank into his greatcoat and slowly left the meeting place. The Maasai girl moved to follow him, but when she passed Colvan she turned to face him. He couldn't read her expression. He expected admonishment, perhaps even contempt or disgust, but saw none of these. She appeared about to speak but remained silent.

Long after she had gone he could still see those searching eyes, old eyes for one so young, probing the depths of him. He wondered what she had found there.

1913

The bundle in her carry-sling had stopped squirming at last. Naisua gave it a gentle jiggle to move the weight to its centre. Her two year old was small for his age, he had never caught up following his birth. It had been a difficult time for both of them. Being her first birth she knew not what to expect, and coming as it did so soon after the death of Lenana, it drained the last reserves of her strength. But although he was small, Seggi's leather carry-sling cut into the tender parts of her slim shoulders and the bruises had no time to heal from one long day to the next.

She moved the straps until they felt more comfortable, then waved her stick at the sheep and goats. The bedraggled flock moved off in the direction of the small cattle herd, barely able to raise a bleat of complaint.

Dust clouds dotted the landscape from horizon to horizon. Somewhere within each was a small herd much like her own, with its owner and his children working to press the stubborn livestock forward. Always southward. The wives would be following, carrying a few precious personal belongings and driving a cow or bullock burdened with the household items. Older family members would struggle and stumble in the rear. The weak would not rejoin the family until some time after the camp had been made for the night. Some would not make camp at all, lost to the heat or a predator.

Naisua and the next youngest of her sister-wives shared the herding tasks, including two pack-steers laden with household effects. Each woman had a few personal items hung in a bundle under one arm. The other wives carried similar loads and supervised the children.

After Lenana's death, and in accordance with his wishes, Naisua had assumed the role of clan leader and *laibon*. Nobody objected. It would be a trying time for any leader.

Within the immediate family, the women's bond had strengthened following their husband's death. It came with the realisation that Sendeyo's curse doomed them all to a life of widowhood. Children were even more important to a Maasai man than cattle. It was known that Lenana's widows were cursed if they bore another girl-child. If a man could not have children, marriage was not worth the dowry. Naisua's situation was no better. Although she had borne a son and might avoid the curse if she continued to produce male children, every eligible male in the region considered it too great a risk that a daughter would arrive and thus end her child-bearing days.

While the women's bond was comforting in the days following Lenana's death, in the desolation of the Rift Valley it became essential to survival. Alone in the vast grasslands, the women fended off marauding carnivores that threatened the stock and angry landowners who threatened their lives. They suffered the heat, the thorns, the thirst and the hunger. They suffered more as the torments took their toll on Seggi and the four little girls. The children rarely cried these days. In the first few weeks of abandoning their *enkang*, they had been in constant need of care and consolation. They missed the love and comfort of the extended Maasai family. But on this forced march, the four women were essentially a tiny community set apart. It could be days, even weeks, before they would see a friend or even a fellow Maasai.

Occasionally, one of the women would quietly weep. There was no particular pattern. It might be in the company of her sister-wives at the end of a day, perhaps not even a difficult day, but never when the children were near. Or on a peaceful night, when the stock and the killers that prowled in the darkness were silent. A quiet night could be distressing to a woman accustomed to the *enkang*'s carnival of life; could lead her to believe that only she and her pathetic little bunch, out of all the thousands of living beings who had commenced the journey south, remained alive to complete it. In the darkness, tears were invisible. Or it might be early one morning, a dry beginning to another unknowable day. A woman could be lost out there in the dust on the herd's flank, where the sun's golden curtain could enfold her. She could be forgiven if she shed tears. Dust can do that.

When a sister-wife was found weeping, no one would ask why. But by day's end, each woman would have found some way to lighten her sister's emotional burden.

The forced march and weather took their toll on the herd and flock, their only asset. At first it was a cow here, a goat there. But as they descended into the Great Rift Valley, stock numbers dwindled in the face of the unrelenting heat. They were not alone in this heartbreak. Like all the dispossessed northern Maasai, the four women had often suffered the distressing sight of one of their cattle, sheep or goats dropping to its knees and, with the stubbornness of a beast drained by endless suffering, refusing to take another step.

NAISUA WAS TENDING TO AN injured bullock, patting a concoction onto its matted flank, when Colvan rode into sight. She smiled as he dismounted.

'*Sopa*, Naisua. It's so good to see you again.' He led the horse towards her.

'*Sopa*, Colvan.' She knew his first name but preferred Colvan. It sounded strong.

They shook hands. Her hand was small, but the grip firm.

'You are a good sight for my eyes too.' She smiled up at him a little shyly. 'You are welcome.'

'You have travelled far these last few weeks.'

'Oh, no! We are like hippos in the mud. Too slow. Too slow.' She noticed that his hair was longer and the blue eyes, which she secretly thought were the most fascinating eyes she had ever seen, still held the kindness she had sensed on her first sight of them. 'You are well?'

'Well enough. And your tribe?' He always referred to her little group of women and children that way.

'We too are well enough.'

'It has taken me two days to find you. I was looking further to the north.' He peered into the carry-sling. 'How is little Seggi? He looks comfortable there.'

'I think so. And he is healthy again. My milk was lost for some days and the cow's milk did not please him.'

He smiled. An awkward silence developed. She returned to study the bullock's infected flank.

'The infection is bad,' he said, looking over her shoulder. 'I hope those potions of yours can heal it.'

'My *dawa* and the cattle are weak and the thorns strong. We lose too many. Nearly half are gone.'

'It won't be long now. You will soon be in the Loita Hills.'

'And you will be gone, back to England.' She shrugged, then said more cheerfully, 'Your Maa is improving, but you still sound like a Nairobi Maasai.'

'I need more practice out here in the Rift Valley. But perhaps we should speak English.'

'Oh no, it is bad. Since old Mr Mackecknie went home there is no one to correct me.'

His smile faded. 'I have news. From the governor.'

'I know it is not good. If it was, you would have been shouting it as you rode in.'

'He received the appeal. I did everything I could, but he won't change his mind about the resettlement.'

'I see.' She dropped her eyes. 'And Mount Kinangop?'

'He says he made a mistake when he offered access. Mount Kinangop is now included in the resettlement terms. It is no longer Maasai land.'

'Even for use during the *eunoto*?'

'I'm afraid so.'

She looked out over the savannah. A vulture circled a distant dust cloud. 'I understand.' She sighed and stooped to gather the leaves of the medicinal potion.

'I'm sorry, Naisua. He is a stubborn, ignorant man.' He scooped leaves into her basket and placed his hand under her elbow to help her up.

'It is all right, Colvan. I know you do your best for us. The failing is mine. I am just a Maasai woman. Even Governor Sir Percy Girouard knows I have no authority. No authority to speak for my family. No authority to speak for the Maasai.'

'He just doesn't understand.' His hand remained cupped at her elbow, the soft underside of her arm warm at his fingertips.

'Thank you.' She patted his hand. 'One day Seggi will be the *laibon*. Perhaps we can then reopen the matter.'

'Perhaps.'

THE AFRICAN TWILIGHT DRIFTED TOWARDS night. Far away on the eastern edge of the valley, the escarpment rose from the valley floor, disconnected from it by a purple-blue heat haze. Beetles made chirruping calls. Somewhere in the gloom nocturnal hunters awaited their chance on the night stage. The Great Rift Valley held its breath.

Their camp was near the western escarpment. It soared above them, silhouetted against the remnants of an orange and gold sky. Colvan began his magic games with the children. They sat in an awed semicircle on the opposite side of the cooking fire. Even the four year old was quiet. The routine had not changed since Colvan invented it on the first night of their trek, but the children never tired of it.

He pulled his tartan bandanna from his pocket. Four pairs of bright black eyes, reflecting the firelight, followed it. Up, down, then around to show both sides. Then, 'Tah-dah!' — a food can appeared from the bandanna. The children giggled and clapped their hands and the women, standing behind, said, 'Ai-ai-ai!'

'Tah-dah!' Cans continued to appear. Soon nearly a dozen were arranged in a row at the fireside.

When the tricks were done and the cooking pots were brimful with bubbling concoctions, Naisua spooned thick *ugali*, the stiff maize porridge popular with Swahili traders, into wooden bowls. Colvan added the tinned beef or mutton with a flourish. The children received a little milk, which had been coaxed from one of the few cows still producing.

By the end of the meal, the night had set in. Stars cascaded down the inky sky to the east and west, touching the escarpment two thousand feet above the valley floor. In the north and south they dissolved in the faint luminescence clinging to the horizon.

The children went contentedly to bed with full bellies. The sister-wives soon followed them to the simple sleeping shelters thrown together for a single night.

Colvan pulled a blackened pot from his pack and poured a sparing amount of precious water into it.

'Would you like tea, Naisua?' he said when the water boiled.

'Tea? What is tea?'

'It's a very popular drink made with these dried leaves and boiled water.'

'Is it modern?'

'No. It's been around for many, many years. An Englishman can't go long without it, but I've had trouble getting some until recently.'

'Well, tea is modern for a Maasai. I will try your tea.'

He poured the tea into two small tin cups and handed her one. 'Careful, it is very hot.'

'Ugh! It is bitter!'

'Have some milk with it. It might help.'

'Help? Why help? You Englishmen are strange. If you think it is good to drink, it should not need help.'

'It's just an expression.' He smiled and blew into his mug before he also took a sip. 'Well, I *have* made better tea. It must be the water.'

'I think I will like tea. Until then, I will use the help.' They laughed as she reached for the milk gourd.

Naisua and Colvan sipped their tea in silence. Beyond the light of the fire, the cattle could be heard snorting and complaining in the makeshift stock enclosure. A distant roar and a screech of pain or terror came from further out in the night — the hunter and the hunted.

'The lion draws near. I must go to the cattle.' She put down her mug.

'I'll come with you,' he said.

They walked past the *boma* with its dozen cattle and small flock of sheep and goats. The moon was not full, but in the cloudless sky it was enough to light their path.

'I don't think your *boma* will keep out a lion.'

'No, it is not possible. There is very little thorn bush near here, and no time to make a strong *boma*. So we must keep watch, my sister-wives and I. The pride could frighten the cattle through the *boma* fence. It would be a feast for them.'

'How do you women manage against the lion, out here alone?'

'Lions like our cattle but they very much do not like the Maasai. It is not just the *moran* they fear. We can keep them away if we watch through the night. I will sleep when the moon is there.' She pointed to a position in the night sky. 'Then one of the others will watch.'

They were content in their silence for some time, strolling the perimeter of the small cattle enclosure, then Naisua turned to him. 'Colvan, you are a good man. You help us so much. Why?'

As always, her guileless question caught him unawares. 'Well, I . . . I am the liaison officer for the resettlement. You are one of my flock.'

They had stopped at a small pond, the shrinking remains of a creek. A frog's melancholy call was answered by another somewhere in the darkness.

'Oh, so now I am a sheep? Or is it a goat?'

He sensed the smile in her voice. 'Oh, nothing so boring. If you were an animal in my flock it would be, let me see . . . a gazelle. An impala.'

'Impala? I like impala. Do you?'

'Yes, they are beautiful.'

'Perhaps I am a horse. Do you think horses are beautiful too?'

'Yes, horses are also beautiful.'

'Do you know, Colvan, the first time I saw a horse it nearly killed me.'

'What happened?'

'Oh, the owner, a *mzungu* man, rode the horse over the top of me.'

He had a look of horror on his face. 'My God! What a stupid oaf!'

'Yes.'

'Why are you smiling?'

'It was so long ago. I was a small child. But yes, I think the *mzungu* was a little bit weak in the brain.' Her smile broadened further.

'I'm sure I would not be so forgiving if I were you. Why, I would —'

'But he gave me a wonderful gift.'

'Oh, really? Then I hope it was many, many cattle,' he smiled.

'No, I was too young for cattle. But I still carry the gift.' She reached into her shoulder bag and pulled out a glass prism. 'Look.'

'A lump of glass?'

'No! It is beautiful! You see? It has lights. No, you cannot see them here. Come, let me show you.' She took his hand and led him to the sandy embankment on the dry creek. 'Sit here.' She pulled him down beside her. 'Now watch.' She lifted the glass to the moon and moved closer to him as she shifted the plane of the prism to catch the light.

A memory of a similar prism stirred in his memory, but he could feel her warmth beside him in the cool night air. If he moved slightly, their cheeks would touch.

'It was a wonderful gift, yes? The lights are even better in the sun. Is it not beautiful, Colvan?'

'Very beautiful.' He turned to face her. They were inches apart. She didn't retreat. 'So beautiful.' He could feel her breath on his lips. He slowly moved his hand to her cheek and ran a finger along the high cheekbones to her nose, then down to the curve of her mouth. He gently caressed the line of her chin to the silky smooth muscle behind her ear, then retraced its path back to her cheek. Her skin was warm. She closed her eyes, keeping her cheek to his hand. When they opened, they held his.

He slipped the folds of her long garment from her shoulder. It fell to her waist. Slowly he moved his fingertips to gently stroke one nipple before his hand cupped the full firm warmth of her breast. A shiver ran through her when he put his tongue to her, licking a dry drop of mother's milk from her nipple. She held his face to her as she lowered herself to the sandy bank. Lips touched lips.

Without breaking the embrace, Naisua slipped her garments aside. Colvan ran tiny kisses down her neck and shoulders to her breasts and belly. Her fragrance was of the Rift Valley: salt, silver *leleshwa* and dry grass.

She looped her fingers through his hair as he returned to her breast, then nibbled and teased at the nape of her neck. He swung his weight to one side and slipped the notch on his belt as she pulled one sleeve of his shirt from his shoulders. Naisua rolled on top of him and they became entangled while he tried to lever one boot off with the toe of the other.

She was on him, around him, and surrounding him, arousing him with her mouth and her hands. He rolled with her to be above her, his body pressing her down.

When he entered her, she pulled him to her with a strength that surprised him. His breath escaped in a rush. Their movement was an increasingly urgent rhythm. A frenzy. Naisua's short panting gasps quickened. Colvan held her and held her, until he could hold it no more.

Time passed — he was not sure how much — but he reached for her with eyes closed lest the feeling was lost, and began to stroke her cheek. He made long gentle strokes, feeling the rise and fall of her breath. Feeling the shape of her under his fingers.

When he did open his eyes, she was watching him with a sad smile.

'Your prism wove some magic for us this evening,' he said.

'It has. But it is not Maasai magic alone. The sun-stone once belonged to you.'

'To me?'

'Yes. You were the clumsy *mzungu* who ran me down with his horse.' Her smile was neither teasing nor accusing, simply languid, as were her eyes. 'And you were the one to give me this precious gift.'

'I thought I recognised it! But that was years ago ... a snotty-nosed girl ... You!'

'Of course, me. And I have kept it to remind me of your kindness ever since.'

'But I am here. You don't need a cheap trinket to remember me, surely.'

'Yes, you are here. But it will not always be so. One day ...'

She held the prism in her hand and touched it to her lips before touching it to his. 'Ronald Colvan,' she said, 'you, and this moment, are captured for ever in my sun-stone.' She moved the prism around his face, touched his eyes, ran it down his nose, rolled it across his cheek and pressed it against his lips. 'This image that I have of you now is captured in the stone. When you leave me, and when I grow lonely for you, I will call you back from the stone.'

Her eyes glistened in the light of the moon. 'You will be in the stone, and with me, for ever.'

CHAPTER 7

PEABODY'S GUIDE TO EAST AFRICA (5ᵀᴴ ED):
During the Emergency, the Home Guard was responsible
for undermining and neutralising the Mau Mau organisation
through their spy network and punitive measures.

Corruption and torture tactics reached scandalous
levels in the Home Guard, with both white colonial and
native troops equally guilty of brutality against civilians.

The amnesty of 1955 was declared to encourage Mau
Mau guerrillas to surrender, but it also absolved the Home
Guard from any future prosecution.

The Thorn Tree Café was buzzing with activity as usual.
Lunchtime customers milled around the entrance, some trying
to settle their accounts, others to catch the waiter's eye to find
them a table.

Mengoru pushed past them and picked his way around
crowded diners to a table in the corner overlooking Kimathi
Street. He squeezed onto the bench seat; his ample gut tilted
the table making the saltshaker topple and the sugar bowl
clatter. Almost before he was seated, he snapped his fingers,
calling for a beer.

Mengoru's thick frame contradicted his Maasai lineage. He
was considered a Maasai by his tribe, and in his heart felt he
was, but his grandfather had stolen a Kikuyu girl in a raid and

she became Mengoru's grandmother. His Kikuyu side was apparent in the thickening of his legs and arms and the substantial midriff, though this might also be from good Kenyan beer, which he consumed in quantity. His nose had the curve of the Maasai, Roman in shape, but was broader and thicker at the nostrils. Above it, his brow was permanently furrowed between bushy eyebrows, which, in combination with the nose, gave him a hawkish look. He was a head shorter than the average Maasai, this too came from his grandmother's side.

His grandfather was quite taken by his Kikuyu trophy and eventually formalised the union in a Maasai marriage. In reward for her hard work and faithful attention to all matters expected of a good Maasai wife, his grandmother was allowed to resume the connections with her tribe. So Mengoru was recognised as part Kikuyu by the Kikuyu and all Maasai by the Maasai. It was a situation he found greatly to his liking. And since the leader in the fight for independence, Jomo Kenyatta, claimed a Maasai connection somewhere in his obscure lineage, Mengoru felt in good company.

He scanned the tables and was glad to find young Onditi was not yet there. He would have time for a couple of beers without feeling obliged to offer him one. As a nephew of Nicholas Onditi, he was surprised the young man was not doing better for himself. Mengoru smiled; clever Uncle Nicholas was probably testing his nephew before offering him fruits from higher in the tree.

When Mengoru first met young Onditi, his immediate thought was that here was a perfect husband for his wayward daughter. But on reflection he realised it would not work. As a Kalengin, Onditi could not be part of a traditional Maasai wedding. And without the proper wedding, Mengoru could not impress the Maasai party members as he had promised Nicholas Onditi he would. No, better to keep with his original plan. A compliant older Maasai man, perhaps one with two or three wives already, was a safer strategy. Young Onditi could find a wife of his own kind.

He referred to him as 'young Onditi', although the man must be at least thirty. At his age, Mengoru was still in the

Home Guard. They were good days, he thought. A time when everybody was too busy worrying about the Mau Mau to bother with a little business on the side; a young bull here, a few goats there.

Mengoru had ordered a second beer and still Onditi had not appeared. It was disrespectful. He would let him know he expected better. He could not refer to him by his given name. Using first names — James, in this case — was another flashy *mzungu* habit of which Mengoru heartily disapproved. But since everyone used the family name, Onditi, for Nicholas Onditi, the Minister for Lands, his nephew was forced to accept various alternatives. Bad luck.

The beer arrived and Mengoru drank deeply, smacking his lips in appreciation. He glanced around at the other patrons. Tourists and office-workers. I should be at Le Château, Mengoru thought ruefully. There had been occasions when he spent appreciable time and money at the popular lunch venue for Nairobi's government leaders, in the hope of catching the eye of Nicholas Onditi or one of the other party-faithful. But he'd had no luck and had remained an outsider until, finally, many years ago, he managed to find a toehold on the sheer cliff-face of setbacks, frustrations and pure bad luck that had blocked his climb to wealth and power.

On that typical Nairobi June day in 1963, the featureless cloud cover shrouded the city in dismal grey. The more usual joyful golds and blues were nowhere to be seen. Even the brilliant red and purple bougainvillea seemed to lose heart, and with it their colour.

Nights had turned cold enough for houseboys to set a fire in the parlour to warm the cold stone mansions of Parklands and Mathaiga. At the club, cashmere sweaters became *de rigueur*. As persistent cloud and Nairobi's high altitude combined to thwart the usual warmth, many of the white inhabitants would escape on a short safari down to stylish Bells Inn in Naivasha, or even an hour further to Nakuru and the lake, perhaps for the weekend. The Rift Valley was always awash with brilliant tropical sunshine, guaranteed to take the chill from the soul.

The *mzee*, the father of Kenya, was in Nairobi on that grey June day. The crowded Nairobi street hummed like a tightly drawn bowstring. Jomo Kenyatta, ex-freedom crusader, ex-prisoner of the British, was inside the government offices, taking the oath as Kenya's first Prime Minister. In a year he would be proclaimed President of the new republic.

Mengoru had pushed through the crowd to the police cordon. He scanned the gathered KANU officials standing in small groups on the wide flagstone steps. The area was surrounded by Kenyan police, mostly black, under the control of a bushy-moustached white officer with a swagger stick. He was hoping to find his benefactor: the Big Man who had given him his chance to make a name for himself; the chance to become a Big Man in his own right.

Mengoru waved his arm. 'Onditi! Mr Onditi!'

Nicholas Onditi glanced at him but let his gaze move on along the line of excited faces.

'Mr Onditi, it's me. Mengoru!'

Onditi turned back. He hesitated then nodded at the policeman. The rope lifted and Mengoru slipped under it to join him on the steps.

'My friend, this is a great moment, is it not?' Mengoru beamed, pumping the other's hand. Onditi grunted.

Mengoru edged up another step to stand beside his benefactor. He squared his shoulders towards the crowd, some of whom were watching with mild interest. It was pleasing to be seen with Onditi, the man most Party members believed would be the Minister for Lands in the first Kenyatta cabinet.

'I thought you were in Isiolo,' Onditi said, barely moving his lips.

'I was, but we have some problems there.' Mengoru had been hoping to raise the matter more subtly.

'Problems? Then fix them. That is your job in this, isn't it?'

A murmur rustled through the crowd as the doors opened and Kenyatta's entourage spilled onto the steps.

'Yes, of course, but I need some assistance. The Somalis are becoming difficult on the price.'

When Kenyatta emerged, a roar went up from every throat.

He wore his usual coloured cap and carried the white colobus monkey-hair flywhisk. The trademark beaded Maasai *kinyata* girded his ample belly. He played the crowd then held his hand aloft to silence them. It was minutes before the buzz retreated to the end of the street and the crowd held its breath for his words.

'This is one of the happiest moments of my life. We are now embarking on the final brief stage, which will lead this country to Independence. It is not a celebration by one Party as its election victory. Rather must it be a rejoicing of all the people of this land at the progress towards the goal of independence.'

'Then meet their price,' Onditi hissed, taking care to maintain his smile for the crowd.

'But I will need more cash. The truck ... and the first delivery was such a high price.'

'But as we celebrate, let us remember that constitutional advance is not the greatest end in itself. Many of our people suffer in sickness. Many are poor beyond endurance. Too many live out narrow lives beneath a burden of ignorance.'

Onditi flashed a sideways glance at Mengoru. 'I thought you were a businessman,' he spat through tight lips. 'You must sell some of the ivory first, you fool. To build your capital.'

'But how do I get to it? The Somalis are very fierce ... '

'As we participate in pomp and circumstance, and as we make merry at this time, remember this: we are relaxing before the toil that is to come. We must work harder to fight our enemies: ignorance, sickness and poverty.'

'I thought your brave *moran* were fighting men. Use them. Or are you not their leader as you suggest?'

'Yes, of course. It will be done.'

'Good. And don't forget our arrangement.'

'I therefore give you the call: Harambee! Let us all work hard together for our country, Kenya.'

There had been times when Mengoru had suffered from Onditi's fierce temper but he never ceased to be enormously impressed by Onditi's success. The Minister was a man of about his own age, and had started from similar humble beginnings quite near his own village. Onditi became the local Big Man, then KANU candidate for Nyanza Province and, shortly after, a

Minister in the government. That was a man to emulate, Mengoru reflected. Nicholas Onditi was a master at squeezing tea money from every constituent, aid donor or corporate magnate. A true genius. As Minister for Lands he was able to quietly sell off road easements to grateful corporations hungry for space. New residential land releases were another gift he could bestow for bounty, as was his approval for any major development plan.

Mengoru rarely engaged in introspection; such habits were self-indulgent and a sign of weakness. But if, at sixty-three, he were to reflect upon his life, he would have to concede that the wealth and power he craved were still out of his reach.

In recent times he had skimmed good profits from ivory and rhino horn, and was successful in managing the primitive tribesmen in the wild northern frontiers, largely due to his naturally aggressive nature rather than inspirational leadership. But the big money, the kind Nicholas Onditi could command, eluded him.

But Mengoru was feeling optimistic that day. With the President's crackdown on poachers, ivory had soared in price. His latest shipment from Marsabit would bring handsome profits. He would need it.

He believed that if he could just get into the Party's inner circle, the rewards would follow. Nicholas Onditi wanted to cement the loyalty of the Maasai block in parliament. It was Mengoru's chance to impress. He would arrange a traditional Maasai wedding, invite all Maasailand and have Onditi as guest of honour. The Minister would be delighted. More so if Mengoru's own daughter were the bride — a traditional bride.

Young Onditi's swagger was unmistakable even from the far side of Kimathi Street. Something in his walk reminded Mengoru of himself at that age. He watched him cross the street and plunge through the sidewalk crowd outside the New Stanley. Moments later he appeared in the café entrance. Mengoru beckoned him over.

'*Habari.*'

'*Mzuri.*'

They shook hands African style, clasping palms then grasping thumbs.

James ordered beers and they exchanged polite small talk until they arrived. When the waiter had poured the drinks and departed, Mengoru rested his weight on his elbows and leaned across the table. '*Sasa*, let me make sure the plans are quite clear.'

James nodded and sat forward.

Mengoru took a mouthful of beer. 'One of my people is in Marsabit now. He will meet you early tomorrow morning in Isiolo, on the north side of the checkpoint. You know the truck. His name is Njuguna. He's a good man. So you organise things at the security checkpoint. *Si ndio?* You have the tea money? Good. But don't give these little people too much. Not too much.'

James nodded. '*Ndio.*'

'Now, listen carefully. You stay with the truck all the way. Okay? We meet at Isuria.'

'I understand. Do you want me to take the truck to the lake?'

'No. The boat will not be there for three, maybe four days. I will go to Muhoro myself.'

'Good.' James raised his glass. 'To success.'

'*Ndio.*' They touched glasses.

James ran a finger down the frosting on his beer glass. 'And the money?'

'After I get mine,' Mengoru rumbled. It always annoyed him when people wanted to talk about payments before the job was done.

'Of course.'

Mengoru took another mouthful. 'And what of the girl?'

'Your daughter? Yes, it's coming along nicely. Very nicely.'

'And her address?'

'Not yet.'

Mengoru drained his glass and burped. 'I thought you said you had her in the palm of your hand?'

'Sometimes these things take time. She is a little shy, but I'll know where she lives within a couple of days.'

'Hmm. I'll be back in Nairobi next Wednesday. We will meet here again. At one o'clock.'

●　●　●

THE NORFOLK HOTEL STOOD FOR nearly a hundred years on what used to be called Government Road. From providing basic overnight accommodation for idealistic young farmers en route to their tranche of land in the White Highlands, to a prestigious temporary home for what Hollywood in those days called 'heart-throbs', it had witnessed a lot.

Government Road was renamed Harry Thuku Road after independence, in honour of the man who, in 1922, stood within earshot of the Norfolk and accused the British of stealing Kikuyu land. Harry Thuku urged his black brothers not to work for the white man any more. He was arrested then exiled to Somalia without so much as a trial.

When, some thirty years later, the charismatic Jomo Kenyatta, leader of the push for independence, addressed a rally at the nearby Central Police Station to protest the imprisonment of his supporters, things got out of hand when Mary Nyanjira lifted her dress and thrust her highly prized merchandise at the line of policemen guarding the gaol. The policemen stoically withstood Mary's loud aspersions upon their manhood until, frustrated, she called upon the crowd to rush the gaol and free the inmates, at which point the police opened fire in a panic. The white Kenyans on the veranda of the Norfolk, sportsmen all, took pot-shots at the fleeing Africans, killing twenty-five according to the next day's *East African Standard*. Probably closer to two hundred, said others.

It was unlikely that Harry Thuku ever entered the Norfolk. Kenyatta did, but not until he was President. In those days the Norfolk was at its zenith, the preferred lodgings of the rich and powerful. Visiting dignitaries, of whom there were many in the early days of the republic, would reserve suites for weeks. But it wasn't until the 1980s that the veranda at the Norfolk emerged as the meeting place and mixing bowl for the chic, young and socially mobile elite of Nairobi. A place to be seen in the first cool breath of evening before departing to a restaurant or dinner party.

Jack felt there was something special about Friday evenings at the Norfolk. Nairobi office-workers would start to arrive around five. By six it was standing room only and by six-thirty the wide open veranda was a thick mix of office girls and businessmen, safari operators and up-country ranchers, dealmakers in white shirts and fake Rolexes.

The hotel's resident guests would not appear until eight, and never on the veranda. These tended to be serious older men in cravats or ties, and jackets, the ladies in elegant dresses and pearls. They would confine themselves to the five-star splendour of the tessellated inner courtyard, then move to the quietly opulent dining room hung with Isak Dinesen oils.

Jack arrived from the office at dusk to find Bear at one of the high drink stands on the Norfolk's veranda in a small circle of men. One of them was a member of the Parklands Club where Jack had started to use the gym and tennis courts; he knew him to be an expatriate Rhodesian rugby player simply from overhearing him at the poolside. Two others were vaguely familiar faces from the UN office: an effusive Italian, and a Scot with an impenetrable Glaswegian accent.

Jack responded to their greetings and eased into a space between the rugby player and the Italian. Bear was opposite, extolling the benefits of the latest Land Rover. Jack nodded to Charles for a round of drinks. Charles was a big Rendille man with a smile as white as his starched shirt. His face was etched with the story of the northern desert and was as black as his satin vest. Minutes later he brought over a tray of cold amber Tuskers. He ripped the tops off one-handed, and passed them around the group.

Jack gave him a hundred-shilling note. '*Tafadhali*,' he said. Charles nodded, smiled and moved on through the throng.

The rugby player leaned conspiratorially towards the Italian. 'As I was sayin', Angelo. Black pussy. The best. I mean *the* best.' He glanced around the table; the others were in another conversation. He looked over his shoulder then lowered his head again. 'Black pussy will just milk you dry.'

The Italian leaned across Jack, turning his ear towards the rugby man above the clamour of the bar. He nodded to him to continue.

'They go crazy for white guys, ya know?'

The Italian, grinning, leaned closer still.

'I tell you!' said the rugby player. 'You'd give yer left testicle for just one night. Take 'em to a restaurant. I mean, a nice restaurant. Know what I'm sayin'? Well, not too fancy. Give 'em a meal. A few drinks.' He tapped the side of his nose and winked. 'They'll fuck yer brains out.'

The Rhodesian's lurid descriptions were becoming irritating. Jack decided to move to Bear's side of the drinks bench. He retrieved his beer from under the Italian's nose, mumbled an *excuse me*, and left them in rapt conversation.

Two women hovered at the outskirts of the group. Jack eased around the rather large rear end of one. The other was facing him, with a coquettish smile in her twinkling dark eyes. Jack noted the short skirt, neat button-up blouse and jacket — standard female office-worker attire. He returned the smile feeling quite sure that they must have met somewhere. Perhaps the UN office.

'Hi!' she said.

'Hi,' he replied, his smile wavering slightly.

'Are you lost?'

'Perhaps just a little.' He wished he could recall her name. She was cute, with high cheekbones tapering to a dimpled chin.

'I haven't seen you around,' she said.

'Oh, I've been here five, maybe six times.'

'So you're new. I'll look after you.'

'Sounds good to me!'

'I'm Monique. This is Nancy.'

'I'm Jack. I thought you were someone I should have remembered from my office.'

'Jack! How could you think that? Honey, you would never forget me.' She put a hand on his arm and continued before he could reply. 'Are these your friends?'

'Oh, these guys? Look, I take no responsibility for them. A bunch of ferals, especially this big bastard here.' He nudged Bear standing at his side.

Bear turned. He looked from one woman to the other before saying, 'Jack! Goddamn! You *have* been busy.' He planted the cigarette in the corner of his mouth and extended a hand. 'I'm Bear.'

'Hi. I'm Nancy,' interposed the larger one. 'This is Monique.' Nancy's eyes didn't leave Bear as she edged to his side.

'Pleased to meet you. Has Jack offered you a drink? No? So rude of him. But then he's an Aussie, you know.' They laughed.

'Margarita for me,' said Nancy.

'G and T,' Monique added.

When Jack returned with the drinks, Bear and Nancy were chattering away like a pair of lovebirds. Monique accepted the gin with a smile, slipped her hand under his arm and squeezed his bicep. 'Happy days, Jack.' She clinked his glass.

THE CARNIVORE RESTAURANT AND NIGHTCLUB was built on the eastern boundary of the Nairobi National Park, where the incursion of expanding suburbia halted at the National park's simple strand-wire fence. Following the disappearance of a few neighbourhood dogs, believed taken by one or more park inhabitants, the National Parks authority reluctantly agreed to replace the wire strands with a two-metre chain-wire fence. It had proved to be more for show than effect, and residents were again becoming agitated.

Carnivore's management were grateful to the lions for the distraction. It diverted residents' ire from the growing issue of the disco's late-night noise.

The four diners found a table close to the dance floor, where strobe lights swept the tightly packed crowd seething to the penetrating beat of four huge speakers. Bear returned with the drinks and Nancy dragged him off for a dance before he could sit. He made a token objection then flung himself into it with abandon. Monique pleaded with Jack; when he finally stood she gave a series of excited little squeaks and they plunged onto the dance floor.

In the numbing din of the sound system, Jack could see her mouth moving but heard not a word. He smiled and nodded at what he hoped were appropriate moments. His body began to absorb the throb of African drums, the deep bass of massed male voices and the trilling and ululating interplay of a woman's voice, teasing them at an octave higher. Instead of absorbing the sound, he felt he was being absorbed by it, as his body began to move without conscious effort. The beat moved his feet and his body followed.

Above, on towering wooden poles, a colourful profusion of flowered creepers coiled in the cathedral spaces beneath the *makuti* roof. Openings in the woven grass walls revealed hibiscus gardens in an expansive lawn. Spotlights hidden beneath grotesquely twisted frangipani boughs made ghostly shapes against the blackness beyond.

After a few dance brackets, all four returned to their drinks. The spell was broken as Monique and Nancy became engrossed in mindless trivia. Jack excused himself with, 'Back in a second.'

He walked through one of the wall openings towards the toilets, then turned off the path and into the garden area. It was nearing the end of the dry season; the night air was still yet moist. Away from the bright lights, the stars came alive, filling the impenetrable blackness from horizon to horizon.

He wandered along, enjoying the relief from the pounding music and Monique's mindless chatter. Frogs sang in the ornamental pond as he passed. At the very end corner of the boundary he propped a foot on the white post-and-rail fence. The land fell gently away towards Nairobi Dam. The city's lights rose above the new housing estate on Langata Road. Somehow the contrast between the disco and the warm, silent darkness gave him a hollow feeling. He took a deep breath, drinking in the air, rich, cool and laden with dew, then released it with a loud sigh.

The air reminded him of nights in the outback; nights when cattle station managers would lose track of the conversation and invariably return to speculation about rain. He could imagine, even taste, the dry savannah grasses and the shrubs in the garden opening every petal and leaf to absorb the wet night air. Another deep breath. His lungs swelled with the cleansing dew.

The sky was filled with unfamiliar gems. The stars were almost as bright as they were in the outback, but the Southern Cross was in the wrong place.

An image of old Joe Scales came to his mind. Joe was the head drover at Moonlight Tank station. Had been for years.

He had the same weather-beaten skin as many older men of the land, but Joe, being part Aboriginal, also had black wrinkles eroding his face and deep-set eyes that for ever searched the horizon. Jack had sometimes had the feeling the old man could see beyond it, which might explain the slightly bemused expression Joe always seemed to wear.

Joe would often wander by the station-house veranda and sit with Jack as the sun settled for the day. He wouldn't refuse one of Jack's beers, sipping it one-sided while a soggy roll-your-own dangled, as usual, from the corner of his mouth. Three or four Aboriginal children, who he would completely ignore, invariably followed him around. Ignoring them allowed him to tell outrageous stories for their benefit. His yarns about the bunyip monster that lurked somewhere up in the folded gorges of the Pillaroo Ranges delivered them into spellbound silence.

'Big as a bloody elephant 'e is, young Jack,' he would say in a quiet voice that easily carried to the children, open-mouthed along the veranda edge. 'He musta bailed up that big grey bull las' night. My bloody oath!' Joe's stories were so compelling even older children wanted to believe the truth of them. 'The ol' fella came inta the home yard here, quiverin' like a kitten. That big ol' bunyip plurry scared the spots off 'im he did, young Jack. Jus' wanted to be patted and petted. Poor ol' fella.'

The children's saucer eyes would be riveted on Joe, who sat, deadpan except for the faintest twinkle in his eye, puffing his roll-your-own and squinting towards the point where the hills met the red western sky.

In the African night, under those alien stars, the outback was infinitely distant in time and space. Even Friday nights in Sydney were only vague memories. He tried to remember their routine. Maybe he and Liz would go with friends to a restaurant or a nightclub in Manly or Kings Cross. Funny, he thought, how distance can make recent memories fade fast.

He thrust his hands deep into his pockets and turned back to the nightclub. The DJ had put on a slow number, an indication that the night was approaching its end.

A couple was silhouetted near the fish pond. The woman's voice held a note of exasperation. 'James, it doesn't matter whether it's business or not. I don't want to see you. And stop following me around.'

Jack was close enough to hear the reply. Although it was in Swahili, there was no mistaking the snarl it contained. The man grabbed her roughly by the arm, pulling her to him.

'James! No! Leave me alone!'

Jack was only paces away. 'Hey! Are you okay?'

She shrugged her arm free. 'Yes. Thanks.' She was mid-twenties. Tall. 'I can handle this.' The way she said it and the way she held herself, almost as if she was above the conflict rather than in it, made him think she probably could.

The black man took a stumbling step forward. He was heavy-set and obviously drunk. With the light now full in his face, Jack recognised the Department of Regional Development's James Onditi.

'What do *you* want?' Onditi said, squinting into the bright discotheque lights over Jack's shoulder. 'Bloody *mzungu*!' He took another step forward. 'Mind your own fucking business!' And threw a round-arm right.

Jack saw it coming and easily stepped inside it, instinctively shooting a jab into the other's short ribs. The black man doubled over with a gasp. Jack waited for him to straighten just enough to get a clean line to his jaw, then hit him with another jab that spun him about. He finished him off by footing him into the fish pond.

'Ahhh!' Onditi gasped, more in shock than in pain as he spluttered to the surface covered in lily fragments. Jack grabbed him by the collar of his jacket, pulled him up then thought better of it and let him slide down the cobbled edge into the pond again.

The woman was already walking away. Jack followed. 'Are you all right?' he said to her back.

As he drew alongside she turned to him, brushing her beaded braids from her eyes. 'Yes, I am. Just ... just leave me.' She blinked away brimming tears.

He could see her face in the light of the large paraffin

burners that lined the garden. She had almost Egyptian features, fine nose, high cheekbones and slightly almond eyes. Her skin was a delicious dark brown.

'I'll walk you to your car.'

'I'll get a taxi.' She continued briskly towards the exit.

'Fine. I'll walk you there.'

'Look, I'm okay. Okay?' She was a head shorter than him, about five seven, five eight. Great legs.

'I just don't want that goon to follow you out here.'

'He won't,' she snapped.

'Hey, lady!' Jack replied in kind. 'What's your problem?'

A taxi stood waiting at the turning circle. The doorman opened its door.

'Did I ask you for your help? Uh? Did I? No. So just leave me.' She slid onto the back seat and swung her long legs in after her, pulling the door shut.

'Well, thanks for nothing! Who the hell do you think you are anyway?'

'Who do I think I am?' she said through the window, her anger barely under control. 'Do I have to be an African Princess to be left alone?'

'Look, I wouldn't care if you were the Queen of friggin' Sheba.'

'Well, bad luck,' she said. 'I'm Maasai.'

The taxi lurched forward. He watched the dust settle in its wake.

CHAPTER 8

PEABODY'S GUIDE TO EAST AFRICA (5TH ED):
The Hash House Harriers began in the 1930s at a British expatriates' club in Malaya. Running was considered a good way to work off the club's terrible food, hence the nickname Hash House.

With their odd cries and blasts on a hunting horn intended to keep the pack in touch, the Hash House Harriers occasionally startle local villagers along their route.

False trails are used to bring the so-called 'Front Running Bastards' back to the field.

The objective, as always, is to be first to the beer at trail's end.

Jack waited for the office girls in front of him to step out of the elevator first, then headed across the foyer towards the front entrance. He strode past the armed guard without a second thought. Three months ago, he would have been careful to avoid sudden movements, believing youth and AK47s to be a hazardous combination.

He skipped down the steps and turned into Harambee Avenue which was its usual shambles. Cars were double-, sometimes triple-parked.

The heat hit him before he had gone a hundred metres and he slowed his pace. Combined with the effects of the altitude, he would be sweating in minutes. Until his car arrived from Australia, the transport alternatives were not appealing. Taxis were out of the question — hot, dirty rust-buckets, intolerable even in the desperation of a drunken late night.

He wore a tie with his pale blue short-sleeved shirt, the slacks from his grey suit and black lace-up shoes. He had considered wearing the jacket when he dressed that morning, but decided against it. The meeting was no big deal, just a project person at the American aid agency. It didn't warrant the discomfort, even if it was their first meeting.

The leper was in his usual place, selling papers on the corner of Moi and Haile Selassie Avenues. Three grim-faced US Marines supervised Jack's entrance to the American Embassy. It was the only building in Nairobi with metal detectors installed. The directory in the foyer listed AmericAid on the fourth floor.

'Jack Morgan to see Malaika Kidongi,' he said to the young male receptionist.

'Just a moment, please,' he said, and vanished into the partitioned offices.

Jack wandered to the window and began to trace the wide path of Haile Selassie Avenue. It wound up Nairobi Hill beside the Railway Sports Club to where he had recently leased an apartment in the Bishops Gardens estate. Perched on the ridge, the place commanded a northeasterly aspect with views over the city and Uhuru Park. He had secured it with a month's rent as soon as he heard his personal effects were about to arrive in Mombasa. He hoped to check out of the Jacaranda Hotel within the week.

At the sound of the office door opening, he turned from the window. The receptionist was returning to his place at the desk. Behind him, an African woman approached with an economy of motion that was both graceful and sexy. She wore a crisp pink blouse and a black skirt that hugged her hips and thighs. Her braids, beaded at the tips, were pulled back to reveal small gold studs nestling in her ear lobes.

It was the walk he recognised first. He'd had plenty of time to devour it on the way to the taxi rank — as compact and graceful as a leopard's stride.

She extended her hand. 'Mr Morgan?'

'Your Highness,' he said with a straight face.

'Excuse me?' Her smile widened but her brow furrowed with the question.

'Or do you still prefer African Princess?'

There was a moment of recollection then her hand went to her mouth. 'Oh, my God! It's you. From Carnivore!'

'Humble servant, Highness.' He made a shallow bow. The receptionist grinned.

'Malaika, just Malaika. Mr Morgan, I ...' She had trouble meeting his eyes, choosing instead to search the reception area for any witness to her embarrassment.

'Jack, just Jack.'

'Oh, my God. This is so ... so ... I'm blushing! Not that you would know, I suppose.'

The receptionist was riveted by their conversation.

Malaika gave him a look that killed his smile and sent him back to his paperwork. 'Um ... please. The conference room is this way.' She turned and headed towards the corner room. Jack followed, his attention again drawn to her hips and graceful stride.

She had regained some of her composure as she closed the door behind him. 'Mr Morgan, I ... perhaps I owe you an apology.' They both remained standing. Jack rested his hands on the back of a chair.

'It's just ... well ...' She wrung her hands and began to pace. He remained silent, raising an eyebrow ever so slightly.

'That man, he's ... well, never mind him. What I was going to say is, I suppose I could have had better manners. And it just popped into my head ... the part about the African Princess.' She appeared to become uneasy again as Jack maintained his silence. 'Mr Morgan ... ? You don't say much, do you?'

'It's still Jack. And I don't know why I should. You were the one doing all the talking last time.'

'Well, yes, but I told you, I didn't need your help.'

'Oh yes.' He moved away from the chair to stand at the window, arms crossed and an index finger tapping his bottom lip. 'Let me see,' he said, turning to face her. 'That would have been just before your boyfriend took a swipe at me.'

'Yes. I mean, no. He is not my boyfriend.' She straightened and forced her hands to her sides. 'Why should I explain all this? Ah?'

'Maybe 'cause I was just a guy minding his own business,' he made a sweeping theatrical gesture, 'who sees a lady struggling with some drunk in the dark and, like an idiot, nearly gets his head knocked off trying to help her.'

'Oh, *help me*, is it? Who asked you to help me?' She took up a position on the opposite side of the conference table. 'Anyway, by the look of you ...'

'Not so much as a *thanks for your help* ...'

'... you were in some kind of bad mood ...'

'... then slams the taxi door in my face.'

'Are you always like that, I wonder?'

'What was that? Did you say *bad mood*? Do you think I was looking for a fight?'

'Showing off your muscles. I suppose you win a lot of women that way.'

'Jesus! I don't believe it! You would have to be the most ungrateful, egotistical ... person I have ever met.'

'And you, Mr Jack Morgan, are ... Oh, this is too much!' She gathered her papers and slipped them into their folder. 'I suggest we reschedule for some other time.' She walked to the door. 'Some time when you have your adrenaline or your ... your ... what do you call it? Your *testosterone* under control.'

JACK HURDLED A MUDDY HOLE in the middle of the track through the squatter settlement. He was at the head of the pack that included the Nairobi Hash House Harrier's best runner, Muni Shan, the bugler. These days Jack wouldn't dream of missing the Monday Hash run. With nearly three months' acclimatisation under his belt, he had become good at it — a regular figure among the leaders.

For the first three or four weeks, Bear had enjoyed waiting for him at the end of a run with a half-empty beer in his hand. But for some time now, Jack had been regularly getting the better of him. He wondered where Bear was in the field today. He smiled to himself, knowing he wouldn't be far behind, but hoping he and the leaders took a wrong trail and would be forced to sacrifice their advantage trying to find the right one again.

The pack ran past a promising track to the right. It had been some time since they had spotted any flour markers. Unless they found one soon, they would have to double back.

He glanced at Muni who gave a blast on the trumpet. 'On! On!' came the cry from another. Well, Jack thought, they seem confident enough. He pounded around a corner, leaving the last of the Kangemi shacks behind.

BEAR PUSHED HIMSELF TO THE limit. His tongue was dry and swollen and his mouth felt like sawdust. Leg muscles threatened to turn to jelly and sweat trickled into his eyes. He brushed it away quickly, trying not to lose his stride. He concentrated on his breathing — tried to lock its rhythm to that of his pounding feet, which were leaden and slow to respond. But the pack leaders were still in sight and he was well clear of the next runners.

Perhaps he was getting too old for this. Apart from the Hash, he hadn't played any serious sport since his days with a rugby club in Johannesburg. He'd loved the game, the only redeeming feature from his miserable years at an English boarding school. Rugby was a man's game, and he had played it hard and dirty. Something to prove. It was the same with the Hash. These days he ran as a statement of capability rather than for enjoyment. *Forty-seven!* Maybe it was time to admit to everyone, including himself, that he was actually fifty-four, before it killed him.

He tried not to think of the burning pain in his thighs.

Jack probably wouldn't have been interested in the Hash if he hadn't opened his big mouth on that first day. And Mondays would have been a whole lot more civilised. But tonight would be a different story. 'One way or another, young Jack,' Bear muttered to himself, 'I'm gonna kick your ass tonight. Or die tryin'.'

And Jack was good. Too good. He had a cross-country runner's build — long and lean. Good musculature without the bulk that became a burden on an obstacle course such as the Hash. His chest was wide of beam rather than deep through the shoulder blades. A chest for a middle-distance runner. Jack and Bear shared the view that running could be fun, but winning was important.

Bear found it hard to accept defeat, by man or beast. He had spent fifteen years sparring with Africa. Bobbing, jabbing, weaving. Counting it a victory whenever he overcame one of its seemingly endless challenges. Smouldering for revenge when it dealt him a blow. But in victory or defeat, there was no doubt that Bear Hoffman was a man of Africa. He had the credentials. It wasn't just that he was big and tough. He was reckless. Africa favoured the reckless.

Recklessness had shaped Bear's life. His mother raised him in Berlin at a time when it was tough to be a kid in that city. His father had died on the Russian front; somewhere in the blood and mud his body simply disappeared. Bear was told his father had been brave. Maybe he was just reckless. When he was a child he had wondered what it would be like to have a father. Even a father in a cemetery.

The pack leaders disappeared as the track took them around a thicket of trees and shrubs. When they came into view again, they seemed slightly further ahead. Bear shut everything else from his mind — the rusty iron roofs of the packing-case huts, the bitter-faced squatters who watched him pass from cardboard doorways. He concentrated all his energies on his run.

When his mother took the US colonel into her bed, Bear was sent to a boarding school in England. It was his tenth birthday. He didn't cry as his mother put him on the train with a guilty look and tears rolling down her face. The colonel was happy to pay. 'Anyway,' he'd said, 'it's not a good place for a kid. Especially while the occupation forces are here.' When the colonel's tour of duty was completed, they collected Bear from boarding school and moved to New York.

Somewhere ahead, the bugler confirmed the continuation of the flour trail. Jack's pack followed him up the left fork. Bear sensed it was a false trail. It would be the first tonight and usually there were three or four per run. If the right-hand path was the true trail, Bear would pick up time — at least five minutes. He might still be able to show Jack an empty beer bottle at the finish.

He swung down the right-hand track, which immediately grew darker as it plunged into the valley. The squatters' huts were behind him as he pitched headlong down the overgrown path. He ignored another turn-off, staying loyal to his instinct. The downhill running was a relief but the track was becoming narrower by the moment. Bear gathered speed as he neared a turn at the base of the slope. Before he could react, he slammed into a chain-wire fence and hung there, his fingers curled into the mesh. Feelings of exhaustion and disbelief swamped him.

'Shit!' he yelled, and kicked the wire mesh as hard as he could. It bounced back. 'What the fuck is a fence doin' in the fuckin' jungle?' he said through clenched teeth. It was ten feet high and topped with razor wire. He shook it angrily. The fence rippled in defiance. On the other side, where his path continued on its way, he could see bulldozer tracks and newly cleared land. It was the beginning of a housing estate. He smashed his palm into the mesh. 'Shit!'

Head down, he began to retrace his path up the hill with plodding steps. Now he would be ten or fifteen minutes behind the leaders. An ignominious finish with the tail-enders.

A pair of muddy bare feet blocked his path. Bear's eyes travelled up to torn and dirty trousers, to army-issue shirt, missing the sleeves, and a muscular arm holding a lump of wood poised above eye level. The cold eyes held a sour, desperate look. Bear ducked. The club bounced off his shoulder, grazing the top of his head. On hands and knees in the soft mud of the track, instinct compelled him to roll sideways. The club thumped into the mud beside him. Bear grabbed the attacker's arm, pulling him off balance. As the young thug toppled forward, Bear swung a right to his jaw. It missed, but he followed it with another that caught him flush under the ear. Bear called upon his remaining strength to struggle to his feet. With a snarl like a wounded lion, he lifted the man by the hair and planted a knee into his face. It hoisted him off the ground and into the foliage to the side of the track. Bear swung a large mud-encrusted running shoe into the man's ribs; as he did so, three men, hanging back until their leader had tried his hand, rushed him. The first caught him in the midriff with a rugby tackle.

'Ooof!' Bear bellowed, landing flat on his back with an attacker on top of him. He rolled from side to side, dodging the raining blows from the others' clubs. Bear used his assailant as a shield but a heavy blow caught him on the temple, and moments later another struck him above the eye. Warm blood trickled into his ear. There was a fogginess growing at the edge of his vision.

Through the blur, a tee-shirt and shorts appeared above him. The nearest attacker went headlong into a tree. Bear blinked his vision clear to see Jack throwing huge looping rights and lefts at the next guy standing above him, a solid brute with a shaved head. Slam. Slam. He set the attacker back on his heels, with a straight left and short right jabs.

'Hah!' said Bear, finding his second wind. He muttered curses in German and English and flung the tackler off. He struggled to his feet. One of the others broke from the foliage at the side of the track brandishing a piece of lumber. Bear ducked it and grabbed him around the waist. The pair stumbled backwards over the man on the ground and continued to wrestle in the mud.

Jack had almost finished with the first of his assailants when another charged from the foliage, blood streaming from a head wound, and grabbed him. 'Bastard!' Jack said, with the exasperation of a man given another load at the end of a hard day. One man held Jack in a bear hug while the other landed punches to his ribs and abdomen. Jack leaned back and delivered a vicious, well-aimed kick to the groin of the man in front. He dropped in a ball of agony.

Bear decided he was sick of wrestling in the mud. He was sick of missing with his best punches too, and most of all he was sick of being on the receiving end of theirs. But he couldn't land a telling blow with his man all over him, and he knew that if he and Jack couldn't get into a position to protect each other's back, the muggers would take them out one at a time. Bear called upon all his bar-room brawling experience. Elbows. Teeth. Head-butts. He flung his fists in all directions, cursing. He lashed out with feet and knees. Half his blows made contact but the two men were also seasoned brawlers. Their combined weight kept him pinned to the ground.

An unearthly cacophony erupted on the path above them. The bugler, closely followed by four other runners, rounded the bend and fell into the mêlée. A bugle note was strangled mid-blast — a frightful squawk.

The attackers fled into the bush.

Jack put his hands on his knees, panting for breath above Bear's prone body. 'Trust you to go picking fights with the locals,' he said between gasps. 'It's supposed to be a fun run, you dumb shit.'

'Well, who asked you to butt in?' Bear said through a lopsided mouth. His jaw had already begun to swell. 'I had it covered. Hell, I was startin' to have some fun. Then you had to come along and stuff it up!'

THE MOONLIGHT WINKED THROUGH THE tree canopy. Jack was in what he called his retreat — a place he had found, a territorial space, where he could escape the feeling of being a guest. The Jacaranda wasn't a bad hotel, smallish, three star, but Jack hated feeling like a tourist and occasionally needed the isolation of the garden. His space was a corner difficult to find by day and perfectly concealed from the prying eyes of the ever-helpful hotel staff at night. A little removed from the main pathway entrance, it was close enough to observe the comings and goings if he needed the distraction.

There were times when he simply wanted to disengage his brain and let the night wash over him. To cleanse. To let the trivia of a quiet Nairobi suburban hotel divert his attention from memories of distant places.

A taxi came to a stop at the entrance gate. Fumes from its shuddering motor turned red in the tail lights. A couple of thirty-something tourists tumbled out, laughing. They'd probably been into town for a meal and a bellyful of cheap Zimbabwe wine. She plucked a purple jacaranda blossom while he paid the fare. They wobbled hand in hand to the foyer.

Two men in suits came from the car park, deep in conversation. Swahili.

From the dining room came the faint clatter of plates.

The garden was soothing.

He gently touched the sensitive place on his side. The bruises he'd won in the fight on the Hash run were just emerging in green and purple blotches down his ribs. He didn't look as bad as Bear, who sported a shiner that had started the whole office gossiping. Bear ignored them all, his injured pride hurting more than his wounds.

It had been a bruising week in more ways than one. Jack had still to find a way to smooth over the disagreement with the AmericAid woman. He knew it was going to be difficult. Diplomacy was not a skill he possessed in any great quantity.

A police car stopped at the entrance and an overweight uniformed man poured out. He sauntered to the reception counter with a lazy air of authority while his partner remained seated in the darkened car.

Uniforms had lost some of their menace. It wasn't so long ago that a uniformed man's sideways glance could bring a catch to his throat. Like at Sydney airport, where the official had flicked open Jack's passport. He'd glanced at the ID page, then at the face through the glass. Jack had fought the urge to swallow. They had traced him. They knew who he was. The immigration man looked at him a second time. Longer. It seemed minutes. Jack held his gaze.

At last the official thumped a stamp on the open page, slammed it shut and thrust it back at him. 'Have a safe trip to Nairobi, sir.'

'Thank ... Thank you.'

The fear had its nuances. At the outset, it was primeval — the fear of the unknown. What would happen if they connected him with the tragedy? Retribution and punishment. Public vilification. *Coward!* they would scream. He imagined he was in the dock. The prosecuting attorney, pacing. *Take us through the events on the beach, Mr Morgan.* Demanding all the facts, the circumstances. The salacious details. A gasp from the jury. The press scurrying to call in their stories.

But fear had a redeeming feature. So long as it dominated his mind, it protected him from the far more damaging emotions that followed as his thoughts returned to O'Hara. She became a person again. Although he had known very little about her, was even unsure of her name, she had been someone's friend, lover or wife.

He had grown depressed. The panic attacks worsened.

Liz knew something was wrong. He needed to hide from her gaze until he found a way to cope with her questioning eyes.

With time he felt he could get it all into perspective. So he went bush, on a contrived field trip. But the regret of a life lost and a trust broken haunted him during the hot outback nights and he would awaken with a sob in his throat, his cabin closing around him like a corrugated-iron straitjacket.

One night, when the panic brutally assaulted him, when he could not get control of it, he bolted out of the hut stark naked. He didn't stop at the muddy edge of the water hole but plunged in, thrashing about. Eventually he crawled out, covered in mud and cow dung.

The policeman returned to the car with a swagger, opened the door, swung inside and pulled it shut. He showed a small fistful of notes to his partner. Muffled laughter from within. They drove off.

Jack remained in his garden hideaway until after midnight but the memory of it would not leave him.

He cursed himself. He cursed O'Hara.

Why didn't he stop it before that beautiful body lay dead on the beach, brains spattered on the white Hawaiian sand?

JACK STABBED THE PAPER KNIFE into his desk. It wobbled back and forth. He grabbed at the telephone, paused, then slammed it back on the cradle. After three paces towards his office door, he returned to his desk and threw himself into his chair.

'Hey! My man Jack. How goes it?'

'If you must know ... bloody awful.'

'Whoa! What's up, buddy? You look like somebody just shit in your hat.' Bear reverse-straddled the visitor's chair.

'Can you believe that bitch? Can you?' Jack spun his chair from side to side.

'What bitch? What are you talkin' about, man?'

'That ... that smart-arse over at AmericAid. Thinks I'm trying to hit on her or something.'

'No shit! Are you?'

'No.'

'So why does she think so?'

'Because I popped this guy who was bothering her.'

'Another one?' Bear's smile was one of disbelief. 'Man! You are one helluva feisty sucker, aren't you?'

'No! It's the same one. The one from Carnivore.'

'The woman with the legs? I thought you *were* tryin' to hit on her.'

'Well, I'm not.'

'Shit, man. You've lost me. On Friday night, on the way home, you were tellin' me what a great piece of ass you'd found that night.'

'I said, what great-looking women the Maasai are.'

'Whatever. Now you're tellin' me she's a bitch 'cause ... Wait a minute! Did you say AmericAid?'

Jack nodded, looking miserable.

'Oh shit!'

'Exactly. The old man's gonna be pissed off if I lose AmericAid on this one.'

Bear shook his head. 'Oh, man.'

Jack slapped his hands on the desk. 'Stuff it! I'll call her.' He picked up the phone and put it down again. It would be better to wait until Bear was gone. 'Gotta do a few other things first.'

'Sure, like find your fork.' Bear stood, pushed the chair towards the desk and paused at the open office door.

'Fork?'

'Isn't that what you use to eat humble pie?'

Bear ducked the pencil. It clattered against the door as he made his escape. Jack could hear his laughter trailing down the office corridor.

THE NUMBER RANG AND RANG. He was about to hang up when a silken voice said, 'Malaika Kidongi.' At least she had calmed down again.

'Hello, it's Jack Morgan calling.'

'Yes.'

'From the UN Development Programme.'

Silence.

'Ms Kidongi?'

'Yes, I'm listening.'

'Look, you don't say —' He stopped, cursing himself.

'You don't say much. Is that what you were about to say? Ah? I don't say much ... Now let me think about that. I think the answer is, *why should I*?'

'There's no need for these personal matters to get in the way of our business discussions, you know.'

'A discussion? Is that what we were having?'

He dropped his forehead onto his hand. This wasn't how he'd planned the conversation. 'Okay, so we didn't get off to a good start, you and I. On the project. So can we just forget all that and schedule another meeting?'

An unnerving silence followed, then, 'I suppose so.'

'Good. So let's say tomorrow morning?'

'Hmm. Sorry, I'm busy. Make it three, Thursday afternoon.'

'Thursday afternoons are difficult for me.'

Silence again from the other end.

'Okay, okay. Thursday afternoon it is.'

'Fine. Goodbye, Mr Morgan.' The line went dead.

THE SAME RECEPTIONIST SHOWED JACK to the conference room. 'Ms Kidongi will be with you shortly,' he said, with what appeared to be a conspiratorial, man-to-man smile.

Jack placed his folder at the head of the empty table. He looked at it from behind the chair and stroked his chin. After a moment's thought he slid it to a seat at the side, its back to the window. He sat down and tried to look relaxed, an arm slung nonchalantly over the seat back, appearing, he hoped, to be studying the view. The window faced a wall criss-crossed with plumbing fixtures. Below it, the alley behind Haile Selassie Avenue meandered dismally through a sea of paper junk.

He was about to try a third seat when she burst into the conference room, a bulging sheaf of papers under her arm. He straightened with a start.

'Sorry I'm late, Mr Morgan.' She took the chair at the head of the table.

'Oh, that's no problem.'

'This is Miss Githu. She will take the minutes.'

They nodded at each other.

'Coffee is coming,' she continued. 'So, should we start?'

'Certainly.'

Jack placed his slim manila folder on the table. He hadn't bothered to bring the official file, which was an endless stream of inconsequential memos and meeting notes. Crap, he had succinctly described it to Bear. The project was going nowhere until Malaika Kidongi entered the scene.

She slid him a typed agenda and began. Jack was immediately struggling to keep up. Most of the acronyms were foreign to him.

The first few items defined the scope of the project. The Integrated Development Programme targeted the Nyanza Province, which covered the area around the main town of Kisumu on Lake Victoria. The pilot project would commence in a remote, underdeveloped area on the edge of the Great Rift Valley near the Masai Mara National Reserve. As an aid project it was typical, but, as Bhatra was proud to point out at every opportunity, it was the first project of its type to combine the resources of two great technical aid organisations: the United Nations Development Programme and AmericAid.

The programme schedule was an important item. Jack knew that Bhatra wanted to be able to report a solid start at the upcoming triennial review. He was relieved to see that AmericAid were able to commence work immediately.

When the item on budgets arose, Jack started to feel uncomfortable. In the cost column at the end of the transport budget line was the comment: *To be confirmed by UNDP/NPWS.* Jack already knew the answer to that one.

When he had finally managed to make contact, Onditi told him that the National Parks involvement was refused. 'A policy matter' were his words. Jack could imagine the satisfied smile across his ugly face at the other end of the line. He hadn't handled Onditi well at all. If a successful career in the UN required diplomacy, he was thankful he was only on a twelve-month contract. He sighed.

'Is there something wrong?' Malaika asked.

'No! Nothing at all. Please go on.'

She covered the budget and he let it pass, hoping for a better opportunity to reveal the transport problem.

A long pause brought Jack back from his thoughts with the realisation that Malaika had completed the agenda and that he was expected to make some kind of report. The silence grew between them across the wide conference table. He felt trapped. Returning to the transport matter would make it a big issue — which it obviously was — but since he had failed to bring it up earlier, that would make matters worse. Malaika's eyes were on him and Miss Githu's pencil was poised above the pad.

He decided he needed more time. Clearing his throat, he said, 'You've done a great job on this.' He meant it. Her research was impressive, and the briefing papers were succinct and professionally presented, making him feel worse about his own poor preparations. There was nothing further to do except get the project papers authorised and start work.

'Thank you,' she said quietly.

'So it seems we're ready to roll. I mean, the administrative side is finalised — that is, between the UN and AmericAid. It's all going very well. Very ... well ...' He realised he was beginning to ramble.

'Yes,' she said. 'AmericAid will do the health work and the UN will look after soil, crop assistance and telephones.'

'Great.' He put the top back on his pen.

'And transport.' She flipped one folder closed and pulled a second out. 'The Nyanza Province report,' she said, glancing up at him. 'You've seen it?'

Jack uncapped the pen again and tilted his head in a gesture that could have meant yes.

'Well, here's a list of our problems in the Lake area,' she continued. 'I have a copy for you.'

'Thank you.'

'You can see why it is so important to get transport fixed up.'

Jack concealed his expression, which he felt sure would reveal his guilt, by dropping his eyes to the list.

'These Nyanza Province people ... Ah? Not a single vehicle for us.' She looked up from her papers. 'By the way, have you spoken with National Parks about transport yet?'

Jack kept his eyes on the list for as long as he could then said casually, 'Yeah. It would have been great to get their transport, but —'

'Would have been? What do you mean, *would have been*?' She looked concerned. 'I thought it was approved already.'

'Yeah. Except for National Parks' transport.'

'Well, what are we going to do? I mean, how am I going to get our medical supplies to the clinics? Or the test specimens back to Nairobi?'

'Bureaucrats, eh? It's just terrible.' He shook his head.

'This is a fine time to tell me.'

'What can I do? We had some problems with Regional Development.'

'Regional Development. Is there something you're not telling me?'

'What do you mean?'

'I mean, is this another one of your games with James Onditi?'

'What do you mean *games*? Onditi had no idea it was me at Carnivore. Anyway, don't get so excited, will you?'

Miss Githu looked uncomfortable. At Malaika's nod, she quietly scooped up her papers and excused herself.

As the door closed behind her, Malaika swung back to Jack. 'You don't give a damn, do you? Do you even know what's going on here? We *need* that transport.'

'Take it easy! I'll work it out. But I'm not going back, cap in hand, to that boyfriend of yours. Public servants like him are the same the world over and I don't play their little power games. Not for some tinpot aid project, for chrissake.'

'Is that it?' She had lowered her voice, but the ominous edge of anger returned. 'Is that what this is to you? A tinpot project? You have no idea, have you? There are so many sick people ... sick children, with diseases that you *wazungu* know nothing about. Things like hookworm. Do you know about hookworm, Mr Morgan? Stops them growing; turns children into ... into zombies. One dose of tetrachloroethylene will stop it. That's all. It costs about ten cents. And ... and trachoma — it damages the ... what do you call it? The eyes ... the cornea! It damages the cornea. For a few cents we can fix that too. Stop them going blind.' She stood and took a step towards the window but swung back, eyes blazing. 'For once,' she took a breath, 'for once I have the money. For once I have got around that ... those people in Regional Development. All I need is transport. If we can just get to these people, simple things can change their lives.' Her eyes fixed on Jack, who was unable to move or speak. 'The children ... Children whose families cannot take them to care centres. Children whose parents have already died of one awful disease or another. The AIDS kids. Children who have been left with grandparents in the village, a village already too poor, now with orphans to care for.' Her voice grew ragged. 'You don't understand, do you? In your cosy hotels. The Hilton, or wherever you have your little drinks. You could never understand.'

She stopped abruptly. Her outburst had brought tears of anger to her eyes, which she blinked away. She took a deep breath. Leaning on the back of her chair she searched his face, perhaps for some sign of connection if not understanding. She seemed to find none and, turning her back on him, she folded her arms and stared out the window. 'Well, that's it!' she said. 'We can't go on.'

'Huh?'

'We can't run our clinics without transport.'

'You can't do that! I mean, there must be another way around this.'

'Well, Mr Morgan, I'd like to hear it.'

'Let me think about it. Give me a few days.'

CHAPTER 9

PEABODY'S GUIDE TO EAST AFRICA (5TH ED):
The Maasai's life is circumscribed by ceremony. All ceremonies share certain features, including: ritual head-shaving, body adornment, singing, dancing and feasting.

The major ceremonies are: *Alamal Lengaipatta:* preparation for a boy's circumcision; *Emorata:* the circumcision ceremony, elevating a boy to warriorhood; *Eunoto:* the graduation of *moran*, or warriors, to elderhood; *Olngesherr:* confirmation as an elder.

1941

Naisua dragged the fine steel blade across her son's scalp. The milk and water balm ran down Seggi's shoulders. His face was composed, as if in sleep, but Naisua knew he was not at peace. She sensed his dilemma in accepting his fate.

This would be her final act of motherhood for her son. She looked at him in the growing morning light. He was a son any mother could be proud of. A loving son, as much as any Maasai mother could wish. Well, a mother could always have more love, but he was certainly a caring son. And brave. Yes, he was brave. He had many fine qualities.

She dipped her hand into the milk balm again and poured it onto his braided hair. The milk ran through the red ochre to his chest, where it carved thin pink lines in the chalk patterns adorning his torso. The shaving would soon be finished and his scalp, which had not seen the sky for twelve years, would be painted red. The blessings would follow and he would dance one last time with his age-mates. He would leave her and begin a new life. Like a chrysalis responding to the warm morning sun, he would proclaim his new self in his new clothes, with his new name and his new life. He would become a responsible member of the elders, take his first wife and begin building his family and his legacy.

Naisua again reminded herself that he had been a good son. As soon as he was circumcised, at age eleven, he had stood like a man beside her to help protect their grazing lands and their animals. Then suddenly the years flew and he was a *morani*, a warrior, and the protector of herself and the *enkang*. These were the good years. Life improved for Naisua. He had provided for her, defended her. At last she could lead a more normal life, although it was a lonely one at times.

And, in her turn, she knew that she had been a good mother to Seggi. She had been able to provide for him through the difficult times as a child, she had tended to him in the years in the *moran's manyatta*. She cooked for him and healed the wounds of the hunt and the raids and the bloody tribal skirmishes, as a good mother should. She was getting older but she didn't care about that. Life was proscribed by duty. Hers was to raise her son. As an elder he would become the *laibon* in her place. At last she could pass on the responsibilities. The position brought too many worries to her gathering years.

The razor was at the back of his neck. Braids dropped, one by one. Seggi looked resigned to his coming change of status. But she knew he was far from happy with his fate. No *moran* cheerfully made the transition from warrior and carefree bachelor to elder and family man. His final days of warriorhood had been an orgy of aggravation, crammed with reckless raids and fierce fighting.

Naisua's hand tightened on her son's shoulder. It pulled at her heart to see his sadness. It could not be helped: he was a man now and beyond the help of a mother. But at the back of her mind there remained a nagging fear that Seggi would always need her. For all his strength and bravery, he had none of the wisdom of his father and, she reluctantly had to recognise, his elderhood and the coming of the years were unlikely to grant it. When too many choices were thrust at him, he became anxious or confused. He was a good son but she wondered if he could make the successful journey to elder, family man and *laibon* alone.

The last defiant braids fell onto the pile at her feet. She poured the remaining milk into the palm of her hand and rubbed it gently over his naked scalp. It reminded her of the milk baths she had given him so long ago. She felt an almost unbearable urge to hold him to her, as she had when he was a baby on the Laikipia plains. When the roasting sun and cold nights, the famine or disease, threatened to take him from her, she had fought for him with an unrelenting strength of will.

'It is done, my son.'

'Yes.'

He remained on the ground a moment longer, one leg straight and his arms wrapped around the knee of the other. Then he stood, ran a hand over his bare scalp and sighed.

Naisua smiled and stood back to admire him. 'You are a fine man, Seggi. Your father would be so proud if he could see you, his only son, become an elder today.'

'HHUUNH-HUH!' THUD. 'HHUUNH-HUH!' Thud. 'Hhuunh-huh!' Thud.

Naisua could see Seggi leaping above the dancing group like a speared impala. Around him, the twenty-two members of his age-set shouted *oohs* and *aahs* as each rhythmic leap exceeded his last. Their newly shaved, red-ochred scalps and red *shukas* set them apart from other males, who forged a wider ring of spectators. The women and children formed the outer ring, and here Naisua stood with the other proud mothers, a huge grin adding further wrinkles to her weathered face.

She was wearing her finest ornaments for the occasion. The principal piece was a wide beaded collar, red, green and blue with white edging. It had taken weeks to complete using the latest beads available from the coast traders. The beads were brighter now than when she was a girl, but smaller, so the work was tedious for her aging eyes. But it was her best so far.

There had been few opportunities in Naisua's life for an indulgence such as vanity. But she knew her beadwork was excellent, for she had been first to use them in her ornaments and she was always working on ways to improve them. In the early days, her break with tradition shocked the women of her tribe — not only in her village but women in neighbouring villages too. Now, women visitors to the Loita Hills would seek her out, to study her work and beg her to teach them the skill. Before long, all Maasailand was discarding the old iron bands and following Naisua's art.

She was wearing new earrings too, but couldn't bear to forgo her older pieces. She wore a dozen of them, new and old, and they pulled heavily at the large hole in each ear.

As a mark of respect, she wore the ancient iron armlets that her grandmother had given her before she died. Spirals of copper — the spoils of one of Seggi's raids on the railway telegraph lines — hung to her waist on a string of beads. A further thirty pounds of copper encircled her lower legs. They made it difficult to move quickly but that didn't hinder her leading the mothers' ululations. Their voices rivalled the chanting from the men's circle.

'*Hhuunh-huh!*' Thud.

Seggi soared like an arrow, high and straight, then seemed to hang, suspended for an instant, as he rolled his head. His friends howled encouragement. Next leap he repeated the movement, but with a shimmy that flicked down his long body before he thumped down, sending small dust explosions onto the breeze. Sweat streamed from him but he didn't seem to weaken. Finally another body joined him in the centre and Seggi retired to the circle of laughing, dancing young men.

1950

Naisua listened with her mind. With closed eyes she cupped the small stones between her palms and rattled them over the smouldering fire.

Voices came, faint at first. She hummed her soft chant of welcome.

'Spirit of Mbatian, come. Hmm-uh.

Spirit of Mweiya, come. Hmm-uh.

Spirit of Lenana, come. Hmm-uh.'

She felt for the bowl of crushed roots at her knee and sprinkled them on the embers.

'Spirit of Mbatian, come. Hmm-uh.

Spirit of Mweiya ...'

A high-pitched note filled her head. It might have been the keening of a black kite, although it was much stronger, more human-like; but the resonating tone was one no human voice could sustain. It was part of her, yet came from outside, rushing at her from a great distance.

'Spirit of Mweiya, come. Hmm-uh.

Spirit of Lenana, come ...'

A glow, warm and as colourful as the morning, filled the void in her mind she had prepared for it. Her hands and feet began to tingle, her body to tremble.

A vision formed of a huge silver moon shedding luminescent rain on the rocky crests above her son's *enkang*. A stream of silver slivers ran down the slopes and through the village. The shards formed a pool and the pool swelled to make a silver ball. The ball changed shape. It was the face of Penina — Seggi's four-year-old daughter and Naisua's only grandchild.

The child arose from the sparkling bed and tottered, chuckling and smiling, towards her. 'Grandmother!' she mouthed.

Naisua smiled, she hadn't seen the little one for over a year, and raised her arms in the darkened hut to catch the sweet bundle in the dream-vision.

Suddenly little Penina was gone and Naisua saw Seggi's face, contorted in ecstasy. He fell naked into the embrace of his wife, Agnes. The silver bodies lay motionless, except for their laboured breathing.

Seggi melted into the silver pool.

Agnes came forward with a handful of dry grass and a single leeyua flower. Naisua wondered at her gift — a peace offering. Naisua searched Agnes's worried face for an explanation and reached a hand to her. But Agnes was being drawn backwards. The faster Naisua walked towards her, the faster Agnes was sucked away from her. She made a soundless scream but Naisua could not reach her. She slipped backwards into a vortex changing from silver to grey, then black.

The vortex flashed and rumbled.

Agnes was gone.

THE HYENA HALTED, LIFTED ITS head and gave a sinister snigger. Naisua threw another stone but it fell short again. The hyena had followed her throughout the four hours it had taken her to walk across the flat lands to the banks of the Mara River, where she now stood. The dry season had begun and had rendered a telling blow to the river, but its flow towards Lake Victoria, a hundred miles west, was still swift and deep enough to make the crossing difficult.

The hyena was just another annoyance to Naisua's frame of mind. She was tired and in no mood for such a companion. All the previous day she had forced herself to keep moving, stopping well after dark and only then because she nearly stumbled into a herd of bad-tempered buffalo. She slept, cold and fitful, in a tree. The dreams that had started her on her journey returned to trouble her. She prayed they were false visions, but she would not rest until she reached Seggi's *enkang* and found the family safe and well.

She had been following the river all morning. Boisterous hippos bellowed and blustered in the deeper pools. The bulls were fighting territorial wars with parries and thrusts of their massive jaws. It was not a good time to be invading their territory. Further on, lazy Nile crocodiles basked with glassy eyes on the riverbank. Naisua came suddenly upon five of them and thumped her stick on the ground to send them slithering out of sight into the shallow muddy waters.

Now the river must be crossed. Here, the Mara made a long sweeping curve to the south. Its annual flood waters had swept sand, shrubs, even whole trees, into the bend before dropping them to create a number of small islands. Between the islands the river ran through swift narrow channels. Apart from wart hogs taking nervous sips on the distant bank, there were no animals in sight. It was her best opportunity.

Water in such abundance was a thing to fear, but she had been bracing herself for the crossing all morning. Dead wood was plentiful and she collected it into a bundle, which she tied with a leather thong to form a float. Her walking stick tested the gathering depth of her first tentative steps.

The hyena whooped a parting insult, then skulked over the embankment and out of sight.

Naisua swallowed hard and allowed herself a congratulatory smile when she reached the first of the islands. The river had not come above her knees.

The channel of the next, broader section dropped quickly and soon she was using her float to keep her head above water. Her garments trailed behind her, weighing her down. It was only twenty paces across, but she was exhausted by the time she had kicked her way to the next island. Her courage flagged as the last channel — wider, faster and deeper than the first two — awaited her.

She shrugged her top garment over her shoulders, baring her thin, drooping breasts. She began to unwrap her lower garment. Being naked outside her hut was something she had not experienced for many years. After a self-conscious surveillance of her surroundings, she also dropped her lower garment and slung them both over the wooden float.

A shudder ran through her frail body as she picked her way through debris into the fast-flowing channel. She was almost halfway across when she stepped into a hole and the water swept her off her feet. It carried her downstream at a frightening pace. She froze in fear and clung to the float as the waters spun her around. Summoning all her resolve, she righted herself and began to kick her way towards the opposite bank.

In mid-stream, her foot struck something large and leathery. With a gasp she curled her legs up, but this caused her to roll under the float. She risked another kick.

The hippo burst from the water beneath her, huge jaws agape and what appeared to be the entire river's surface rising with him. Naisua slid down the animal's back, off its fat rear and into its wash which swept her into the current again. The hippo plummeted back to the depths, searching, she feared, for the dangling legs that had flagrantly invaded its territory.

When she dared another kick, she felt the sandy river bottom and scrambled to the bank.

THE ISURIA ESCARPMENT IS JUST another ripple in the tortured topography of the Great Rift Valley. Unlike the Mau Escarpment and the steep rises near Limuru, which soar to their summits, it climbs in fits and starts to an unimposing crest.

The Maasai village below it was modest — even for a Maasai village. The small *enkang* at Isuria, some twenty or so huts, clung to a rocky fold in what were considered by the neighbouring pastoralists to be barely passable grasslands. But after years of wandering the Great Rift Valley looking for pasture and water, the clan who settled there considered themselves fortunate to have found it.

Other Maasai tribes in the Mara area were perplexed by their neighbour's choice. Perhaps the clan leader, in his wisdom, had found something in Isuria they had been unable to see. Their bewilderment dissolved in time. There was no doubt that Seggi Kidongi was a fine-looking man, with a reputation of being a fierce warrior in his day. But he seemed a little slow-witted for a *laibon* and leader. The consensus in the area was that, eventually, the clan at Isuria would be in need of charity, if not pity.

SEGGI PACED THE OUTSKIRTS OF the *boma* in silence. Mengoru was at his side. 'You worry for what, my friend?'

Mengoru's use of the familiar term vaguely annoyed Seggi. Mengoru was fifteen years younger than him. It was almost improper for men of different age-sets to socialise as he did.

'She is having a difficult labour, Mengoru.'

'Difficult? What is difficult?'

Seggi sat on the root of a euphorbia tree. Its candelabra branches threw good shade. Plucking a blade of grass, he began to shred it with his thumbnail. He frowned, threw it away and began shredding another. Mengoru annoyed him for a number of reasons, but mainly because he didn't seem to understand the problems that came with responsibilities. All Seggi wanted was silence and a chance to think.

'A good Maasai woman would have popped out a son for you by now,' Mengoru continued. 'But it will soon be over. Then you will laugh to have worried for nothing.'

'Well, I pray it *is* a son,' Seggi mumbled. Why Mengoru spent so much time with him was a mystery. He was a *morani* and could be — *should be* — with his age-set in the *manyatta*.

'Every man prays for a son, Seggi, but there is no need to worry foolishly about your woman.' Mengoru lowered himself to another of the tree roots. 'You know, if you had taken my advice, you would have had a second wife by now.'

Seggi scowled at him.

'Well, I mean she would be able to help in the birth, of course.'

'The midwife is with her,' Seggi snapped. He regretted not sending for his mother to help in the delivery, but he knew she would disapprove of this second pregnancy. Praise Ngai if it is a boy, he thought. His frown deepened. It was difficult being an elder, being responsible for all manner of complicated decisions. How he wished he were still a *morani*, like Mengoru. Out on raids, or up to some other mischief.

'My God!' Mengoru muttered.

Seggi watched him stand and followed his gaze to the north. 'What is it?' he said, moving from under the tree to stand beside him.

'I don't know.'

'It is not a storm cloud. It has a strange colour ...'

Mengoru took another step forward. 'I think it is coming towards us.'

'Listen!' Seggi raised his hand to silence him. 'Listen!'

Mengoru looked back at Seggi, who had cupped his ear and now stared at the tree root in concentration. 'What?' he asked.

'There! Did you hear that?' Seggi said.

'I heard nothing!'

'Wait. It comes on the breeze.'

The euphorbia rattled its bony limbs and the men exchanged glances. 'Now you heard it, Mengoru?'

He nodded. 'But I do not believe what I have heard.'

'It sounds like many snakes, does it not?'

'Ahhh, Seggi!' Mengoru spluttered. 'What are you talking about? Sometimes you ...' He turned back to the cloud. 'It is changing colour. See?' He pointed. 'Black in the centre. Brown on the edges. Even red.'

The hissing grew and the cloud climbed higher.

The hissing became a buzz.

A locust struck Seggi on the cheek. Another hit him on the chest. The men were peppered with thousands of stick-like legs and brittle wings. The sound was now like a cloudburst on dry leaves, snapping and smattering. They threw their arms about, trying to swat them away, but the insects assailed them, invading their mouths and stinging their skin.

An eerie twilight fell across the savannah as the locust cloud covered the sun.

Seggi heard a faint cry and turned towards the *enkang*. Penina came running through the swirling locust storm. She shielded her face with her arms as she stumbled towards him.

Seggi shouted, 'No! Penina! The *boma*! Stop!'

The noise was deafening. A low rumbling added to the screech and crackle of the insects.

'Papa! Papa!' Her voice was almost lost in the maelstrom.

'Penina!' he screamed, but she plunged into the vicious acacia thorn barrier.

'Mengoru! Come. Help me!' Seggi dashed through the *boma* gate and was with his daughter in a moment. His hands plunged into the clawing thorns to stop her thrashing among the barbs. 'Be still, child. I will get you. Be still.' He worked frantically at the thorns. 'Mengoru!' he shouted.

The rumbling increased and he now understood its cause. It shook the ground beneath him. The thunder was racing towards them through the teeming locusts. He knew he had little time.

'Papa! Papa!' she wept.

'Hush, Penina. I have you. Be still, little one!'

'Papa! Auntie said ...' She spat out a locust.

'Hush, Penina. Tell me later. They will get in your mouth.'

'Papa! Auntie said you must come! Come quickly. My mother ... the baby ...'

NAISUA'S HEART SANK WHEN SHE saw the locust cloud. It had been many years since she had seen a plague. This one was bigger than the last. Much bigger. It swept across the grassland from horizon to escarpment like a huge vulture. Black and grey, ugly and dangerous. A dust cloud rose red and brown to join with it. It was directly ahead, rushing from Isuria towards her.

The village was another hour away. She hurried on, as impala and gazelle bounded past her, fleeing the swarm.

She threw a fold of her garment over her arm to shield herself from the dust and flying insects. She could see no more than a few paces ahead. A gazelle bounded into her path and swerved away at the last moment. The remainder of the herd streaked past.

She searched for a safe hide. The gazelle had startled her and, from her childhood memory, the larger animals would soon follow.

The thundering of the stampeding game grew. Three giraffe galloped past with graceful, slow-motion strides. A small herd of zebra bolted helter-skelter through the dust clouds; a half-grown colt dealt her a glancing blow. She fell to the dirt and crawled into the shelter of two large rocks as a buffalo came out of the dust and bounded over her. She wedged herself behind her barrier as the herd thundered past. One huge animal, she knew not what, crashed into the rocks above her.

When the earth was still again she emerged from her shelter. Dust settled on a landscape that had no sign of living vegetation. Squabbling scavengers already surrounded a number of animals that were dead or mortally injured. Nearby a cheetah was trying to drag down a fully grown bushbuck whose broken hind leg hung from a scrap of skin below the knee.

Naisua shuddered and hurried west.

• • •

THE WEARINESS SHE HAD REPRESSED during the three long days of her journey threatened to overcome her as she faced the last incline. Beyond it was the village. She dreaded what she might find when the remaining steps were taken.

Her anxiety increased as she drew closer to the crest; she heard none of the usual village sounds from beyond.

Reaching the ridge, her breath caught in her throat. Above the village, an evil air hovered like a grizzled vulture whose death belly hung fat on the lives it had plundered.

Naisua had known that death was there long before she climbed the ridge. It was the silence, the dreadful silence. A thief, she had called it when first it visited her tribe on their trek from Laikipia years ago. And she knew it to be a heartless thief when it came to a Maasai *enkang*, for it would boast of the things stolen. The laughter of children and the bawling of calves. Even the lowing of the cattle and the hollow clonk of their wooden bells, which usually went unnoticed, left a strange emptiness when gone. Mothers' songs were also taken, and the chatter of the old. Who could imagine a thief as cold-blooded as this one; who could bear the silence of a village once death had paid its visit?

Naisua walked slowly through the remains of the thorn *boma* to what had been the centre of the village. Simple kitchen items lay scattered amongst the debris of the huts that had contained them. A few villagers picked through the rubble to retrieve an item here and there. Some stood, stunned, beside the crushed and broken body of a loved one.

The scene confirmed two of the three predictions in her dream-vision. The silver rain of her dream was the locust swarm. The black vortex was the death it would bring. What of the third — the vanishing face of Agnes? She dared not untangle it until she must.

At the head position of the village, the site of the *laibon*'s hut, Seggi stood leaning on a broken spear. A mass of flies swarmed at a gash in his left thigh; others invaded the dust and dung covering the cuts on his torso and arms. There was nothing in his eyes of the proud *morani* she had helped prepare for his *eunoto* years ago. Again, she wanted to hold him, to shield him from the worst of his pain. To take it from him if it were possible.

She searched his hut with foreboding. In what had been the sleeping chamber, a wildebeest bull lay dead, a spear point protruding from its back. Most of the kitchen and entry vestibule walls were gone.

Seggi was slumped on his broken spear shaft like an old man. Naisua followed his eyes to the rolled-up calfskin mat on the ground. The beaded anklets on the feet that protruded from an end were familiar. She had given them to Agnes as a wedding gift.

So the third and last part of the dream-vision was answered. Naisua felt forsaken by her god. With all her prayers, how could *Ngai* be so cruel? Had they not suffered enough? It was as if Sendeyo's curse had been unleashed again. But that was not possible. Seggi had but one daughter, Penina.

'My son ... I weep for Agnes.' She placed a hand on his shoulder. 'I have come to share your suffering.'

He nodded. His jaw was slack and behind his eyes she sensed a mind at war with an unseen foe.

'And Penina?' The dream-vision had shown that her granddaughter would be safe, but she needed his assurance. 'Where is your daughter?'

He turned to her with a childlike smile and the look of complete innocence she had often seen peeping out of his carry sling as a baby. 'But, Mother, I have two daughters.' His voice was as dry as the dust storm. 'Penina is ... there.' He pointed to the hill. 'With the women. Until we bury our dead.' He dropped his arm as if the effort was too much. 'My other daughter is here.' He nodded to a tiny bundle of *kanga* cloth lying beside the calfskin mat. 'Here ... with her mother.'

He walked away, dragging his shattered spear shaft behind him. It scratched jagged lines through his footprints.

CHAPTER 10

PEABODY'S GUIDE TO EAST AFRICA (5ᵀᴴ ED):
Kisumu (population 197,100) became a place of
importance in the new colony when the last piece of track
for the Uganda Railway was laid to the shore of Lake
Victoria on 20 December 1901.

Ronald Preston was the railhead engineer for almost all
581 miles of the project. The authorities named the last
station on the line Port Florence, in honour of Preston's
wife, who had accompanied him during construction,
enduring the heat, lion attacks and skirmishes with the
marauding tribes along the way.

Jack put Bear's beer on the table next to his squash racquet
and sat opposite him, facing the pool. He mopped his face
with the towel hanging around his neck, and watched a few
Indian children duck-diving for stones. He took a sip of beer.

'She's gonna kill the project?' Bear said.

'So she says.'

'What are you gonna do?'

'Well, as I told her, I'm not going back to that prick, Onditi.
Got to think of something else.' He put his beer down and
wiped his mouth with the back of a hand. 'Who do you know
in the west who might be able to give us some transport?'

'Give? Nobody.'

'Okay then, *sell* me some transport.'

'The provincial office bombed out, right?'

'Yeah. Bhatra tried that up front. Drew a blank. That's when he gave me his pep-talk about *creative solutions*.'

'I guess you'll think of something.'

'Hope so. We've got the regional conference to kick it off next week. I'd better find out whose *personal motivators* I have to be creative with.'

'Are you having it at the Hotel Florence?'

'Yeah. The Admin people set it up.'

'You could speak to Emma Ouko. She runs the Hotel Florence. She knows everyone in town.'

'It's worth a try, I guess.'

'Is the AmericAid lady going too?'

'Yeah.'

'Going together?'

'Are you kidding? I'd rather go bare-arsed all the way.'

'Now you better be nice to her, man.'

'Nice to her? I can promise you, mate, there's not enough charm in all of Africa to get to her. Talk about a hard-nosed bitch!'

'She could make life very difficult for you if the boss hears about this.'

'Yeah, well, the boss isn't going to hear about this, because I'm gonna fix it before he does.' Jack drained his remaining beer in a swallow.

THE HOTEL FLORENCE SAT ON a small rise looking through a thin scattering of trees to the papyrus-lined shores of Lake Victoria. A well-kept lawn surrounded the building and Jack's walk from the car park took him through a neat avenue of flowerbeds.

The foyer was small but, as part of a larger area making clever use of shrubbery to separate bar, reception and coffee shop, it conveyed an illusion of spaciousness. The woman at the reception desk fitted into her beige suit with no room to spare at breasts or hips. She smiled from behind the vase of flowers she was arranging as Jack lowered his overnight bag to the floor.

'Good morning! Can I help you?'

She was perhaps late forties, although Jack was beginning to understand that African women seldom showed their age. 'Good morning. I'm Jack Morgan, United Nations. You have a —'

'Mr Morgan! *Karibu*. Welcome. I have your reservation. For a single room, yes?' She highlighted the line in the register and turned it towards him to sign. 'How was your *safari*?'

'Not bad, thanks.'

The *safari*, the journey, had started before Nairobi's morning rush hour but it was now almost noon. Lengthy segments of the highway were under repair, slowing the stream of cars, trucks, tourist buses and various dilapidated conveyances to a crawl.

She handed him the key with another flash of her smile. 'Room number sixteen, on the first floor. You turn left at the top of the stairs.' She pointed through the lobby.

'Thank you. And would you please leave a message for Ms Ouko? I'd like to speak with her if possible.'

'I am Emma,' she smiled, extending her hand. A jangle of thin gold amulets hung from her wrist.

'Jack. Pleased to meet you. And Bear Hoffman said to say hello.'

'Oh, Bear! Is he coming too?'

'No, not this time, I'm afraid.'

'Oh, what a pity he's not here. Dear Panda Bear.'

Jack nodded, careful not to show his delight at receiving this enlightenment. 'Yeah, good old Panda Bear.'

'All the additional conference arrangements have been made.'

'Additional arrangements?' He had only asked for half-day use of the conference room.

'Requested by the lady at AmericAid, Miss ... ah ...'

'Kidongi?'

'Yes, Miss Kidongi.'

'How nice.' He wondered what she had found missing.

'The white board and overhead projector are already in the room. Morning tea and coffee at ten and a light lunch at twelve. I'm doing the flowers right now. Aren't they lovely?'

'Perfect.' He made a poor attempt to match Emma's smile. 'Ms Kidongi is her usual efficient self, I'm pleased to see.'

He stooped to collect his bag but, remembering his plans for the afternoon, put it down again. 'Emma, Bear said you might be able to help.'

He explained the project's need for weekly transport in the district and the background to the local authority's refusal of the initial request. He avoided mentioning his own inept efforts with Onditi in Nairobi.

Emma nodded. 'So the Provincial Commissioner has a truck, but no money for the truck repairs?'

'That's it.'

'Ahh ... and that one has the big workshop in town.' She gave a wry smile.

Jack bit at the corner of his lip and nodded. 'How much do you think I would need? I mean, to get the truck fixed?'

'Let me make some calls. Have you eaten? Then go to the coffee shop and come back when you have finished.'

'SASA, THIS IS WHAT YOU DO.' She had joined him at his table as he finished lunch. 'You make a payment to Onunga's company for the first repairs. He's the PC,' she said when he looked puzzled. 'Then you can have the truck for once a week.'

'Great! How much?'

'This truck, it is very expensive,' Emma said, shaking her head.

'So I figured. How much?'

'Well, fixing is the first thing. Then also there will be regular repairs, you know.'

'Yes, I guess there will be.' He knew he could squeeze transport maintenance costs out of the other budget items, but the initial cost couldn't be hidden. It would have to come out of his pocket if the project was ever to get started. 'So what's this first cost?'

'Forty thousand shillings.'

'What? That's over a thousand dollars!'

Emma shrugged. 'And no tea money for me, even!'

He looked at her open smile and knew she was telling the truth. 'Thanks, Emma,' he said. 'I owe you one. How about dinner?'

'*Mungu angu!* And now he wants to buy me dinner in my own hotel?'

'A drink then?'

'Only?' She gave his arm a playful squeeze. 'Okay. You buy me one drink before dinner. But my husband wants you and Ms Kidongi to join us tonight. For dinner. A thank you for all the UN's business.'

'Done.'

'Now, I must go to market. And you will take me,' she said, pulling him to his feet. 'On the way I will show you the PC's office.'

THE PROVINCIAL COMMISSIONER'S OFFICE WAS on the top floor of the six-storey Lake Victoria Line building, one of the tallest in town. It was a block from the wharf and enjoyed a panoramic view of what Jack initially thought was the lake. After a quick study of the wall map in the PC's reception area, he realised it was only the Kavirondo Gulf. The immensity of the lake proper lay beyond the horizon.

The PC's desk reminded Jack of Bhatra's. Not a lowly pencil or sheet of paper debased its high-gloss surface, just a gold-embossed diary with a fat gold fountain pen sitting neatly upon it.

The Provincial Commissioner, Joseph Onunga, shamelessly counted out the greater portion of Jack's meagre savings. 'Twenty thousand is correct, Mr Morgan,' he said, obviously pleased. 'And you say you can send the remainder?'

'Yes, as soon as I get back to Nairobi. If that's okay.'

'Certainly, certainly.' His chin and jowls wobbled as he nodded emphatically. 'Please deposit the other twenty thousand directly into an account for me. That is, into the repair shop's account.'

'Sure.' Jack forced a conciliatory tone, reminding himself that it was his sharp tongue that had got him into trouble in the first place. 'No problem at all, Mr Onunga.'

'Excellent. I have the number here somewhere.' Onunga rummaged in his top drawer, removing a folder to search underneath it. 'I seem to have mislaid the account number. Would you excuse me a moment?'

Jack nodded, ruefully watching the pile of currency disappear into Onunga's ill-fitting trousers. The PC lifted his considerable bulk and waddled out of the office.

Jack sat drumming his fingers on his chair arm, furious with himself for having been driven to take part in this sham. After some minutes, he became restless and stood to catch a view of the lake. The stiff breeze was throwing up a short white-capped chop that pummelled the sides of the small craft at their moorings. A large ship with two rust-stained funnels lay alongside the main wharf. A forklift was shuttling a pallet of bulging hessian bags between one place and another.

Jack turned from the window to resume his seat. The name on the folder sitting in Onunga's open top drawer almost leapt off the cover. *Onditi*. It was too much of a coincidence. With a glance at the office door, Jack pulled the folder out. Beside the name was written a Nairobi telephone number. He fumbled for his pocket diary and flipped through the pages to the day he'd called James Onditi at the Regional Development office; the day he was told, none too politely, that his transport plans had been trashed. It was the same number.

He opened the folder. It contained a few notes, a shipping schedule and a map of the lake. Port Muhoro was circled. He closed it again and noticed a second name on the cover in the same fountain-pen blue: Mengoru. It meant nothing to him, but he was intrigued by Onditi's involvement in shipping on the lake.

BROWN PAPER BAGS SURROUNDED EMMA, who was fanning herself in the shade of her huge yellow umbrella when Jack returned to the car. As he drove back to the hotel, he asked, 'Do you know a place on the lake called Muhoro?'

'Muhoro? Muhoro? Oh, I think it is a village near the Tanzanian border. About two hours in this car.' She slapped the heavy dashboard, indicating her approval of Rover's products.

He glanced at her. 'What kind of shipping uses the port?'

'I don't think it is used these days. Maybe it has a wharf. The lorries have taken all the shipping business. The little places have closed down.'

'I see.'

'Are you taking a drive down there?'

He looked at his watch. 'Yes, I think I will.'

HE DREW THE CAR TO the side of the dirt road. Massive granite boulders lay scattered about the dry grass, as if intended for a giant's game of marbles. Below him was the town of Muhoro, with its long wharf jutting into the golden waters of Lake Victoria.

During the thirty-kilometre journey from the main Kisumu–Tanzania road, dust rising to find every concealed point of entry to the Land Rover's cabin, Jack had a growing suspicion he had embarked upon a futile search. He wondered what interest James Onditi could have in such a remote part of Kenya. The more he thought about Onditi — nightclub predator, urban sleaze-bag — the more he believed Port Muhoro was not his scene.

When he arrived, his suspicions were confirmed. Muhoro was a sleepy backwater. The only feature of note was the wharf, which was disproportionately large. As Emma had said, the little town had seen better days.

Only a few vessels were berthed at the wharf, the largest being fishing trawlers, of which there were two or three of a decent size — forty feet or more. A large rusting metal hulk, resting on its side in the shallows, told of happier days, perhaps when the ships of the Lake Victoria Line sailed proudly between the great ports of three new nations.

Whatever it may once have been, Muhoro was not a den of iniquity.

Jack smiled at the melodramatic turn his mind had taken since becoming involved in petty bribery. He slipped the Land Rover into first and headed back to the Hotel Florence. He was looking forward to that cold drink he had promised Emma on his return.

CHAPTER 11

PEABODY'S GUIDE TO EAST AFRICA (5TH ED):
In the push for land rights and independence, a secret society grew in Kenya. Established principally by Kikuyu warriors, the society adopted a deadly oath to ensure the loyalty and unswerving fanaticism of its followers.

Breaking the oath was a crime the Mau Mau punished with death.

It was Wednesday, the day before payday. The Thorn Tree Café was quiet, except for the usual throng of low-budget tourists who seemed to enjoy the kerb-side dining.

Mengoru took a large mouthful of beer, burped and wiped away the froth with the back of his hand. Young Onditi was late again. When he eventually arrived at one-twenty, Mengoru snarled, 'Where have you been?'

Onditi sat, taking his time to reply. 'Working. On your behalf.'

'Doing what?'

'I'll tell you in a moment. What about the shipment last week? Did it go well?'

'Very well. Our friends are pleased. They want more.'

'Good. And when will that be?'

'In a few weeks. But what have you heard about the girl?'

'Ah, that's my news. I went to City Hall. I have a friend there. He was sure he could trace her. But as it turned out, nothing.'

Mengoru used his fingernail to pick at a piece of meat trapped in the space between his front teeth.

'Then I checked in our records office. So many papers! All a big mess.'

'And ...?'

'No luck.'

'Papers, papers! Why are you wasting time with papers? Just make her tell you!'

'She is too careful, that one. And she is not easy to get talking.'

'I've come all the way from Isuria for you to tell me you cannot find where a silly girl is living?'

'It takes time,' Onditi said, becoming angry at the older man's suggestion he could not stand up to a mere girl. 'She is stubborn.'

'Hah! Stubborn, is it? In the old days you had only to go to a man's house and you would find all his women there. No running around in those days.'

'Well, times are changing. Some of them do as they please.'

'Is that why we fought for independence? Ah?' Mengoru spat on the floor. 'You should have been there in 1952. I was just a young man then. Let me see ... just twenty-six years old. Humph! You young ones get everything for nothing, while we, we had to do the hard work. Go into the jungle. We fought for freedom. We did it all!'

A SHORT PATHWAY, FLANKED BY stalks of sugar cane and arrowroot, ran under an archway of woven pandanus palms to a food table spread with banana leaves. It might have been a garden party in any well-heeled Nairobi suburb. The small group congregated beneath the canopy of a purple bougainvillea in the flickering yellow light of oil burners on bamboo poles.

But in Pumwani in 1952 there was no wealth, and the 'garden' was simply a temporary clearing in the accumulated garbage beside a once crystal-like water course. Now the stream served as a sewer for the immense squatter settlement on Nairobi's outskirts, its stench pervading the new housing developments encircling Pumwani's sprawling squalor.

Fred Kubai, the stocky bearded son of a Kikuyu farmer, was dressed in a long white cloak. Ostrich feathers fluttered at his shoulders and his face and short-cropped hair was plastered with the thick red soil of eastern Nairobi.

Mengoru shifted from one foot to the other under an oil burner wafting black smoke into the night. He was naked except for a single piece of goatskin that barely covered his groin and a garland of woven grass draping his neck. Nine other men in the clearing were similarly clad.

Kubai lifted his bloodshot eyes to the full moon and raised a clenched fist. His whispered voice carried to all of them.

'If you ever disagree with your nation or sell it, may you die of this oath.

'If a member of this Society ever calls on you in the night and you refuse to open your door, may you die of this oath.

'If you ever sell a Kikuyu woman to a foreigner, may you die of this oath.

'If you ever leave a member of this Society in trouble, may you die of this oath.

'If you ever report a member of this Society to the government, may you die of this oath.'

Mengoru knew these were forbidden words. Taking the oath of the Mau Mau secret society was an offence under the administration's Emergency laws, which had declared death to terrorists. His skin became clammy.

Kubai, a member of the Mau Mau Central Committee, performed all the oathing ceremonies in Nairobi. He was a founder of the society but the reason he conducted the oathings was because Kubai understood the power of ritual. Every performance was carefully planned. Every theatrical movement, every carefully chosen word, was shaped to forge the Mau Mau mark on the brain of the initiates, as a red-hot branding iron marks a bull.

A goat tethered to the bougainvillea bleated nervously as Kubai approached. He grabbed its horns and levered the head over his thigh so its throat was exposed to the knife. The goat kicked once as Kubai's blade passed across its throat with the sound of a razor slicing silk. It gurgled and died, and its blood was caught in a gourd. Kubai cut open the chest and pulled out its heart, lungs and liver. His assistant, who now moved out of the shadows with a machete, chopped off the forelegs and used Kubai's blade to slit the beast from anus to throat. With a few additional nicks and slashes, the skin was deftly stripped from the carcass in a single piece. He spread the skin on the ground and sliced a long thin strip of hide from its outside edge until the spiral reached the centre. Kubai took the hide and tied its ends to form a large ring into which he gathered the men.

Mengoru cracked his knuckles and tried to be calm as the other nine were initiated. Finally Kubai's wild eyes were upon him. Mengoru's throat closed. His upper lip glistened wet in the firelight and he felt an unbearable urge to retreat from the piercing glare.

'What are you?' Kubai demanded, the blade hovering over Mengoru's upturned arm.

'I am Mau Mau!' Mengoru croaked, his existence reduced to a speck in Kubai's indomitable presence.

Mengoru's lip whitened as the blade slowly made the seven cuts, the evil number of Kikuyu superstition. Kubai added a few drops of Mengoru's blood to that of the others, dipped a finger into the bowl, and with it made the cross of Gikuyu and Mumbi, the mythical ancestors of the Kikuyu, on Mengoru's forehead.

Weak with nausea, he managed to take his seven bites of the steaming offal before leaving the circle, as the others had done, to return through the archway, reborn a Mau Mau.

Kubai wiped the blade in the grass and told them to eat. The ceremony was over.

Mengoru picked around the tables of *ugali* and *matoki* stew. He wished there was something to drink. The worst was over, he was now a sworn member of the forbidden secret society. His vow had dedicated him to overthrow white power in Kenya and to reclaim African land stolen over a period of fifty years.

He glanced around to be sure he was not observed, then wiped the blood from his arm with a banana leaf. It was worth all the work and the pain, he decided. He would be a

Big Man in the movement when they won control. Then his real rewards would come.

But the rewards didn't come. Not for him. Not for the Mau Mau.

When it was clear that Kenyatta was distancing himself from the Mau Mau, Mengoru made his move.

His desertion was carried out with aplomb. He simply marched out of camp one morning and two days later found himself a proud member of the Home Guard. In the face of escalating Mau Mau activities, the British had begun to recruit native members. The strategy was to use them to persuade villagers to report the terrorists among them.

The rewards were not as grand as Mengoru had hoped; the pickings sometimes small. But just occasionally he stole a sweet fruit from the tree. Like the time he was sent on a search and destroy mission in the Aberdares.

He remembered the day was a miserable one. Mists drifted up the rocky valley, hiding the mountain behind a grey cloak. His Home Guardsmen's unit trudged into a small clearing on a gentle slope between the forest and the mist-covered gorge. The officer called a break to read the newly arrived orders. The men dispersed into the clearing, conversing in whispers, as if in a church.

Out of the silence in the valley below came a rustle, barely discernible from that of the breeze moving the high forest canopy above them. But it became more insistent. The men began to shuffle towards cover, searching the flat, grey shroud of mist for a clue to the direction of the sound, pulling their coats and collars about them.

The squall burst from the gorge. It lashed the jungle, tearing down small branches and sending a whirlwind of leaves above the men. They took shelter where they could as rain bombarded them with a fusillade of stinging pellets.

Mengoru, who had bullied and cheated his way to the rank of corporal, sat on a root at the base of an enormous cedar. Even such a large tree could not hold the rain for long. In moments, fat raindrops cascaded through the canopy. He had never been so cold in his life. The Aberdare Range was no place to be during the long rains. Apart from being constantly wet, the paths were overgrown and cutting through the bush was sometimes the only way to make progress. All day yesterday they had pushed through a bamboo forest. The shafts were as thick as a man's leg and the razor-sharp leaves left not a soldier unbloodied at day's end.

He didn't like patrol duty. The mountains were a dangerous place. Three days ago they came upon some allies, a platoon of British regulars who were returning with the body of one of their men. In Mengoru's opinion, which he kept to himself, it had been a lion attack. Some of the British soldiers said that it was the Mau Mau, but Mengoru knew otherwise. His old Mau Mau squad would have made a better job of it. The genitals were intact and, although the skin was shredded, it was indiscriminately done. Mau Mau torture was much more sophisticated.

The patrols were a waste of time. The Mau Mau were always a step ahead, fleeing their camps hours before the Home Guard arrived. Mengoru didn't mind; he didn't want to engage some fanatic in hand-to-hand combat out there in the jungle.

He turned up the collar of his greatcoat and pulled down the brim of his cap. Water trickled into his lap.

The officer, a large Yorkshire man who had been seconded from the army to the Home Guards, shouted an order. Fifty wet and bedraggled Home Guardsmen struggled to their feet.

'All right, you bastards! Listen hard.' He waited for the stragglers to form up. 'We got orders. Search and destroy. You know the fuckin' drill. We'll start with that fuckin' village we passed a while back. Mbakathi! You go and take out the food gardens. Mengoru, do the village. Weberu, you and your men come with me. Questions?'

The men began to shoulder their weapons.

'Okay, we'll meet at base camp five. Be there by dark or you're on your fuckin' own for the night. Understand? Now, get out of here!'

Search and destroy. Mengoru was pleased. He was something of an S & D expert. The Mau Mau had taught him well.

The Home Guard officers ignored the little sideline

Mengoru and his squad ran. The villages were easy pickings and a surprise visit might not only produce livestock and trinkets, but uncover some entertainment too.

The Mau Mau had used S & D to intimidate the uncommitted Kikuyus into their ranks. Now the British were trying to do the reverse. But life was far better with the Home Guards and Mengoru was comfortable with his prospects for the future. There would be no retributions when the British side inevitably won the war. The Mau Mau were finished. That's why he had deserted them. They would never hold power now that Kenyatta had publicly denounced them. Even if, as everyone suspected, Kenyatta had only done it to please his powerful overseas backers, he could never go back on his word in government. The Mau Mau, having led the struggle for independence, were doomed to ignominious irrelevance.

When Mbakathi's men peeled off to destroy the food gardens, Mengoru's squad continued at a fast trot to the village. The alarm went up and two young men bolted towards the jungle. They were shot before reaching it. The villagers were then shepherded into the centre of their circle of crude huts. The Home Guardsmen systematically stripped everything of value. A couple of old men shouted a string of insults but a thrashing soon silenced them. Nobody else made a sound after that.

Mengoru strutted through the village with a crooked smile on his lips. As he estimated the haul the little village would deliver his smile broadened, revealing a startling gold tooth. It was an extravagance indulged in after a particularly lucrative earlier raid.

A family group, a mother and her two daughters, were being bundled out of their small hut. One of the girls, no more than ten, fell at Mengoru's feet. He pinned her to the ground with a boot as she tried to get up. Her mother grabbed Mengoru's arm but he dealt her a sickening blow with his rifle butt. Then he grabbed a handful of the girl's tightly curled hair and dragged her to her feet and back into the hut.

'Out!' he snapped at the two Guardsmen rummaging through a small pile of belongings. He flung the girl to the rear of the hut. She watched him like a mouse caught in a cobra's hypnotic stare, before darting first one way, then another, to get to the door.

For a big man he was quick. He grabbed her around the waist and swung her up. She kicked her bare feet in the air. Mengoru laughed and threw her onto the bed. She bounced up and made another dash for the doorway. Mengoru's face darkened in rage. He snarled as he caught her by the hair and, swinging her around to face him, punched her hard in the mouth.

The girl flew backwards into the wall and dropped without a cry.

Mengoru slowly slipped out of his greatcoat and started to unbuckle his belt.

CHAPTER 12

PEABODY'S GUIDE TO EAST AFRICA (5TH ED):
From the time of the ancient Egyptians, the mystery of the
Nile intrigued geographers and scientists. For centuries
they could offer no explanation as to why the Nile could
be in full flood when all known regions lining its long
course were simultaneously experiencing their driest
season.

The answer lay far away in central Africa, where
torrential seasonal rains poured into the vast reservoir of
Lake Victoria.

Malaika felt so much better after her shower. She patted the
water from her braids then rolled them up into a turban
fashioned from the towel.

The train ride from Nairobi had taken most of the day.
When it reached the Mau Escarpment, the train had slowed to
a walking pace to manage the gradient and hairpin bends. It
was about then that the Ugandan moved to her side of the
compartment and tried to engage her in small talk.

He was a tall, thin, balding businessman with discoloured
teeth and bad breath. Probably happily married in Kampala,
was her opinion. His half-hearted attempts at seduction would
not normally have bothered her — you couldn't be a young
female in East Africa without fending off similar attempts on

an almost daily basis. But he bore a vague resemblance to the uncle she had lived with in her early days in Nairobi, which made her flesh crawl.

She knew the Ugandan would have felt no qualms about cheating. Having more than one conquest was the African way. For many, polygamy was allowed. The remainder generally had a wife and a number of girlfriends; all the benefits with none of the attendant responsibilities.

She took her black skirt from her suitcase and vigorously shook the creases from it, then sat on the edge of the bed to pat-dry her braids.

Yes, she thought, African men have the power. It was an attribute that both attracted and repelled African women. In Malaika's case, it was the latter. She had never met an African man with a shred of empathy, except for Jai's father, Dr Hussein, who was Indian anyway. The only genuinely gentle black man she ever knew was her stepfather, Hamis. But that was too long ago to remember. More typically, they were men like James Onditi: confident, often arrogantly confident, in their masculinity. The nation had been forged by the raw use of power. It was noble to fight for what you wanted. Except if you were a woman. Women were expected to know their place, and that place was under a man — both literally and figuratively.

Malaika believed it was wrong that women were denied many basic rights, whereas an African man could do no wrong. Even the law was slanted in their favour. It was rare that a divorced woman would win custody of her children.

She idly fingered the bed-cover fabric. It was a neutral colour. As she scanned the four walls she realised the whole room was neutral. With these plain fittings and curtains, it could not be called an African style. Nor could it be called European. Or Indian. If she had been magically put down in this room with no knowledge of its situation, she could believe she was anywhere at all. It had no stamp of ownership. It had no roots. No past.

It occurred to her that she had been trying to achieve just such anonymity for as long as she could remember. She knew why. The events of her childhood were so unbearably painful she could scarcely believe they had occurred. Her defence was to forget them.

Being the only Maasai child at the school in Mwanza had made her the butt of every nasty prejudice. Later, leaving home without her mother's blessing brought her great sadness, and although her stepfather had tried to help with an introduction to Nairobi, that too had led to unhappiness. What happened there shook her confidence in herself and etched in her mind a deep mistrust of all men. It set her resolve to remain apart from her home and family; for a long time she felt shame without knowing the cause. But she got over it. It didn't do to linger on the emptiness.

Jai was the only light she carried with her from those days in Nairobi, but soon he was also gone.

The big city made no concessions for her. A woman seeking a career, a Maasai woman at that, was an aberration not to be encouraged.

She set about remaking herself when she joined AmericAid, comprehensively removing any thoughts of the life she had left behind in Mwanza and, before that, in the dim dark recesses of her family's village. By denying her Maasai origins she could reinvent herself.

Malaika wondered if things would have been different if she'd met someone after Jai had decided to stay in America when he graduated, choosing to settle there with his new love. But although his absence left a void in her heart, she later realised she was grieving for a lost soulmate more than a lost lover.

Although on some nights she was drawn by the irresistible urge to touch herself where Jai had made her feel so full and alive, and longed for the release his smooth brown body gave her, she could not bring herself to take the first steps towards finding that relief in another man.

Time would resolve things. It had in the past.

She slipped the dress over her black underwear and quickly buttoned her blouse. The room-service menu stood propped beside the clock radio. It was 5.45 and she was hungry. The incident on the train resolved the matter of dinner — she'd often experienced similar intrusions while eating alone in hotel dining rooms. She decided to eat in, but before retiring with her book and a Chicken Kiev, she would confirm that the conference room was ready for the following morning. She threw the menu on the bed and locked the door behind her.

A busload of tourists was monopolising the check-in desk so she took a stroll around the lobby. She picked up a magazine at a rack and flicked through the pages. A woman's laughter from the bar on the other side of a row of potted shrubs caught her attention. She was a reasonably attractive woman, in her forties, Malaika guessed, a woman accustomed to winning and retaining male attention. Perhaps a little over-dressed for that time of day. From behind, the white man's broad shoulders and dark hair looked familiar. He turned and caught her looking at him.

'Malaika!' He looked as surprised to see her as she was to see him. Although it made sense to stay where the conference would be held, she had thought he would stay at one of the bigger hotels.

'Hello, Jack.' Malaika kept the potted plants between them. 'You're staying here!' What a dumb thing to say, she immediately thought, looking from him to the woman, who could even have been an up-market prostitute.

'Yeah, I arrived this morning. Would you like to join us for a drink?'

'Oh, I don't want to ... I was just on my way out. To meet some friends.' The woman was older than Malaika would have expected. It surprised her. She had imagined Jack Morgan would be more interested in the Nairobi Hilton version — chic, informed, younger.

'Emma and I were just killing some time before dinner. Oh! Excuse me. Emma Ouko, this is Malaika Kidongi.'

They exchanged smiles and nods.

'Malaika, hello,' the woman said, running an appraising eye over her. 'I understand you're Jack's assistant?'

'Oh, no,' Jack said hastily. 'Malaika's in AmericAid and has been doing all the work so far. I've kind of come in on the end of it.'

'Well, have a nice night,' Malaika said with a lame wave. They appeared to be settling in for a comfortable evening.

'I hear you are doing some good work in the villages,' the woman said, refusing to let her go.

Malaika smiled as she backed away from the potted shrubs. 'Well, it's just my job.' *But probably not so well paid as yours.*

IF SHE HAD AVERTED HER eyes the instant she saw him coming towards the coffee shop, he might not have felt obliged to join her and she could have finished her breakfast in peace. But she couldn't help studying him over the rim of her cup.

He strolled through the entrance, one hand stuffed into a pocket of his black slacks and his newspaper captured under an arm. Such composure. In the light of last night's dalliance with Emma, she had to reassess her notion that he was a man of integrity, despite his crass manners. She was generally quite good at judging character. Maybe she had been fooled by the way he engaged the eyes, like a small boy does when struggling to explain a difficult concept. In a man it conveyed strength of character. She had liked that about him.

Her miscalculation had somehow made her angry. She began to explore this discomforting realisation, but at that moment their eyes met. He gave the waitress a nod towards her and a moment later was at her table.

'Mind if I join you?' he asked, looking as if he would be relieved if she declined.

'Not at all.'

He flicked the napkin loose and settled it on his knee. 'How was your evening?'

'My evening? Oh, I just took it easy. Very quiet.' *While you and the lovely Miss Emma ...*

'Didn't your friends take you out on the town?'

'My friends? Oh, my friends! Well, they're really stay-at-home types. We just had a simple meal at their house.'

'It was a pity you couldn't join us.'

She raised her eyebrows. 'Join you ... ?'

'Yes, you met Emma. She's a lot of fun ...'

I'll bet!

'...And Simon. We had a good night.'

'Simon?'

'Yes, Emma and Simon Ouko. The owners. Our hosts.' He gave her a questioning tilt of the head. 'Didn't you get your invitation?'

She had seen the card on the table. *Your host and hostess cordially invite you to join them at their table for dinner this evening.* She had thought it the usual type of promotion for the restaurant. 'No. I don't think so.'

'Just to show their appreciation of our patronage.'

The waitress took his breakfast order. When she had gone, he leaned back in his chair and said, 'By the way, the transport problem is fixed.'

Her coffee cup paused halfway to her lips. 'It is?' She thought he looked incredibly smug.

'Yes. I sorted it out with the Commissioner yesterday.'

'You did?' She put the cup down. 'I thought the UN had already tried that.'

'Yes. Well, the office people tried, but sometimes you need some ... ah, some creative solutions. You know, serious negotiations, man to man.'

'I see.'

'But, as I suspected, it was no big deal in the end.'

'Congratulations.'

'Thanks.' He tore his bread roll apart.

If it hadn't been for that self-satisfied smile, she might have let it go. She folded her napkin and placed it neatly on the table in front of her then, standing, said, 'Well, if your creative solution cost more than twenty thousand, you've paid too much.'

His mouth opened like a fish out of water, but he was unable to muster a response before she collected her key tag between thumb and forefinger and, with a dazzling smile, said, 'See you in the conference room.'

THE LAST OF THE CONFERENCE attendees filed out of the Florence Hotel's meeting room, leaving Jack and Malaika alone at the head table. Malaika collected her papers together and slipped them into her briefcase.

'How do you think the meeting went?' Jack asked, surveying the lunch remnants on the cardboard sandwich platters.

'Better than I expected. Your idea for a big free dinner in Nairobi helped.'

'Yes, I guess it did.' He didn't add that it was at Bhatra's insistence.

'Can you really do that thing, linking the outposts together with telephone lines?'

'So my telecom man tells me.'

'It's a great idea.'

'Well, I started thinking that if your nurse has a few thousand square kilometres to cover, we ought to make some contingency plans. At first I thought mobile phones. But Bear tells me there's no reception. Then I thought, hey, what about the plain old telephone? In a booth. Why not make the booth an outpost? And the outpost a small clinic? My man designed it all with really cheap radio links. And the UN bought it.'

'You did all that?'

He had a mouthful of ham and cheese sandwich. 'Mmm,' he mumbled. 'You sound surprised.'

'Oh! Not really. It's just ... Thanks for chairing the meeting without warning.'

'That's okay, but why not you? You've done all the work.'

'I couldn't. African men get very uncomfortable when a woman is in that role. They hate losing control. And when it comes to business, important things ...' She shrugged. 'Well ...'

The meeting's polemics had been interesting. The men — there were no women on the Nyanza Provincial Council — had listened patiently to Malaika's ideas, but steadfastly refused to endorse anything without some indication of Jack's thoughts. A nod, a word of support from him, and one by one they would voice their approval, never once acknowledging the originator of the idea. Regardless of her bristling indignation, she had managed to keep cool in the hostile environment and he again found himself admiring her professionalism.

'Anyway, thanks for your help,' she said.

'You're welcome.' He wiped his hands on a serviette and

followed her into the lobby. 'Well, I'm going to have a swim before I hit the road.'

'Next Wednesday for our usual project review meeting?' She extended her hand. 'Safe trip.'

He took her hand. 'Thanks. What time's your train?'

'I'm not going by train. I've decided to get the express bus. It's ... quicker.'

'I heard the bus service is hopeless. So unreliable.'

'Actually it's good. Very good. It leaves just outside the hotel in fifteen minutes. I'll be in Nairobi by eight.'

'Okay. See you.' He turned to go, but waited for her to collect her key from the reception desk.

'I can give you a lift back to Nairobi,' he said, 'if you like.'

'Thanks,' she said with a polite smile. 'But the bus ...'

'Yeah ... the bus. Okay. Well, safe trip. *Kwaheri.*'

'Bye.'

He watched her walk to the stairs. Her red blouse was nipped in at her narrow waist by a wide belt and her black skirt, hugging her hips and thighs, accentuated the long curved muscles of her calves.

CHAPTER 13

PEABODY'S GUIDE TO EAST AFRICA (5TH ED):
The Kunono tribes of East Africa have been blacksmiths to the other tribes for generations. Their skills with metal are in great demand, and are admired by all, except the Maasai.

The Maasai consider the Kunono unfortunate souls who carry the burden of a talent condemning them to a life of manual labour and therefore, in their eyes, servitude.

1959

Any hunter — any big-spending hunter that is — flying from Nairobi to the Mara River area and its teeming herds, would be unlikely to spot the Narok–Kisii road. It was made of the same sandy, powdery dirt of the Rift Valley through which it ran. Perhaps if the small plane crossed as one of the occasional four-wheel drive vehicles raised its dust plume, he might suspect a road was there. But he would certainly not see the slab timber and corrugated iron shop and its makeshift outhouse. Even those in a vehicle on the potholed Narok road would have been unlikely to notice the flaking wooden sign, *Patel's Duka*.

The *duka* was at the junction of the Narok road and a track leading to the small village of Isuria, about a kilometre away. In the great expanse of the Rift Valley, passing trade was always going to be scarce, but Patel had built it in the hope he might win some trade from Isuria. It was not one of his better business decisions.

Patel was seldom at the *duka* these days. He ran the haberdashery in Narok, selling red cloth by the bolt to the Maasai. Maina Mwenje, a Kikuyu, managed the *duka* and was constantly trying to cheat the patrons in order to make a reasonable living. It would have been more lucrative to cheat Patel, but Maina knew that Patel had the nose of a baboon and could smell out short stock the moment he entered the *duka* on one of his irregular inspections.

Beside Patel's *duka*, a pair of rock-hard ruts formed the track to the village of Isuria that wet season. It had been just a foot trail meandering through the thorn bushes until the first vehicle arrived some years ago. The deep ruts cast in the black-cotton mud became an enduring reminder of the tax collector's visit.

Mengoru pedalled along the hump between the ruts. It was an airless morning and the sun beat mercilessly on his back. But even on home leave he allowed no further regression into inappropriate dress than a pair of neat black trousers and a long-sleeved white shirt. He dodged the larger stones, being careful not to wobble off the fringe and risk a thorn in one of his tyres. He hated the bicycle. It was demeaning. But one day that would change.

A pair of dik diks, the size of hares, scurried from the track. The buck paused beneath a thorn bush, sniffing at Mengoru's approach, his tiny front hoof raised in mid-step. After a moment he plunged through the thorns after his mate, and out of sight.

Nearing the *duka*, Mengoru saw Seggi at the window opening, head slumped over his usual table. It enjoyed the advantage of shade from the lifted shutter and the occasional stirring of air along the valley. Years ago he sat in the back, at a table beside the bar, away from the glare. Nobody knew why he'd moved, but the old prostitute from Buka sat there these days. She would cough and spit and sip at her drink, if she had one, and proposition everyone who entered. She was cheap — a cigarette or a shot of *chang'aa*.

Seggi wore a dirty red and blue checked *shuka* and a faded red tee-shirt with a picture of palm trees by the ocean and the words *Plaza Hotel — Mombasa* on the back. He was seldom seen without it, except when his mother, Naisua, could get it from him to wash and patch it.

Mengoru dismounted, unfolded the hinged strut from the rear-wheel fork and carefully tilted the bicycle to stand against it. Resting his right foot on the rusted drum beside the entrance, he rolled down the cuffs of his trousers and patted his shirt to smooth the wrinkles.

He nodded to Maina from the doorway then stood over Seggi, who held an empty enamelled mug nestled in the curl of his fingers.

'*Jambo*, Seggi.'

Seggi lifted bloodshot eyes to Mengoru then dropped his head. When he lifted it again, he gave Mengoru a bleary smile. '*Sopa*, Mengoru,' he slurred. 'My friend. Sit. Here, sit.' He gestured to the other side of the table.

Mengoru pulled out the stool. 'Maina! *Chang'aa!* And a Tusker for me, *tafadhali*!'

'Oh, so?' Seggi laughed ruefully. 'Cheap whisky for Seggi, is it? Beer for Mengoru. Hah!' He shook his head, chuckling. 'Tusker beer, *tafadhali bwana*,' he said, mimicking Mengoru's haughty Swahili accent. Mengoru did not find it amusing. Seggi continued, 'Tusker beer for the *bwana*. *Chang'aa* for the *mzee*. Ai-ai-ai.'

Mengoru sucked on the inside of his cheek, resisting the taunt. Seggi was becoming annoying. One moment he would be agreeable, even sensible, and the next, belligerent or moody. After a few drinks — two, five, ten, who could know — Seggi would become maudlin or, worse, simply pass out. Either way, at that point Seggi became useless to him.

Maina clonked the beer bottle on the table in front of Mengoru and flicked the top off. Then he poured a clear liquid from a brown bottle into the mug, spilling some on the table and Seggi's fingers, still wrapped around it.

Seggi took a gulp of the brew. His eyes brimmed, threatening to overflow. He stifled a cough then sniffed loudly. Opposite him, Mengoru sipped warm beer from the bottle wondering about Seggi's age. *Forty-nine?* It was hard to believe. He looked sixty-nine. When Mengoru was barely a teenager, Seggi was a *morani*. One of the best. There was nothing left of that man. No sign of the elegant strength in the long line of his jaw. It was slack and weak. The slender nose had been bent out of shape by numberless falls. His skin was dry and leaden. Slumped on his stool and peering silently into the mug, he looked like a miser clutching his moneybag. Yellowed and bloodshot eyes peered morosely from hollowed sockets, and his scalp, which should have been proudly clean-shaven as a sign of his position, was a mottled cluster of short bristles and scabs. Overall, Mengoru decided, Seggi had the appearance of a marabou stork, the ugly scavenger of rubbish dumps and carrion. He had second thoughts about his plans, but his patience was at an end. He would raise the matter regardless.

'So, Seggi, have you thought about my offer?'

Seggi drained his drink, ignoring the question. 'Maina!' His voice was a little throaty. 'Maina!' He clunked the mug on the table. Maina was at the counter, folding a piece of red checked cloth while an old Maasai woman counted from a pile of small coins.

Mengoru waited, tapping his fingers on the tabletop, until Seggi's mug was refilled. 'Do you remember what we discussed yesterday, Seggi?' he said, when Maina had returned to the counter.

Seggi raised questioning eyebrows over the rim of his mug.

'Of course you remember. How many times have I spoken of it? Penina. The marriage.' He glanced around the *duka*. Maina was raking handfuls of coins from the bench. The old Maasai woman tottered out the door, her red cloth draped over an arm.

'Hmm, Penina,' Seggi said. 'Too young.'

'What are you talking about?' Mengoru hissed. 'She is ready for circumcision. She is nearly fifteen years.'

'She is but a young girl.' Seggi's brow creased. 'Her *kokoo*, her grandmother, says you are too old for her. You must find someone else.'

Mengoru's fist clenched but he kept it pressed hard against his knee and out of sight. Naisua had been a nuisance ever since she had arrived in Isuria. She tested his patience with her disrespect and jibes — ever since her first day, when in front of the whole *enkang* she had accused him of cowardice during the locust plague. It had been years, but it was not forgotten. She would pay one day. And now her interference in her granddaughter's affairs ... It was men's business, the arranging of marriages. He would deal with old Naisua another day.

Mengoru drew his seat alongside Seggi. 'Now, you listen to me, my friend! We will settle the matter of marriage.' He paused. 'But first we will settle the matter of the money.'

Seggi's mug stopped short of his lips.

Mengoru was pleased. He was not as drunk as he appeared. 'I hold all your debts, my friend. Every one of them. Your bar bill. The cattle feed from last year's drought. Your gambling debts. Everything. It is time to settle.'

'You forget your place, Mengoru. I am your *laibon*. I watch over you. Over the whole *enkang*. I heal ... protect ... protect against ... evils. Yes, against evils ... an enemy's magic ...'

'The superstitions of an old man.' Mengoru spat. 'I don't need your potions. They are finished. Gone like all the other rubbish. Village leaders like the *laibon* — gone. All of them. There is no place for them in Kenya now.'

Seggi's gaze was a little out of focus and his brow furrowed. His breath hit Mengoru, who recoiled before resuming. 'Haven't you heard of independence, old man? Well, it is coming. Very soon. The new government will have no use for you and your old ways. You are finished.'

'I don't care about the government. We are *Ngai*'s chosen people. We Maasai will never change. We rule ourselves.'

'The Maasai? Hah! There is no power there. Kenyatta will lead us. Not you.'

'Ai! Who is this Kenyatta, ah? I hear he is a black Englishman. He will not lead the Maasai.'

'Enough! What do you know, old fool? You sit here like an old woman dreaming your crazy dreams —'

Seggi lurched to his feet, knocking his seat backwards. It toppled to the floor. 'You are a disgrace to my *enkang*! How dare you speak to your *laibon* in such a voice —'

Mengoru was quick to his feet and, in a single movement, brought the back of his hand across Seggi's jaw, knocking him backwards. The older man stumbled over the upturned stool and fell heavily into the wall.

'Do you think you deserve respect? Look at you.' Mengoru snatched the mug from the table and flung it at him. 'You don't even pay for your own *chang'aa*. I pay! Do you hear me, old fool? I pay! And you owe me.'

The alcohol trickled into Seggi's eyes and tears welled. He blinked them away, mouth open, but was unable to form a reply.

Mengoru squatted beside him. 'I have no pity for you. You talk of shame? You shame yourself! Look at you. You will pay your debts. Or I will have your cattle. Your daughter can stay unmarried as far as I care. I have had enough.'

He reached down and clutched Seggi by the front of his tee-shirt. Seggi flinched. Mengoru stopped abruptly, releasing his grip on the shirt. Seggi slumped to the floor, his arm still shielding his head from another blow.

Staring down at him, Mengoru chewed his cheek. He pulled a piece of tattered cloth from a pocket and wiped it across his forehead before righting the stool. 'My friend,' he said, helping Seggi to his feet, 'there is no need for such behaviour between friends, ah? We are like brothers, you and I.'

Seggi nodded, blinking his watery eyes.

'How many years have we been friends, ah? All I want is to make Penina my wife so I can care for her. For all of you. You see?'

'My cattle…' Seggi's mouth hung open, a drop of spittle clung to his lower lip. 'You would not take my cattle, Mengoru?'

Mengoru seated himself again. 'There is no need for such unpleasantness between friends. I will look after you. As a good son-in-law should.' His smile was intended to be engaging. The gold tooth held prominence in a crooked and discoloured row.

'Because I am a Kidongi … I am the *laibon* … I …'

'Of course. After the wedding, the debts will be settled. Your cattle are safe in your *boma*. All will be well.' Mengoru's thin smile slipped into a sneer of disgust, but resumed its warmth when Seggi glanced at him.

'Ai, the buzzing in my head!' Seggi passed his hand across his face and rubbed hard at his eyes. 'This *chang'aa* is strong, ah?' His nervous laugh hinted at his relief.

'I am pleased it is settled,' the younger man said. 'I will make the arrangements.' He stood, tossing some coins on the table. 'Here, my friend — *chang'aa* for celebration. *Kwaheri!*'

Mengoru rolled up his trousers, raised the pedal to horizontal and, without a backward glance, swung his leg over the saddle. He smiled as he wobbled onto the Narok road. Overall, it had gone well. The heavy fist had worked on the old man. He hadn't expected it to, otherwise he would have tried it sooner.

Yes, everything was falling into place. As the husband of one of the Kidongi clan, he was one step closer to control. Through Penina he would command a block of votes. People in Nairobi would take notice. Word would get to the top, maybe even to Kenyatta. People would know him. Important people. He would rise within the party.

Independence was coming and, when the whites were finally thrown out, he, Mengoru, would be there.

SEGGI STUMBLED DOWN THE RUTTED track from Patel's *duka*, mumbling in the dark. Mengoru had tricked him again. The marriage to young Penina was now two months past and still no bride price had been paid.

'*Ngai!*' he swore. 'Bride price must be paid. It will bring bad luck.'

Mengoru had also denied the agreement to forget the debts. Seggi was so sure it had been part of the arrangement. Maybe he'd got it wrong again. But the tribe's traditions were another matter. He had warned Mengoru that his new position in the clan did not mean he could ignore the rulings of the elders.

He continued to mumble as he walked. 'I'll call a meeting of the elders about this...' The snap of a twig beside the track stopped him.

'*Sopa?*' He called a greeting. '*Habari?*' The night was silent. He waited a moment then stumbled on, continuing to mutter. 'Not right ... A meeting of the council...' He stopped at the creek. The sound was behind him. 'Who is it?'

The half moon appeared from behind a cloud as he began to pick his way over the rocks. A shadow fell across his path.

'Mengoru!'

1971

It was the season of the short rains, the sixth since Malaika Kidongi was born and the seventh since her grandfather, the clan's *laibon*, Seggi Kidongi, was found drowned in the creek behind the village.

The Isuria *enkang* had grown in that time. Not that there was general prosperity — indeed, many older clan members could recall better days; even occasions for singing and dancing — but it was undeniable that the Isuria herds had grown steadily, especially those of the Big Man in the village, Mengoru, who was seldom seen in the *enkang* and never in attendance upon his herds. He was able to pay a small wage, maybe a lamb or even a calf, to a diligent herdsman for a season tending his cattle.

The younger generation doubted that Isuria had ever seen either prosperity or good times. Not like in the towns, where there were so many things to see and do. A young *morani* from Isuria would happily make the three-hour journey to Narok to gape as the simple events of town life unfurled.

There were the *Wahindi*, the Indian shop-owners, like Patel, who owned the *duka* near the *enkang* and a haberdashery in the town with all manner of materials. Ribbons, laces and printed coloured fabrics, wools and cotton thread and needles to work them.

And Biram Singh, a large man, who stood like a doorman at the entrance of his general foodstuffs store and waved prospective customers inside. An ancient double-barrelled shotgun stood in a corner at the end of a high counter. He had a strange assortment of coloured confectionery, powders, dried leaves and roots, black and green tea and coffee beans in dimpled glass jars. They were arranged by size in regimental order and filled shelf upon shelf from counter-top to ceiling. He also had tins. Round tins, square tins, oval tins. Tins with gold and silver pictures of beautiful buildings and handsome women. Tins with strange scrolling and symbols.

And there was Sudhoo, the livestock and grain merchant, who had a merry fat wife as well as a nasty look for anyone who glanced at her twice.

If the shopkeepers of the town were not Indian, they were Kikuyu. Kamau sold meat in the centre of an enormous swarm of flies. He had fine goat's meat and mutton, purple-red, with generous strips of fat. His best cuts were hung outside, above bloody shallow trays of offal.

The young men of Isuria would amble into town with flowing red capes and self-conscious smiles. At street corners they stood in groups of six or eight, gawking at passers-by and giggling and whispering among themselves. They would pose for hours, trying to impress the girls, who hid their smiles behind a hand cupped to their mouth. Few Maasai girls were allowed in the town so a tall Maasai boy would flirt with others, perhaps a young Luo girl. By mid-afternoon, sideways glances might be encouraged by a smile, and, after dark, the young people would make their first tentative moves towards one another. And the nights ... oh, the nights in Narok were the best times for the young Maasai of Isuria.

NAISUA ENTERED HER GRANDDAUGHTER'S HUT humming an ancient song. She carried a milk gourd and a few pieces of wood. At the fire the old woman lowered herself slowly to the hearth-side stool with a sigh.

She greeted Penina, who sat on her heels at the cooking fire, listlessly stirring a pot of leaf vegetables. 'Thank you for the wood, Grandmother,' she said, keeping her face turned away.

'Hmm,' Naisua answered, 'you are trying to hide your bruises from your *kokoo*. Do I not expect them each time he visits the *enkang*? Let me —'

Penina interrupted. 'Did you see the boy out there?'

'Yes, your son is standing guard like a little *morani*,' Naisua chuckled. 'He feels he is a great Maasai herdsman at last. Oh, I could see he was never happy with the sheep. But now he has his first herd, well...' Her smile sent the many wrinkles of her lips to join those at the corners of her eyes. 'His spear is taller than himself. And such a fierce face. My, my. He is expecting a lion attack at any moment.'

'And Malaika?'

'Oh yes, at her brother's side as usual. Until he chases her away again.' Aged ten, and soon to begin his journey into manhood, the boy was acutely embarrassed by his little sister, who seldom let him out of her sight. The women smiled together.

Naisua's smile died as she caught sight of her granddaughter's swollen eye. 'I am an old woman,' she said, 'and maybe these days I do not understand the ways of our men. But I raised you as my daughter when your mother died. So I will speak now although good manners would forbid it.'

'Grandmother —'

'Hush! I must. I do not understand this husband of yours. What kind of Maasai man is he? How can he treat you this way? Ah?'

Penina glanced at her grandmother then returned to the cooking fire.

'Does he have no pride? No self-respect?' Naisua pulled hard on the beads of her necklaces, as she did whenever agitated. 'You are *siangiki capisa*, as the Swahili say, a true wife. You have given him two beautiful children. You repair his hut. You tend his cattle and flock. You feed him — when he chooses to come home, that is.' The old woman spat in the dirt. The beads moved around her scraggy neck, blues, reds and yellows. 'Him and his fancy women in the town. Oh yes! I am old, but the flies have ears.' She shook her head slowly. 'I knew he was a bad man even when he was a young *morani*. No courage. No heart.' She seemed to drift off for a moment. 'And what he did to my son ...'

Penina reached a hand across the fire to her. 'Grandmother, you know my father drowned.'

'No! The spirits have shown me. Seggi was drunk, yes, but Mengoru struck him and pushed his face into the mud. Sat on him with Seggi kicking like a waterbuck in the jaws of a crocodile. And in the mud we found him...' Her tears welled and she blinked them away.

'Oh, Grandmother...' Penina could think of nothing to say.

Naisua took a deep breath. 'But that is over. Seggi is gone. You are here. And my oath to *Ngai* is to keep you and your children safe from him. He is an evil man.'

'It was the *chang'aa* again,' Penina said after some time. 'Mengoru came home late last night. Drunk. I did not want to lie with him and he knew it. So he beat me and forced me.' She sniffed. 'He wants more children.'

Naisua remained silent, to encourage her granddaughter to release her pain. 'Talking is the *dawa*, the medicine for the spirit,' she often said.

'I am afraid to have more. I can still see the death in our village. My mother and my just-born baby sister.' She covered her face with her hands. 'Oh, how I hate him!'

'Then, child, you will leave,' Naisua said calmly.

'What? What are you saying? Grandmother, that is not possible.'

'I don't know how it will happen, but I have seen it.' And she described how she had been sent a dream from the spirit world. She saw a great expanse of water. In it stood huge boulders like giant stone Maasai warriors surrounded by a floating garden of violet flowers. 'The water rose and fell as if moved by the beating heart of *Ngai* himself,' she said, indicating with her hands the motion. 'The heartbeat sent water rolling to a pebbled bank, where the wave was spent. A moment later, another came. And another. And so on.'

Penina wished she could see it too. But more than that, she wished she could conjure fantasies as easily as her grandmother.

Malaika burst through the entrance in a shaft of sunlight, carrying an armful of camphor leaves, silver and green, with long thin loreats of pale yellow. She put the flowers into her great-grandmother's lap and reached for the milk gourd in the same motion.

'Oh, Malaika, flowers for your old *kokoo*. Thank you. *Asante sana*. Now, what do you say in Swahili?'

'*Haya*. You are welcome, Kokoo.'

'Very good, little cactus. Very good.'

The child took a few gulps of milk and was gone in a moment.

Penina returned to the pot, stirring it slowly. Malaika's appearance had revived a question that had been lurking in her thoughts for some time. 'Kokoo, why are we Maasai women circumcised?' she asked.

'Oh! My child, what a question.'

'All I can remember is the pain.' The day of her circumcision was still etched vividly in her memory. She had heard the scream in a faraway place in her mind and had wondered who, or what, could have made such a wild animal cry. For a moment it lifted her from the agony that flooded every part of her body, and when she brought her attention to it, she realised that the scream was hers. It was a sound she could not believe herself capable of making — a profane, untamed and alien thing. But it was hers.

When Naisua had collected her thoughts, she said, 'I asked the same question when I was about your age. When it was important. The answer was: it is normal. That is all I was told. Oh, and: it has been that way from the beginning.'

'All my friends, my cousins, speak of it in the same way.' Penina remembered her cousin telling her, 'I couldn't believe it was possible to hurt so much. Even my ears and eyes ached.' And an aunt, warning, 'You had better hope she gets everything with the first cuts. Otherwise she will have to cut you again.'

'But what is the purpose of it?'

'Maybe fathers like to stay with the old ways. Mothers want their daughters to find a good husband. Men don't want their wife to be different. So many things. Who could know all the reasons?'

'But what did they say in the beginning?'

'Nobody knows. Nobody gave us a reason. It is just done.' Naisua shook her head. 'When I asked my mother, she told me the story of one of our ancestors whose wife ran away with a

146

man of an enemy tribe. She fell in love and betrayed her tribe by informing the enemy of her tribe's weaknesses. They attacked and defeated them. The men have never trusted the women since that time and they cut them to keep them close to home.' She sighed. 'It is only a legend.'

Penina thought for a moment. 'Some say that lying with a man is not so pleasurable afterwards. Not like when we were young and played the love games with the *moran*. Well, me, I have never enjoyed it with Mengoru, but he ... Is it the same, Grandmother?'

'Now you are asking a very old woman to remember the child's games of so many years gone!' She turned away to the fire.

'Some things are not forgotten.'

Naisua's eyes were black pools where the reflection of red-hot coals glowed. She smiled. 'Yes, it is true. Some things are not forgotten.'

'Well, is it the same?'

Naisua's narrow shoulders lifted and fell. 'Yes, I remember the pleasure of those love games. How we *entitos* would wait until dark then steal into our boyfriend's *manyatta*. There were many happy days back then. The smallpox was behind us and the cattle herds had grown again in numbers. We had food in our bellies. And the *moran* were sleek and long-muscled and oh, so beautiful and proud.' The fire held Naisua's eyes and a small shy smile flickered at the corners of her lips.

Penina noticed the glass prism in her grandmother's hands. In the dim light of the hut her hands looked younger — the hands of a girl before being torn by thorns and ragged firewood, or by years of working the hides.

Naisua lifted her sun-stone to her cheek. 'I remember a man ... We met long after I was circumcised. After your grandfather died. A man from far, far away. Strong and proud. He spoke little, but when he did, men would listen. But he was gentle. And so kind. Oh, that smile made my heart sing with happiness. I remember we would fly across the Laikipia on his horse, the wind in our faces.

'Our time together was always brief. He had a wife in Nairobi and a job. It was the time when we drove our herds to the south, as the British had demanded. He worked for them, but hated what they were doing to us.

'Once we went to Lake Baringo for three days. I can still remember the cool waters and the silence of the lake. The hippos playing in water reeds. The sweet short grass studded with tiny flowers. And just we two . . .' Her voice lost its way. 'That was a man I loved with my whole body. Not just . . . *there*.'

Penina let the silence enfold her grandmother and returned her attention to her cooking fire. Suddenly she said, 'I do not want the old ways for my daughter. I don't care. I do not want her circumcised.'

Naisua slipped her hand into Penina's. 'Then we, you and I, will see that she is not.' And she nodded, as if she knew exactly how they would break the tribal imperative.

A DETERMINED CLUSTER OF CLOUDS hung above the western escarpment, throwing great dark shadows on the distant grasses, lush with the rain of recent weeks. Penina hummed softly while she trimmed the goatskin. The air was bright and clean and the morning sun, when it broke through the clouds, was warm. It was a good day to stretch hides.

The Kunono man was at the next hut. She pretended not to notice him as he fussed with an assortment of hammers and pieces of iron. He had been in the village for many days, lugging his haversack of metal objects and tools on his muscular shoulders. She pitied the Kunono tribe, the butt of many Maasai jokes, which the menfolk would recall with great hilarity and within his hearing. But Hamis ignored them with a good-natured smile and would simply continue to pound at the spear point or the branding iron that he was forming. After a few days the Maasai tired of the jokes and he was left to ply his craft in peace.

Penina had first been embarrassed by his regular and polite conversation, then amused. But now, as he hoisted his load to his shoulder, she was pleased to see him approach out of the corner of her eye.

'*Jambo, mtoto* Penina,' he said in Swahili, setting down his load at the edge of her goatskin.

'*Jambo*, Hamis. And if you do not stop calling me a "small child", I will hit you with one of your own very fine hammers.' Penina's Swahili was passable, due to her grandmother's persistence. '*Mtoto* I am not!'

Hamis laughed, a wonderful rumbling sound from deep within his barrel chest. He showed a row of straight white teeth. 'Now, now, Penina, you must forgive me, for when I see someone of your size, someone I could easily pick up with one hand and carry up Mount Kenya, I see nothing but *mtoto*.'

She smiled in spite of herself.

'But I will call you *mama* if you prefer.'

'No, thank you. I am still too young to have such a nickname. To be truthful, I sometimes cannot believe I am a mother at all.'

'Yes, you are too young. You should be out there, finding the world. Have you ever been to Narok?'

'Of course I have!'

'What about Nairobi?'

'No.'

'Kisumu?'

'Well, no, not Kisumu either. But Mengoru might take us to Kisii on the *matatu* when my cousin's boy is circumcised next month.'

'Be careful on those noisy, smelly *matatus*. The drivers are all money-mad boys racing to the next fare. But Kisii is a nice place. You will enjoy it. Oh, but if you could go on to Kisumu … my, my, my! You should see the buildings there!'

'Yes?' Her eyes widened.

'Oh, yes. They have very fine hotels in Kisumu.'

'Bigger than the one in Narok?'

'Much bigger. And better too. Inside there is polished stone on the floors, I swear! And tables with glass tops. And so much food. Even a dance hall.'

'A dance hall?'

'Yes. Young people go dancing. Every week!'

She wanted to ask about the dance hall, but she was ashamed to show any further ignorance. He was such a knowledgeable man. She dropped her eyes to hide her embarrassment and noticed his heavy pack. 'Where are you going today?'

'To Kisii. I am finished here. There is usually plenty of work there, and then I go to Narok, Nakuru and Kericho.'

Penina stood and dusted her apron to hide her disappointment.

He reached into his pack and pulled out an amulet. 'Until then, it would please me if you would keep this heavy trinket to lighten my load.'

It was copper woven like leather into a wide band. Thin strands of white metal entwined with the copper, highlighting intricate patterns through the middle and along the edges. She slipped it up her arm to the elbow. It was a perfect fit. 'But it is so beautiful!'

'As is the small one holding it.'

She expected to see him teasing her again, but his face was serious. She dropped her eyes to the amulet. 'You are ... Where are you going now?'

'I told you, Kisii.'

'Yes, of course.'

'I will be coming by on my way west. On my way home to Mwanza.'

'You have a wife there?' She shifted her attention to her fingertips.

'No,' he smiled, 'just my bad-tempered old *babu*. My neighbours keep an eye on him when I am on *safari*, but I worry. He has been a little strange since my mother died.'

'Well, then, maybe I will see you pass by.'

'I will make certain of it.' He smiled at her and stooped to gather his things. She watched his muscles leap as he hoisted the weight. She liked his generous mouth. And that smile.

'So...' he said. She knew he was waiting for her to meet his eyes, but she was too shy. She studied her fingertips instead.

'*Kwaheri*,' he said to the top of her head.

'Yes. Goodbye.' She glanced up at him as he moved away.

He was at the *boma* gateway and turned to find her watching him. He smiled again. She waved him goodbye, and wondered if he would really come back on his way to Mwanza. Wherever that was.

CHAPTER 14

PEABODY'S GUIDE TO EAST AFRICA (5ᵀᴴ ED):
May you have a hand of leather. (Maasai curse, referring to
calluses. In other words, may you have a life of manual
labour, or farming.)

1971

The hills at the base of the Isuria escarpment had begun to
lose the verdant gloss they had enjoyed during recent weeks.
The gold of the dying grasses now on the ridge tops would
soon tumble down to adorn the plains with the crisp burnt
colours of the dry season.

Malaika ran ahead of her mother, pouncing on pieces of
firewood and handing them back to her. Penina dropped them
over her head into the basket on her back. But she wasn't
thinking about the firewood. Her path, high on the slopes of
the escarpment, was aimless. She didn't see the beauty in the
golden savannah that undulated into the violet heat haze on the
far side of the Rift Valley. Nor the rock face above, circled by a
pair of keening martial eagles. She was even oblivious to the
flies that clustered on the dried blood above her blackened eye.

Her heart had distanced itself from the cruel world of Isuria.
Even in the worst days following the locust plague, she had not
felt so bereft of hope. When they buried her mother and
newborn sister, she felt real grief for the first time in her life. It

was as much as a child could bear, but she knew it was transitory. And although the deaths were cataclysmic for all the villagers, she gained strength from their acceptance that it was part of the cycle of life in that harsh land, and that it would pass.

But now her suffering was not due to the pendulum swings of chance, which brought equal shares of good and bad, but was caused by the cruel manipulation of a brutal and hateful man.

Mengoru's moods were becoming increasingly violent. They could spring from a real or imagined affront, or because one of his many schemes was thwarted, or come from the *chang'aa* he seemed to prefer to beer these days. In the past, she would have left him to rant until his mood was expended, but of late he had insisted that she hear his complaints. If she didn't display support and sympathy, he would turn on her and berate or beat her until she fled. She learned to sit in the corner of the hut, a mute witness to his fury as he tried to provoke her into an argument. But now she had come to the sickening realisation that his tirades were simply an excuse to beat her, and that the beating stimulated a sexual arousal he was unable to achieve by any other means.

To her even greater concern, she noticed his violence was having an alarming effect on Malaika. In the past, Malaika would flee the hut at the first sign of his temper. Now she seemed to be frozen with fear, and retreated into a corner of the hut, where her cries sounded like those of a small forest creature caught in the jaws of a terrifying predator.

Three days ago, when Mengoru found Hamis's gift, he flew into a frightful rage. Penina's body was slowly mending from his foul abuse, but her heart and mind felt mortally wounded. Her life would have been unendurable had she not found some escape in an imagined world where she lived with an imaginary husband. A kind man who had loved her and who cared for her and the children. That man who had loved and cherished her all those years had no name, no face. But in recent weeks he had taken on the appearance of Hamis. Hamis with the huge shoulders and strong arms. The kind smile. Hamis, who had the strength to pull her from her misery.

'Hamisi!' Malaika's cry startled her. It was as if her daughter had been reading her mind. When she turned, she was looking at a scene from her imagined world. There was Hamis, walking hand in hand with Malaika, smiling that smile. Penina could find no words, but a wave of relief swept over her as if a death sentence had been lifted.

Hamis's smile fell away when he was close enough to see her injuries. She covered her face, feeling an inexplicable shame. He took her gently by the wrists to look at her eye. She burst into tears and fell into his arms. He held her until the sobbing stopped.

'When did this happen, Penina?'

'Three days ago,' she sniffed.

'I will deal with him.'

'No! You must not! He has a gang of thugs with him these days. They will kill you!'

'I am more afraid for you.'

'I will be all right. But you must go.'

'Come with me.'

She stepped away from him. 'That is impossible. He will find us. You must not speak like that. I ... ' She wiped her face and lifted her head, but could not meet his eyes, looking instead to the valley beyond him. 'How ... how did you find me here?'

'At the village, they told me you went towards the escarpment.'

Her heart sank. Mengoru was sure to hear of it. 'You are back so soon. It has been only three weeks.'

'I was in Narok. I left everything to hurry here so I could see you before I continue to Nakuru.' He reached out a hand. 'Come with me. Bring the children and come with me now.'

'No.' She stepped back again. 'Malaika! Come! We are going back.'

Hamis stood awkwardly, foolishly. He looked so embarrassed she regretted her brusqueness, but she dared not entertain the idea he had planted in her mind. She took Malaika's hand and turned for home without risking a backward glance.

• • •

153

MENGORU ALMOST FELL THROUGH THE door of the hut. His trousers were covered in mud. He stumbled towards the cooking fire where Penina stood with a pot of hot millet. His breath had the sour smell of *chang'aa*.

'So,' he slurred, casting bleary eyes around the hut, 'my wife is alone, ah?'

She turned away from him.

A small sound came from the corner. Malaika was cowering against the wall. Her eyes were wide as she tried to strangle her whimpers by stuffing all four fingers of one hand into her mouth. Penina dared not respond to her daughter. She was afraid any move might enrage him. Maybe he would fall asleep when he was finished with his foul abuse.

'Very nice for you to be alone,' he continued, menace growing in his voice. 'That's how you can see your lover, isn't it?'

She shot a frown at him, but swallowed her protestation. To disagree was dangerous.

'Oh, yes. You're surprised that I know, aren't you? You slut! Do you think I don't know what's going on in my own hut?'

Malaika's pathetic whimper became unbearable to Penina's ears. She moved slowly towards the corner where her daughter was curled into a tight ball, but Mengoru caught her, pulling roughly on her outer garment. It tore from her shoulders as the force spun her into the wall where her head struck a timber support. The millet pot smashed on the floor. Malaika gave an ear-piercing scream.

Mengoru hunched his shoulders and lumbered towards Penina, his face contorted into a vicious sneer. 'Do you think I don't know? Slut! Well, I hope you enjoyed the Kunono *mboro* in you, because it will be the last you will ever have.'

She clung to the wall, trying to clear her head of the ringing sounds. Before she could retreat, he hit her hard across the side of her face and she went spinning across the room and fell onto the bed platform.

Malaika's screaming became hysterical.

Mengoru tore off the last of Penina's small garments as she tried to scramble off the bed and struck her again. She fell backwards, gathering clouds of unconsciousness preventing her escape. He fell over her like a heavy sack.

Penina opened an eye. Her grandmother stood over him, wielding a heavy war club, waiting for him to move. He didn't.

A figure crashed through the doorway. Naisua swung around, shouldering her club for another swing. It was Hamis. He rushed to Penina and threw Mengoru's inert body from her. He took her gently in his arms. Penina began to sob and clung to him.

Naisua dropped her club and went to Malaika. She was beating her head with two small fists, her eyes tightly shut. Naisua held her while she gulped and choked on the sobs that racked her body.

Hamis held Penina tight in his arms. 'Take me away, please,' she said. 'Just take me with you.'

'It is all right. Hush. Of course I will take you. There, hush. I am here. I will take you away.'

'You must go quickly,' Naisua said, trying to lift the trembling child who remained curled into a protective cocoon. 'He won't sleep for long, and his thugs are here in the village.'

'Can you bring the boy?' Hamis asked Naisua. 'We will go immediately.'

She nodded and let Penina take her sobbing six-year-old daughter. Hamis circled them both in his arms.

When Penina had dressed and stuffed a woven bag with the few items she possessed, Naisua returned with the boy. He looked at his father lying inert on the bed. His sister, for once, did not rush at him, but sat in a corner wide-eyed, her fingers buried in her mouth. Penina began to explain what she intended to do. She chose her words carefully for it had been difficult to communicate with him recently. It was so preposterous she almost lost her resolve. To leave her village with another man — a Kunono of all people — was absurd. Her son was ten years old, an age at which a boy was expected to spend most of his time in the *moran's manyatta*, learning about what awaited him in warriorhood. His absence had spared him the worst of Mengoru's outbursts.

The boy listened in silence to his mother's plans. Then, 'I am not leaving,' he said, squaring his shoulders.

'But you must come. I cannot leave you here, with him.' Penina took her son's hands, trying to reach him with the intensity of her grip.

'Mother, I am about to be circumcised. To become a man. It is all arranged. If I go with you I will never become a man. And never join the *moran*.'

'But you can have a new life. A new way to live.'

'There is no way but ours. I do not want another life.'

'My son, I want you to come willingly ...'

He remained sullen and unmoved. 'If you make me go I will hate you. I will run away.'

Penina hid the shock and pain his words brought her. In desperation she said, 'Grandmother, can you not talk to him?'

The old woman had been watching the boy; she now turned to Penina. Her wrinkled face held sadness, but the old strength was still evident. There were times when Penina thought those ancient eyes could hold the whole world in check while the power behind them gathered itself. Penina realised she was holding her breath. Her grandmother's hesitation worried her.

'Penina, your son is no longer a child,' Naisua said at last. 'If he was any other boy in the village, I would say, yes, take him. He will find a new life with you out there.' She looked at the boy standing stiff and silent at the edge of the lantern light. 'Many other boys will leave the village as soon as they can. Some don't even care to go through the circumcision ceremony. They are sick of village life. There is too much in the towns to interest them and nothing here. But this one,' — she moved to stand beside him, her hand patting his shoulder — 'he has always been a Maasai boy. He hunts well. He has learned to make weapons and joins the *moran* in their mock battles. He has the blood of the Great *Laibon* in him, and one day, if he proves worthy, he will become a *laibon* himself.'

Penina knew her grandmother was torn by the grief she was inflicting upon her, but spoke, as always, from the heart. 'He would shrivel like a lily in the desert if you took him away,' she said in conclusion.

Penina looked from her grandmother's sad smile to Hamis, the mountain that now seemed to give her strength. She swept her daughter into her arms, seeking a familiar comfort while she collected her thoughts, but the small body was stiff in her embrace. Yesterday, leaving the village with another man had been an unspeakable sin. Now her grandmother was suggesting she also leave one of her children behind. How could she make decisions that only an hour ago were beyond her comprehension?

Her son stood before her, defiantly awaiting her response. Penina found something in his eyes that was not there the day before. He had grown, not in size of course, but in other ways. She could see a young man. It seemed only days ago that she had borne him, but now, at age ten, he was on the verge of realising the only ambition he had ever confided to her — to become a real man, a Maasai *moran*. Looking at him now, the way he held his head with the self-assurance of the totally commited, she knew she would for ever lose him if she insisted he go with them.

'Leave him with me,' Naisua said, seeming to read her thoughts. 'When he becomes the *moran* he must be, he will be man enough to come to you for your blessing.'

THE KENYA–TANZANIA EXPRESS BUS pulled into the Mwanza bus terminal at dawn, ten hours late. The *konda* climbed to the roof rack and threw bags and bundles to the sleepy-eyed throng below. Hamis waded through with his heavy tool bags and Penina's small bag of possessions.

'Come, let me get you away from the crowd while I fetch Malaika.' He led her across the road to a sandy verge, put their bags at her feet and returned to the bus for the child. Penina had slept little on the journey, although it had been nearly two days since they had fled Isuria. On the occasions that exhaustion overwhelmed her and she slept, she would awake in a panic until she found Hamis's strong forearm.

The yellow dawn struggled through a mist that hung over a stony beach enclosed between massive granite boulders. Hamis joined her with Malaika on his hip, her head against

157

his chest. 'It is so … beautiful,' Penina said, looking across the flat grey water. Gold streaks spread from the shore, rippling on the wave crests from a warm breeze.

'Lake Victoria,' he said.

Water hyacinths made green and violet rafts in the lee of two huge boulders a stone's throw offshore. Clumps of thick papyrus reeds swayed in the ebb and flow of the gentle swell. Waves flopped onto the pebbled beach with a soothing regularity. She felt an overwhelming urge to rush into the cleansing waters and wash away all memories of Isuria. Except for two. A young boy, on the verge of manhood, and a magical old woman who had already seen this place in a vision she had found difficult to describe, because even she could not believe such beauty existed.

I have seen you beside columns of great stones that stand like warriors, guarding the water that flows from a sky of gold and is so vast that the far bank cannot be seen. There are tall reeds with tops like the feathers of the crested crane. Violet flowers surround you. The wide golden water moves, though it has no current. Rising and falling like a heartbeat.

I know that you will be safe and find love with the man who leads you there.

Find the waters of the beating heart, and you will find the peace you seek.

CHAPTER 15

PEABODY'S GUIDE TO EAST AFRICA (5ᵀᴴ ED):
Kericho, with its high rolling green fields, is the tea capital
of Kenya.

   At almost any time of day, the tourist is likely to see
teams of women wading through the chest-high bushes,
plucking leaf ztips and dropping them into wicker baskets
on their backs.

Fifteen pairs of eyes watched the white Land Rover, with a
blue laurel cluster circling the initials UNDP on the door, pull
out of the Hotel Florence car park. It lumbered along the
gravelled verge of the quiet road then shuddered to a halt a
few paces past the bus stop. The fifteen travellers watched in
silence, some sitting on overstuffed suitcases, others flapping
makeshift fans. Conversation had long ago evaporated in the
heat of the afternoon. They had been waiting at least two
hours for the bus. The delay was not new to any of them and
they endured it with the patience that rural Africans learn
from childhood. Only the young Maasai woman in the black
skirt and red top, who had placed her leather bag in the heavy
shade of the flame tree and paced the length of the bus stop
for all of the first hour, seemed incapable of accepting the
delay. She had finally retired to the deeper shadows under
the tree.

The Land Rover's arrival was a welcome distraction for the travellers, again with the exception of the Maasai girl. She alone ignored the car's arrival.

There was a metallic clunk and the car reversed and stopped again, this time directly opposite the bus stop. The *mzungu* sat looking at the Maasai girl for a long moment. The handbrake squawked, and fifteen pairs of eyes watched the man open the door, climb down and walk slowly across the road, his gaze upon the young woman. He was tall, with the face and arms of a man who had felt the sun. His shoulders were squared and his stride well balanced, like a warrior ready for action. None of the travellers could read the thoughts behind his grey eyes. The swing of his sinewy brown arms suggested careless indifference, but his fingers toyed with the ring of car keys as he drew near the Maasai girl, and his faint smile was not so confident as his stride.

The girl avoided his eyes when he spoke. Although the *mzungu* seemed to know her well, they were clearly not lovers, for she remained as distant with him as she had been with her fellow travellers. He thrust his hands into his pockets, looked around, and shifted his weight from one foot to the other. Now his smile had melted and, with a step towards the Land Rover, he seemed to be on the point of leaving. But he went back to her, this time with a softer tread and perhaps with more pleasing words, his head cocked slightly to one side. She gave him no more than a glance before her eyes fell to her hands where she studied her fingers intently. The *mzungu* man spoke softly and raised a hand towards the west, from where they all hoped a bus would soon appear. Fifteen pairs of eyes followed his gesture. The road was deserted except for an old woman driving a small herd of goats. He nodded his head to the east and Nairobi, and shrugged before thrusting one hand in his pocket and turning the other towards the Land Rover.

The Maasai girl picked up her bag and strode to the car without a word. The *mzungu* slowly shook his head and followed her.

The many watching eyes found just the faintest hint of victory in his smile.

MALAIKA FELT SHE COULD HAVE been more gracious. After all, she might have been waiting for ever for that bus. It was just that he had such an annoying way of being right at the worst times. And now here he was, driving along in the most infuriating, casual manner.

For the first sixty kilometres or so from Kisumu, Jack persisted with attempts at conversation. He told her about his car and household effects that would arrive in a week or so, and how glad he would be to escape the Jacaranda Hotel and some lunatic who drove him to the office every day. She gave him monosyllabic replies. His efforts to carry even a one-sided conversation waned as they drove through the sprawling tea plantations that straddled the high country between Nyanza and Nakuru provinces.

'We must be getting near Kericho,' Malaika said, after a silence of about thirty kilometres.

'Yeah?' His voice held a hint of surprise.

'Yes, tea. Kericho is famous for its tea.'

'It's beautiful country. Like Kisumu. In a different way, of course. I mean, Kisumu is beautiful in its own way.'

'Lake Victoria is lovely.'

'Yes! Really ... lovely.' An uncomfortable lull threatened to develop again. 'But you must have seen it all before.'

'Yes, I have.' She paused. 'But not at Kisumu.'

'Oh? Where?'

She felt him glance at her as the silence grew. 'Mwanza,' she said at last. 'I was raised in Mwanza.'

'Mwanza. Where's Mwanza?'

'In Tanzania.'

'Oh? I assumed you were a Kenyan.'

'I am. I went to Mwanza as a child. Look,' she said, pointing to the south, 'our pilot project is somewhere down there.'

Jack looked down the rolling ridges and valleys, green as far as the eye could see. 'Didn't I read that the pilot was in a dry area?'

'It is. It's in the Rift Valley. Miles away. The people down there have nothing like this. They are just little people.'

'Little people?'

'Yes. In Kenya we have big people — important people like politicians and businessmen.'

'You mean like Nyanza Provincial Council?'

'Hmm, not quite. Now you're teasing me. And we have little people. The *wananchi*. All the others, who don't seem to matter to the big people.'

'I see.'

'The Rift is full of little people. Small farms. A few cattle.'

Jack was silent for a while, then said, 'That stuff I said — you know, about this being a tinpot project. Well, I didn't mean it. I'm sorry it came out that way. I know it's important to you ... and I'm beginning to understand why.'

The resolute set of his jaw made her want to believe him. He returned her gaze for a moment before giving his attention to the road again.

She mumbled, 'I'm glad,' feeling surprised that she could affect this seemingly impervious, insensitive person to the extent that he felt the need to defend himself.

The Land Rover laboured on a steep winding ridge. Jack changed down a gear. On the downhill side, the road followed the tea plantation's undulations to a small town nestled into a fold of the distant hill.

'You have a degree in agriculture,' she said.

He shot her a glance. 'How do you know that?'

'The agencies get all the details. Why, you look worried, Mr Morgan,' she said with a smile. 'Have you got some terrible secret?'

'No! Not at all.'

He seemed to have missed the joke and she wondered if she had offended him in some way.

'Why do you mention it?' he said.

'I was just wondering, will you be doing the soil conservation work ... or ...'

'Oh, I see. No, I'm not doing the technical stuff. Not this

time. I'm just setting it up. Handling local arrangements.' His smile returned. 'Are you a medico?'

'No. I've had some medical training, with AmericAid. But I'm like you — administration. I'm supposed to get things started. Get government approvals.' James Onditi and his leering innuendo intruded on her thoughts.

They were entering the village on the ridge. The tattered road sign read: *Welcome to Kopsiti*.

'But after we get it going, I will move on to something else,' she finished. 'There's so much to do.'

Jack muttered as the Land Rover bounced out of a pothole at the road's edge.

'Is there something wrong?'

'It's just this idiot in the truck behind.' He looked into the rear-vision mirror. 'Keeps trying to pass me on these corners. Is he crazy?'

Malaika glanced over her shoulder. The truck, with a high green canvas tarpaulin flapping above it, was hugging the tailgate of the Land Rover. 'Careful. These people don't know how to drive.'

'That's for sure! He'll go over the top of me if I slow down here.'

As the truck began to overtake, it hit a hole and bumped the Land Rover sideways into a roadside culvert. They bounced out of it, becoming briefly airborne. Jack tried to nurse the vehicle out of a slide in the soft dirt, but the rear end began to creep around in a slow pirouette.

A small crowd waited at a bus shelter, directly in their path. Malaika shouted, 'Jack!' He tried to correct the four-wheel drift as the terrified group scattered in all directions.

Splintered wooden planks clattered around them. Chickens squawked and disappeared in an explosion of feathers. The car jolted to a halt. Dust settled over them like a blanket.

Malaika held her breath in the airless cabin. Waiting. Waiting for any sign of injury or death. It was sound, Africa's voices, that measured tragedy. Jack touched her shoulder. 'Are you all right?' His voice was a whisper. Before she could speak, an unearthly wail arose from behind them at the bus shelter.

Jack sprang from the cabin. Malaika joined him. A woman was crying hysterically, an unconscious teenage girl cradled in her lap. The crowd was quickly forming a tight circle around the pair, gawking and yabbering to one another. Malaika pushed through, fell to her knees beside the injured girl and began to examine her, lifting open each of her eyelids and feeling along her back and limbs.

Jack said, 'Can we move her?' She was checking the soft indentation on the side of the girl's head. It had begun to ooze blood from a nasty depression. Finally she said, 'Yes. Very carefully.'

Jack slid his arms under the girl and carried her to the Land Rover where Malaika opened the back door. He put her gently on the seat. Malaika returned to calm the woman, wrapping her arms around the ample frame and patting her shoulders. When the wailing subsided into despondent sobs, Malaika's soft words and quiet manner drew out the information she needed. Looking at Jack over the woman's shoulder, she said, 'There's a hospital in Kericho.'

'Let's go.'

Malaika joined him in the front seat, squeezing against him to allow the other woman, who was substantially broader across the beam, to get in beside her. She kept an eye on her patient as Jack eased the Land Rover out of the shallow ditch where it had finally come to rest.

'How is she?' he said without taking his eyes from the road.

'I don't know.' Malaika's concern was for the head wound; it might be superficial but the girl's pupillary response was absent. 'The head injury is the problem.'

She took the old woman's hand into her lap and patted it. 'She says the girl's sixteen. She is her aunt. She has no mother. Her father is in Kisii, picking tea.'

The late-afternoon traffic slowed them as they entered the town. Malaika turned to the aunt to ask, '*Je, hospitali iko wapi?*' The woman stifled her weeping to give her the directions. Malaika translated for Jack.

She was dismayed when they reached it. The hospital was no more than a series of connected sheds with sheltered walkways leading to an older two-storey brick building. 'Jack, there's the door,' she pointed.

Jack pulled on the handbrake under a sign, *Bahati Nasibu*, and in smaller letters, *Casualty*. He vaulted around to the rear door. As he gently lifted the girl, he turned to Malaika and said, 'She's going to be okay, isn't she?'

A note in his voice brought her eyes from her patient to study his face. What she had assumed to be silent composure in the gathering crisis now appeared to be the onset of shock. He was pale and beads of sweat gathered on his upper lip. 'I think she'll be okay.' She put a hand on his arm, feeling guilty for not noticing his condition earlier. 'The doctors will know.' She led him to the entrance where he placed the girl's inert body on a parked trolley.

She ran ahead, almost colliding with a group escorting an old man to the exit. She hurried an apology, then shouted into the empty corridor ahead of her, '*Kuna hali ya hatari!*' The old man's group stared from Jack to the trolley to Malaika, now hurrying down the hall, and finally to the aunt, who had commenced wailing again.

Malaika found a doctor and explained the situation as she hurried him back to where Jack waited with the young girl. The doctor made a quick check of the girl's condition then whisked her away. Jack started to follow but Malaika called him back. 'Jack, let them go. We can't do any more.'

His eyes followed the disappearing trolley before he returned to the casualty area. Malaika took the aunt's arm and led her to a bench seat that occupied the better part of one wall. Her face was wet with tears and tight with misery. She was twisting her colourful *kanga* into a knot. She had a headscarf to match and Malaika guessed that she and her niece had been on their way to somewhere important, maybe an elder's house. In her *chondo*, which she still had over her shoulder, there was probably a small gift for their hostess. Perhaps a couple of maize cobs or some sweet potatoes.

Jack joined Malaika and the aunt on the bench, but was not seated long before he began to fidget. He stood, then sat again. Finally, he commenced stalking the casualty room, a silhouette against the dusty louvred windows, now lit by the setting sun's splash of gold.

MALAIKA AWOKE TO THE STERTOROUS sounds of the aunt snoring beside her on the bench seat. She checked her watch: nearly 1 a.m. The last casualty, a road accident victim, had been admitted around ten, but otherwise the night had been quiet for a casualty ward. The doctor had last visited them three hours ago, with no news other than that the girl was under observation.

Jack must have finally succumbed. He was slumped in a wheelchair opposite her, his head resting on the handle and his forehead against the wall. She watched him stir, fingers twitching in some hidden dream scene. For someone she had branded heartless, he had surprised her by his obvious concern for the girl. The accident was not his fault. In fact, it could have been a lot worse had he not managed to manoeuvre the car away from the main group at the bus stop. Yet he seemed tormented by an unwarranted guilt.

He grunted and twitched violently, causing his head to slip between the wheelchair handle and the wall. Malaika stood and stretched her aching body. Wondering if she should wake him, or put him in a more comfortable position, she leaned over the wheelchair. He suddenly let out a strangled cry and almost leapt from the chair. Malaika jumped backwards, barely keeping her feet.

His eyes were wide but, for a moment, uncomprehending. As realisation flooded back, he let his body slump into the chair, his face in his hands. His shoulders rose as he gathered a large breath, and fell as he let it escape with a rush. Abruptly he sat up. 'Is she all right?' He studied her face intently. 'Is the girl all right?'

'I don't know. I was just now going to find the doctor.'

He ran his hands down his face and climbed from the wheelchair. 'I'll come with you.'

In the corridor they met the doctor coming towards them. He removed his glasses and rubbed his eyes. Malaika asked about the girl. Outside, an owl made mournful calls to the moon.

She listened to him in silence. When the doctor turned away she thanked him.

This was not the first time she'd had to break such news, but it had never been more difficult. 'Jack ... I'm sorry. She's dead.'

THE SUN HAD JUST LIGHTENED Nairobi's eastern sky as Jack turned the Land Rover through the rusty steel gates stuck wide open on dropped hinges. A creeper, some kind of pea with tiny violet flowers, had run rampant over the right-hand side.

He killed the motor. The silence of early morning settled around them. Malaika's apartment block had once been a large family home in the older section of Parklands, not far from his club. Bear said the area had been popular with the Indian business class years ago, but that most had moved to houses at better addresses. Green wooden shutters framed the windows on both floors. The patchy lawn had totally given up the battle beneath two very large mango trees that dominated the garden.

He became aware of bird sounds. Malaika climbed down and collected her bag and briefcase from the back seat. As he began to open his door she was at his window saying, 'I can handle these.'

'Are you sure? I'll carry your bag up.'

'Really, it's okay.'

'You look beat.'

'So do you.' She hesitated a moment then put her hand on his arm. 'Get some sleep.'

He waited for her to slip silently through the green door of the old mansion before starting the motor.

IN THE JACARANDA HOTEL CAR park, Jack hauled his bag out the back door and slammed it shut. The slanting rays of dawn fell across the Land Rover, revealing for the first time the damage caused by the truck. He dropped his bag and squatted, staring at the paint scrape. It began as a streak of the truck's dark green paint on the front door and ended as an indentation towards the rear mudguard. He ran a finger along it. Not much to show for a life, he thought. A touch of paint and the car would be restored. But the girl . . . It was an obscene disparity.

He dragged himself to his feet and trudged to the reception desk for his key. A sleepy attendant handed him a telephone message: *Don't forget to pick me up for the office. Bear.*

He fell on his bed fully dressed, and stared at the ceiling in the semi-darkness. The death of the young girl had revived unwanted memories. The nightmare that had wakened him in the Kericho hospital proved he had yet to put the white sands of Hawaii behind him.

A breeze against the drawn curtains sent early morning shadows dancing up the walls. He took deep breaths, willing the bunched muscles of his shoulders to relax.

'MEET ME AT THE END of the beach.' It sounded like she was calling from the house phone in the lobby.

'Tonight?' She knew he was leaving on an early-morning flight. They had said goodbye at lunch.

'I changed my mind. This is not going to end. You know that. You're into this as much as I am. And if you think you've had the best, think again.'

In the silence between sentences he could hear her every breath, the mouthpiece pressed to her lips, perhaps with a hand cupped over it for good measure. No ounce of seduction must escape. He counted her breaths, stalling, trying to find the strength to deny her.

'You don't want to miss this one. I have something special. Very special.'

Now he could hear his own breath, in time with hers. 'What time?' He felt the excitement growing.

'Eleven.' She hung up.

• • •

THE BEACH WAS EMPTY. LONG white breakers thumped into the shallow water. Sweeping froth hissed up the sand before falling back to be caught in the following surge. The constant motion was hypnotising. Jack became absorbed in the play of surf and sand. An image of Liz came to him. He forced it aside, as he had on every occasion she had threatened to invade his thoughts over the last five days. The person who inhabited his body now was alien to him. But to examine that man and deal with his conscience was a matter for another time, another place. The flight tomorrow would give him time to think. This was not who he was. He would leave this surreal experience behind and return to his other, normal life. And then he would deal with his conscience.

He had been lost in his thoughts for maybe half an hour. She had not come. Just as well, he thought. When she had mentioned it never ending, she had alarmed him.

He turned to walk up to the hotel.

In the months that followed, he would ponder how his life might have been had he not made that final glance along the beach. Chaos theory — the beat of a single butterfly wing deep in the Amazon, and the inexplicable effect it may have on rainfall in the Himalayas.

The person was barely visible through the surf spray. There was an inward curve of the beach, before it ran out to the cliff. It gave the figure a backlight of iridescent foam. He knew it was O'Hara.

He hesitated.

You don't want to miss this.

His shadow, flung across the sand by the hotel's floodlights, led him back to the beach.

Her red dress was a wet sheath that hugged her full curves. He grabbed at her breast and mouthed the salt at her throat. She threw her arms around him then led him to a depression in the low dunes, which nestled under a shoulder of rock before climbing slowly to the height of the headland above them. The onshore breeze carried the muted sound of the waves into their hideaway. She pulled him down beside her and began her exquisite opus of hands and mouth and tongue. The ache for her body began to build.

'Take it,' she said. She shook the sand from the black snub-nosed revolver.

He moved his eyes from the gun to her face, which was pale and still dripping saltwater. 'It's The Game,' she said. 'The last one.'

The weight of the gun surprised him, but it lay perfectly balanced in his palm. A beautiful, potent machine, was his thought. Sleek and smooth. It was made to be caressed and fitted his palm so well the maker might have used Jack's hand for the mould. 'What's this for?'

O'Hara began to un-notch his belt.

'Wait a minute,' he said. 'What's this for?'

She had his trousers undone, her hand on his growing erection. 'It's The Game,' she whispered.

'But what's this got to do with it?' He raised the gun.

'Risk and consequence. That's what it's always been about, lover. We've done risk — the risk of being caught. But the consequences ... the danger ... Dangerous sex is the best.' Her voice was breathless with excitement. 'Do you remember the time we did it while you leaned me over the balcony? It was sensational. It's the imminent terrible consequences that stimulate lust. Brings it alive. Adrenaline ... the ultimate sex drug.'

Her eyes had the smoky, unfocused look he saw in the passionate throes of sex. Abandonment.

He had never held a handgun before. He was fascinated by it. It reeked of menace.

'See, this is how it works.' She took it and flipped open the cartridge chamber. 'There's one bullet in the six chambers.' She flicked it shut with a snap, spun the chamber, then returned it to his palm. 'You fuck me from behind.' She was breathing heavily as she slipped the straps of her dress from her shoulders. 'You put this to my head. Pull the trigger. Take your time. Count them. Measure the risk.'

'You're mad,' he whispered under his breath.

'You haven't complained so far,' she said with a snigger, and slipped her hand around his scrotum, giving it a gentle squeeze. 'Don't worry, you're in control. You stop when you want. You have the power.' She ran her tongue lightly over his lips. 'Extreme risk. The equation. Remember?'

She pushed his trousers open. He caught his breath as she took his penis into her mouth, doing that thing with her tongue that drove him mad. Then she somehow turned under him and guided him into her warm inviting body.

'Do it!' she whispered.

He put the gun to the back of her head.

He squeezed the trigger.

Click!

HIS EYES FLEW OPEN.

Sunshine on the curtains, the bedside phone ringing.

He put the handset to his ear.

'Where the fuck are you, man?'

CHAPTER 16

PEABODY'S GUIDE TO EAST AFRICA (5ᵀᴴ ED):
Avoid freshwater bathing even if you see the natives doing
it. Most natural water sources contain parasites that can
penetrate the skin, such as Schistosoma, which produces
the disease known as bilharziasis. The parasite is common
in Lake Victoria.

Swimming pools in upcountry lodges are safe.

1972

It was the third time that Hamis had been told to leave. This
time the midwife used her considerable size to bullock him out
the door. The chickens scattered ahead of him, disappearing
into the banana trees that clustered between the kitchen and
the wooden outhouse.

He wandered to the front of the small concrete-block
house. Malaika was sitting cross-legged on a rock near their
garden plot, her elbows on her knees and chin on her hands.
Hamis placed his hand on the girl's head and watched
the *matatus* roar up and down the road, dodging potholes
of sinister black water. The conductors, *kondas*, hung
precariously from open doors and bawled out the bus route:
'*Pansiansi! Twende! Twende!*' on their way to the Mwanza
airport, and '*Saba Saba! Twende!*' on their way back.
Twende, the universal call of the *matatu* operator: *Let's go!*

To be first at the next pick-up point meant a bigger share of passenger revenue.

He looked down at the little girl and wondered again what was going on inside her pretty head. He had been wondering that since they had arrived at the Mwanza bus stop that golden morning nearly nine months ago. At first they thought she was just tired. They all were. The rush from Isuria had left them drained and on edge. But as hours turned to days, to weeks, Malaika had remained silent. Penina had tried to draw her out by talking about Isuria, her friends, her games, her brother. Hamis could see that this came at a price for Penina, whom he knew desperately missed her son and village life. But he also sensed that it was making Malaika retreat further into her silent cocoon.

They discussed sending her to school. Hamis had no children of his own, but his observations of his brothers' many offspring suggested to him that she needed the company of other eight year olds. But after only two days, the teachers sent Malaika home. They said they couldn't spare the time to teach an idiot child. Both Penina and Hamis did what they could at home, but the lessons were slow and difficult. The child seemed bright enough, and appeared to be able to hear and understand. But behind the intelligent eyes were unspeakable memories that had not only struck her dumb, but had taken away her smile. They decided to wait and see if time would heal her.

Hamis found it hard to believe nine months had passed. So much had happened. Penina's belly grew, and her worries with it. Not just about Malaika's continuing silence, but her fear that the unborn child might be Mengoru's and a girl. Hamis didn't believe the tribal superstition but there seemed to be nothing he could do to reassure her that she and her children were safe with him.

The shriek rose above the *matatus*. Hamis bolted across the garden, through the kitchen, to the bedroom door. The cry had stopped. Penina, drenched with sweat, lay on the bed in the stifling room. The midwife was wiping her body with a damp cloth and gave Hamis a look that said she would tolerate his presence, but not for long.

Penina opened her eyes and reached a hand to Hamis, beckoning him to the bedside. 'Hamisi, I'm afraid.'

He took the cold, sweaty hand. 'Penina, you are going to be —'

'Not for me. But what if it's a girl? What might happen to you and Malaika? Promise me you will take care of Malaika, and this new one, if something happens to me?'

'I will, my love, I promise.'

She was gripped by another spasm. The midwife elbowed her way to the bedside, dismissing Hamis as she did so.

An hour later, the midwife, smiling at last, placed the baby in his arms. '*M'sichana*,' she said. A girl. 'You men!' Shaking her head. 'Always expecting trouble!'

He made a protective hollow for the baby by an awkward hunching of his big shoulders and arms. This bundle, no thicker than his forearm, was complete with ten brown clenching and unclenching fingers and an animated, wrinkled little face. He smiled at Penina who tried to smile back. The baby in his arms made a soundless grimace and wrinkled her nose in great agitation. He didn't understand the curse that Penina said had been put on her family. He wasn't sure that Penina understood it either, but he decided he really didn't care if this was his or Mengoru's baby. Here was a gift of God and he loved her already. They would call her just that: God's bonus. *Ziada*.

'Ziada,' he said softly, testing the sound of it. Then again, 'Ziada!' He looked at Penina, very pleased with himself.

He became aware of Malaika under his elbow. Her face, lifted to his and the child in his arms, had the light of curiosity. He dropped to one knee to let her see her new sister. Malaika gazed at the baby with awe. Every detail of her tiny features, her fingers, toes, wisp of black hair, was studied. Finally she appeared satisfied with what she saw.

Her eyes brightened and a small smile teased at the corners of her mouth. 'Ziada,' she whispered.

1975

Malaika dawdled past Bismarck's Rock. Lake Victoria never

quite managed blue; today it was blue-grey, the best it could do. She should have been at her parents' market stall by now, but she scuffed her bare feet along the sandy pathway between the road and the lake, dragging her school bag behind her as ten year olds were prone to do. Her teacher had kept her back for fighting again. It was the fourth time this term. *It isn't fair,* she thought. *Why should I get three of the cane and have to clean the schoolyard when it was Faridah Pemba who started it all? The last time it was Sekela Macharia and he wasn't punished either. It was unfair.*

Now her mother would be angry. She and Hamis would not be able to finish at the market stall because Malaika was late to take little Ziada home. Hamis wouldn't mind. He seldom got angry. But he would stand there, wringing his hands and looking worried until Mama finished. Then he would smile with relief and, later in the day, find some excuse to call her aside. He always had something, like a curious piece of twisted metal that could be untangled and tangled again like a puzzle. Then he would ask, *What do you say?* It was Hamis's idea of parental guidance: basic good manners. And she would have to answer, *Thank you, Hamisi.* She never called him Father, although in every other sense he was. She wanted to call him Papa, like two-year-old Ziada did, but the word would not come. It was strange, because she had no memory of her real father, seldom thought of him, except in nightmares where he wore the mask of a monster. In fact, she had no recollection of life before Mwanza. It was a curiosity but it never bothered her.

She passed the New Mwanza Hotel. The patrons at the patio bar were as noisy as usual. Crossing the street she turned into the narrow road leading to the part of the market where her mother and Hamis had their stall. It was in ironware, beyond the poultry section with its usual riot of squawks and quacks and feathers. And disagreeable smells.

At the first stall in poultry, an old woman hung two live birds, their legs bound with twine, from a carry-pole. They twisted their heads towards Malaika, giving her an indignant stare. Up ahead she could see Hamis, towering above a customer in obvious dispute about the fairness of a price. Hamis seemed resigned to a long struggle, shrugging his shoulders with palms upturned in a gesture of futility.

Her mother, with Ziada in a carry-sling on her hip, was arranging the beaded pillows and aprons she sold as a sideline to Hamis's metal tools and cookware. When her mother caught sight of her, she scowled and came from behind the counter.

'Malaika!' she hissed. 'Where have you been? Ah? You are late again. Do you care how much I worry? Do you care? No! And your sister is so tired.' She lifted the two year old out of the sling and handed her over. Ziada clutched her sister with fingers sticky from the ooze of an over-ripe banana. 'Now hurry up! Get yourself back home *upesi*, *upesi*, or you will feel my hand.'

Malaika hurried down Nyeri Road, avoiding the places where the children of her school might be playing. Nearer home, where there were no more side alleys to use, she stopped to move Ziada to the other hip and prepare her final rush to the safety of her doorway.

Two boys she knew were running a car tyre down the street, steering it with sticks slipped into the rim. They ignored her as she hustled past. Malaika slowed her pace at the corner of her street. It was empty. Hitching Ziada higher on her hip, she rounded the corner at a smart pace without appearing to rush.

'Hey! There she is!' Four boys were kicking a soccer ball in a vacant lot not far from the corner. Her house was a hundred yards away. Don't run! she told herself as the boys bounded alongside her. They were a year ahead of her at school, but she could almost meet them eye to eye.

'Hey, Maasai girl,' one said in a loud voice. 'Show us your thing.' They encircled her but she pressed on. 'Show us the little thing between your legs.' They all laughed.

'How did the old Maasai witch doctor cut it? With a razor?' a second boy said.

'Oh, no!' said another. 'She is a Maasai, it must be an axe!'

'I am not Maasai,' she said in a fluster, not daring to make eye contact. 'I am not Maasai.' She bit her lip.

'Oh! Not a Maasai! Look at her. All teeth and legs and she is not a Maasai! Hah hah!'

She fought her way through, regretting her outburst. It always made them worse. Ziada was cradled in her arms, but she began to whimper in fear. The house was in sight and the boys were emboldened in their efforts to draw a reaction. One ran a hand up under her school dress and managed to slip his fingers between her thighs.

'I did it! I touched it!'

The others roared with laughter and began to fondle and pinch. One groped at the buds of her young breasts. They pulled at her school clothes. At the gatepost she tried to force her way through but they blocked her. Ziada was clinging to her in terror and wailed when one boy shoved a hand at Malaika's breasts, tearing her blouse in his attempt.

'Hey! You boys! What are you doing there?'

The boys turned at the neighbour's demand, allowing Malaika to dash to her door. The seconds it took to unlock were an agony but she flung it open, slammed it behind her and pressed her back against it with a gasp.

Hugging Ziada to her chest, she whispered soft words to calm her while fighting back her own tears of self-pity. She would not let them win. She would not weaken.

1980

Penina stood, hands on hips, in the centre of the lounge room, looking to Hamis for support. He was sitting in his armchair, appearing a little uncomfortable as he always did when parental discipline was needed. He raised his eyebrows and shrugged his broad shoulders. Should have known better than to expect support from that one, she thought.

'And what do you expect to do with yourself if you don't go to high school?' she demanded of Malaika, who sat, head lowered, in the chair opposite Hamis. The discussion had been going around in circles for an hour. Days really. Ever since Malaika had announced that she would not go to Mwanza East High School next year. Or any other school at any other time, for that matter.

Malaika looked miserable but determined, as Penina knew she could be. 'Oh, I don't know! I'll find something. Maybe in the market with you.'

Her mother tilted her head to one side. 'Hah! Did you hear that, Hamis?' she said, not taking her eyes from Malaika. 'Helping in the market! This from one who moans and complains because she must spend just two hours there each day.'

'Well, a shop somewhere.' Malaika sensed it was doomed as it left her mouth. She quickly added, 'I could work in the kitchen at the hotel. I could become a cook.'

'A cook!' Her mother made a theatrical gesture with her arms before flopping onto the vinyl-covered sofa. She mopped her brow with her apron. The electric fan on the sideboard barely moved the air and shuddered alarmingly at the end of each sweep. Hamis had promised to install a ceiling fan, but, as usual, he had not. It was the same with the front fence, the broken hinge on the outhouse door and the leak in the roof over the kitchen. She could go on and on. It was always the same — tomorrow. She shook her head. '*Haki ya Mungu!*' was all she could mutter. Oh, my God.

'Oh, Mama! You can't make me go back to that horrible school. I hate it! It hates me!'

Penina could see her daughter was growing up. No longer a child, she had started menstruating when she was eleven. Now her young breasts were turning heads at the market and her long legs had given her a grace of movement where only a year ago she had been bumbling and awkward. She understood why Malaika wanted to leave. Mwanza had not been a happy place for her. In most school activities she seemed out of step with her classmates, preferring to stand on the sidelines. Not that she was lacking in ability. But she would only participate when compelled to do so, and then became so intense in her endeavour to succeed that her mother felt sure she could not possibly enjoy it. With few friends, she spent most of her time with Ziada, amusing her with little adventure stories and games that she seemed able to invent for any circumstance. In the games, Malaika was the fearless hunter or the life-saving doctor, and Ziada the hapless prey or dying patient.

'Please!' Malaika pleaded, sensing some softening in her mother's attitude.

'Malaika.' Hamis climbed out of his chair and ambled to the window. 'If you don't study, how will you ever become a doctor? Isn't that what you want to be?'

Malaika bit her lip and ran her fingers through her hair, absent-mindedly teasing it up into the Afro she had been trying to grow for months. She sank further into her chair, a look of despair on her face. He had touched a concern that she had been trying to forget. The determined lines on her face dissolved.

'You do want to study.' It was a statement more than a question. 'So,' he said, glancing in Penina's direction, 'so what if it was not in Mwanza?'

Penina looked up at him. 'What do you mean, Hamis?'

'Well, I am thinking this girl has never been a good student. Good results, but not a good student. Now, myself? I was also never a good student, but me, I failed all my school tests too. That's why I have these.' He showed them his large callused palms. 'But if Malaika wants to be a doctor, or something important, she knows she has to be a good student and also get good results. *Si ndio?*' He looked from one to the other for a response. 'Yes!' he said, when none was forthcoming.

Penina waited for him to continue. It was about the longest speech she had heard Hamis make in all the nine years she had known him.

'What I am thinking,' he said, 'is that Malaika is unhappy in school here. That is why she gets into trouble with fighting and such.'

Penina hoped this was not the limit to his observation, because that much was clear to anyone who knew Malaika. She grabbed one of her beaded pillows and began to knead it irritably.

'I think Malaika is even unhappy here in Mwanza. So, I think that Malaika would…' He glanced at Penina again, '…would be a better student in Nairobi at a new school with new friends and new teachers,' he finished in a rush.

'You mean leave home?' Penina said incredulously. 'She is barely fifteen!'

'She is older in her head than fifteen years. Look at her.'

'I don't have to look at her to know she is a reckless child. She needs strong parents more than a good school. You are the one who should look, Hamis. Or do you not have eyes? She is always getting into trouble or doing dangerous things. She cannot be trusted to go to the *duka* on the corner without getting into a fight!'

'She fights for a reason. And yes, she is too proud and too quick to temper. But if she makes mistakes, she will learn from them. It does not mean your promised big tragedy will fall upon her head.'

'Hamis! What...' She spun around to Malaika. 'Malaika! Go fetch your sister from Mama Salama's house!' she snapped.

Malaika poked fingers into her springy hair and clung to fistfuls of it. She looked at Hamis with a pleading frown.

'Go!' her mother screeched as she got to her feet. Malaika left the room, slamming the door behind her.

'Hamis, what do you mean I want a tragedy? I worry about her safety because she is careless. While you!' She jabbed a finger at him. 'Why, you don't even know where she is. You think she can look after herself. Do whatever she wants. You say, everything is going to be very fine. No matter what.'

'Look at you, Penina! Can you hear yourself? Even after all these years you are still expecting a mountain to fall on us. You are so worried about these girls, you have forgotten your own life. Our life. Do you not see her, Penina? Does she look like a demon is about to swallow her? And Ziada. She is nearly eight but you treat her like an infant — a baby needing your constant attention.' It was unusual for Hamis to raise his voice and he checked it before it became as strident as that of his wife. 'For Allah's sake, forget the curse. There is no curse.'

'If you have seen what I have seen, you would not call on your Allah. I tell you, the curse is real. I have seen it. But do you listen? No! Or you listen, but do not want to understand. My mother, my baby sister, lie dead because of this evil curse.'

'The curse is nothing, Penina. Nothing but an excuse. Yes, an excuse. For not being happy.'

'How dare you say that?'

'Because I am sick of seeing you use it for every wrong that happens to us. Every time we have a poor day at the market, *it is the curse*. Every time one of the children falls down, *it is the curse*. The Maasai tribe will not die out because old Sendeyo put a curse on your grandfather. And our family will not die of it either.' He opened his palms to the heavens in emphasis. 'But I tell you this, Penina, our lives together will die if you do not let it go.'

Penina threw the beaded pillow onto the sofa and stormed towards the kitchen. She had never been so angry with him. So this was why he refused to help her discipline the girls. He thought she was mad! All these years he had been ignoring her, even when the signs were clear.

Malaika appeared at the kitchen doorway, Ziada's hand in hers. Her mother's accusing finger was in her face. 'Do you see the trouble you bring to this house?' Her face was clouded with rage and her mouth a line drawn between taut lips. 'Well, I am finished worrying. It is on Hamis's head. You go to this Nairobi. But take care. You will get no pity in this house if you find yourself in trouble there.'

'DON'T GO, MALAIKA. PLEASE DON'T GO,' Ziada said, sniffling. She was sitting on her bed in the room that she and Malaika had shared since she was born. Her tears had dried into salty tracks down her plump cheeks.

'I must go, Ziada. You know what Mama said. Anyway, I want to go.' The cloth bag Malaika was packing lay on the floor. All her clothes, and the few personal items she had chosen to take, covered her bed.

'But what about me? Who will be my friend?' Ziada had been using the same argument for a month, since their mother had told Malaika to go.

'You have your friends. They don't tease you and call you names.'

'But you could have some friends too. Some day.'

'I don't need them. Anyway, I will make new friends in Nairobi.'

'Oh, can't you take me to Nairobi too, Malaika? Please?'

Malaika took a piece of cloth and wiped Ziada's nose. She sat beside her on the bed. 'Kidogo,' she said, using the word for 'little' that was the nickname she had given her when she was born, 'I told you. You are too young. And I will be too busy to play with you.'

'But what will you do there? Where will you live?'

'Hamisi has an uncle in Nairobi. He works in a hospital. They have many nurses and doctors there. Hamis said his uncle will try to get me a job.'

'As a doctor?'

'Well, maybe. After I do more study.'

'Take me with you, take me with you, take me with you ... Please.'

'Kidogo, I can't. But one day I will come back. When I have money. Then I will take you to Nairobi.'

Ziada threw herself onto the bed face down on the sheet.

'Don't cry, Ziada. Look, here is my necklace — keep it until I return.' She eased it over her Afro and held it out to her sister.

Ziada sniffed and wiped her arm across her nose. 'Your necklace?'

'Yes. You know I love it, so now you must believe I will be back to get it.'

'Your beautiful necklace...?' She held it in the palm of her hand. 'Your very expensive and beautiful one?' The malachite stone was the size and colour of a green pea with swirls of darker green. Three red trade beads were threaded at each side. Malaika had collected empty soda bottles for weeks to buy the stones and together the sisters had threaded them onto a piece of fishing line.

'Yes, but it is only until I bring you to Nairobi. There is so much malachite in Nairobi you can have all you want. And even more beautiful.'

Ziada threw her arms around her big sister's neck and hugged her. 'I love you, Malaika. I hate Mama. It's all her fault you are going away. I hate her.'

'Shh,' Malaika said, closing her eyes and holding her tight. 'Shh.'

SHE WAS THE LAST TO climb down from the bus. The bus station was awash with traffic. Buses queued to the corner, blocking the whole road. Cars, motorbikes, carts, *matatus* and trucks all crushed into a space too small for half of them. Tooting. Trying to manoeuvre around the jam. And in every space between the cacophonies of traffic was a moving throng of people. Kikuyu, Luo, black Turkana and Pokot, tall Maasai and Samburu, proud Swahili men in flowing robes with veiled women following in their footsteps carrying baskets and children.

And where was Uncle? Why had she not paid more attention to Hamisi's description of him? She doubted if she could even find her mother in this crowd. Hamis had warned her there would be many people at the Nairobi bus stop. But so many! It was beyond imagining.

The swirl of people and traffic flowed around her as she clutched her cloth bag to her chest. The faces she searched meant nothing to her. *A tall thin man, not much hair,* he had said. It could be almost any of them. *Few teeth.* What else had he said? *Wait at the bus station, he will find you when he finds the bus.* She fumbled for her malachite pendant. Her breath stopped before she remembered she had given it to Ziada to dry her tears. The memory brought a lump to her throat.

Her bus roared into life, sending a cloud of diesel smoke over her. It was her only hold on Mwanza and now it was rumbling and bumping away down River Road. A crush of people filled the void it left, but it was a short-lived victory. Three *matatus* pushed into the space, tooting, and sending Malaika and the throng scurrying to the footpath.

She was less than twenty-four hours into her new life, but it was not how she had imagined it. Her bag hung limply from her fingers.

'Ho, Malaika! Is that you, Malaika?' The man was tall, thin and balding. 'Is it?' he grinned. Four discoloured teeth punctuated a gummy orifice from which came disagreeable breath. She nodded. Unable to speak, she tried to smile.

'So you are Hamisi's little one, ah?' He wore a dirty white tee-shirt under an ugly brown jacket. 'Ho, not so little. Look at you! Tall already. And even little *maziwa* too!'

She hid her chest with her bag and dropped her face to cover her embarrassment.

He lifted her chin. 'Aren't you pleased to see Uncle?'

She had been, but now she was not so sure.

'Ho! A shy one. Now come, Auntie is waiting. Do you have *matatu* money?'

The question took her unawares. She nodded, remembering the Kenyan note Hamis had thrust into her hand at the bus stop in Mwanza.

'Where is it?'

He took her bag as she fumbled in the small pocket of her beaded belt. 'Fifty shillingi!' He plucked the note from her hand, letting the bag drop to the ground. She scooped it up and wiped the dust of River Road from it. 'Come,' he said, and was paces away before Malaika realised the introductions were at an end.

Malaika tucked her bag under her arm and trotted to catch up. Her heart was in a turmoil. The fifty shillings was the most money she had ever owned and she could not dispel the feeling she might never see it again. A day and a night she had travelled with that fifty shillings in her belt, fighting her hunger and fearful that if she pulled it out she might be tempted to spend it all. That, and the fact she was terrified to reveal it to her fellow passengers, who looked honest enough, but her mother had warned her to be careful on the bus. And in the big city to be especially wary of men, as they were usually after one thing. Malaika assumed her mother had not been referring to her fifty bob.

She followed a step or two behind her new uncle, trying to discover something to admire. Bare ankles, skinny and dusty, showed between the bottom of his navy trousers and his brown, laceless, scuffed shoes. There was a grease stain on the elbow of his brown jacket.

He led her along River Road at a brisk pace. Some buildings had columns defining impressive doorways and wide ornate verandas on the second storey. Others were more modest, of bare timber, although it appeared they may have once been painted. Turrets and towers adorned some, reminding Malaika of the mosque in Mwanza. There were street stalls selling cooking utensils and hardware; others carried all manner of clothing, hats and shoes. Sprinkled throughout were the ubiquitous food and refreshment vendors, tormenting Malaika with their irresistible aromas. Kiswahili tunes thumped from many doorways where young men stood, smoked and made loud comments about the passers-by. Uncle joined one such group outside a corner bar, joking and slapping their hands in greeting. He went into a huddle for a few whispered words and the group roared, looking pointedly at Malaika, who stood mortified on the kerb. She and Uncle moved on, leaving the laughter behind in the crowd.

River Road opened out to reveal tall city buildings on her right and the sprawling expanse of low-level houses across the river to her left. Uncle strode out, arms swinging and coat-tail flapping. He said, 'Machakos Market,' as they passed. The items on the stalls were similar to home, but this market was much bigger than the Mwanza Municipal Market. On the right was a bus terminal. Malaika wondered if her bus was there, hidden amongst the many that slumped, exhausted and lopsided, on flat tyres or sagging suspension.

They crossed a bridge over a river that was more mud than water. It smelt awful. 'Nairobi River,' Uncle said, without pausing in his brisk stride. Malaika had no trouble keeping pace but she was hot and thirsty and began to doubt that any part of her fifty shillings would go towards a *matatu* fare.

They entered a maze of houses, some neat and tidy, others squalid and overgrown. Uncle paused outside the Pumwani Maternity Hospital. 'There,' he said with some pride, 'is where I am working.' He expected no reply, for which she was grateful, and marched on, through small laneways, past building lots crammed with ramshackle huts, where toddlers stood naked at doorways, staring.

They arrived at a dwelling — actually a rickety collection of building materials, where mud brick and iron sheeting predominated. Without a word he pushed open the door and stepped in. Malaika assumed she should follow.

The room was a kitchen with a bed squeezed into one corner. A flap covered a doorway on the far side of the kitchen. Malaika guessed there was probably a bedroom beyond it. Wooden shutters were propped open on sticks for the light and to allow the air to flush the wood smoke from the small cooking stove.

Auntie — Malaika could only guess it was she, having received no introductions — looked up as they entered. On first sight she appeared too young for Uncle. A toddler sat naked on the floor playing with a broken pot; a baby whimpered in a cot made from half a truck tyre. But the woman's eyes, which paused briefly on Malaika's face before quickly appraising the rest of her, were bloodshot and yellow where they should be white. And they were tired. Very tired.

'So, you have come,' she said, continuing to mix chopped green vegetables into a mash of *ugali*.

'Yes ... I have come ... from Mwanza.'

Uncle slipped through the flap to the bedroom without a word. Malaika stood where she had entered, her bag under one arm, feeling too tall for the small house. There was nowhere obvious for her to retreat. She scanned the room again and returned to find Auntie's eyes on her while she continued to mix the corn flour and vegetables. Malaika felt ashamed of her small breasts and again covered them with her bag.

'There is a bed there,' Auntie said, nodding to the one in the corner of the kitchen. 'You must share it with Mayasa. She is six, my oldest.'

'*Asante sana*. Thank you, Auntie. I will be no trouble for you.'

The woman was silent, her eyes on her hands which she slowly wiped on a kitchen cloth. Uncle strode from the bedroom and out the door with a grunt of farewell.

Auntie sighed and took slow steps to a chair under the window. 'What is your name, girl?' she asked as she eased herself into the chair.

'Malaika.'

'Malaika?' She frowned. 'A strange name for a Maasai.'

'I am not!'

There was no condemnation in Auntie's expression, only mild surprise at the brusque reply. She lifted the toddler who had crawled to her and now pulled at her dress.

'No,' Malaika said more politely. 'I am not Maasai.'

Auntie let it pass, opening her blouse for the child. It sucked and gurgled at her breast.

Malaika, chastened by her bad manners, needed to make a peace offering. 'I will be no trouble, Auntie. I plan to get a job. At the hospital.'

'Humph! I suppose that one,' she nodded her head in the direction of the street, 'told your father he could get you a job with him?'

'I . . . I think so . . .'

'Well, you would be better off taking yourself there. Your uncle has been put off. For drinking.' She hoisted the baby to a more comfortable position on her lap. Milk trickled from the toddler's pursed lips. 'Now he thinks he will make money with the *chang'aa*. Humph! He drinks more than he sells. Him and his whoring friends.'

Malaika's shoulders dropped. Her whole plan was built around getting a job, no matter how lowly, in the hospital. It had started as a story to appease Ziada, but in the telling it had grown. By the time she had boarded the bus she had convinced herself that she would soon be a nurse and, by whatever means — the details would reveal themselves soon enough — become a doctor. Saving lives. Delivering babies. Doing deeds of great humanitarian value.

Auntie must have noticed her expression. 'But go, child. Try. You could . . .' She shrugged, unable to find any words of hope.

IT WAS A MONTH AFTER she arrived, and two months before Uncle found her alone in her corner bed, that Malaika met Jai Hussein. He was waiting at the steps of the hospital, as she was, but he looked too well dressed to be begging for work. He had been pacing the length of the stone steps for some time. Wearing cotton tracksuit pants, a white tee-shirt and a peaked cap with *Reebok* written on it, he looked ready to take to the soccer field or tennis court at a moment's notice.

She stole glances at him when she felt it safe to do so. He was nearly six feet tall in his thick-soled running shoes, but his beard looked like he had been trying to grow it for some time and it didn't quite bridge the gap between his jaw and the thin soft finger of hair at his temples. Without the beard he could be an angel. That is if India had angels. His brown-skinned, heart-shaped face was perfectly proportioned with a long straight nose and full soft lips. His eyebrows arched over beautiful dark brown eyes.

He startled her when he spoke, telling her he was waiting for his father and would she like some of his *nyama choma*. The smell of freshly barbecued meat had been wafting from the vendor's cooking cart since she had arrived an hour ago, but she thanked him. 'No.'

'Are you working here?' he asked, diving his hand into the rolled newspaper cone and popping a piece of meat into his mouth.

'Not yet. I am looking for a job only.'

'What do you do?'

'Anything. I will do anything.'

'Do you live around here?'

'Yes. Over there. With my uncle and aunt.'

'Hmm. Are you sure you won't have some *nyama choma*? It's very good.' He pushed the packet towards her. The aroma was irresistible.

'Well, just a piece.'

'Take plenty. There's too much. And I'm playing basketball in half an hour.'

'Oh, you play basketball . . .'

'Three times a week. Do you?'

'Play basketball? No. I used to play it at school. Oh, but that was a long time ago.'

'How old are you?'

'Me? I'm fif . . . almost eighteen.'

'You look like a good basketballer. Want to come and watch me play?'

She was too shy to say yes, she would love to watch the boy-man with the long lashes and dark brown eyes play basketball. She shook her head.

When his father arrived and drove him away in his Peugeot 404, she wanted to change her mind. Instead she wandered home, hating herself for missing the chance to be with the most beautiful creature she had ever seen. But two days later, beside her Prince Charming, with Dr Hussein at the wheel of the 404, she sat like a princess on worn velvet upholstery.

THE HOSPITAL LAUNDRY WAS HOT and steamy, but Malaika hummed a song as she folded and stacked the warm linen on the wheeled pallets, ready for delivery to the wards. Of all her jobs, she enjoyed taking linen to the wards best. There she was able to see the workings of the hospital, and meet other workers — an opportunity she seldom had for the majority of her day, tucked away in the basement laundry.

She was happy to have found work. But she was even happier to have found Jai. He seemed to like her. Last time he came to the laundry he had held her hand and kissed her with his soft brown lips. Then he touched her breasts, ever so gently. It was an electric feeling. She was sorry when he stopped, but he had backed away, a little shyly, saying, 'Late for basketball.' She was worried he may not try again.

As the afternoon progressed she began to fret. What if he didn't come? Thursday was one of his basketball days. He always visited the laundry before going outside to wait for his father to drive him to the game. But if he wasn't here soon . . .

'Hello?' It was Jai. 'Malaika?'

'I'm in here! In here!' She pushed her Afro into shape and straightened her clean white hospital uniform.

'Hi!'

'Hello.'

'I'm back.'

'Yes. It is basketball again this afternoon, yes?'

'Yes, but a late game today.' He walked around the laundry, running his hand over the piles of sheets and towels. 'Phew, aren't you hot in here?'

'I think maybe I am getting used to it.' Two weeks after she'd started she almost fainted. Jai's father, Dr Hussein, told her she must keep up her fluid intake.

'I don't know how you do it. Look at me! I'm sweating already.' He pulled his tee-shirt over his head. She watched the lean muscles of his chest leap and ripple as he struggled with the tight garment. 'That's better,' he said, flinging the shirt onto the table.

Even when he noticed her staring at him, she couldn't drop her eyes. His body drew her to him and she ran her fingers over his sleek brown skin. Every rib could be counted, but his shoulders and arms were taking on the shape and proportions of a man. She began to tremble and clung to him, feeling the silky smoothness of the light chocolate flesh against her cheek.

Jai's fingers fumbled at the buttons on her blouse. At last she felt freed of the person she had been in Mwanza — the target of everyone's cruel taunts, the object of every boy's leering jokes. She saw for the first time what the beauty of her body could do, as Jai sighed and clicked his tongue when he took her blouse from her.

When she lay with him, her victory was complete. She felt more powerful than she had imagined possible. Jai was her victim and her saviour. Her heart soared with the joy of being a person rather than just a lowly member of a ridiculous tribe.

But when, three days later, Uncle found her alone in her corner bed, all that changed.

The house was empty. He was drunk. And he hurt her. But his worst crime was that he destroyed the wonderful feeling of power that only days earlier she had taken as the first gift of her womanhood.

CHAPTER 17

PEABODY'S GUIDE TO EAST AFRICA (5TH ED):
As far as capital cities go, Nairobi was a mistake. If not
a mistake, an accident. It should have simply remained a
railway storage depot in the pestilential swamp at mile
325 of the Uganda Railway.

Perhaps upon arriving there, the engineers needed a
place to recover their zeal after losing scores of men to
the man-eating lions at the Tsavo River crossing. Or
maybe they were exhausted from fending off the raiding
Kikuyu. For whatever reason, Nairobi grew in spite of
itself.

Now, ninety years on, Nairobi is the cosmopolitan
jewel of East Africa.

The Exotica Café in Muindi Street was anything but exotic.
But Malaika and her colleague from AmericAid, David
Shakombo, used it on those irregular occasions when they
combined a social lunch with the opportunity to catch up on
office matters. The food and prices were local, in contrast to
the expensive tourist venues nearer their office.

Shoppers from the Municipal Market bustled past their
pavement table carrying full *chondos* or trussed hens, squawking
and flapping. The narrow side street was cluttered with three-
wheeled pushcarts stacked high with slatted wooden crates

crammed with ducks or brimming with fruit and vegetables or layers of blood-red carcasses.

David tucked into his roast meat dish with a gusto that belied his lean frame. 'We have not spoken since you came back from Kisumu,' he said. 'How was the meeting?'

'The meeting went very well,' Malaika said, pushing the green vegetables around her plate.

'Hmm, good. Are you not eating your *ugali*?' He pointed his fork at the maize mash untouched on her plate.

'No, you take it. I've had enough. They are getting interested at last.'

'The Nyanza people? Good.' He scraped the pile of mash onto his plate. 'Why do they have this change of heart?'

'It seems like the UN have finally done it.'

'The UN? Mr Morgan? The one you thought was another lazy *mzungu*?'

'Yes, Jack Morgan. He made a good presentation. Some new ideas. He proposed two or three unstaffed outposts with telephone lines for the circuit nurse and project people. He really did quite well. I might have misjudged him.'

'And our programme? How is it?'

'They all seem happy with our health service programme — now that it's coordinated with the UN's agriculture and vet services.'

'That is very good, my sister,' he said, using the colloquial term for a female friend. 'When do you start?'

'We start the pilot programme in a week or two. After the dinner dance.'

'What dinner dance?'

'The UNDP want a party to celebrate the wonderful Integrated Development Programme. It's at the Intercontinental.'

'Goodness! The Intercontinental Hotel. So much money, uh? Who pays for this party?'

'They do.'

'My, my. If we could get that money ... How is it with Machakos?'

The Machakos project was the next one she and David

hoped to get started, but she had yet to get the Department of Regional Development's approval.

'Nothing. It's Onditi again.' She put her fork down on her unfinished lunch and pushed the plate aside. 'I'm getting nowhere.'

'Now, do not worry, my sister. God will find a way.'

'David, how can I not worry? Everything about Onditi worries me. He is so obvious. I can't believe he came to our office the other day. What does he need my home address for, ah?'

'*Haki ya Mungu*, Malaika, I should not have told you about that. Now you worry. But he will not ask again. I chased him away. Yes, he fears me.'

David seemed to have appointed himself Malaika's personal carer shortly after joining their office a year ago. He was fresh out of college when he started, and Malaika took him under her wing until he got going. After she helped him and his young girlfriend through a difficult time following a miscarriage, he was for ever grateful. But she doubted that even his fierce loyalty could overcome James Onditi's physical advantage. 'Thank you, David,' she smiled, 'but it's more than that. I can't get my projects out of the department without first passing them through Onditi.'

'*Sasa*, so this is what you do. You go to Mr Kibera and you say this: Mr Kibera, it is not my fault that I am having trouble with my job. It is this bad man, Mr Onditi, who is playing snakey-snakey games with me.'

Malaika smiled in spite of the situation. *Snakey-snakey* was as far as a good Methodist like David Livingstone Shakombo would go to describe sexual harassment. But she suspected even David understood that his advice was unrealistic. She could not go to Joe Kibera and explain what James was doing. Joe was of the old school: African women were expected to cope with such things. Boys will be boys.

As if a bad dream were coming true, she caught sight of James Onditi shoving his way through the clutter of Muindi Street shoppers and traders, tourists and worshippers. He had not seen her yet. There was time to flee. She reached for her *chondo*, the strap of which was tied to the leg of her stool. Then she stopped herself and slowly resumed her position, straight-backed at the table. She placed both hands on its smooth wooden top and carefully entwined the fingers of one hand into the other. She would not be chased away from her friend and her lunch by the likes of James Onditi.

Out of the corner of her eye she saw him pause at the kerb nearest their table. She held her breath. David was absorbed in trapping the last morsels of his lunch on his spoon.

'*Jambo*,' Onditi said, now at her elbow. '*Ms* Kidongi.' He hissed the westernised title. 'Eating at the low end of town I see!' he sneered. 'How are you today, my dear? *Habari yako?*'

'She is well enough,' David snapped, puffing himself tall in his seat.

Onditi ignored him but his eyes burned into Malaika's cheek. 'I haven't seen you in our office for some time. Is AmericAid on holiday? No projects? What about that one in Tsavo? No, it's Machakos, isn't it?'

'The papers are still with you,' she said, keeping her eyes from his direction.

'Really? Then I must have overlooked them. Why don't you come over and we can discuss them further?'

Malaika pushed her stool from the table. 'Come, David,' she said, 'it's time to go.'

'Yes, don't be late. So much to do.' Onditi laughed into David's face as he stood. 'Oh! Mr Shakombo. So sorry. I didn't see you there. But you must hurry along.'

David drew himself up in an attempt to be at eye level with Onditi but failed. 'Yes,' he said with as much dignity as he could muster, 'we are going.'

Onditi's laughter was lost in the blare of nearby Jamia Mosque's loudspeaker sounding the call to prayer.

JACK WAS ENJOYING THE COFFEE at Idi's pavement stall and the warmth of the morning sun, which had yet to develop its bite. More importantly, he felt no guilt about his pleasure. In the two weeks since returning from Kisumu, he had felt unable to enjoy anything without the memory of the dead girl in Kericho banishing it, leaving in its place a feeling of unworthiness. Even the simple pleasure of a coffee had been subverted by guilt. He was also pleased to have the visit to Police Headquarters behind him. For two full days the threatened interview had unsettled him. And it had annoyed him that it did. Hawaii was the better part of a year behind him, but the threat of them finding a link to O'Hara's death, unlikely as that might be, still induced a cold sweat of fear.

Although initially unsettling, his report to the police on the road accident had helped to relieve his conscience. He had completely overlooked the legal requirement to make a statement — the impact of the event itself had consumed him. In the end, it wasn't the legal requirement that drove him to Central Police Station, but Bhatra, who, aghast when he heard of it, had insisted he go there at once. As he had pointed out in his usual verbose manner, Jack had already committed a serious breech of Kenyan law by waiting nearly two weeks to report the death.

With it now behind him, Jack was grateful for the respite. Grateful that the matter had reached some kind of closure. From experience, he knew that the recollection of the car accident, whilst remaining a painful one, would mercifully recede with the passing of the weeks and months. Soon it would become just another unpleasant but distant memory.

Time heals. Mostly.

In allowing himself to move beyond the Kericho incident, he should have been able to put his mind at ease. But another disturbing development loomed. Was there no end to the mind's ability to inflict torture?

It was Malaika. Her attitude seemed to have changed at Kericho. She seemed ... more human. And because of this, she was almost unbearably more attractive. Now the dreams that came to him in the night's half-awake, half-asleep time were of Malaika. Her almost feline eyes, her full lips parted to receive his. Then, as he lowers himself onto her sleek body, he has the unbearable urge to do something wild. Something ... dangerous. He wonders if he can ever enjoy a woman's body having once been an addict of O'Hara's deadly game?

In horror he sees the gun in his hand again.

Click!

'Good morning!' Malaika breezed up to the table, taking the seat opposite. The morning sun bounced off a malachite clasp pin in her braids.

'Good morning.'

'Oh.'

'Huh?'

'You don't look well.'

'No, I'm okay. Just a little . . . '

She inclined her head to one side. 'Still upset about Kericho?'

'Yes, I guess that's it.' He told her about the police report.

'So, it's done.'

'Yes.' Although he was pleased to have the diversion from the more disturbing memories of O'Hara's erotic equation, he didn't want to dwell on Kericho either. He let the Banda Street traffic fill the silence while he searched for another distraction. Three-wheeled bicycle carts darted between cars, earning toots from motorists.

It was Malaika's suggestion that they hold their weekly project meeting at Idi's. The coffee was good and, even with the bustle of Banda Street, it was a more agreeable venue than her conference room.

'I couldn't wait so I started without you.' He indicated his coffee. 'Sorry.'

'No, it's okay. I was running late again.' As she spoke, Idi appeared at her elbow with a coffee. She thanked him.

Jack started to tell her about meeting one of her AmericAid colleagues when a girl, four or five years old, with a snotty nose and tattered cotton dress shoved a small dirty palm under his nose. She stared up at Jack with soulful eyes. He dropped some change in her hand as Idi returned to chase her away. 'An awful lot of beggar children around Nairobi,' he said as the girl scuttled to the next café.

'AIDS kids.'

'What do you mean?'

'It happens a lot these days.'

'What does?'

'One or both parents dead. From AIDS.'

'I didn't realise it was such a problem.'

'It is. We, AmericAid, are looking at putting more time into it.'

'Right ... That's good.' He watched the urchin move on to yet another café. 'Well, as I was saying, I saw Joe Kibera yesterday. I didn't know he was your boss.'

'Yes. Joe's my boss.' Malaika added a spoonful of sugar to her cup.

'He told me only a few people from AmericAid are going to our sponsors' dinner.'

'That's right. Joe doesn't really approve of drinking. That probably goes for all other forms of enjoyment too.' She shook her head. 'Very churchy.'

'Are you going?'

'Afraid so.'

'What do you mean, *afraid so*? I've heard the Intercontinental's great.'

'Yes, me too. And I wouldn't mind going but ...'

'But?'

'It's getting there and back. I don't like taxis. Especially late at night in Nairobi. What about you? Are you going?' She doodled on her napkin.

'Yeah. The boss hasn't been too subtle about it. Half our section will be there.'

'You don't sound too happy about it yourself.'

'You know how it is. Everyone's there, paired off. Then there's Bear and me.'

'And what is wrong with this ... Bear? Apart from his mad driving.'

'Well, for starters, he's not my type.' He smiled.

'I see.'

'And when we dance, he'll probably insist on leading.'

Jack liked the sound of her laughter. An idea grew in his mind as they watched a nearby motorist ease his vehicle's front wheels over the kerb between two parked cars. The driver sauntered by with his briefcase, leaving the car's rear end protruding into traffic.

'Malaika, I have an idea. There's another way we can do this.'

'Do what?'

Traffic chaos was building behind the illegally parked car. Jack leaned forward to be heard above the din. 'Why don't I take you to the dinner?'

'Take me? I can't get there myself?' She clattered her cup onto its saucer.

'Huh?'

'You think I'm one of those silly white girls? Helpless?'

'No! But what you were saying ... about taxis —'

'Because, let me tell you, I can get to the Intercontinental ... if I want to.'

'Hey. Hey.' He raised his hands. 'Just hold it right there.'

She threw herself back in her chair, her arms rigidly folded across her chest.

'Is it ever possible to offer you a simple courtesy? I mean, without getting into an argument? It's just a suggestion. You know, a courtesy. People do it all the time. Maybe it's a language thing. Or maybe I'm just not the diplomatic type.' He pushed his coffee cup aside. 'Oh, let's just forget it.'

An uncharacteristic silence hung over her side of the table.

He decided he had more to say. 'You know, that night in Kericho was bad. Really bad. For both of us. But for a moment there, we worked together. As a team. For just a few hours we weren't at each other's throats. You actually seemed like a normal human being.' He shook his head in resignation. 'And we got through it.'

'Normal? What do you mean?' Her scowl lightened.

'Strange as it might seem to you, I was trying to be helpful. About the lift. I didn't mean anything by it. You can take it or leave it. Just once in a while give me a small break, will you?'

She lowered her eyes to her fingertips, which she examined closely. 'I thought your car was still on its way from Australia,' she said in a voice so low it was almost lost in the traffic noise.

He took a breath. 'It's coming pretty soon now.' His shoulders relaxed. 'There was a foul-up in the paperwork.'

She nodded, studying a speck on the tabletop. 'That's, um, good news. You won't have to travel to the office with … Bear.'

'Yeah, the kamikaze driver.' He kept his voice soft, feeling a little guilty for his outburst. 'But I'll borrow the Land Rover again for the dinner.'

Her eyes were still on the table, watching her finger make small circles in the spilled sugar grains. 'You're right, it could be a nice evening. And I *could* use a lift.' She looked up. 'If you don't mind.'

The malachite clasp glinted in her braids.

MALAIKA STUDIED HERSELF IN THE full-length mirror. White was definitely her colour. She turned around and looked over her shoulder. Her bra couldn't be seen through the white dress. Nor could the elastic of the matching panties with the loose French cut. The only other time she had worn them she'd had the naughty feeling of wearing no underwear. It had excited her. She turned to look over the other shoulder. The dress material looked good, the way it shaped her buttocks.

'Sandra, what do you think? Black shoes?'

Her flatmate looked up from the magazine. She was still wearing her Kenyan Airways uniform. 'Are you wearing stockings?'

'No. Why bother? Black skin, black stockings.'

'The Intercontinental tonight, right?'

'Yes. They say it's dressy.'

'Black shoes then. How are you getting there?'

'Jack Morgan's picking me up.'

'Who's he?'

'Someone from the UN. We're working on a project in Nyanza together.'

'What's it like?'

'What's what like?'

'You know, doing it with a white guy.'

'How would I know? Honestly, Sandy!'

'Just asking. Isn't he interested in sex?'

'I have no idea.' She shook her head before fitting her earrings.

Sandra shrugged and picked up another magazine. 'Are you still being hassled by that guy in Regional Development?'

Malaika sighed. 'No. Not at the moment. Thank God.'

Sandra flicked over a few pages. 'I've heard they're not as bad as everyone says.'

'Who?'

'*Wazungu*. White guys. You know, in bed.'

Malaika decided to ignore her, concentrating instead on hitching her shoulder straps higher so her breasts and the lacy edges of the imported bra were better covered. She did not have the time to sew them up so she let the straps drop again. To hell with it. Tonight she would have cleavage.

AT A LITTLE AFTER EIGHT there was a gentle rap on her apartment door. Jack was wearing black slacks, grey jacket and a charcoal silk shirt. He paused in the doorway until she invited him in with a smile. 'Jack,' she said, 'this is Sandra. Sandra, Jack.'

Sandra studied him and offered her hand without rising from her seat. 'Jack. Pleased to meet you.'

'Me too.' He took her hand.

'Sandra's my flatmate,' Malaika said, wondering why she often felt compelled to state the obvious for Jack's benefit.

'You two could be related,' Jack said, looking from one to the other.

Sandra laughed.

'What's so funny?' Jack shoved his hands in his pockets, his smile fading a little.

'Jack,' Sandra said, 'I'm a Kikuyu. Malaika is Maasai. Our tribes have been at war since for ever. This place might be the only peace zone in the entire nation.' She pronounced it *en-tire*.

'Sandra and I have been sharing here for years,' Malaika added.

'We know everything to know about each other,' Sandra said. 'And we don't keep secrets, do we?'

'Well, Jack and I have to run, Sandy,' Malaika said, avoiding her flatmate's eyes.

'Okay. I'm leaving soon too. Some of the girls are going to Bubbles.'

Jack said, 'Nice to meet you, Sandra. Bye.'

'*Kwaheri,*' Sandra replied, then continued in Swahili for Malaika's ears, 'and you will tell me how he is in bed when I see you tomorrow. *Si ndio?*'

THE WAITER LED THEM TO a table on the far side of the dance floor. Jack introduced Bear to Malaika and, at Jack's invitation, Malaika sat beside him, Jack opposite her. Bear introduced the others sharing their table, one black couple and one white.

'Well, that should set some tongues wagging,' Bear said, as the others at the table returned to their conversation.

'What?' Malaika said. She had felt what seemed to be all eyes on her when they crossed the floor.

'The arrival of the zebra couple.'

'Zebra couple?' said Jack.

'Yeah. Like, black and white.'

Malaika smiled, glad that Bear had seen her tension and dispelled it with a joke. But she thought that Jack looked a little annoyed.

'Any drinks, sir?' The waiter was at Jack's elbow.

'Would you like something, Malaika? Some wine?'

She was unsure whether to let him order for her. After all, it wasn't a date. How do white people handle these occasions? she wondered. Insist on buying the next round? 'Um, what are you having?' she asked.

'I thought I might have some white wine.'

'White wine . . . Yes. I'll have white wine too.'

'Good,' he said.

She got the idea he was also feeling a little awkward.

'And you, Bear?'

'Just another beer, buddy.'

'That'll be two for wine. Let's see . . .' He ran a finger down the wine list. 'How about an Aussie chardonnay?' He looked across the table at her.

She gave a noncommittal shrug.

'Okay. A bottle of the Rosemount and another Tusker. Thanks.'

'AmericAid, huh?' Bear said.

'Yes,' she answered with a smile, suddenly conscious of being the centre of the table's attention. The others — she had already forgotten their names — had reached a hiatus in their conversation and seemed to hang on Malaika's every word. 'Um, yes, our office is on Moi Avenue. Well, actually on the corner of Haile Selassie.'

'Oh, sure. The US Embassy,' Bear said.

'Yes.'

One of the army of stiff-shirted waiters interrupted to serve entrées. With the lull in the conversation, Malaika felt it safe to glance around the nearby tables. The delegates from Kisumu were well into the spirit of the evening already. Probably arrived on the five o'clock train and had been at the bar since. She noticed a few people from AmericAid. There must have been a hundred and fifty in all. Quite a party for two aid agencies, she thought.

Bear seemed to be well acquainted with the others at the table and, as another waiter interrupted to serve them drinks, joined in their conversation.

'How's the chardonnay?' Jack asked as silence fell over their end of the table. Malaika thought it was the best wine she had ever tasted. 'Hmm, not bad.'

'I really miss the wine from home. There's no Aussie wines on the UN's duty free list.'

'Oh, that's sad,' she said, smiling.

'Yes, it's tough in the tropics.'

Bear's conversation had moved on to something to do with radio equipment. Jack said, 'I'm really glad you could come, otherwise I might have had to pretend an interest in telecommunications.'

She smiled back.

'Nice dress.'

'Thanks.'

'White suits you.'

● ● ●

AFTER DINNER, COFFEE WAS SERVED. The music became slow and mellow.

'Would you like to dance, Malaika?'

The question took her by surprise. For some reason she hadn't taken him for a man who would happily volunteer to dance. There were a few other couples on the floor and the lights, although lower, had not reached the very late, very intimate level. She stood and placed her folded napkin beside her wine glass. He waited at the end of the table to let her take the floor ahead of him. His hand was at the small of her back and he led with confidence. This was too much. Without exception, her dance partners were invariably shufflers or, worse, drunken shufflers.

Jack held her gently as he navigated the floor amid the handful of other dancers. Not too close, but as he took her into a slow pivot he drew her into his chest. He was making small talk about a rock band he and some friends had tried to form at university. She listened, but mostly she was exploring the strange sensations of being close to him, and him being so charming.

'There were four of us. I played drums.'

She could imagine him on drums. Her nose was at the level of his chin. Aftershave. Just a hint. Musk.

'The others were guitar players of course. We were going to be the Australian version of The Beatles.'

He was really quite a good dancer. She began to relax. The wine, and the feeling of release, letting him guide her around the floor, was heady. They stayed for another bracket. It was slower. And another. The lights dimmed to the very late, last-dance level. Her cheek brushed his shoulder.

He took her arm as they descended the steps outside the hotel. The car was parked at the rear of the building, beyond the garden. The night's dry warm air was a gift that only a city at that altitude, and a hair south of the equator, could offer. The wine made her feel a little high, more relaxed than she'd dreamed possible. She found herself actually humming something from the last bracket of dances. It had been a long time since she had enjoyed herself on such an occasion. And tomorrow was Sunday. She was going to have a lazy morning, wash her hair, read the morning paper, then catch up on some paperwork in the afternoon.

'Oh, shit!' she said, and her hands flew to her lips. 'Sorry!'

'What is it?' He had unlocked her side of the car and paused at the open door.

'I forgot to get the project papers from the office. I was going to ask you to stop by on our way here tonight. But I forgot.'

'No problem. I'll take you now.' He was at his side of the car where the hotel security guard stood smiling at attention. Jack tipped him then climbed into the driver's seat.

'What time is it?' she said, helping him lift his sleeve to find his watch.

'Just after midnight.'

'Oh, no! The building is closed down now. Full security. I can't get in.'

'Is it important?'

'I was supposed to do our amendments to the — oh ... what is it called? — the health services contract. It was for typing and signing on Monday morning.'

'Well, I have a set of the papers at home. Will that help?'

'You won't need them?'

'Are you kidding? Tomorrow's Sunday.'

'Well, if you don't mind. God!' she howled. 'Why am I so dumb?'

He laughed.

THE SECURITY GUARD ON THE gate at Jack's apartment block smiled a greeting, then saluted when he noticed Malaika in the passenger seat. Jack parked the Land Rover under a jacaranda tree and turned off the headlights.

'I won't be a moment.'

'Jack, this is really nice of you,' she said. 'I don't know what I was thinking. Now I've taken you out of your way, and it's late.'

'Hey, no problem. It's only ten minutes to your place from here and this will only take a minute.' He opened his door then turned back to her. 'Would you like to come up for a coffee while I hunt out these papers?'

'No, thanks. I'll be okay here.' She looked around the compound. 'Won't I?' The moonlight on the pool floated eerie reflections up the apartment building wall.

'Sure. The security guard's back there somewhere.'

The gate entrance was hidden by the tree canopy, which hung darkly over the drive. 'Perhaps I will have a quick coffee.'

After leaving the elevator, and leading her along the dim corridor to the door of the sixth-floor apartment, he stepped back for her to enter ahead of him. Reaching around her, his body brushed hers in the darkness. She stiffened and held her breath for the moment it took him to find the switch. Finally there was a click, and by the time her eyes had adjusted to the light he was at the glass doors, sliding them open onto the balcony.

Malaika moved tentatively into the room. Jack switched on two standard lamps then flicked off the main light. The lamps cast a subdued light, gently revealing stylish white leather chairs and a sofa. A tall ebony Maasai warrior guarded a black glass stereo cabinet against the near wall. A chrome gismo, one of those mechanical toys that go for ever when you give them a push, sat on a simple coffee table. The far wall carried a large framed photograph of the Sydney Harbour Bridge and Opera House. A black and white batik portrait of a Swahili girl filled half the wall space opposite it.

He waved towards the balcony. 'Would you like to enjoy the night air?'

A myriad of stars formed a diamond-studded bubble over Nairobi. Wow! she thought.

'Make yourself comfortable.' He indicated a cane sofa. 'I'll put on the coffee. Or would you prefer a glass of wine?'

The cane sofa, overflowing with colourful cushions, was barely visible in the light that spilled from the lounge room. 'Look, I've changed my mind,' she spluttered. 'I've taken up enough of your time already, so I'll ... I'll just take the papers and let you ... and I can get a taxi from the gate.'

He had his back against the city lights. 'Sure. I'll get them for you.'

She tried to catch a glimpse of his profile as he passed. It told her nothing and she wondered if she had offended him.

'Be right back,' he said as he walked from the balcony.

'Jack?'

'Uh-huh?' He turned at the lounge room door.

She wasn't sure what she had intended to say. 'Thanks,' she said finally.

He nodded and left the room.

She threw herself down on the cane lounge and punched the cushions in exasperation. What *was* it about her? It had been a wonderful evening, so why couldn't she enjoy it? It had been nearly ten years since the incident with her so-called uncle soon after arriving in Nairobi, but over the years she had managed to overcome the feeling that every man who glanced at her was about to do her harm. She could not blame the past.

Perhaps she had been corroded by her more recent experiences with James Onditi? She tried to forget him.

Nairobi's streetlights rolled off to the dim horizon. But the thought of Onditi would not go. At the outset she had simply chosen to ignore his comments as clumsy attempts at flirtation. But as she continued to refuse to play his game, he had become increasingly threatening, until he began to physically intimidate her, leading to the scene at Carnivore when he had grabbed her violently by the arm. That was when Jack had stepped in. It worried her because it was seriously affecting her work. She hadn't been back to Regional Development since the chance meeting with Onditi at Exotica Café last week. She just couldn't face him again. Not yet.

She wished she were like Jack. Of all the people she knew, he seemed able to deal with Onditi. He appeared calm enough, but behind those cool grey eyes was someone always alert. On his guard. He gave the impression that he was always prepared to take control of a situation. She liked that.

Was it the wine, or had she really discovered something important, something different, about him tonight? Perhaps she had been too hasty, putting him in the same category as

Onditi that first time at Carnivore. But now she wasn't so sure. Who was he? And what else had she missed about him? Sandra's question about *mzungu* men as lovers popped into her mind. How would they, the white men, treat their women? As partner or chattel? Was there something about the way a man danced that could give a clue? The memory of the brush with his body in the darkness at the apartment door rushed back to her.

'I've got them.'

She almost leapt to her feet. As it was, she flung up an arm, knocking the papers from his hands. They spilled onto the balcony floor.

'Oh, shit! Oh, sorry!' There it was again — cursing twice in the same night. What would he think of her? She fell on hands and knees before he could make a move to help and swept the papers into an untidy bundle. Now, feeling utterly lacking in decorum, scampering around the balcony floor like a cockroach, she leapt to her feet again. The top of her head collided with something solid. It made a crunch, like hitting a hanging pot plant. Or teeth.

Jack reeled backwards, going into a crouch and clasping his jaw.

Her hand flew to her mouth in horror, releasing the bundle of papers which fluttered to the floor again. Her thick braids had cushioned the top of her head, but the blow to Jack's jaw must have felt like a haymaker. 'Oh, my God!' she cried and hovered over him, making solicitous sounds.

He straightened, gingerly rubbing his jaw.

'Oh, you poor thing! I'm such a stupid ...' She moved to him and cupped his face with her hands. 'Have I broken your teeth?' she said, peering at his lip. 'Let me see you.' She took his fingers in hers and lifted them aside. 'Oh, it must have hurt.'

She felt the fingers entwined with hers tighten, and became aware of the closeness of him. She withdrew one hand but he held her other at his mouth. 'You didn't hurt me.' His arm slipped to the small of her back as it had on the dance floor, but his eyes held another meaning, and she realised they were hazel, not the steely grey she had previously seen.

'You're ... you ...' she began, feeling the press of his chest against her breasts.

'I'm okay,' the hazel eyes said.

There was a moment when she felt sure he was going to kiss her. A moment when she began to panic with the indecision of returning it or pushing away. But he let his eyes slip from hers to their entwined fingers. He unravelled his from hers and let her hand drop to her side.

It was as if she had been struck.

She snatched up her handbag and ran to the door.

CHAPTER 18

PEABODY'S GUIDE TO EAST AFRICA (5TH ED):
The annual migration of the East African herbivores is best seen from September to November and is triggered by the return of the trade-wind rains that commence on the Indian Ocean off the Kenyan coast.

An irresistible wet aroma floats westward across the continent to the dust-bowl plains of the Serengeti. This siren's whisper triggers an ancient call to grazing animals in their hundreds of thousands. Zebra, Thompson gazelle, impala, hartebeest, buffalo, giraffe. And wildebeest. Particularly wildebeest.

Jack was pretty sure he heard a wildebeest fart. Not that he was an expert. In fact, in spite of the endless hours he had studied the wild kingdom as a boy, he realised that he knew absolutely nothing about wildebeest. So it could have been something else. Like a cough. Probably that.

'Murp.'

There it was again.

'Murp' from another. Well, if it wasn't a fart, it was certainly not communication. The herd shambled about in stagnant pools of dust, staring at the stationary Land Rover. They seemed even more brainless than he remembered from TV documentaries. Close-set eyes, vacant expressions. A cud-chewing, mindless mob roaming the grassy plains of the Masai Mara Game Reserve.

He was glad he hadn't mentioned the fart to Bear, who had stopped briefly at a signpost before slamming the Land Rover into first and lurching in the direction of the border. It would be too much to describe Bear as a mild-mannered person. Polite, yes, but there was always the hint of a contained aggression lurking behind a veneer of civility. So to say that his Dr Jekyll character was transformed into a Mr Hyde when behind a steering wheel would be going too far. But it was also true that in the driver's seat Bear was seldom in the mood for foolishness. Mention of the fart would have tested him to the extreme.

They were returning from Kisumu where Jack had signed contract papers with Joseph Onunga, the PC who had pocketed his bribe money on his first visit to the town. Bear had found an excuse to be there and then taken the initiative to arrange a side trip through the Mara to the Serengeti National Park before returning home.

Jack was thrown against the passenger door as the car bucked through a series of corrugations. 'Christ, Bear! What's the hurry?' If there was an answer it was lost in the roar of the diesel before Bear clunked the vehicle into second.

Jack felt a trickle of sweat slip down the back of his neck. The sun beat like a kettledrum on the Land Rover's roof. He leaned forward, without releasing his grip on the swing handle above the door, and peeled his tee-shirt from the wet patch on his back.

The car hurdled a pothole like a startled antelope. Bear's driving was not much better in Nairobi, but Jack, having accepted Bear's offer, felt compelled to continue sharing transport to the office until his own car arrived. It had now been over four months and in that time there had been occasions when Jack knew that if he were to die in Africa, it would be in Nairobi's chaotic traffic rather than in the jungle. And it would be at the hands of a demented German-American driver rather than under the fang and claw of a lion.

The Serengeti Plains unfolded ahead of them. On its wide straw-coloured canvas was painted the teeming herds of the East African migration. Hundreds of gazelle, thousands of zebra and perhaps a quarter of a million stupid, murping wildebeest. It was the Africa that Jack had dreamed about as a boy, ever since seeing his first *Tarzan* movie.

Dust crept cowardly through the Land Rover's door linings, gently coating everything in a soft beige talc. They were moving at a slower speed, avoiding the worst of the potholes. A frenetic line of wildebeest stretched like an elastic band ahead of the car, galloping faster and faster to keep the conga line intact ahead of the Land Rover. When the car finally broke through the elastic line, the panicked animals on the wrong side of the road dashed frantically behind the passing vehicle to rejoin the departing herd.

An hour later, the Kenyan immigration officer gave each United Nations passport a perfunctory stamp. A mile further on, the Tanzanian border entry post was unattended. Jack opened the gate. Bear drove through.

'What's going on? No paperwork on this side?' Jack asked.

'Sometimes they do, sometimes they don't. Welcome to Tanzania.'

On the road again, Bear was arm-wrestling the steering wheel. Jack had realised, during the daily trips from hotel to office, that it was useless trying to have a sensible conversation with Bear at the wheel.

Jack noticed the sign: *Seronera Lodge — 80 km.* He said, 'Tell me again why we're camping.'

'To experience Africa.'

'Right.'

To the left of the car a family of wart hogs took off in a pompous trot, the flywhisk ends of their skinny tails held vertical like Sunday-best parasols. Jack watched them disappear into the scrub then asked, 'I don't suppose we could experience Africa in the Seronera Lodge?'

'No.'

THEY REACHED THE SMALL SETTLEMENT of Seronera as the sun slanted long shadows through their trailing dust. Jack had taken a turn at the wheel and followed the sign along a narrow track, past simple staff accommodation, to the game lodge.

The wall behind the vacant reception desk, which proudly displayed the lodge's four-star rating, shed paint like confetti onto dusty travel brochures and registration forms. Outside, the pool water was avocado-green. The barman arrived ten minutes later and served them a warm beer. In faltering English, he gave them directions to the National Parks office.

It was a grey concrete and corrugated-iron building half a mile down the gravel road. They paid about a dollar to the game warden, a pleasant fat man wearing a frayed shirt with *National Parks Authority of Tanzania* on the epaulettes. It took him ten minutes to complete the paperwork for the camping permit. He handed them the official receipt for five hundred Tanzanian shillings. It had three corrections on it.

An acacia tree was a black silhouette against a purple western horizon as the Land Rover turned at the weathered sign, *Seronera Camping Reserve*. There was nothing to distinguish the reserve from the surrounding dry savannah. No buildings, no obvious campsites and no fences. They drew to a stop beside a stunted tree and some large flat rocks. It seemed as good a place as any.

Jack stretched and looked around the deserted camping ground while Bear unrolled a tiny hike tent on the ground beneath the tree. 'You could probably squeeze in here too, buddy, but I snore and fart somethin' fierce.'

'Thanks, Bear, I think I'll pass.'

Bear found a stick to prop up the string line; its other end was wound around the tree trunk.

'That tent looks like something you'd wear rather than sleep in. Aren't you a little big for it?'

'Yeah, I hang out a bit at the end, but it keeps the dew off the rest of me. One day I'll probably get me a bigger one.'

Jack poked around the Land Rover and found the lever to release the back seat. It folded forward with a clunk, creating a space almost long enough to accommodate him. Jack decided it would do, and pulled out the car fridge, threw his pack and sleeping bag in and slammed the door. 'Done! Want a beer?'

• • •

BY EIGHT O'CLOCK THE COOL of the evening denied the heat of the day. A full moon filled the eastern sky, washing the sandy camping grounds in a pale yellow tint.

Canned vegetables and another of meat were soon brought to a bubbling concoction on the gas cooking-ring. They ate quickly and in silence, tearing lumps of bread from a loaf and using it to soak up every drop of the juices. At the end of the meal the plates were wiped clean and Jack threw them into the shallow cooking pan, pouring enough water into it to cover them. He placed it all on the burner to boil the plates clean. Fishing around in the icebox he pulled out a dripping bottle. 'Great! They're still cold. Want another beer?'

'Nope, I've got a better idea,' Bear said, climbing into the Land Rover. A moment later he reappeared with a bottle of Black Label from which he poured two generous portions into plastic cups. He sat, gave one to Jack and sipped the other with a sigh. 'Ahhh, now that's a smooth drop.'

Jack took his whisky and joined Bear on the rock. 'But I'm going to have my beer and take it very easy on the scotch tonight.'

'You don't like scotch?'

'It doesn't like me, remember?'

Bear looked puzzled.

'The night at Buffalo Bill's. After my first Hash.'

'Oh, yeah. You were shit-faced, man.'

'And as sick as a dog the next day.'

'I don't need to make no excuses for a grown man like you, but under the circumstances, your first run and all, I was surprised you lasted as long as you did. By the way, you never did tell me ... does the lovely Benice live up to her name?'

'I don't know.'

Jack saw his expression. 'It's true. I sent her home.'

'Sure. Not your type, right? Now if you had any sense at all, which I doubt, you would patch up your differences with that Malaika lady from AmericAid. That chick's got real class.'

Jack covered his hesitation by taking a mouthful of his beer. 'Mmm. That's business.'

'Business, huh? And I suppose you're gonna tell me you and Monique didn't do the business that night after Carnivore either.'

'That's right.'

'Man, that's the greatest load ... Get out of here!'

That's what he liked about Bear, Jack decided. He was loud and nosy but one would never die wondering what was on his mind. 'Okay. Don't believe me.'

Bear shook his head.

A comfortable silence grew between them, Bear contentedly sipping at his whisky, Jack with his beer, recalling Benice on that first Monday-night Hash. From the moment she gave him her beautiful open smile, Jack was hooked. But later, in the hotel room, the memory of O'Hara's Game came back to him and he was suddenly afraid to test if he needed its excitement to be able to enjoy sex. What if it was all a bore? In his more logical moments he had rationalised that it was unlikely to be an enduring need. It was almost certainly a transient titillation — wildly stimulating at the time, but now passé. Perhaps Benice would have been an ideal test of the hypothesis? But he wasn't thinking too clearly at the time. He'd begged off, muttering something about being married. Guilty conscience. She seemed to accept the excuse and kissed him passionately when he saw her off in the taxi. The girl he had met at the Norfolk, Monique, was another matter. Talkative, scatty and a little too professional for his liking.

Bear broke the silence. 'You know, Jack, you're not the kind of guy I generally expect to find in Africa.' He scratched the length of his narrow beard, his brow creased in thought.

'I'm not?' Jack had drained his beer. The plastic whisky glass was in his hand.

'No. Single men who come to Africa ... Well, they're usually one of two types. Do-gooders, usually Methodists, boring as all shit. Or tear-ass cowboys who shoot up the wildlife and, when they're done with that, try to charm the pants off all the married women. Or they go for any bar girl who looks at them and end up dead drunk, or just plain dead, in some bar.'

'Thanks, mate!' Jack rested himself on an elbow. The night air was becoming cooler but he could feel the warmth of the rock on the back of his knees. 'So which camp have you put me in?'

'Oh, I didn't say they were all like that. There are some real mysterious types. Like you. They probably ran away from some female.'

Jack searched his face. Deciding it was only a guess, he let it pass.

'Hah! Hit it on the head? Right?'

Jack forced a smile to his lips, shaking his head.

'Oh, man!' Bear threw a hand in the air. 'There you go again! Can't get a word out of you!'

'What's to say? Sorry I don't fit into one of your boxes?'

'Man, you are impossible.'

'So who was the female?'

Bear turned to him. 'Huh?'

'Well, you named all the boxes, and I don't think you're one of the cowboys. And you're definitely not a churchgoer. So you must be running from a female, right?'

'Awww, no use runnin'. I'm a three-time loser. Not a one of 'em could handle the overseas postings. Oh, it's fine for a while, then the excitement wears off and they want you to get a real job.' He took a slug of whisky. 'So my postings ain't exactly the glamour spots of the world. But it's what I do. Wanted me to settle down. Uh, uh.'

'How old are you now?'

'A pup! Forty-seven.'

'And married three times.'

'How do you think *I* feel? I'm a slow learner but even I've figured out that halving your wealth and giving it to some stranger every few years is a helluva way to get rich.'

Jack smiled. 'Is that the worst of it? The money?'

'Nah. Guys go on and on about the alimony. It's more than that.'

Jack sipped at his scotch.

Bear said, 'I met the first when I was young and still in the merchant marine. Radio Operator, Second Class. I was at sea for seven months in every eight. So I joined the UN. Figured

I'd get a long-term posting somewhere nice like Rio or Suva. But long-term postings were hard to come by in those days. We did three years in Africa — the longest posting was four months. Never really got to know Regina.'

He finished the dregs in his cup and poured himself more. 'Want some?' He passed Jack the bottle. 'When I got home on my first leave after that divorce, I found the girl next door. Wife number two. She left me in Mogadishu. Can't say I blame her either. Somalia was a shit-hole in '73.'

When Bear fell silent, the night sounds seemed to drift back. There was a murmuring cacophony surrounding them. It was impossible to say whether they were small noises close by or big noises in the distance.

'Then there was the third.' Bear sighed. 'Elizabeth was a South African. One of the English tribe. Now, I thought, here's someone who knows Africa. Just gotta be right this time, I tell myself.' He took a gulp of scotch. 'Well, I guess she knew Africa too well. Or thought she did. They found her body at a set of traffic lights in Soweto. Never did find her Volvo. I was somewhere in Angola at the time. Didn't know about it until three weeks later.'

The moon was high in the sky. It hung like a huge yellow ball on spangled velvet drapes. Rocks and boulders glowed with a faint luminescence in its eerie light. Distorted tree limbs were starkly etched by the moonlight and razor-sharp blue shadows rendered the landscape two-dimensional. It had the look of stage scenery — flat, with colours chosen to set a melodramatic mood.

'Looking back on it all,' Bear said with a note of resignation, 'can't say I did a damn thing right.'

Jack studied his cup of whisky. The night sounds faded and he became acutely aware of the almost tangible silence that had suddenly enveloped them. He would rather not have heard Bear's confession because now Jack felt obliged to reciprocate. A man could not be allowed to bare his soul like that without an offering in return. Something from the heart. Jack held his breath, wondering if a plausible fiction could be concocted in time.

The question finally came. 'What about you?'

He couldn't lie to him. 'Never married. But Liz and I had been living together for about three years or so. Everything was fine, but, well, we split up just before I came over here.'

'That's too bad.'

'Yeah ... It was.'

'Your choice?'

Jack wondered how far he could go with it. If there was ever going to be a time and place to share at least some of his story, it would be with this rock of a man, here in the middle of Africa.

'Hey. Shit, buddy,' Bear said, 'I know I'm a mite inquisitive at times. Personal stuff. You don't wanna talk about it? Fine with me.'

The soft sounds of the night floated to him: the peculiar barking calls of zebra punctuated by the whooping cackle of hyena. 'It's not that. It's just a long story, I suppose.'

'Sure.'

Jack felt an urge to unburden himself. Africa was one enormous, empty land. Another world. He felt safe to do so. 'I had an affair. At worst, it should have been a one-night stand. At the beginning I was pretty damn sure even *that* wasn't going to happen. I mean, I'm at a five-day conference; back home there's Liz. I'd never cheated on her.

'I have to admit I found her attractive. Not what people would call a knockout. Average looks. But attractive in a sexual way. She had a thing she did with her tongue, it kind of slipped over this tooth and ... well ...

'She was pretty sure of herself. Assertive. Maybe sexually aggressive is closer to it. Everything about her challenged me to come on to her. But that wasn't going to happen. At least that's what I was thinking at the start.

'It was some kind of theatre. My part was to play the scene and exit gracefully. No crude walk-off with a plain good night! It had to be done with class. It had to be done with the same style she used in her seduction routine. And she was good. So subtle. She would *accidentally* brush her leg against mine under the table. She would put her hand on my thigh as she reached for her dropped napkin. Things like that. My defence was Liz. I knew I wouldn't cheat on her so I played along. Lighting her cigarette with a hand cupped on hers. Just like in the movies. Flirting a little.

'I was still confident I could walk away as we got to her door. Then she did that thing with her tongue as she said good night, and ... I guess I paused a moment. She reaches up like she's going to flick some lint from my shoulder, then ... she kisses me. I'd never been kissed like that before. I mean, straight off the cuff, no preliminaries. Never expecting it ... It was the most sensational feeling. And that was it ... I was gone.'

'I guess your girlfriend, Liz, found out about it?'

'No. I mean, yes. That's right. She found out and that was it.'

'Hey, sorry 'bout that, Jack. So, did you take up with what's-her-name?'

'Her name? Um, Carla. How about that? I nearly forgot her name. Her name was Carla.'

'So?'

'Oh! No, I didn't see her again.'

'Why not?'

'She was ... She lived too far away. North Queensland. Impossible. Anyway, it was just sex.'

'I understand,' Bear said, nodding.

Jack said nothing.

'So what's your plan for Kenya?' Bear sipped his whisky.

'Plan? I plan to hang in there. I can handle anything for twelve months.'

'Watch it, buddy, it'll grow on you.' Bear retrieved Jack's cup and topped it up. He refilled his own. 'I said that when I came here. It's outlasted three wives.'

A roar came faintly from the distance. It could have been a lion or an elephant. It was hard to know.

'I doubt it. In a year I'm out of here.'

EARLY MORNING IN THE SERENGETI. Fine overnight dew glistened like diamonds on the dry grass stubble — a delicious scent. The sun had edged up over the distant low hills, pale gold and hinting of the heat to come.

Jack climbed down from the Land Rover in his jocks and stretched. He found Bear drinking a cup of coffee. 'Hey! Good morning! You're looking pretty good for this hour.' The Black Label sat almost empty on the rock.

'Yeah, I'm fine. But I must have been out like a light 'cause about four o'clock a hyena came into camp and munched our big cooking pot.' He nodded in the direction of the saucepan. 'Carried our water container into the bush too. I found it about half an hour ago, after it got light enough. He put his teeth through our pot.'

Jack picked up the aluminium saucepan. 'Wow!' he said, turning it over. 'They're like bullet holes. Just crunched the whole pot!' He put it back on the rock. 'Anyway, how do you know it was four o'clock?'

''Cause the bastard woke me. Started pulling at the end of my sleeping bag poking out the tent. When I woke up he high-tailed out.'

'Jesus!'

'It was a bit hard to get back to sleep after that. Been sittin' here ever since, drinkin' coffee.' He looked at Jack. 'What are you grinning at?'

'Mate ... caffeine? Dangerous stuff.'

CHAPTER 19

PEABODY'S GUIDE TO EAST AFRICA (5ᵀᴴ ED):
As far back as human history can grope, the monsoon winds
have brought the great trading *dhows* of the east to Mombasa.
Their crab-claw lateen sails swoop down on the north-
easterlies, or the *kazkazi* in Swahili, from October to April,
and return on the *kazi* during the remainder of the year.

The *dhows* brought supplies to the Arab settlements on
the coastal strip and, at change of season, would sail away
laden with ivory and gold, frankincense and myrrh, and
human cargo of concubines, servants, labourers and
miners, to golden sultanates in faraway desert lands.

The meeting in the UNDP's conference room had commenced
in predictable fashion. Bhatra, of the UNDP, and Joe Kibera,
head of AmericAid's Kenyan office, spent five minutes politely
insisting that the other accept the role of chairman. Joe finally
won and Bhatra harrumphed his way through the agenda.

Kibera was assisted by Malaika, who provided the detail on
health clinic services. Jack and Bear were there to make Bahtra
look good in front of the traditional half a dozen senior
UNDP brass, who were always in attendance at triennial
meetings. They provided a worthy audience for Bhatra's
impressive chairmanship.

With Bear's assistance on technology items, Jack completed his status report.

'So in summary, Mr Morgan, all parties are now agreed to this project being the first in our Integrated Development Programme?' Bhatra said.

'That's right.'

'And Mr Kibera? From your report it appears AmericAid is ready?'

'Yes, Mr Chairman, we are.'

'Very fine. Very fine indeed.' He ran his finger down his briefing notes. 'So, as far as I can see, Mr Morgan, all you are needing is the few items of equipment?'

'Yes. It's in Port Mombasa now, waiting for customs clearance and shipment to Nairobi.'

Looking over his glasses at Bear: 'And that is the radio equipment, if I understand it correctly, Mr Hoffman?'

'VHS base station controller and outstation transponders. We have the other stuff.'

'Yes, yes. Technical things.'

'If I may make a suggestion, Mr Chairman?'

'Certainly, Mr Kibera! Please do.'

'Chairman, in our experience at AmericAid, customs matters can take a very long time. Even for small items of medical equipment there is paperwork and delays. And then, who knows if it is delivered to the right place, eh?'

Heads nodded sympathetically around the table.

'We find it far better to send a representative to Mombasa. A little push can do wonders.'

'An excellent idea, Mr Kibera. Excellent idea.' Bhatra turned to Jack. 'Mr Morgan, may I suggest you attend to this? The grass roots, eh? Excellent suggestion, Mr Kibera!'

Jack suppressed a groan.

Bhatra closed his notes. 'But as our partner ... sorry,' a broad smile, 'our *integrated development* partner, perhaps AmericAid would care to be involved?'

'Most generous, Mr Bhatra.' Kibera swept an arm in Malaika's direction. 'Ms Kidongi will attend on our behalf.'

• • •

APART FROM A POLITE HELLO at the management conference, Malaika hadn't exchanged words with Jack since the night of the Intercontinental dinner party. It wasn't that she was avoiding him — although she was dreading their next meeting, whenever it might be — there hadn't been a pressing reason to meet. No reason until Joe Kibera graciously accepted UNDP's offer. Now she and Jack Morgan had been thrust together for forty-eight hours in Mombasa. In the same hotel.

To make matters worse, on returning to the hotel after a hot and harrowing day on Mombasa's waterfront, the hotel manager told Jack he had won some promotional prize: dinner for two on the Tamarind Dhow — a floating restaurant.

Jack seemed as reluctant as she to spend an evening together, but he had shrugged and asked lamely, 'Care to go?'

Malaika couldn't think of a plausible reason to refuse without making an issue of it. 'Oh! Um ... Lovely.'

What she had thought might be a quick sweep around the harbour and a dinner of finger food was quite different, and a pleasant surprise. The old trading vessel had been beautifully renovated with all modern conveniences. Dinner was silver-service, complete with candles and string quartet. They were seldom able to see the bottom of their wine glasses before a dinner-suited waiter glided in to top them up. While the quartet played classical music, the chef prepared their seafood banquet in the galley, and the *dhow* rocked on the gentle swell of Kilindini harbour. Conversation was a little wooden for the first hour, but as the wine and the music had their combined effect, Malaika relaxed.

They skipped sweets and ordered coffee. Somehow they had started recounting stories of first loves. She laughed at Jack's telling of his pitch for a girl in first-year university. At the time he had a very old car with the unnerving habit of dropping part of its steering mechanism without warning. The solution was a replacement from a bag of bolts he kept in the boot.

'Anyway, she agreed to be my partner to a friend's engagement party. This was my big chance to impress. But as we drove out of her house, the tie-rod bolt must have worked loose again because, at the end of the driveway, the left front wheel turned left and the right front wheel turned right! The car came to a shuddering halt. So, as cool as can be, I climb out the car, walk to the left wheel and line it up with the other one. Back in the car, I say nothing and complete the turn.'

Malaika tried to control her laughter but tears threatened to roll down her cheeks.

'I thought I'd got away with it. But before we made it to the end of the street she yells, "Stop! Stop the car! I heard all you Science guys were crazy. Now I'm sure of it!" And leaps from the car. I never had the nerve to ask for another date. End of first love affair before it even started.'

When she had wiped her eyes he nagged her until she told him her story.

It was about Jai. 'The most beautiful creature in the whole world,' she said, laughing at his feigned gagging. But when he pressed her for the whole story, the reason the love affair died, she changed the ending to a more amusing one. A story about rape and how it can affect even profound infatuation was not one that should be told that night. If ever.

They took their coffee to the upswept stern to watch the lights of old Mombasa Town twinkle and dip in the wake.

'You handled everything at the customs office very well today,' he said as they stood at the railing, coffee cups in hand.

'You mean the tea money?'

'Tea money! Even the name makes me puke. I just can't do all that stuff very well.'

'I know,' she said smiling, remembering his clumsy efforts in Kisumu.

'Yeah, exactly! You know what I mean.'

The cannons on ancient Fort Jesus threw long shadows up the walls from powerful spotlights concealed beneath them in the rocks.

'Look, about the other night ...'

Oh, no! She didn't want him to raise it. Everything was going so well. Why not just forget it?

'After the Intercontinental ... I acted like an idiot ...'

'No, it's okay. I was not feeling well and ...'

'...I wasn't myself. Been having a tough time lately.'

'Well, what with the project and ...'

'No, I don't mean at work. Well, what I really wanted to say was, that I went and spoiled a perfect evening. Everything was great until ...'

'Until I nearly knocked you out?' She smiled.

His frown turned into a smile. 'Yes, until you nearly knocked me out.' He put his cup down. She was afraid to part with hers, keeping it held to her chest between them.

'No, it's more than that. Malaika, this has been a bad year for mistakes. Some big ones. And I didn't want to make any more where you're concerned. I wanted to be sure I could trust myself. And I wanted you to trust me.'

'Why shouldn't I trust you?'

'You should! What I mean is, some time ago ... an incident, one terrible mistake, made me lose respect for myself. Now I'm trying to put it back together. To be the person I was a year ago. I ... I think I'm finally getting there.'

'If we're not careful we can let a single thing ruin our lives.'

'You're right. But what's the answer? How do you undo those things?'

'You can't. But you accept it. You live with it. Sometimes, if you are lucky, someone might help you put it behind you.'

'You have to be very lucky to find a *someone* like that.'

'Yes, very lucky.' She recalled her luck. The luck of meeting Dr Hussein, Jai's father. Learning to trust him, when she may well have turned against every man she ever met. 'In my case, my *someone* found me. One of the kindest men I ever met. He saved me from a really bad situation. He got me my start in AmericAid.'

'Did you love him?'

She smiled. 'No, it was not like that. He was more of a father. But in the beginning I found it hard to trust him. He was a doctor. He healed me.'

'Where is he now?'

'He ... died. Three years ago.'

'I'm sorry.'

The *dhow* bumped the wharf and she fell into him, her empty coffee cup clattering on the saucer against his chest. He held her while she regained her balance.

'Thank you, ladies and gentlemen. We hope you enjoyed the Tamarind Dhow this evening. Mind your step on the plank as you disembark.'

HE OPENED HER DOOR AND held out the keys for her. As she reached for them he took her hand in his and pressed it to his lips, kissing her fingers. Then he kissed her mouth, softly. Her lips parted to feel his tongue. She was disappointed when he stopped, but after a moment reading her eyes, he kissed her firmly and with a passion that took her by surprise. It was the flood that follows the first of the long rains. It swept over her and drew her along in its wake. He kissed her, nibbled at her bottom lip and teased her mouth until she was racing in the same torrent, trying to catch him — to ride the wave with him.

She leaned on the door, pushing it open, and drew him in after her. He kept his lips on hers, closing the door with his heel. In his arms she let herself sink against the enveloping warmth of his body. For the second time since she had met him, she felt the bliss of release, this time to Jack's lips and tongue and to his exploring hands. He caressed her so gently that it was a butterfly's wings touching her face, her arms, her hands. He lifted her fingers to his lips, kissing each fingertip in turn. He sucked her little finger, rolling his hot tongue around it.

When he buried his face between her breasts, she pushed the edge of her gown aside, hungry to feel his lips on her. With a tweak of thumb and finger, her bra snapped open, exposing her breasts to his searching mouth. First one nipple, then the other, contracted into tight little peaks. She ran her hand into the soft hair at the back of his neck. It was a strange and erotic sensation. So soft, so able to gently conceal the corded muscles of his neck. She let herself drift to vaguely notice the other enjoyable differences — the texture of his hair, long and thick, but at the same time, silky fine — the slight abrasion of the beard stubble at her breast. She lifted his face to hers and enjoyed the different feel of his lips — not so full as some, but no less sensuous, with tiny muscles able to build sensation upon sensation. They were magic lips.

In the dim light of the room, his fingers played up her spine and fumbled a moment at the catch of her dress. The zip made a delicious sound as he drew down on it. With deliberate care he slipped the remaining shoulder strap to let her dress and bra drop to the carpet.

Time seemed to falter. She sensed every individual movement in acute detail — the fall of the beads in her braids onto his shoulder, each one a red, blue or yellow jewel — long fingernails indenting the slippery fabric of his shirt — Jack's infinitely slow breathing as he planted gentle, slow kisses on her eyes, her nose, her shoulders.

She ran her fingers across his chest. Inch by inch they crept along the electric silk to find the buttons. She teased them loose, enjoying each button as an exquisite sensation in itself. Then, like a person in a dream, she slid the shirt over his broad shoulders. It fell softly to the floor. She nibbled his neck. He sighed — the sound of a man released from a prison.

Warm hands slipped down her ribs to the French-cut panties and slid under the loose lacy edges to caress her buttocks, sending an involuntary rush of pleasure through her. He tugged them, and bent to slide them down her long legs.

When he straightened again, she loosened his belt and slid down the zipper. His trousers dropped where he stood. She felt his erection through his shorts, thrusting against her.

'Malaika,' he whispered and, taking her hand, led her to the bedside.

She pressed her cheek to his chest, clinging to him so tightly she could hear the short bursts of his breath. His heart was like a hammer.

From the pillow, she could see him in the dim light, removing his shorts — the size of him in silhouette.

She opened her arms as he knelt on the bed beside her and slowly, slowly, she drew him to her.

THE LIGHT INTRUDED UPON HIS sleep, a deep sleep languidly visited by strange and exciting warmth on the other side of the bed. He wanted to preserve the dream-like quality of his half-awake, half-asleep state, and used a childhood trick to prolong it. He parted his eyelids just enough to see through the lashes. A sleeping vision lay beside him and, in her tranquillity, was more beautiful than he remembered.

He resisted the morning's intrusion into his consciousness. The clarity of daylight could be delayed a little longer as he wafted in and out of sleep ...

The faint thumping of breakers on the beach. O'Hara was below him, her buttocks thrusting as he plunged into her. His gun hand was on her shoulder, the muzzle against her blonde hair. The first click had sent an electric pulse through him. Intoxicating. He enjoyed the weight of it in his palm, the slight resistance of trigger pressure on the fingertip.

Slowly, slowly he squeezed.

Click!

He took a deep breath and let it escape in a long silent sigh. It was no longer the gut-wrenching trauma of months ago. But it was there.

He looked at Malaika asleep beside him. It was a relief. A relief to lie there, knowing again the beauty of making love — not just fucking. That's all it was with O'Hara. A mindless coupling. A mistake.

Malaika's soft warm breath touched his arm. She stirred. A fluttering of eyelashes. She was waking. He took a long last secret look at her. The shape of her eyes was accentuated in sleep. They curved up at the ends, the lashes and brows following the line. One red bead from her hair lay in the corner of her mouth. Her lips twitched at it, sending it sliding to her throat where it moved again as she swallowed and parted her lips. Her eyes opened: soft, dreamy and with a hint of surprise.

'Good morning,' he whispered.

She smiled.

He watched her become aware of her surroundings. Her eyes roamed the extent of the dim bedroom that she could see without moving her head, then they returned to his. 'Good morning,' she said with a voice full of sleep. Pulling the sheet up to her chin, she rolled onto her back, taking in the remainder of the room.

He propped himself on an elbow and looked down at her. She blinked and smiled at him. 'What?'

He didn't know the answer, but it was the kind of thing he would say when trying to avoid being first to speak. Instead he said, 'Sleep well?'

'Mmm.'

'Comfortable?'

'Yes.' She looked at the ceiling. 'At last.'

'What do you mean, *at last*?'

'I hardly ever felt comfortable with you.'

'You were uncomfortable with me?'

'Uncomfortable. Often angry. Frequently frustrated ...'

'Okay, okay,' he said, smiling. 'I get the message.' He ran his eyes over her face. Tiny gold studs peeped from her ear lobes. Her beads made small clicking sounds as she moved her head. He placed a gentle kiss on her. Her mouth clung to him, sticky- soft with sleep.

'Maybe I was just playing hard to get,' he continued. 'Or seeing if you could be frightened off.'

She retrieved her arm from under the sheet and ran a long red fingernail down his beard stubble. 'Somewhere inside, I'm Maasai.' She moved her gaze from his lips to his eyes, holding them. 'It takes a lot to scare us.'

THE MID-MORNING DOWNPOUR HAD MADE the hard-packed dirt corridors between the market stalls treacherous. The market itself was awash with colour. Veiled and jewelled women swept through the throng, baskets on their heads or over an arm. Children trotted behind, some stopping to gawk at the white man with the beautiful black woman.

They had decided to take an extra day, it being Jack's first time on the coast. An early Monday morning flight would see them back in Nairobi not much later than ten.

'Jack ...'

'Uh huh?'

'This is going to sound silly, but ... um, not here.'

'What am I doing? You mean putting my arm around you?'

'Yes.'

'What's wrong with that?'

'Oh, I'm sorry. How do I explain this to a new *mzungu*? You do know *mzungu*, don't you?'

'Of course. White person.'

'Good! That's your first Swahili lesson. The second is, showing signs of affection like this is, well ... it's not done. It's, you know, too personal.'

'Too personal? Wow. Okay, how about this?' He took her hand.

'Not so bad, but ...'

'Not even hand-holding?'

'Not really. Maybe in Nairobi ... but Mombasa, the coast, these people, the Swahili, are very — what's the word? Conservative. You will never see them holding hands and when a zebra couple do it, well, they just stare. Haven't you noticed?'

'But I'm a compulsive hand-holder. I feel strange not holding my girl's hand. Like I'm some visiting out-of-town cousin.'

'I'm sorry. It's my fault. I get mad when they stare, so the best thing to do is ... you know ... wait for later.'

'So I guess a quick fondle is out of the question?' He smiled.

She gave him a push.

'So what do I do? It's not fair. Kenya or no Kenya, it ain't fair.'

'I know it isn't. But okay, we'll have a secret kiss. When I do this,' she placed her hand against his cheek for a moment, 'that's my secret kiss.'

'Hmm, cute.'

'Okay?'

'I guess it'll have to do.'

She gave his hand a quick squeeze, then released it.

THE SMASH OF METAL SPEARS on rock-hard buffalo-hide shields rolled like thunder through the confined space. The ten Maasai *moran* circled one of their number, a very tall, handsome young warrior, who began to leap in the air in time with the beating of their shields. His short red *shuka* flapped and his red-ochred hair spun as he threw his body into mid-air contortions.

The auditorium at Bomas of Kenya was full of weekend tourists. It was really a large circus tent sitting importantly in a neat garden on the southern outskirts of Nairobi. Inside, high-powered stadium lights pinned the dancers to their multiple shadows on the sandy arena.

Jack was focusing his telephoto lens on the dancing Maasai. Snap. Whir. Malaika was becoming bored and wished it would soon end. The Maasai, in their short red lap laps, were the sixth tribal group to appear and it looked like being a long afternoon. She and Jack were in the tiered seating surrounded by busloads of tourists. Flashbulbs popped silent exclamations around the arena. Malaika swirled the remnants of her Seven Up with her straw. She thought about getting another. It was hot and dry under the canvas roofing, but she felt that Jack would probably insist on fetching it, and he seemed to be engrossed in his photography.

Snap, whir, from the camera. Thud, thud, from the floor of the arena.

Malaika found herself drawn into the beat in spite of her guarded indifference. Each compelling clash of spear on shield was exactly one heartbeat apart. Thud. Thud. Thud. But another sound began to insinuate between the beat of the shields. Like a train climbing a distant hill, the whoosh of heat and steam announcing its ascent, the Maasai's chant began. 'Hhuunh-huh!' A crash on the shields, then, 'Hhuunh-huh!'

A long-forgotten image flashed into Malaika's mind. An image from another life, the life of a child, but laced with dim, disturbing memories. A mother. A brother. An old woman. The chant and the thud of iron on hide were things familiar to a different part of her. A ghost sound.

THE GIRL SLIPPED HER HAND *from her mother's grasp and crawled through the cluster of women. She scuttled among the skinny black legs and broad flat feet that stamped dust clouds into her face. Above her, the women's high ululating cries gathered in strength. Their voices played with the deep other sound. They threaded their song through it and over it. They tried to lock it with theirs. But the other sound, the one that drew her, would not listen. It denied the taunts and flirtations of the women's singing, droning on, resolute and unmoved. And it pulled her away from the women, the old ones and mothers. It pulsed through her and pulled at her tummy and pulled at her mind. It pulled at the beat of her heart and bound it in its unrelenting rhythm.*

She emerged from the tight band of women and hesitated before taking slow, slow steps towards the men, gathered in numbers around the sound. It frightened her but compelled her forward. Little boys were running wildly about. They jumped and clapped their hands in the space between the women and the men and they were not afraid of the sound. Her brother's face loomed before her. He laughed and danced around her before running off with the other boys.

She sensed that she should not be there, near the men, so close to the sound. But it pulled at her, and her legs, with the beautiful new bracelets of red and yellow beads and red metal wire that her mother had tied there that morning, obeyed. The wall of old men blocked her path. They paid her no attention. She sensed that they knew the sound, were intimate with it. It was of them, but not theirs. It belonged to other, younger voices. Stronger voices.

The women's singing grew with the challenge. They teased and tempted the sound but it grew deeper, contemptuous of their seduction. No power could change its relentless rhythm. 'Hhuunh-huh!' it said. Again, a moment later, 'Hhuunh-huh!'

In the forest of legs she found a gap. With eyes grown large and her breath held tight in her chest, she saw them, the fearsome young men of her tribe, glistening and tall and almost naked in their short red shukas. She knew the sound filled them too. Their bodies were consumed by it; pulsated with it. 'Hhuunh-huh!'

In the counterpoint, as the warriors' chins dipped to their chests, and chests swelled for the next bursting exhalation, came the thunder of iron spears against hard shields. Thud!

It bounced from the rocks surrounding their valley. 'Hhuunh-huh!' Thud!

In the middle of the circle, a morani *was leaping as straight as an arrow shaft. Higher and higher he leapt with each beat. 'Hhuunh-huh!' Thud! Higher. 'Hhuunh-huh!' Thud! Higher and higher. The sound propelled him upwards, ever higher upwards, until it seemed he would touch the sky. Sometimes, hovering high above them, he swirled his long red-ochred braids about his head, suspended until the crash of spear on shield released him to return to earth.*

She knew that she would never again see anything quite as beautiful, or quite so awesome, as the young warriors of her village. As she felt the wonderful sound, and the dance, and the whirling colours, were about to carry her away for ever, a hand found hers and dragged her gently from the circle of men. Back to where she belonged, with the mothers and children.

The sound released the child. She became herself again, just another skinny Maasai girl.

CHAPTER 20

PEABODY'S GUIDE TO EAST AFRICA (5TH ED):
An aid agency in East Africa, studying AIDS cases among
young street beggars, made the following analysis in 1985:
physiologically, HIV gets into the defence system and
wipes it out. Sociologically, it gets into the extended
family support system and wipes it out too.

Driving the Subaru was a strange experience. It was quiet and
easy to manage. In comparison to the rollicking Land Rover, it
hugged the road and handled like a sports car. It hadn't
arrived a day too soon. He had been pushing his luck this last
month or so since he had started seeing Malaika. The UNDP's
admin manager, a hostile Sikh, was becoming increasingly
difficult whenever Jack asked to have the Land Rover for the
weekend.

Malaika was drumming her fingers to a track on the tape
player as Jack motored along the leafy avenues of Westlands.
They pulled up at the high steel gate on Peponi Road and
tooted the horn.

Jack had been to Bear's Westlands house on only two
occasions, and never inside. Bear's invitation was for an old-
fashioned roast beef meal while they made plans for a weekend
safari to the Mara. 'Come around twelve. You might like a swim
before lunch,' he had said. Jack glanced back along the narrow

road with its Tudor-style houses, grassy verges, clipped shrubs and shade trees. It could have been an English country lane on a fine summer morning except for the frangipani and the hibiscus hedges.

He was about to toot again when a uniformed guard poked his head through the gate opening. Malaika leaned out the window and said something in Swahili. Jack heard her say, '*Bwana* Hoffman.' A moment later the gate swung open and the *askari* bent to smile into the Subaru as it rolled into the paved courtyard. '*Jambo, bwana!*'

The Land Rover sat wet and gleaming at the edge of the bitumen driveway. Jack pulled in between Bear's vintage Sunbeam Talbot and the row of terracotta pots that separated the parking area from the gardens surrounding the house.

'*Jambo,*' Jack said to the guard as he climbed out. The *askari* wore the uniform of Nairobi Nightwatch, the company that manned the gate at his apartment compound at Nairobi Hill.

From basalt footings, the sombre brick walls rose to Tudor-style timber bracing under a red gabled roof. Each window sported a little red gable above it, while golden zinnias overflowed from flower-boxes on the sill. Jack took Malaika's hand as the *askari*, chatting and smiling, led them to the door. Jack heard '*Habari*', one of the few Swahili words he knew; literally, 'the news', but more usually used as a greeting. Malaika didn't seem to want to get drawn into a conversation.

The front door opened as they approached. An old man in a white apron nodded and, without a word, indicated that they should enter. Bear called from somewhere down the panelled hallway, 'Henry will show you to the sitting room. Give him your drink order. I'll be there in a moment.' They did as they were told, following Henry down a short corridor.

The sitting room had once been a wide open veranda, for the enjoyment of the back garden and the distant green hills. A low panelled wall and sliding glass windows, looking very much a recent addition, now enclosed it. Sisal matting and curved cane furniture accorded a feel of the tropics. It made a mockery of the austere formality dominating the front rooms of the house.

A tangle of purple bougainvillea had claimed the lower branches of a huge cedar tree near the side fence, where a gardener was raking a mound of its bracts towards a corner. Some had escaped to become tiny purple skiffs, chased around the swimming pool on the warm breeze. Through the greenery beyond the fence were the manicured lawns of neighbouring houses. They were of solid brick with gables, turrets and stone chimneys.

Henry tottered in with three drinks on a silver tray. He handed a cola to Malaika and a frosty beer to Jack. He was about to put the third glass on the coffee table as Bear joined them. 'Thanks, Henry.' He took the glass and raised it to them. '*Karibuni!*' he said. 'Welcome.'

'Cheers,' they answered. Glasses clinked.

'Ahhh!' Bear said after a long swallow. Jack smiled. Bear always said *Ahhh* on his first sip.

'Jack, I should have told you to try one of Henry's gin and tonics. They're fantastic.'

'Since when did you become a G and T man?'

'Best thing the English ever invented. But you can't use the local limes. Not quite the right punch. I get my lemons from the highlands.'

'You have a big house, Bear,' Malaika said, looking from the garden into the room beyond the doorway.

'Oh, it's comfortable, I guess. Been here for five years now.'

'Five years?' Jack said.

'Yeah. You sound surprised.'

'I suppose I am. It's just that, well, it's so formal for someone like you. The house, the rose beds, even the gardener has a uniform!'

'It's the system. And it works. Oh, I know it's trendy to dump on this stuff as colonialist crap, but the goddamn Brits had them a system goin' here.'

'Oh, great! You're talking about the benefits of colonialism?' Jack wondered if it was too early in the day for serious discussion.

'No, not the system. What I mean is, well ... take house help. The Brits trained the best servants around. Not many

235

like old Henry left. Part of it was the colonial tradition. Uniforms. The formality. *Bwana* Bear. All that shit. But it carried through to everything. Look at this house,' he swept his hand around. 'Steep roof to stop snow building up. Small windows to keep the heat in. Perfect for England. Really dumb for the tropics, right? But the Brits made no concessions. The formula made Britain great. So why change?'

'But that's so much bullshit today, isn't it?' Jack said. 'Why not pith helmets and puttees while we're at it?'

'What I'm saying is, the system makes it easier for everyone. We all know our place.' He jiggled the ice in his glass. 'There are rules for all of us. I treat my people with respect. I pay a fair wage. Maybe they steal a little food here and there. But they do their job.'

'I've seen a lot of these old-fashioned houses around the town, Bear,' said Malaika. 'But never been in one.'

'A tour? Sure. Follow me.' Bear led them first into the kitchen, which was large and simple. An electric cooker was against one wall; a refrigerator, the size of a Mack truck, against another. A small table and a single chair stood in the centre of the floor. The surfaces were finished in small white vitreous tiles, fifties style. Elsewhere the flooring was timber parquetry, highly polished and scattered throughout with oriental rugs.

The lounge room had a tall mirrored sideboard, a sofa and three overstuffed and faded floral armchairs. A smoker's stand reared its head to the arm of one of them. On the mantelpiece above the fireplace stood two silver-framed photographs. One, a photo of a young girl, had faded into sepia browns. The other was of a white-haired lady in a dress with laced collar and cuffs. Bear said they were of his mother. At the geometric centre of the room was a glassed coffee table and, on it, a pile of magazines in a neat stack. *World Boxing News* was on top.

The dining room was only just large enough to house an oval table with settings for eight. It would be a squeeze to get between the crockery stand and the high-backed chairs.

Walnut wardrobes dominated three of the bedrooms, with a single bed cowering in a corner of each. The master bedroom was much bigger and commanded a view of the garden.

The gentleman's dress stand and oriental storage box complemented a huge four-poster bed. A mosquito-net tent was tied at each corner post like furled sails, ready to drop and carry the bed out the bay window.

Bear finished the tour at the pool. The late-morning sun was hot.

'Let's have a swim!' Malaika said.

'Too freakin' cold for me,' said Bear. 'Anyway, I've gotta duck out for some champagne. You guys go ahead.'

Bear was right. The pool was icy. Malaika gave little squeaks as she took to it from the shallow end, a step at a time. Jack launched a running jump and came up bellowing like a bull seal. 'Whoa! It's cold!'

'Jack, you splashed me!'

'I'll do more than that if you don't get off those steps!'

She dived in as he swam towards her. A splash fight followed and then they were laughing in each other's arms. Jack hugged her to him and swung her around in circles, feeling her breasts against his chest through the thin bikini.

He nuzzled her throat, remembering their last day in Mombasa. They had found an isolated stretch of sand. The water was inviting and the day, hot and humid after the rain, had demanded a swim. Malaika dropped her clothes in an instant. Her body aroused him, but she had run to the water while he was still kicking off his shorts. He had come up behind her as she was wiping saltwater from her eyes. She turned into his embrace.

'Oh, look! It floats!' she had said, looking down into the crystal water in the gap between their bodies.

'Darling, that's not floating.'

'Oh!' she had giggled.

In the pool, Malaika pushed him away with a laugh. 'Race you!' She took off. When Jack looked up after two laps she was pulling herself up the pool ladder.

'Hey! Where're you off to?' He watched the gleam of her sleek brown legs and the curve of her buttocks, exposed by the high-cut bikini. She turned, leaning forward to gather her braids before throwing them back over her shoulders. He had a view of the deep valley between her breasts.

'Too cold for me but I think you might need a little cooling off.'

'Oh?' he asked innocently.

'Jack, that thing just won't stop floating,' she said, and ran across the lawn to her towel. It took minutes in the chilling water before he could rearrange his shorts and climb out with any amount of propriety.

When Bear returned from his shopping trip an hour later, laden with cardboard boxes and bottles, Henry served first course at the pool. The prawns were fresh from Malindi on the Indian Ocean coast. Bear said he had a connection to a fishing co-op, but made a big fuss about the need for secrecy before giving Jack the details, under pain of death if he divulged them. They ate the prawns in the shade of the poolside shelter and worked steadily on the champagne until the bottle lay, defeated, nose down in the ice bucket.

Zimbabwean red wine accompanied the main course, which was served in the dining room. Bear sliced the roast beef on an enormous platter. Adding roast potatoes, pumpkin and boiled peas to their plates, he waved them to commence.

When conversation waned towards the end of the meal, Bear turned to Malaika. 'You know, this guy has been hogging all your time. I hardly know a thing about you. You know that?'

Malaika smiled. 'What is there to know?'

'Oh, there must be plenty. For instance, how long have you been in AmericAid?'

'I started a few years after I came to Nairobi.'

'You must have been a baby!'

'Seventeen. But the first four years was study.'

'They sent you to school?'

'Yes. Secondary school and a few special courses. Why?'

'Just a bit unusual, I guess.'

'I had a friend who got me started.'

'Who was that?'

'Bear!' Jack said. 'Not another of your inquisitions! I don't even know this stuff.'

'Just tryin' to get to know the lady a little better is all.' His smile suggested he was teasing Jack as much as getting to know Malaika.

'Have you ever considered a career in the secret police?' Jack said, giving Malaika a helpless shrug.

Bear ignored him and turned to Malaika again. 'So a friend got you into AmericAid and then you finished school. That must have been ...'

'Three years ago — 1986.'

'And since then?'

'Since then, whatever needs to be done. My last project was a clinic for Hansen's disease in Lamu.' She sat back, allowing Henry to clear the table.

Bear suggested they move to the lounge room where they could finish their drinks in comfort. As Jack rose from the dining table he had the uncomfortable feeling of having over-eaten. Henry had proved to be an accomplished, if uncommunicative cook.

In the lounge room Jack flopped into his chair and said, 'Great meal, mate. I'm stuffed!'

'It was delicious,' Malaika added.

'And so much of it,' Jack said, crossing his leg over a knee. 'There's still a mountain of food out there.'

'It won't be wasted. Henry will see to that. If he can't use it, it goes to the gardener or the guard. It'll find its way to someone's table, that's for sure.'

Malaika nodded. 'We send food parcels from Nairobi to our clinic in Kisii.'

'Food shortages in Kisii?' Bear said, topping up Jack's wine glass. Malaika declined. 'Every time I go through Kisii, the food gardens are overflowing.'

'Yes,' Malaika nodded. 'Good soil and good rain. But still not enough food.' She explained how, in Kisii tradition, as each son married, he received a share of his father's land. In return, the sons ensured that their parents were cared for in their declining years. However, in recent generations, the divided lots had become too small to provide subsistence for the sons and no surplus for the parents. The Kisii had been forced to find alternative means of providing for their children, and for themselves. The popular alternative for poor families was to scrape together sufficient cash to send one child to secondary school, and therefore win a chance at a job in the city and sufficient cash flow to care for the family back home. The father's chosen child was invariably one of the sons, usually the oldest. The opportunity was given to the boy showing most promise in primary school. A failure to complete secondary school was more than a personal failure; it was an economic disaster for the whole family.

'Sounds like a good idea,' Jack said. 'The kid with the best chance. Where's the problem?'

'Nothing, so far,' Malaika answered. 'In the village, it's difficult for the parents. You know, money is still hard to get. Well, they knew that. They struggle for a few years.'

'And then?' Jack said, as she paused.

'And then the boy gets a job, maybe a clerk in a big office. The old people in the village see that as a great success. But the boy, the young man, is away from his family. In the city there is freedom never known in the village. They have fun. Some get married and have children.

'Anyway, the children — that is, the grandchildren — are usually sent home to Kisii. That's part of the plan. A little bit of money goes back too. Not much, because city rents are high, even for a one-room — what do you call it? A one-room shack.' She stopped, looking down at her hands.

'That's when the big problem comes up,' she went on. 'Maybe five or six years after they leave home, one of the couple gets sick. Sometimes both of them.' She squeezed the fingers of one hand with the other. 'They call it the slimming sickness. About one in five catch it.' She looked at Jack. 'In the west you call it AIDS.'

Jack frowned. 'One in five! Did you say the married couples?'

Bear answered. 'It's not a gay disease here. In Africa, it's everyone. And everywhere.'

Malaika shrugged, a gesture of defeat. 'Mainly the young ones.'

Jack shook his head. 'And they were the hope of the team ...'

'Yes. It's bad enough to lose your son or daughter, but they were also the one big chance. For the whole family. All their hopes were in that young man. Finished. And now with grandchildren to support as well ...'

'Jesus, Malaika, that's ...' Jack couldn't think what to say. 'I didn't realise.'

She gave him a weak smile. 'That's part of the problem. The rich countries don't understand. Maybe they don't want to know. In Africa, AIDS is killing a generation. The educated generation. The ones who could have earned the money. What did you call them, Jack? *The hope of the team.* That's what they were. Now the old people in the village have children to raise. And still not enough land.' She took a deep breath. 'It's bad. So bad.'

Jack started to understand the scale of it. 'It must affect the whole economy, the whole country. Isn't anything being done? How did it all start?'

'They say it started after Tanzania's war with Uganda. That was around the time I came to Nairobi.' She told them the history or, more correctly, the folklore of the African AIDS pandemic. How the soldiers marched home like heroes after the 1979 victory over Amin's Uganda. And how the women were happy to give them a big welcome. They didn't know, nobody did, what the men carried. It would be five years before the symptoms began to appear, and ten for them to be understood. By then it was too late. She said that in border towns on the long-distance truck routes, like Bukoba and Mwanza, infection rates ran as high as sixty per cent.

'Is there any education going on? Is anything being done?' Jack asked.

'There's no money for health. There's never enough money.'

'But what about education? That can't cost so much.'

She shook her head.

'What about condoms? Free condoms?'

'No. It doesn't work. This is Africa. An African man wearing a condom?'

'But the women ... Don't they have anything to say in all this?'

'It must be hard to understand, Jack,' she sighed, 'but an African woman just can't do that. I don't know what it is. I speak to many of them about being careful. To use condoms. They nod their heads, they go home. Nothing changes. I try to get them to bring their boyfriends, their husbands, in for a test. No.'

'I don't believe it,' Jack said. 'With AIDS around ... What's going on in their heads?'

'I don't know, Jack.' She shrugged. 'Maybe it's just Africa.'

'The African male more like it! Unbelievable! For the sake of a condom ...'

Bear had been silent for some time. 'It's different here, Jack,' he said. 'It's a culture thing. And it's about fear. And shame.'

'Shame?'

Bear reached for the cigarette resting on the smoker's stand. 'Yes.' Inhaling deeply, he leaned back into the padded headrest and shot a long smoke stream upwards. It ballooned and drifted towards the ceiling. He seemed content to have his comment hang there, like the smoke.

'What do you mean, *shame*?' Jack asked again.

'You need to understand that this is, like, from another age. Think of them lepers a couple of thousand years ago and you'll get the idea. A disease so terrible, so cruel, that to have it means that you must have deserved it. You must have been a really bad person.' He topped up his port and waved the bottle at Jack and Malaika. They shook their heads, waiting for him to continue.

'A few years ago I met this gal named Violet,' Bear said. 'I was on my first tour to Kenya. Been here, oh, 'bout six weeks by this time, see. Met her at Buff's. Yeah, it was the same ol' pick-up place then as now, but I guess it was a bit harder to tell the prostitutes from the enthusiastic amateurs back then. But there was no mistaking Violet. She eyeballed me as I walked into the place. Sittin' in a booth with some drunken *mzungu*; she dumped him. Like that.' The snap of his fingers was like a rifle shot in the quiet room, now shadowed with the long rays of the afternoon sun. 'She looked pretty rough, I must say. Red mini-skirt, big red polka dots on her white blouse. Hair tied back with a big red bow. Couldn't miss her in a crowded stadium. So she's gettin' kinda friendly, and that's okay. I was ready for a good time and she had the equipment. Man, what an ass! And me? I'm as horny as a stud bull. Then her boyfriend comes out of the booth like a steam train. I mean he was pissed off!' Bear puffed the cigarette and gave a chuckle. 'So him and me, we're goin' after each other. And the sucker could fight! Surprised the crap out of me, he did. He got in a couple of lucky ones early. And I'm not lookin' too good there. Then, *wham*! Violet breaks a beer bottle over his head. Down he goes like a sack o' shit!'

Jack was enjoying the story but wondered where it was going.

'So Violet and me, we get the hell out of there before the cops come. Go to some bar somewhere near the market. Got plastered together. We sure had a good time that night!' He smiled.

'So, after that, I get to dropping by from time to time, see? Catch a drink or two with Violet. Maybe we'd drop in here for a spell. She lived out in Eastlands, staying with a cousin. Violet had a kid. A boy, about eight.' He scratched the greying side of his narrow beard. 'Got her into a little apartment in Hurlingham. Her, the boy and her cousin. Most of the time she'd be here with me. Well, before you know it, it's been two years. Even took her on leave with me. Bangkok, Rome ...' He blew ash off the end of his cigarette and stared at its glowing tip. 'Violet was a lot of fun.'

He stubbed the cigarette in the smoker's stand. 'When she got sick I didn't know what to do. All of a sudden she starts getting headaches like you wouldn't believe. One night she was throwin' up with the pain of it. I took her to the Aga Khan Hospital. They couldn't find anything wrong. They gave her some tablets and after a while the headaches went away. Then about a month later they were back. And much worse.'

He flipped out another cigarette and straightened his leg to retrieve the lighter from deep in his trouser pocket. The lighter top clicked open and he puffed the cigarette end into life. He clicked the lighter shut and put it on the smoker's stand.

'She fainted from the pain on the way to the Aga Khan. When she came to, I had just about got her to Casualty. Screaming, begging me to help.' He coughed and stared at the cigarette for a long moment. 'They drugged her up with painkillers. When they did the tests, they said she had severe meningitis brought on by AIDS.' He paused again to lift his port glass and took a small sip before he placed it carefully back on the coffee table. He leaned back in his armchair. 'She wanted to know the results, so I told her. I wondered if she'd grasp it 'cause she was pretty much out of it with the drugs an' all. She understood it okay. Didn't say much for a while, but then she kinda calls me over close and she says, "Bear, promise me you won't tell any of my family." I can still see the fear in her eyes. "Don't tell any of our friends. Nobody. Promise me." I did. What else could I do?

'You know, that was the last thing she ever said to me. Not, "Bear, tell me you love me." Or, "Bear, don't forget to feed the cat." Just, "Don't tell anyone I have AIDS."' He puffed on the cigarette. 'She could face death but couldn't bear the thought of people knowing.' He rubbed a hand along his jaw. 'She died that night while I was sleeping in the chair beside her. I didn't even have a chance to get her boy back from the fancy school I sent him to.'

The room rang with the silence.

'You know the thing I regret most about Violet?' He looked at Jack. 'You know the worst goddamn thing about it? I never took her home. My friends back home never knew shit about Violet. Nothin'. And my mother never met her. I was too fucking embarrassed to take her home. Too fucking embarrassed to tell my educated friends and my shitty family about her. Me and my pride. I couldn't take her home 'cause of the way she might appear to them. Her manners an' all.' He took a deep breath and blew it out, like a diver breaking the surface. 'I regret that.' He slowly shook his head. 'I sure as hell regret that.'

The lounge room had fallen into a gloom tinged with gold as the sun made its swift retreat. One of the photos on the mantelpiece glinted, reflecting the dying rays like a shimmering ghost on the wall above Bear's head. It diffused, faded and was gone in moments. The silence remained.

Jack looked to Malaika, who held her clenched hands to her lips. He wondered how long he could wait before it burst from him. But Bear sat there, dragging on his cigarette, looking out over the garden.

When he couldn't stand it any longer, Jack said, 'So ... Bear ... What about you?' The words struggled from his throat, now suddenly dry and constricted. 'Are you okay?'

'Me? Dunno.'

'Don't know? How can you not know?' He was angry but not sure why. Was it because this indestructible man might be dying? Or was it because he seemed so maddeningly detached? Perhaps he had a selfish motive — he was angry because he hadn't asked for this load, this terrible knowledge. Because he didn't need it, any of it, to further burden his life. 'No tests? How can you *stand* not to know?' His voice was a croak as he tried to keep the anger out of it.

'You mean, why haven't I bothered to find out if I'm dying? Is that what you mean, Jack? So I can fret and feel sorry for myself? Mope around and maybe pray for divine intervention. Or a miracle cure? Or is it your social conscience, Jack, concerned that I may not be practising safe sex?'

Jack lowered his voice to a whisper. 'I just don't understand how you can go from day to day.'

'Oh, that one? That's easy.' Bear's smile was calm, without rancour. It was the smile of a man who had faced the question a thousand times before. 'I just live every day like it's my last. If I die early, I've given it my best shot.' He shrugged. 'If I'm okay and I live to ninety-nine, well then, I've not wasted a bit of it, have I?'

PART 2

EUNOTO

CHAPTER 21

PEABODY'S GUIDE TO EAST AFRICA (5TH ED):
Marriage is a matter of luck. It has no eyes. (Maasai proverb.)

The girl slipped through the low doorway of the hut. Her cool necklace brushed gently against small black nipples. They grew tight and sensitive at the thought of being with him. She had watched him like an eagle on the wing, from early evening to moonless night, so she knew he was alone. Not an action had been ignored. Not a word missed. From the dim edges of the firelight she watched. Like a lioness guarding her cubs, she would have leapt upon any other *entito* who made an approach.

In the darkened hut she whispered his name. He grunted a reply.

She fumbled her way towards the voice in the darkness. At the bed platform she slid her hands about until she touched the top of his plaited hair, then traced her fingers down his slender nose. There, the small scar on his cheek where a mock battle had nearly cost him an eye. And there, beneath his full lips, the sweep of his wide jaw.

She asked him how he knew it was she. Her whisper was unnecessary. No one could hear them in the dark forest of the *moran*'s meat camp.

He knew she had watched him all night, like a monkey watching fruit fall among leopards, but in reply told her he was a warrior and missed nothing.

His broad chest was cool in the darkness. She let her hand rest on his belly and asked him if she could stay.

He asked why. He liked to tease her.

She felt his stomach muscles ripple under her fingers as he spoke. In reply, her hand slipped down to the tight hairs at his groin. She skirted them to play along his thigh muscles. There was a tension in them that made her heart glad. She knew this body.

He remained silent but he sucked in a breath as her fingers wrapped around him.

She offered the promise of her body if they married.

It was not the first time this had been suggested during their love games. He thrust his groin to the rhythm of her hand.

She said she craved the feel of his strong spear inside her. To drink its juices. There was great joy in store for him — far more than that permitted with a *moran*. The love games were for children. She was a woman, he a man, soon to be an elder. It was time to marry, she said.

He gave an ambiguous grunt.

She stopped stroking and moved her hand to his thigh.

He put it back.

She began to stroke again — the long slow strokes she knew he enjoyed so much.

He moaned and let his body relax. Her warm soft body was pressed along his side and her hand was there, the stroking rhythm perfectly timed.

She played with him, knowing just when to stop, to make the pleasure last.

His breathing quickened. It was unbearable. He released a loud gasp and his hot sticky juice shot to his chest and belly.

She nuzzled into his side, smiling into the darkness, and licked his salty arm like a cheetah cleaning her cub.

KIREKO SAT IN THE DARKNESS, brooding at the embers of the cooking fire while sipping the *laibon*'s magic brew. Nobody knew its secrets, but everyone knew of the dreams that sprang from it. Of the great courage it inspired in battle. He felt the brew rush through his body like a stream of fire, the fire that Mesianto, or Njisha, could kindle in him three times in a night. He would have taken one of them, any one, if women were allowed in the *olpul* camp. Instead, his discontent grew as the heat of the brew devoured him. His seed would wait.

His two friends and age-set brothers, Noah and Shokeri, were cracking jokes on the other side of the fire. He loved them but they were shallow. His brothers, all the other *moran*, were welcoming their coming elevation to elderhood, while he, Kireko, was the only one grieving the passing of warriorhood. But he was too harsh. It was the old one, the *laibon*, who came with the brew and the stories of the great days, who had cast Kireko into this morbid mood. He should be celebrating the coming *eunoto* instead of mourning it. He tried to lighten his mood. There would be singing, dancing. The young women would be flirting and hinting at games of love.

The *laibon*'s words had consumed him and clung to his mind still. Stories of past battles — raids against enemy and interloper — the glory of the old days, the old ways.

Oh, on a thousand Maasai, the *laibon* said, *the red of the* shukas *form an open wound on the escarpment, brimming with blood before spilling down the ridge. A thousand* moran *on the march to battle. The chant, like a roll of thunder from a distant storm, heard long before the red appears, is a terrifying sound. Sometimes it is enough to settle a battle before it begins. Painted shields. Fearful spears. Towering* olawaru *of ostrich plume or lion's mane. And always the blood-red* shuka, *the badge of the Maasai. Red. The colour of battle. The colour of death. With the power to startle enemies. Fine enemies. Brave enemies. To set them to flight, like so many gazelle.*

Kireko knew that, come *eunoto*, those days were gone like the grass that falls to the firestorm on the savannah. Black and dead.

Oh, you moran *of the Aiser clan. Be proud. You have fulfilled your task as warriors. You have lived the noble life of the* moran, *protector of our people. Now, prepare for your new life. Prepare yourselves for your elevation to elder. For when you leave the warriorhood you must take a wife. Gather your cattle. Raise a family. It is the way of the Maasai.*

'No!' he roared from his brooding dream.

Noah and Shokeri's eyes were wide in the firelight.

'No,' he said when he saw their startled expressions. 'This is not the way to end it.' He put his drinking bowl beside the fire. It toppled and spilt. 'Listen, brothers. We have had five years as senior *moran*. In a few weeks we begin our *eunoto* ceremony to become junior elders. There is no going back.'

They watched him in silence. Noah blinked and rubbed his eye with the back of a hand.

'So, what have we to show for our warrior years?' Kireko continued. 'What stories do we have to tell our children?'

Noah and Shokeri exchanged glances. Noah said, 'Kireko, what are you talking about?' He sloshed more brew into their bowls. 'Just drink, brother. This is the time for celebration.'

'What do we have to celebrate? What memories do we have of our warrior years? You see! You are ashamed. Like me. Two small raids. Three cows and six goats!' He spat in the dirt. 'No more than the childish games of uncircumcised boys.'

'You're not talking about a raid, Kireko?' Shokeri looked uncomfortable. 'Not again.'

'Of course I am! A raid.'

'You know how hard it is. We cannot raid the Luo's cattle. They will set the *askaris* on us. We will be arrested again.'

Kireko unfolded his tall frame and stood above them. Tension tightened his long muscles like the bullock sinew on his bow. At twenty-seven, he was in his prime. 'Do you hear yourselves?' he asked, pacing before them. He always wore a slight frown, like a young man personally responsible for too many important things. Now the firelight flared in his eyes and glistened on his taut jaw. He acted fiercer than he felt. 'Or is it one of the girls who has hidden in our *olpul* camp making these whining excuses?'

Calm, calm; his old grandmother's words came back. Be calm in the storm and conquer it.

He began again, his voice softer, inviting them into his vision. 'Noah, you were the one to grab the horn of the running bullock. It was at our circumcision ceremony. Remember? What a victory you had. And you have proven yourself many times since. Many times.' He let the silence flutter in the night like a hovering owl poised to strike. 'And you, Shokeri. It was you who cut off the buffalo's tail before he was dead. Have you not both proven your courage?' Kireko nodded to underline the truth of it. 'Of course you have. So my friends ... I need your help.'

This won their attention.

'I want *my* chance. A chance for one more raid.' He continued to pace the edge of the firelight. 'A glorious raid. One that will be sung at our *eunoto*.' A trickle of sweat slipped from his heavily ochred hair to the corner of his eye. He blinked it away. 'We will go far,' he said in a rasping whisper. 'Where we are unknown. One last raid ... For your brother.'

'Oh, mama,' said Noah with a smile and a shake of his head. 'Listen to him. One last chance for glory. Will we ever hear the end of this? What do you think, Shokeri? Does this pile of zebra turds deserve his chance?'

Shokeri laughed at Kireko's fierce expression. 'Just look at him! If we don't, I swear we won't leave this fire alive! He will slice us into pieces with his *simi*.'

'My brothers,' Kireko pressed on, 'a raid in the great tradition. The way our grandfathers would have it. Spears, shields and *simi*. Our raid will have greatness.'

Shokeri's eyes drifted to the darkness beyond the flames. 'Yes ... greatness,' he whispered. Kireko's passion seemed to have invaded his drunken lethargy. He looked to Noah who had returned to his drinking bowl. 'You! Noah? Do you hear? Greatness!' He pushed him on the shoulder to rouse him. 'Greatness!'

Kireko smiled. The brew had woven its magic.

CHAPTER 22

PEABODY'S GUIDE TO EAST AFRICA (5ᵀᴴ ED):
Accommodation in the Masai Mara National Reserve may
be enjoyed at a number of lodges, ranging from luxurious
five-star tents incorporating full *en suite* bathroom facilities,
to motel-style establishments. In the latter category are the
Mara Serena Lodge, sited on a ridge overlooking the Mara
River, and Governor's Camp some miles downstream.

For those preferring a more rustic safari, simple
accommodation outside the east gate of the Reserve, such
as Cottars Camp, might prove interesting.

There is something seductive about a *makuti* roof. It compels
a person straying under its low eaves to enter the hushed space
at its centre. There, beneath the high ridgepole, air presses
warmly upon the skin. The sun finds invisible paths through
the woven fronds to somehow bring light to its mute interior,
an eerie light of a kind more usually found in places of
worship. Things that should provoke no sensory awareness
become tangible. Nothingness assumes a physical form.

A modest *makuti* roof makes a hut a hushed haven, a place
to escape the heat. A larger one, like on the reception building
at Cottars Camp in the Masai Mara, creates a place of shaded
stillness, silencing sounds from within but, as if it were a
maestro's orchestra shell, magnifying others that creep from

the garden beyond. The myriad sounds of creatures of the sun
— crickets, beetles, birds, grasshoppers and bees — are
funnelled into the hushed semi-darkness.

Malaika waited alone at the reception desk. There was a
silence and an air of familiarity here too, but she dismissed it
as she had out on the Serengeti. Their drive to the lodge had
been through Maasailand, where forgotten memories stirred
like ghosts in a haunted graveyard.

She waited, her eyes drawn into the higher reaches of the
cathedral-like structure, but nobody came to the desk. Bird
calls from the garden beckoned her and she wandered through
the wall opening to a dining area scattered with slab timber
tables and bench seats. The garden sounds receded. Not a
breath of wind stirred the enveloping trees and shrubs.
Malaika felt a sudden sensation, as though something had
brushed her braids. The skin at the back of her neck tingled.
Although full sun shone from the cloudless sky above the
makuti roof, she hugged her arms to her chest, feeling a chill
pass over her.

A faint sound from the far corner of the garden caught her
attention. The ground was spread with river sand, which an
old woman was sweeping with a broom made of a handful of
hibiscus branches. Red hibiscus flowers lay in her wake. She
put a hand on her rickety knees to help her straighten.
Malaika realised, with a twinge of embarrassment, that she
had been staring and that the old woman must have noticed,
for she seemed to be appraising her, perhaps wondering at her
bad manners. Malaika averted her gaze, but when the old
woman eventually returned to her sweeping, she studied the
wizened face in profile. Old. Very old, and ... A tantalising
revelation hovered somewhere at the back of her mind. What
had those bright eyes said in the breathless moment they had
held hers? Like the fragments of a dream that can only be
gathered in the moments after awakening, Malaika tried to
pull the pieces into perspective before they scattered. She knew
it couldn't be rushed. To capture the vision she must practise
deception, must patiently gather the threads one at a time until
she had the meaning.

'Hello-o-o!' It was Bear's voice from behind her at the reception desk. 'Hello-o! Anybody here?'

'I don't think so,' she said, joining him. 'Nobody but that old Maasai woman out ...' The garden was empty.

Bear dropped his bag. 'Now this is better,' he said. 'This is what I call a *safari* camp.'

Malaika followed his eyes. The décor consisted of slatted bamboo walls and simple cane and canvas furniture. 'No background music,' she said.

Bear walked past her to peer into the garden. 'No fences.'

'And no pool.' Her voice trailed off as she noticed there were no hibiscus flowers on the swept sand.

'No bullshit with the fancy napkins. No starch-assed waiters. I think I'm going to like this.'

From behind the reception counter there was a shout of, 'Bags! Bags! *Twende, twende!*' A stocky African in tan trousers and a navy sports coat had suddenly appeared. 'Good afternoon, sir. Madam.' He flourished a rehearsed smile. 'Welcome to Cottars Camp. I'll have someone collect your other bags.' Without waiting for a response, he shouted again, 'Bags! Bags! *Twende, twende!*' A jagged vein bulged at his temple.

'Don't bother, I think I've got it all,' Jack said, as he came in with one over-stuffed vinyl bag slung over his shoulder and another in his hand. 'We're the Morgan booking. Two rooms, two nights.'

'Certainly, sir. And *karibu*. If you would please sign our register, I will show you to your *bandas*.'

Bear made a flourish of entries and handed the pen to Jack. When Malaika added her details, the manager craned his neck over the book, then clapped his hands again. 'Bags! *Twende!*'

A sleepy-looking man wearing shiny black trousers and a *Harrambe!* tee-shirt appeared from the garden. The manager thrust Bear's backpack into his hands and jabbed the key at him. 'If you would follow Juba, sir,' he said to Bear with a slight bow, 'he will show you to your *banda*.'

'See you guys at the bar. Okay?' Bear said.

'Okay,' Jack said. 'Later. Better give us an hour.'

Jack's arm slipped nonchalantly around Malaika's waist as he waited for their key. She felt the manager's eyes on her, but when she shot a glance in his direction he looked away, making a fuss with a collection of keys. He gave them his manager's smile and said, 'Ah yes, *banda* number twenty-two. Please follow me, sir, madam.' He picked up Malaika's bag and strode purposefully through the dining area and down the path through the garden.

By the time they had reached the path, the manager was out of sight beyond the diphenbacia, fan palms, ferns and flowering shrubs. But a moment later they came upon him, his broad smile awaiting them at the first bend. He marched on as they approached. 'I'm sure you'll have all the privacy that you could possibly want in your *banda*,' he said over his shoulder with a grin. Malaika wondered if she was becoming overly sensitive, or if the comment could indeed be taken two ways. She kept it to herself.

Paths sprouted to the right and left, then the garden receded and in its place was long grass, dotted here and there with spindly scrub. 'As you can see, wonderfully secluded.'

'Remote comes to mind,' Jack murmured from behind Malaika. 'Any uninvited guests?' he said for the manager's hearing.

'You mean animals, sir? Oh, no. Baboons of course. Such a nuisance. Elephants sometimes wander in. But nothing serious.'

'I think we'll need a compass to get back here tonight,' Jack said to Malaika as he lifted a low-hanging branch for her to pass.

'Nothing to worry about, sir,' the manager continued. 'We have an *askari*, a local Maasai man, who will bring you to your *banda* after dinner. Just in case.' He threw a deferential smile back at Malaika. 'The young lady will tell you what excellent warriors and *askaris* they are.'

She gave him one of the looks she used on people who stared when she and Jack entered restaurants. The manager seemed not to notice and, when they finally reached the *banda*'s thatched porch, bid them a pleasant stay.

Jack unlocked the thin door. It was a simple freestanding hut with split bamboo wall linings and a *makuti* roof. The floor had a woven grass mat inside the door and another between the single beds. A kerosene lantern sat on each rough bedside table. The toilet and shower were in a small annexe at the rear. In spite of its basic appearances, Malaika noticed that everything was spotlessly clean.

'What do you think?' Jack said as Malaika kicked off her sneakers.

'If it has a hot shower, I love it!'

Minutes later she disappeared into the bathroom and moaned with pleasure as the hot water washed off the dust of the day. When she emerged from the shower room wrapped in a large pink towel, a cloud of steam surrounded her. She applied moisturiser from a dab in the cup of her hand, enjoying the cool feeling against her warm skin.

Jack sat in a director's chair at the open door, watching her. He had his hands clasped comfortably behind his head, his feet propped on the porch rail. Beyond him, the savannah drifted to the mauve hills on the horizon.

'What are you grinning at?' she said with a shy smile, her hand on the knot of towel at her breasts.

'I was just wondering if you're aware of it.' He lowered his feet from the rail and leaned forward in his chair.

'Aware of what?'

'That you hum one of those quiet songs of yours whenever you're doing some little thing or other, like just now, rubbing on your cream. Or making a coffee. Stuff like that.'

'Do I?' She smiled. 'I don't really think about it.' She lifted her braids and slipped a hand under them, shaking water droplets to the bamboo flooring. 'What was the song?'

'I don't know. Something African, I reckon.'

'Just a silly habit. From the look on your face, I thought it might have been something important.'

'Actually, now that you come to mention it, it was.' He stepped into the hut and pulled the screen door behind him.

'Oh?'

'Yes,' he said, moving towards her from the doorway, 'it

was a vision of Africa.' He kissed her gently, folding her and the towel within his arms. 'No, an African princess.'

'Jack. Sometimes you can be so sweet.' She returned his kiss.

'What do you mean, *sometimes*?' He loosened his embrace and planted a kiss on her nose. 'I think I'm sweet often.' Another peck. 'Always.' He found her lips again and kissed her tenderly.

When she put her arms around his neck, she let the towel drop to the floor. The feeling of release swept over her again and she let herself float off with it. Jack had been able to create that sensation since the first night, when he took control on the dance floor. It was such a heady feeling, one in which she could indulge without anyone knowing, not even Jack. She couldn't remember a time when she'd felt she could just let go like this without putting herself at risk. Jack was ... Jack made her feel safe.

He spread his fingers as he gently traced down the line of her ribcage to her hips. Like a sculptor forming the curves of a woman in warm clay, his thumbs slipped softly into the valley where her legs met the gentle curve of her belly. Then they moved up, leaving exquisite, aching ripples behind them, until they brushed her breasts. He let his thumbs torment her as he ran his tongue along the line of her ear lobe and down, allowing the slightly abrasive edge of his stubble to brush the hollow between her neck and shoulder. When she couldn't stand it any more she stepped back to the bunk bed, pulling him with her.

He slipped down his shorts and briefs and pulled his shirt over his head. As he struggled with his joggers, she again enjoyed the whiteness, no, the *two-tonedness* of his skin. She still found it an intriguing pattern. Tanned, muscular arms and legs, but on his buttocks and torso the skin was fairer. The division was like a shade line at the edge of the jungle, where it meets a sandy beach.

Body hair was another fascination. The tangle of his chest hair darkened as it speared down his abdomen to his *mboro*, where it seemed to point in an exclamation at the size of him.

When he was naked, standing over her at the bedside, she pulled him to her, impatient to feel him inside her.

IN THE HALF-LIGHT OF DUSK, Jack lay beside Malaika on the narrow bed and gently stroked her neck at that part where the tiny tight curls began. He felt a peculiar intimacy in this. Maybe it was because only he knew that those little curls were there, hidden from the world as they were, behind the long braids.

He stroked her neck for a long time, letting his mind wander away from the *banda*, up the path, beyond the lodge, into the immeasurable vastness of Africa. A continent with no bounds. That, he thought, was the essence of its beauty. Not the picture-postcard beauty of Europe, or the splendour of America. But a land able to command attention by its awesome, limitless space. Nothing constrained Jack's visceral flight across the continent. Its vastness reminded him of Australia, but Africa had an added dimension. It was exciting. Dangerous. He stroked Malaika's neck absent-mindedly. Exotic.

He was miles away, flying effortlessly over the wide brown savannah, when she whispered, 'Jack?'

'Hmm?' Her question took him by surprise; he'd thought she was asleep.

'What are you thinking?' Her voice was soft in the late-afternoon hush.

'Thinking? I'm not sure I was thinking anything at all.' He paused, trying to retrace his flight path over the savannah. 'Maybe taking a reality check.'

'What do you mean?'

'Well, here I am, a boy from the bush, a long way from home, and in bed with a beautiful black woman. That's got to give pause for consideration ...'

'Hmm,' she said, preoccupied with her thoughts. Her hand had slipped up his arm and across his shoulder to his cheek, where her fingernails stroked his jaw line.

'What about you? What are you thinking?'

She made a small sighing sound. 'I'm thinking about all this.'

'All this?'

'Yes, you know. You and me. The zebra couple. And I'm thinking, how do I feel about it?' She put a finger over his lips. 'I mean, look at you. You're so ... so white!'

'Not only beautiful — observant too!'

'And I'm so ... Well, I don't know what I am. Different, is what I am.'

'I don't understand.'

'You and me. We're so different. This isn't a good country to be like us. So different. Maybe it's the same everywhere. What about Australia? Would we look a bit strange in Australia?'

Jack had a vision of them queuing for the Sunday, all-you-can-eat carvery lunch at a typical RSL club, or the seafood buffet at a Leagues club. 'Yeah, probably.'

'It's not polite, you know. These people have no shame. You must have seen them, Jack. All those people out there who stare, who whisper, who look back when we pass. You know, those people.'

'Oh yeah, those people. I've seen them all right.'

'Don't they worry you?'

'Not really. Mostly I feel pretty good about being seen with you. Yeah, we get the stares. But usually it makes me feel kinda good. Like I'm walking into a restaurant with a movie star.'

'It doesn't make me feel good, that's for sure.' She ran her fingers through the hair on his chest. 'Maybe it's the same wherever you go. I only met one zebra couple before. They came to AmericAid for a short-term project. They were from America and they were always having problems. She was white. He was the black. She said she thought that's what made it worse. The white guys looked at her like she was a traitor. Some picked fights with her husband.'

'Is that how you feel? A traitor?'

'No! But it makes me mad. I think it's nobody's business. You know what I mean?'

'You have nothing to feel guilty about. You're proud to be Maasai, and that's great.'

'Proud? No, I'm not proud. Or unproud. Is that a word?'

'You aren't? Somehow I got the impression you were really proud of it.'

'Why?'

'I don't know. Maybe it was that night we met at Carnivore. I remember you said you were an African Princess and I said something really dumb like, *Not the Queen of Sheba* and you said, *No, Maasai.* I thought that was pretty cool, being proud of your culture like that.'

'Is that what you thought? Proud of being a Maasai? That's funny! I probably said it to get rid of you.' She gave him a kiss on his chest. 'Jack, when you've been in Kenya for a little longer, you will understand that being Maasai is nothing to be proud of.' She sat up and rummaged through her travel bag on the other bed. She pulled on a tee-shirt.

'I would have thought, all the tradition the Maasai have —'

'Tradition? What can tradition do for people who can't feed themselves? That's something for educated people. The Maasai have so many cattle. But can they sell one for school fees? Oh, no! Stuck in the old ways. Them and their *fucking* cattle! Excuse me. I just get *so* mad with it all.' She stood, grabbed a pair of panties from her bag and stepped into them. 'Their stories, their folklore. They believe that when God created cattle He gave them to the Maasai. All of them!'

'Well, what's wrong with that? Many cultures have their own peculiar view of the universe. Look at the west. We think we're born to rule.'

'Yeah, well in the Maasai universe, if someone else has a cow, it means it was stolen or lost from a Maasai herd. Either way, they take it back. What do you think of that?'

Jack smiled in spite of her annoyance. 'Um ... convenient?'

'Really, Jack!' she said in exasperation.

'Isn't anybody trying to educate them? What about the leaders — what do you call them — the elders? Can't they fix those kinds of things?'

'Oh, they could fix it if they cared. But the Maasai leaders are another story.' She plopped onto the bunk bed opposite. 'Maasai politicians, for instance — they're a joke.' She slapped her hands to her knees. 'One of them tried to pass a law to make the Maasai wear trousers. Can you imagine that?' She shook her head. 'I can't remember his name — it was a few years ago. Ai! Well, after everybody had a good long laugh at the idea, he dropped it.' She stood, pulling on a pair of shorts then sat again. 'So you see? Even the Maasai leaders are embarrassed by the Maasai.'

'I shouldn't be trying to defend them or condemn them,' Jack said, reaching across to stroke her arm. 'You're the Maasai here.'

'Not any more,' Malaika said with a dismissive shake of her head. 'Not any more.'

BEAR SHIFTED DOWN A GEAR as the Land Rover struggled up the dirt road and drew to a halt on a grassy slope beneath an acacia tree. To the west and north a long black smudge inscribed the grey grassland. Through binoculars Jack could see that the smudge was a moving mass of animals whose leaders were now climbing the rise towards them. The acacia, with its spindly limbs and flattened foliage, stood like a scarecrow, trying vainly to stop the herd that surged over the ridge, around them, and down the far side.

'Jack — there,' Malaika said, putting her cheek next to his to draw his line of sight to hers. 'Over the hill there. Can you see?'

Bear had noticed the same circling line of vultures and shifted into gear.

Five minutes later, the Land Rover rolled into a shallow valley. Six lion cubs were defending the remains of a wildebeest carcass from an ominous press of vultures hopping between the grass clumps like grotesque marionettes. The noise of the approaching Land Rover shied the scavengers to the edges of the kill site. Mortal combat in the grey pre-dawn had flattened the grass surrounding the kill. The six cubs, no more than knee-high, noted the approaching Land Rover with mild interest then returned to the scrappy remains.

'Look over there!' Bear pointed to the line of thorn bush two hundred paces away. A male lion and three lionesses dozed in the shade.

'And there,' Jack said. Three more, with adolescent manes, were lazily teasing at a ragged haunch on the side of the track. Malaika gave Jack's hand a squeeze.

The pride, of about fifteen lions and six cubs, was scattered around the wildebeest kill. The adults had eaten first and were now content to retire for a nap; the adolescents were nearby and playful enough to indulge in some lazy wrestling and half-hearted swipes at their siblings. Only the cubs were hungry and at the kill, but they were barely holding ground against the brazen scavengers.

Jack scrambled into the back of the Land Rover and climbed through the roof hatch. He let his legs dangle into the cabin as he fiddled with the video zoom lens.

'I'm goin' over to the big fellas in the bushes,' Bear said as he eased the four-wheel drive off the track. 'Hold tight up there.'

The Land Rover pressed through tall yellow grass at little more than walking pace. Jack let the camera run, trying to keep the bouncing viewfinder on the far edge of the clearing where an imposing black-maned lion was blinking in the half-stupor of a full belly.

The car's left rear side dropped with a jolt. The camera flipped from his grasp and slid along the roof until it hit an old roof-rack fixture. The lens cap caught on one of the thumbscrews. He instinctively lunged for the camera as Bear gunned the motor. The jolt threw Jack backwards out of the hatch, his fingers desperately grasping for anything to stop his slide. Another roar of the Land Rover, another upward leap, and he was thrown over the edge, catching the spare wheel in the ribs. Winded by the blow, he could barely muster a breath and his protest went unnoticed.

Inside the cabin, Bear was rapidly losing his temper as he revved the big diesel and slipped the clutch. The old Land Rover rocked and bucked as Bear crunched between forward and reverse gears. Jack rolled clear, but not far enough to avoid a peppering of dirt and stones from the spinning tyre. Burning rubber billowed from the hole that had swallowed half the rear wheel and the acrid smoke filled his lungs.

A piercing scream ripped through the noise of motor and roaring rubber. Jack felt a powerful blow to his shoulder. He was flat in the dust, a young wart hog in his lap. It bolted with a squeal. Another wheel-spin and a second small wart hog flew past, this time narrowly missing his head. With each rev of the motor, a football-sized wart hog was ejected like a shelled pea. High-pitched squeals followed as wart hogs ran for cover in all directions.

At last the hole was large enough for the Land Rover to gain purchase at the bottom of the burrow. It leapt up and out of the hole in a bound, leaving Jack in the dirt. He scrambled to his feet and stumbled after it but fell into the plundered wart hog hole. The roar of the diesel faded somewhere on the other side of the dust cloud. Jack stood in the hole and muttered an obscenity.

Lions! He had forgotten them!

The black-mane came charging through the knee-high grass. Jack gasped and leapt backwards but, with his legs still in the hole, he flopped onto his backside at its edge and scuttled on hands and buttocks like a deformed crab. A strangled cry escaped him.

Obscured in the grass, the lion's fleeing quarry made a broadside slide, a whisker out of reach of a vicious swipe. The lion went down in the dirt as he tried to take the turn. Both he and the wart hog disappeared in an explosion of dust, not twenty paces from Jack, still on the seat of his pants in the dirt.

A moment later the shrieking animal reappeared, dashing towards a couple of adolescents that had trotted behind the chase. They sat back on their haunches, ears pricked, as the terrified wart hog bolted towards them. It sighted the young lions too late and tried to spin away. One pounced. Two huge paws pinned it to the ground.

Within Jack's circle of thorn bushes were about ten lions of various sizes, snarling and charging at a converging circle of wart hog misery. He was transfixed at its centre.

He didn't see her jump from the Land Rover, but when Malaika grabbed his arm he shot to his feet like a startled gazelle. They ran to the Land Rover. He pushed her inside, then slammed the door behind them.

The cabin filled with dust and Bear's roar of laughter. For a moment Jack gaped in amazement at the big man who laughed even more at his expression. He slapped Jack on the leg. 'Hey, buddy! Welcome to the *real* Africa!' Tears filled his eyes and rolled into his greying beard. Each time he looked at Jack his booming laughter began anew.

Jack commenced to smile, then laugh. Finally he let out a loud whoop of exhilaration.

Smiling her relief, Malaika threw two arms around him, kissing and blessing him with every English and Swahili invocation she could recall.

JACK CAME FROM THE SOUVENIR shop with three bottles of Coke. Malaika's browsing was cut short by an impatient Bear, who made it known they would probably be back at the bar for sundowners if they didn't dally too long.

Twenty minutes later, they passed a signpost saying twenty-five kilometres to the Sekanani gate. Cottars Camp was ten kilometres beyond it. The conversation had petered out. Jack rested his elbow on the window ledge, his head propped on his open hand. It had been a tiring day for all of them. Heat and dust and pummelled by endless rough roads.

Malaika's tiredness had another edge. She had been struggling with a mounting tension ever since they entered the wide savannah of the Masai Mara. Like the constant dripping of water on a stone, the familiar sameness eroded the capsule containing the part of her life that she dare not recall. On the savannah, every acacia tree looked familiar. Every hill and ridge promised to reveal a hidden story. Hour after hour the landscape, increasingly and persistently evocative, took her back. Memories that had no place in her life crept into her consciousness and probed at the tender parts of her mind. They were of a long-ago time, in an alien world.

Malaika noticed a movement on a distant hill. A flash of reflected sunlight. And a shape, moving steadily through the sparse vegetation. The shape disappeared as the Land Rover skirted another ridge. Minutes later she could see it again more clearly. It was a man, running with a spear and shield.

He was wearing red. She noticed two others about half a mile behind the first. She said nothing. But she wondered about the three *moran*. Why would they be running so purposefully through the bush? Such a strange people.

CHAPTER 23

PEABODY'S GUIDE TO EAST AFRICA (5TH ED):
Many scholars believe that the Maasai are descended from
Mark Antony's lost battalion. The military phalanx of the
Maasai, with its locked shields and broad-edged *simi* and
spears, does have some resemblance to that employed by
the soldiers of ancient Rome in the millennium before the
Maasai emigrated from the forests of the Nile. And, like
the phalanx of their Roman predecessors, the Maasai's
wall of shield and steel is only as strong as its weakest link.
Total commitment to the warrior brotherhood is the key
to their success in battle.

The red demon of pain stabbed at Kireko's heel and grew
quickly at the edge of his vision. He denied the demon the
attention it demanded, for he would not be distracted from
running until he reached the heights of the hill ahead of him
— the goal he had set before allowing himself to rest. Instead,
he would summon the *motonyi* bird from its roost.

His imaginary sycamore tree was large and its strong
boughs appealing to the beautiful bird. He whistled the song
the *motonyi* bird so much admired and it appeared in the
sycamore's topmost branches. There it displayed all the
radiant colours of its plumage — stretching its flamboyant
wings and spreading its broad tail. When he called it, the

motonyi glided to him and threaded its long curved claws into Kireko's braided hair. Its gold and red tail feathers formed a cloak for his shoulders and back. Now settled, the bird folded its pale blue flight feathers across Kireko's face, lightly covering his eyes. The pain quickly subsided.

How many times had he blessed his great-grandmother for this cherished gift? The gift of the *motonyi* — her secret spell to dispossess the red demon of pain. The old woman knew the magic.

The *motonyi* also kept his mind from his thirst. Although dripping with sweat, he was not in need of rest. Many times he had run from sunrise to sunset with others of his age-set, in the make-believe children's world that traditionally would have prepared them for a swift strike against an enemy. How he regretted they remained just pointless games.

He reached the hilltop before the sun stood overhead. He slowed to a walk then sat in a cluster of large boulders to examine his foot. The thorn had attached his sandal to his heel. With the *simi*'s edge against the thick butt of the thorn, and his thumb forming the other side of a pincer, he slowly drew it out. The trickle of blood stopped after he pressed a pinch of red earth to it. Only then did he allow the *motonyi* bird to return to its roost in the back of his mind. He bid it safe passage.

Pray to Ngai,
That on your journey,
You accost only things that are safe,
And meet none but blind people.

He sipped water from his shoulder flask, his back in the cool embrace of the boulder, and searched the hillside in the direction his friends would come. He smiled, knowing his age-set brothers would be shy for the *wazungu* to see the manhood beneath their brief *shuka*. So they would take the difficult path through the valleys. At least their shyness did not cause them to favour the longer garment worn by many *moran* these days. It was a pity, but in the old days they would not be so foolish as to wear such a cumbersome garment. No. It was life itself to be free to sweep the *simi* from its scabbard or to lay hand quickly on spear and shield. To be quick was to survive. Like the poetry of the elders, the *moran* must find balance but be unbounded.

Although the family connections were remote, he and his friends were brothers in every other sense. As young boys in the *enkang*, they had played their children's games while their mothers threaded beads or cured hides. They had run through the *enkang*, oblivious to the filth and stench of cattle dung, imagining they were brave *moran*. When it was time to shoulder the responsibilities of herding the lambs and kids, they did so together, pretending they guarded the herds of cattle that would one day make them wealthy elders. The triumph on the day of their circumcision ceremony, and the coming of manhood, was both solemn and joyous. And shared. How they made the young girls run as they shot padded arrows at them for ransoms of honey and milk. They practised the art of warfare side by side. They learned how to anticipate each other's reactions to a feint or charge. Tradition demanded that the *moran* never eat or travel alone for the *laibon* said, *No matter how brave a man is, two brave men are better*. And Kireko, Noah and Shokeri would not travel without at least one of the others for companionship. Their age-set bond was for life. They would live and die as members of the one social stratum, advancing together from boyhood to *moran*, from *moran* to junior elder to senior elder, and beyond. But for now they were the *moran*, the warriors, and their bond, forged in the knowledge that survival relied upon the courage and dependability of their age-set brothers, was absolute.

In a few minutes his friends trotted into view. '*Sopa*,' he said in greeting.

'*Hepa*,' they replied breathlessly as they entered the circle of rocks.

'So, you have taken the easy path and still you are far behind me.'

'Ai! Kireko,' said Shokeri, 'how can you say that? We ran in the bush and creek beds all the way.'

'You did? Why would you do a foolish thing like that?' Kireko said, expressionless.

Shokeri looked at him and, grinning widely, threw a small stone at his leg. 'It's all very well for you to go about showing that big thing of yours to the *wazungu*.'

'He has not yet found a woman who will have him after *eunoto*,' added Noah with a laugh, 'but he waves his cattle prod in the air like a herd boy.'

IT WAS AN HOUR LATER, but it would be several more before the sun would run its long golden fingers over the surrounding hills, when Kireko whistled his friends to a halt. In the cloudless northern sky, over a hill strewn with large boulders, a squadron of vultures was in a slow, spiralling descent.

A slight breeze played against their faces as they cautiously stole up the face of the rocky ridge. Below them was a fresh kill, a full-grown buffalo cow. Five hyenas approached to claim the carcass as the vultures circled. The ever-patient jackals, with nervous heads darting in every direction, were now banished to the sidelines. The hyenas, ill-tempered as usual, were squabbling amongst themselves for precedence at the feast.

A male lion lunged from the far side of a boulder, scattering the cackling hyenas in all directions. The three *moran* nodded at each other, pleased with their unexpected good luck.

Shokeri said, 'Here is a gift from *Ngai*, Kireko. For your *eunoto*. Not a glorious raid, but a glorious kill perhaps.'

They waited ten minutes. Kireko whispered, 'Yes, he is a lone bachelor. Young, but with a mane to make a fine *olawaru*.'

They made their plans. Kireko would skirt the ridge and approach the lion from the downwind flank. Noah and Shokeri would keep the lion's attention from the opposite side and allow Kireko to find the mark with his spear. They moved downhill through jagged rocks split by the eternal cycle of equatorial sun and cold nights.

The *moran* separated. Kireko followed the ridgeline then crept down through the scattered brush and rocks to the far side of the kill. When he was well advanced, Shokeri and Noah moved forward, keeping about thirty paces apart.

The lion was harassed from all sides by the five hyena. He had not yet gained the confidence that full maturity would bestow, and showed it by licking his jaws in agitation as the hyena stole ground. Periodically he would make a short charge at them. They would whoop and scamper off, their sloping hindquarters a hair's breadth from the slashing claws.

Kireko was in a good position behind a small shrub. He noted the lion's agitation with some satisfaction. The omens were good. If the hyena could keep the lion off-guard for a few more minutes, Shokeri and Noah would be in place.

He waited patiently and closed out all thoughts except for the lion. The sun's heat, the chattering bul buls and chirping flycatchers, darting swallows, the incessant buzz of flies, were all gone. He desired to see deep into the lion's yellow-green eyes — to know what he knew, to see what he could see. He wanted to own his lion's life before he stole it from him.

He remembered the dead eyes of his cousin's lion, many years ago. They were full of hate, or perhaps outrage at the indignity of death dealt by mere man. He could see it lying dead, massively dead, in the caked mud beside the water hole, his cousin's broken spear haft in its ribs. Flies had worried its frozen ice-green eyes. Kireko had brushed them away and earned a derisive laugh from his cousin's age-mates.

But this lion was his, and it was fiercely and powerfully alive.

Kireko knew that he or the lion would soon be dead. He prepared himself, carefully lowering his eight-foot-long spear to the grass beside him. His shield was at his left hand. He was ready. It would be perfect. The lion's beautiful brown mane would make a splendid *olawaru* headdress that the girls would honour with a new song at the *eunoto*.

But he pushed such thoughts away and willed his mind into the brain of this, *his* lion. He understood his aggression, felt it rise in his chest as if it were his own. His muscles twitched with each swipe at his tormentors. His heart surged and rushed at the immensity of his frustration. The insolence of the hyena! How they enraged him!

Kireko sensed a movement on the high rock ledge across the clearing. It was only a tail-flick, but he caught it out of the corner of his eye. A moment later the lioness trotted quickly across the ledge in a crouch, her eyes on Shokeri, not twenty paces from her. Noah hadn't seen her either — his eyes fixed on the male lion at the kill. Kireko knew that with the sun at her back, neither would see the lioness until it was too late.

He leapt from his hide with raised spear. 'No-o-o-o-o!' he roared.

The hyenas whooped in alarm. The jackals bolted. Vultures leapt to the air. The male lion spun about to see Kireko rushing towards his kill. At that same moment the lioness launched herself at Shokeri.

Kireko vaulted a stunted shrub at the clearing's edge and launched his spear at the lioness. It was a fraction high and glanced off her shoulder bone. She was onto Shokeri, who was slow with his shield. A vicious swipe of the lioness's massive paw tore down his right side. His spear arm dropped to a sickening angle.

The male lion charged across the clearing at Kireko. Noah, who had sensed the male's reaction, stood and launched his spear in a single motion. It hit the lion in mid-stride, piercing the soft flank revealed by its extended hind leg. The lion snarled in anger and faltered in its leap, but its five hundred pound momentum carried it on, smashing into Kireko and knocking him to the ground. Animal and warrior were lost in a flurry of dust. Kireko, under the lion as it rolled to its feet, grabbed for his scabbard and released the brutal *simi*. He felt the sensuous slice of steel in muscle as it plunged into the lion's side. The lion gave a loud gasp as lung and heart were pierced and it collapsed onto Kireko like a fallen tree. Its head lay in the dust beside him and its large pink tongue rolled out of its cavernous jaws, twitching in a froth of saliva and blood. He stared at the lolling tongue for a moment, but it was the eyes — yellow-green behind twitching lids — that made his heart leap. For a brief moment he feared the lion was not truly dead.

'*Shokeri!*' Noah's cry triggered instant awareness. The lioness! She was shaking Shokeri's body like a jackal with a scrap. Kireko pushed the fallen lion from his legs and began to scramble and stumble across the clearing.

Noah flung his short heavy club at the lioness, hitting her flush on the ear. She sprang from Shokeri with a grunt, dropping his limp body to the bloodied earth before bounding up the ridge. Noah threw his *simi* after her with a roar of utter rage. It clattered off the rocks. He fell to the ground behind Shokeri and dragged his friend into his lap. 'No! Oh, my brother. No,' he sobbed. With arms wrapped around Shokeri's abdomen, he spread his fingers to hold in the mass of entrails which threatened to spill from the torn body. He cradled him against his chest, rocking him, weeping, 'Oh, my brother ... my brother ...'

Kireko dropped to his knees at their side, trying to engage the life force behind Shokeri's eyes. Blood saturated his *shuka*, turning the dry dust around him into a rich red mud.

With a blow as great as that of the charging lion, Kireko realised that his brother was dying. He had never felt so powerless — so useless in a crisis. He cradled Shokeri's face in his two hands, willing him, begging him to live, but felt him shudder, releasing the tension in his convulsing body. He was still.

When Kireko saw the fire in Shokeri's eyes die, his cry, a wild moan of anger and despair, filled the valley.

Noah had not released his hold on his brother's body, but continued to cling to him and rock back and forth, weeping. Kireko gripped Noah's shoulder with a bloodied hand. Noah turned tear-filled eyes to him. His voice, when it struggled from his constricted throat, was a laboured, strangled sound. 'I could not save him, Kireko,' he said. 'I could not do what had to be done. It was too much.'

Kireko knew Noah was right. He could not have done more than he did, one thing at a time. He retraced the events leading to the tragedy, trying to find the flaw in the strategy. The diversion plan had been used for many successful lion hunts. His grandfather's uncle, Marefu, had used it on the Laikipia Plains to secure his *olawaru*, and with it the hand of his sweetheart when he proudly wore it at his *eunoto* ceremony. And there had been a cousin who had also used a diversion with equal success.

But this was Kireko's lion and his responsibility. When the

lion and his lioness made separate but simultaneous attacks, one thing at a time was never going to be enough. And although Noah had done each perfectly, one at a time, a death was inevitable.

'I could not help both of you. My arm was slow,' Noah moaned.

'No one could have done more. And our brother died bravely. We must thank *Ngai* for giving him such a glorious death. There is no finer way to end a warrior's life.'

Kireko tried to lift the body from Noah but fell to one knee with a gasp. The six-inch slash to his right thigh exposed pink muscle, but was a clean cut and the bleeding was light. Noah slowly lifted Kireko's fingers from where he clutched them at his midriff. Blood ran from a long ragged tear and dripped from Kireko's *shuka*.

As was the custom, they arranged Shokeri's body for the arrival of the carnivores that would take him from this world to the next. They placed his spear and shield at his side, his *simi* in his bloodied hand.

'Come, Kireko, now we must get some help for you. I will be your right leg for this journey.'

'Thank you, my brother.' Kireko straightened up, fighting the stab of pain in his gut. 'But I will first take my *olawaru* from my lion.'

AT THE WATER HOLE, NOAH lowered his friend onto a log. He looked to the sun, which was midway in its slide to the west, then walked to the water's edge. The many tracks in the mud told the story of the day. Perhaps less than an hour ago, buffalo drank here. Eight, including two calves, which were the last to drink. Elephant came in the early morning. Baboons, probably with the elephants. And there, the tracks of three, no four, hyena. One had an injured hind leg.

Noah filled the *calabash* and returned to Kireko whose spirit seemed to be drifting in and out of his body. He was worried. Kireko had lost much blood.

'The bleeding has slowed but you look tired,' Noah said, handing him the water flask. He squatted on his heels at

Kireko's side, watching him trickle the water across his lower lip. Not a drop was lost.

'I saw an *enkang* in our outward travel this morning,' Noah continued. 'It is not more than two hours west. We will reach it before sunset.'

Kireko's eyes remained distant and unfocused.

'I will leave you there,' Noah jutted his jaw towards a nearby *kopje*, 'where the rocks give safety, and I will go alone for help. It will be quicker.'

Kireko's spirit returned to his eyes. 'No, brother. We will go to the *enkang* together. I am rested.'

'As you wish. But we should move from here now. The hyena will taste your blood-scent and we will have more trouble on our hands.'

Kireko nodded and let Noah pull him to his feet.

THE *ENKANG* WAS SETTLED IN a shallow valley, the thorn-bush *boma* surrounding perhaps fifteen low dung-covered huts. The children had already returned the goats and sheep to it. The older herd boys were now bringing the cattle into the middle of the *enkang*, safe from the predators of the night. A line of women, with large bundles of wood strapped to their backs, was filing through the gate.

At the *boma* entrance they were met by a junior *morani*. '*Sopa*,' he said, 'I am Elias, of the Yellow Grass age-set.'

They returned his greeting. 'I am Noah and this is Kireko of the Spotted Calf age-set of the Aiser clan.'

Noah explained what had happened.

'I am sad to hear of the death of your brother,' said Elias. 'Thank *Ngai* your lion was not too fast. But he has given you a bloody reminder of your battle, my friend.'

'He was fast, cousin,' said Kireko, 'but also, sadly for him, quite stupid to think he could take a *morani* of the Aiser clan.'

'Oh, so?' Elias replied with a smile. 'Well, he may be stupid but he was not blind. He could see that you were not one of the Purko, for he would have run so fast even a strong Purko spear arm would not catch him.'

'Please, enough, Elias,' said Noah. 'Let us get him into your *enkang.* He needs food and rest. And, if you would be so kind, we need to see your *laibon.*'

Elias, chastened by a twinge of conscience at his poor hospitality, bent to assist.

Kireko raised a hand. 'I thank you for your assistance, but leave me now. I would walk unaided into your *enkang.*'

Noah and Elias exchanged glances. Kireko gently shrugged them off, carefully drew himself to his full height, straightened the *simi* in its scabbard, and took a step.

He fainted before taking two paces towards the *enkang.*

KIREKO AWOKE WITH A GASP. The pain stabbed in his midriff and for a moment his head was an ostrich plume in the breeze, wafting in and out of the light shafts that speared through the gloom of the hut. He sent the silent *motonyi* call and soon the pain cloud cleared from his mind.

He fumbled his way to the entrance, pushed the hide covering aside and squinted into the golden morning. He saw Noah and four warriors wrestling a young heifer to a standstill. It struggled against the noose drawn tight around its neck. The *morani* standing to the side of the bull stepped close with his bow and, after taking a moment to aim, shot an arrow into the bulging jugular vein. When the blocked arrow was removed, another young warrior caught the blood in a gourd. The noose was withdrawn and the puncture pinched closed with a mixture of dirt and dung. The heifer was released and it ambled back to the herd.

Elias took the gourd and stirred the contents with a long twig to collect the blood filaments. He added milk then he and Noah walked towards the hut.

When he saw Kireko standing at the entrance, Noah's smile dropped. 'You should be resting, Kireko. Go inside, I will bring our friend's gourd to you.'

'I can share it here as easily. Better than inside like an old woman at her cooking hearth.'

Kireko sat on the stool at the entrance and felt a moment of light-headedness sweep over him. Noah helped him hold the heavy vessel and he drank deeply of the rich warm liquid.

Noah offered the *calabash* to his host, who politely declined, indicating that Noah should drink first.

A man wearing a *morani*'s *shuka* and many beaded necklaces approached. 'This is my half-brother, Tingisha,' Elias said.

Tingisha was tall even for a Maasai. He spiked his spear into the ground at the entrance to the hut and squatted on his heels amongst them. '*Sopa*,' he said.

They nodded their greetings.

'I hope your cattle are in a good mood.'

'Yes. And yours too, we pray,' said Noah.

'Your *enkang* and all your people. Are they also well?' the tall one asked.

'Very well. Yes. And yourself?'

'I am well.'

'That is good.'

Tingisha turned to Kireko. 'The Purko welcome our Aiser brothers and offer prayers to *Ngai* for your brother. I am sure he died bravely.'

Kireko thanked him. Noah nodded.

'My brother has informed me that your lion tried to deny you your *olawaru*.' He smiled, nodding at the mane at Kireko's feet.

Kireko grunted.

The pleasantries completed, Tingisha's expression turned more serious. 'Perhaps I should see your injuries?'

'I am sure your *laibon* or an elder can help me. It is nothing.'

'Tingisha is an elder of the Skilful Archers age-set,' Elias said, indicating the ceremonial club his half-brother had under his arm.

The two visitors exchanged glances. Noah was the first to speak. 'Tingisha, forgive my bad manners, but the Skilful Archers age-set are already junior elders, and your attire ...'

'Yes, you are correct, my friend.' He smiled at them. 'But I work at the tourist camp. They expect all the Maasai to be warriors. So I must dress like one.'

'Really?' Noah's eyes widened.

'Are you also the *laibon*?' Kireko asked.

Tingisha untied the blood-clotted *shuka*. 'No. We share our *laibon* with the Keekonyokie clan, near Narok.'

Noah was still unsure of Tingisha's status. 'But, Tingisha, my friend, it is surely embarrassing to dress below your rank?'

'It does not concern me at all, my friend. One thing that I learned in school was that there are many traditions in Kenya. The Maasai way is not the only way. Two of us work at Cottars Camp. More could do so, but they cannot read. Most do not speak English.'

'You can read? And speak English?'

'Yes. Elias, the cloth, dip it in the milk.'

'I see.' Noah felt increasingly uncomfortable.

Elias handed him the wet cotton pad. Tingisha began to gently swab the wound.

'So . . . you went to a government school?'

'Yes. We hated it. I can still feel the shame. I walked sixteen miles each day to that school. We left the *enkang* before dawn. Imagine, three young boys in the bush while the leopard hunted still. Of course, we had no shoes.'

Noah shook his head in sympathy.

'And our *shukas* were like nothing against the chill of the cold mornings. At school the other children laughed at us.' Tingisha gently dabbed at the torn edges of Kireko's abdomen. 'More cloth,' he demanded.

Elias tore a chunk from a piece of patterned red fabric.

'And the teachers? How were they?' Noah said, unable to control his fascination.

'They were very strict. They followed the government policy, you know. We had to leave our Maasai customs and traditions at home. They tried to make us farmers, I think.' He smiled, shaking his head in recollection. 'So many years now. But, near the end, I think I grew to like school. A little.'

'But you did not become a farmer!' Noah's horror overcame his good manners.

Tingisha ignored the inflection and continued to clean the wounds. 'Oh, no. Not me. But some of us Purko have done so. Particularly the poor. Those with too few cattle. It helps in the bad times.'

Noah shook his head in disbelief.

'The schooling almost stopped when the Mau Mau chased the British away. We went back to the old ways. My brothers and their children have had no education.' Tingisha was working quickly. He applied the coloured cotton wad to the wound then bound another piece around Kireko's waist to hold the wad in place. He sat back on his haunches with a deep frown and shook his head. 'We must get him to a doctor.' He looked up at Noah and Elias. 'I have nothing here for such a wound. The bleeding has almost stopped but it looks bad. He may have nicked the gut.'

He stood, towering over them all. 'He needs a doctor.'

Kireko said, 'I have no need of the *wazungu* medicine, cousin. But if you can stitch me, we will be away to Isuria for our *eunoto*.'

'Isuria is more than a day's journey. In your condition you may be dead for your own graduation ceremony.'

'Then bring your medicine man.'

'But this wound is not one for the *laibon*'s work with cow's sinew and sheep's fat. Anyway, he is on the other side of Narok. It is nearly as far as Isuria.' Tingisha sighed. 'I will ask the lodge manager to call a doctor.'

'No.' Kireko stood with difficulty. 'Noah and I will continue when I have rested. My great-grandmother will mend me.'

Tingisha raised his eyebrows and turned to Noah for explanation.

'His great-grandmother is a venerable elder.'

Tingisha shook his head in resignation. 'As you wish, cousin. But let me try to find transport for you.'

'Thank you,' said Noah. 'But that will be truly difficult for you.'

'It is an emergency. Once, at Cottars Camp, the manager let us use his minibus. He is a Kikuyu, but he is sometimes understanding.' He looked at Kireko. 'You should rest now.'

Kireko nodded then asked, 'Do you drive this minibus, cousin?'

'I do.'

'Good. I will take assistance from an elder of the Maasai, but no Kikuyu or *mzungu* will carry me injured to my *enkang*.'

Tingisha sighed. 'One so young and yet so set in the old ways.'

'When do you think we can leave for Isuria?' Noah asked.

'If I can get the minibus, we will go this evening. I don't like the look of your friend's injury. His great-grandmother … Well, she may be able to sew him up but I am worried about infection. You will not know for perhaps a day or so, but if it takes hold I doubt she could save his life.' He slung his water *calabash* over a shoulder. The long strands of beading clattered against the brittle gourd. 'But I must leave you, I am already late for Cottars Camp. Keep him to his bed and feed him the blood-milk. He will need all his strength for the journey tonight.'

He turned to go then took another look at Kireko, shaking his head. 'If the choice was mine, I would say take him to a doctor in Nairobi now.'

CHAPTER 24

PEABODY'S GUIDE TO EAST AFRICA (5TH ED):
Kenya's rainfall is essentially tropical, alternating between
periods of relatively dry weather to times when it rains, at
least briefly, every day.

With their customary precision, the British colonists
determined that the Short Rains fell in November and
the Long Rains between late March and June. The rains
may indeed come in those months, or earlier, or later, or
not at all.

In the transition from the dry to the long wet season,
storms can be dramatic, but are usually welcomed as they
bring to an end an uncomfortable period of high humidity.

The humidity made the walk to the breakfast table a task, but
seemed to accentuate the scent of the variegated shrubs and
trailing lianas heavy with hanging blossom. They festooned
both sides of the path. Malaika moved at a measured pace.
She was trying to conserve the fleeting freshness of her
morning shower, which she felt was doomed as the heat
gathered for an assault on the day. Jack followed, swishing a
makeshift fly swatter he had stripped from a shrub.

At a table in the garden dining area, Bear was seated like
royalty, buttering a slice of toast. He wore a fresh white *safari*
shirt and grey cotton slacks.

'Mornin', you guys. Coffee?' he asked, holding the pot over one of the empty cups.

'Not for me, I need a cold drink.' Jack grabbed a pitcher of mango juice from the adjacent serving table. 'Malaika?'

'Hmm, me too, please.' She sat and unfolded her napkin onto her lap.

'How come you look so fresh?' she asked Bear. His hair, which was normally a scattering of unruly loose ends, was combed and plastered flat on his balding head.

'Yeah, how come?' Jack added, handing a glass of juice to Malaika. 'I know! I bet he doesn't have a day's hike from his *banda*.'

'You got it. Just around the corner a spell. How'd you sleep? Hot, eh?'

'Damn right! Humidity. It's a killer.'

'Everybody's sayin' it'll rain in the next day or so,' Bear said, taking a sip of coffee.

'That'll be a relief.' Jack scanned the sky. The thunderclouds that had crept from the horizon each afternoon for days were gone again. 'Are you sure?'

'Me? Hell, no! But about this time every year people start sayin' it's gonna rain any day now. You know, kinda wishing it. *Hell! It's gotta rain soon.* But it doesn't. Me? I'd say give it another month. Maybe more.'

'And no pool,' Malaika lamented, not for the first time. 'Ai! Today I am looking for a cool place to read my book. What are you boys going to do?'

Jack looked at Bear. He shrugged. 'Good question.'

'What about a *safari*?' Malaika suggested.

'I've had enough of that dust bucket for quite a while,' Jack said.

'There's a notice at the desk saying there's a guided game walk every afternoon. They meet at the bar at three.'

'A walk? What do you think, big fella? Want to stare down some man-eaters?'

'I'm in.'

'Malaika?' Jack asked.

'Uh-uh. Too hot for me. But you crazy *wazungu* don't seem to mind.'

THEY ARRIVED AT THE BAR before three o'clock, Malaika with a book under her arm and the men with shoulder-slung cameras. The guide hadn't appeared by 3.15 p.m. and the group — there were four others — had drifted into pockets of small talk.

Stewart, an English journalist, said he was the training editor at one of Nairobi's daily newspapers. But it was obvious that his heart was in politics. He could barely wait to hear what Malaika, an honest-to-goodness local, thought about his newspaper's brave move into investigative journalism.

Jack was cornered by the journo's wife, a scatty American of about fifty with a shock of orange hair that was either a fashion statement or a mistake at the salon. Jack thought the latter. He also diagnosed her as suffering ex-pat wife syndrome: trapped in a world of tennis, bridge and the local amateur theatre. When she began to tell the story of the scandalous resignation of the president of the Friends of the National Museum, Jack excused himself to get another beer. By the time he returned, she had attached herself to Bear and the other couple. The man was mid-sixties, fat and balding. The blonde with him looked at least twenty years younger. Bear was in animated conversation and seemed particularly charming. Unusually so, thought Jack, and let him know it with a grin and a broad wink. Bear pointedly ignored him.

Jack joined Malaika and the journalist.

'But don't you think it's a good start?' the journalist was asking.

'Too little. Too late,' she answered.

'Oh, come, my dear, you're being a bit tough on us, aren't you? We're doing a damn sight better than *The Standard*.'

'*The Standard*'s owned by the government.' In response to Jack's puzzled look, she said, 'Stewart says the poaching is more government corruption —'

'Shh!' The journalist touched her arm. 'Sorry, my dear,' he said, looking around the bar area. 'It's just that, well, you can't be too careful. By the way, you aren't with the government, are you?' He put his palms to his face in mock horror. 'Just joking. Ha! Haaah!'

She smiled politely, and to humour him continued in a lower tone, 'And his newspaper, *The Nation*, is starting to report on them.'

'Oh, yeah,' Jack said, 'I think I read something recently in *The Nation* about poaching. You had a picture of Moi in the Nairobi National Park, setting fire to all that confiscated ivory.'

'Yes, that was us. Window-dressing by Moi. But *The Nation* is getting good support for our exposés. Particularly from the conservation groups. Overseas ones, of course.'

'Can't remember all the details,' Jack went on, tapping a finger against his lips. 'What was the gist of the story?'

'We say there's some funny business involved,' Stewart added. 'The President isn't giving enough support to his Director of National Parks, Richard Leakey.'

'But where's the connection?' Jack asked. 'Between the poachers and the government?'

The journalist looked over his shoulder again. Jack couldn't suppress his smile.

'Nicholas Onditi. The Minister for Lands.'

PEOPLE IN POWER DO STRANGE things at times, James Onditi said to himself as he drove the white government Range Rover through the ramshackle outskirts of Nanyuki. The canvas-covered truck was still in the rear-vision mirror, bumping along in his dust.

He was feeling pleased with himself. He'd got the truck through the checkpoint at Isiolo with ease. The bribe of five hundred shillings was no more than the price of dinner and a few beers. He would tell Mengoru it was a thousand and watch him splutter and moan. That was what got him thinking about people in power and their strange behaviour. Mengoru's obsession with small money, for instance.

And then there was President Moi, burning that huge pile of perfectly good ivory. What a waste, he thought and shook his head. Very strange. He and Mengoru didn't care. It made for higher prices. He smiled again.

That Mengoru, now there is a strange man. Always acting important. But he is just a Big Man in a very small village. And that thing with the Kidongi woman. *Haki ya Mungu!*

Ever since Mengoru overheard him mention the name Malaika Kidongi, the snotty-nosed bitch in AmericAid, he had been obsessed with finding out more about her. He should never have agreed to do it. In the beginning he'd thought it might be fun to get her into bed as part of his job, something of a perk of office, but he had failed. And worse, she had made him look stupid in front of Mengoru.

Mengoru ... Strange indeed.

Perhaps the strangest thing was the look in his eyes whenever Onditi reported on his daughter. Was it anger? Bitterness? It was hard to put a name to it. Vengeance was about the closest he could come to it.

His mind drifted back to Malaika and his jaw tightened at the memory of the night at Carnivore when she had rejected him and that *mzungu* had stuck his nose in. He'd never really cared for the Maasai girl but the bedding could have been fun. No matter, one day she would pay for her disrespect. Onditi suspected that it was not going to be pleasant for the girl when she finally renewed acquaintance with her long-lost father.

He began to tingle at the prospect of taking some part in it.

JAMES ONDITI STOPPED THE RANGE Rover outside the house above the village. Again, he was struck by the absurdity of it. Poised above the traditional Maasai village, it seemed to mock it with its pseudo-Nairobi styling and modern pretension.

'*Habari!*' Mengoru said, climbing down the steps from his porch.

'*Mzuri,*' James replied.

'Ah, you have it,' Mengoru said, looking at the canvas-covered truck below them in the village. 'Come, let me see.'

They walked down the hill to the *boma* opening. The three men squatting beside the truck stood as they approached. Mengoru barked an order and they folded back the rear canvas covering. The truck's tray was packed with shallow crates loosely loaded with ivory. Mengoru climbed up the workman's ladder and, holding one of the stays that supported the tarpaulin, grunted as he swung his leg over the tailgate.

He picked his way through the tusks, feeling some as he went. 'How many?' he asked Onditi.

'Twenty.'

'Tusks or elephant?' Mengoru ran his eyes again over the haul, knowing the answer before Onditi replied.

'Elephant.'

Forty tusks. Mengoru smiled to himself. Only a few of good size. He had never seen a prime pair. They were all cleaned out years ago, before he had made his start in the business. He estimated there was about half a ton of ivory in the truck. Ismail, his Somali supplier in Nairobi, would probably begin by demanding fifteen US a pound. Mengoru would make an offer of six. In the end they would agree on ten. Landed in Uganda he would get fifty. Then there was the litany of outgoings, starting from the top — the Minister.

Ismail was a thug and a thief, but he was the only poacher Mengoru knew who would extend some credit. He no doubt felt his risk was low, as it was well known he had castrated and blinded a small operator who could not pay his debt. Mengoru hated dealing with such scum, but with no capital it was the only way he could operate at the moment. With luck, he might clear enough to buy his own truck.

He continued to stroll amongst the haul. A taller crate was packed with rhino horn in the corner behind the cabin.

'Not much horn this time, ah?' he said to James, who was watching him from outside the truck.

'No, only about twenty pounds.'

Mengoru did the mental calculations, concealing his smile. 'Useless Somalis! You are too soft! Push them harder next time. Horn is the only good market these days.'

He climbed down and motioned with his head that James should follow him back to the house. When they were clear of the truck and had commenced their climb to the house, he said, 'No problems on the road?'

'No. Everything went smoothly.'

Mengoru cast a glance over his shoulder, although they were now well out of the hearing of the men. 'You will thank your Uncle Nicholas for the use of the truck, ah?'

'Yes. I go to his house when I get back to Nairobi this evening.'

'Good. And tell His Excellency I will arrange for his share to be deposited in the usual way.'

'I will.' James slowed his pace as Mengoru's breathing began to labour on the climb up the slope. 'And when will that be?'

'I will see to the loading …' Mengoru rested his hand on a knee. 'Loading the boat at Muhoro … day after tomorrow …' He resumed his climb. 'Monday … So you keep your eyes open in the valley … until Tuesday … I am in Entebbe by then.' He took a long pause, wheezing. Sweat rolled down his face and dripped from his chin. His eyes bulged with the exertion. James dared not smile or comment.

'So it will be in his account by the end of the month,' Mengoru said.

'He will be pleased.'

They had reached the top of the hill. The Range Rover sagged as Mengoru leaned on it, mopping his brow with a dirty white handkerchief. James waited for him to collect himself then asked, 'Anything else?'

'No. Oh, yes! On your way through the valley, make sure those useless police are on duty. I'm not paying for their tea if they're not on the job every day. Such a price they ask these days! I can't believe it. Oh, but thank your uncle very kindly for getting them for me. Now go. I will call you if you are needed.'

Onditi climbed into the cabin slowly shaking his head. Mengoru was such an old woman. He thinks I am a child in these matters. *Check the police station. Don't pay too much.* I could do it so much better. If only I could get to deal directly with the Arabs in Entebbe, I could do some real business.

CHAPTER 25

PEABODY'S GUIDE TO EAST AFRICA (5ᵀᴴ ED):
An elephant makes but a small hole in the jungle. (Maasai
proverb indicating that seemingly important events may in
time prove to be of little consequence.)

It was nearly four o'clock. Conversation around the bar quickly
dropped into silence when a giant of a man eased under the
doorjamb and ambled towards them like a giraffe moving
through an acacia forest. A swathe of red cloth swept like a toga
from shoulder to knees and many strands of colourful beads
criss-crossed his chest. The extended lobe of his right ear was
filled with a large wooden plug and beaded earrings looped
through the other. He carried a slender ebony club across his arm.

Jet-black eyes slowly scanned the tourists below him, pausing
very briefly on Malaika, then to them all he said, '*Jambo*. I am
Tingisha.' He had a deep voice. 'I am, eh … your Maasai guide
for walking.' He made an unconvincing attempt at an engaging
smile, revealing two missing bottom teeth. His frown returned
as his monotone continued. 'Today we walk, eh … near the
Masai Mara Game Reserve. The Masai Mara Game Reserve …
eh, has no boundary fence. We see all … eh, the animals … that
are inside the Masai Mara … but, eh, we be safe.' There was a
contrived pause for dramatic effect. 'If we are lucky.' He applied
the smile again.

A polite chuckle rippled through the group.

'While we walking I will answer, eh ... I will try to answer ... questions. Please follow me and keep, eh, close.' He turned and ambled out, dipping under the door again.

'Say a prayer to those African gods of yours, Malaika,' Jack said, as she walked with him to the car park. 'Bear's dangerous enough in the city. Imagine what he could do out there.'

'You'll be okay.'

Tingisha had turned, waiting for Jack to join them.

'You bet.' He kissed her nose. 'See you in a couple of hours.'

'Take care.' He waited but she didn't respond.

'I guess I know you pretty well these days.'

'Why do you say that?' she said, smiling.

''Cause now I know when you're blushing.'

She dropped her eyes for a moment. 'It's just, well, you know, the zebra couple stuff.' She indicated the group, now at the far edge of the car park.

'Does that mean I don't get a kiss for luck?'

She put her hand against his cheek. 'There. For luck.'

Jack caught her hand and squeezed it before joining the others at the beginning of the path.

Bear was chatting with the blonde and her husband, whose shirt was already stuck in dark khaki patches at the folds of flesh under his armpits and belly and where it touched his lumpy shoulders and back. Tingisha waited for them to bunch up, then set off at a moderate stride, an ancient shotgun in the crook of one arm. The journalist and his wife joined Jack behind him. Before a hundred yards had gone she had tried to engage the Maasai guide in conversation. His replies were brief but courteous.

'Tingisha, I have a question,' she said undaunted. 'Is that old shotgun good enough?'

He glanced down at her. 'We Maasai do not like guns,' he said, looking at the weapon with disgust.

'But I mean, if a lion comes, is it big enough?' She added a nervous giggle, looking back at her husband for reassurance.

'The lion will not come when I, eh, walk with you.'

Tingisha seemed to know the next question before she had a chance to ask it. 'The lion and the Maasai are born enemies. Eh ... they fear us. A lion will run from the *morani*. He will not fight him. If he does, eh, he will die.'

'Oh!' she said in a small voice and soon drifted towards the relative security of the middle of the group.

The sun was dropping lower in the afternoon sky, but with every step the heat seemed to rise on the small puffs of dust that danced at Jack's feet. He wiped his arm across his brow but a moment later the sweat began to trickle down his temples again. It fell in drops from his nose.

The walkers were forced into single file between tall stands of waving grass that lined the narrow track and, at times, cut their depth of vision to a matter of metres. The dusty path muffled their footfalls and the group eventually fell into a silence sympathetic to the intense stillness that surrounded them. Tension was mounting. Silence fed the nervousness. The hair on Jack's forearms became receptive to the slightest touch or puff of air. Behind him the redhead made little skipping steps to keep up. He caught a glimpse of Bear at the end of the column, darting sideways glances at any sound or movement.

Tingisha seemed oblivious to it all. He turned to Jack, now immediately behind him at the head of the line, and asked, 'So, your friend? She will not, eh, walk with you?'

'No. She's tired. Anyway, I'm sure she's seen it all before.'

'Yes. She is Maasai.'

The group emerged from a stretch of tall grass. Sporadic wildlife appeared. Tingisha began a desultory commentary. 'Wildebeest.' He pointed to half a dozen bony individuals staring at the tourists from a safe hundred metres. 'Masai giraffe,' he continued, barely glancing at the animals, keeping his eyes on the path ahead, his stride relentless.

The track wound through the grassland, which was interspersed with scattered spindly scrub. Grasshoppers sprang ahead of them from brittle grass hideouts. Large black beetles, with the aerodynamics of an outhouse, struggled into improbable flight.

Each time the group entered a clearing, they came upon more animals. 'Wart hog ... Burchell's zebra.' The names floated over Tingisha's shoulder like morsels tossed to a pack of following strays.

'...Thomson's gazelle.'

Strangled gasping sounds came from the blonde's husband, whose cheeks were the colours of molten metal.

Finally someone had the courage to ask to stop for a photograph. The Maasai patiently complied, but when the cameras were lowered he moved off without further ado. 'Impala ... Grant's gazelle ...'

Jack's video camera was stuck. He assumed that the fall from the Land Rover had something to do with it and gave up after a few minutes' fiddling with the battery and buttons. On the next photo stop, he joined Bear at the rear of the line. Bear was busy adjusting the focus of his zoom lens onto something like an antelope that was posing under the grotesque naked limbs of a baobab tree. 'There you are!' Jack whispered. 'I thought I'd lost you!'

'Huh?' Bear looked up from the viewfinder.

'Lost you to Helga the blonde German bombshell.'

'It's Inga. And she's Swedish. And don't try to be funny.' His eye went back to the camera and the antelope, still framed beneath the upside-down tree.

'Mate, I wouldn't dream of it.'

'Good.' The shutter snapped. The camera whirred. 'It's a neat walk, eh? What do you think of the *askari* dude?'

'Hmm. Tall. A man of few words.'

'Did you notice that black thing he's carrying?'

'You mean the old shotgun?'

'No, that short black club under his arm. I think it means he holds a special position.'

'You mean like, centre and leading goal shooter?'

'Jesus, Jack. How am I ever goin' to get some Africa into that dumb-ass brain of yours?'

The line moved on.

'...bat-eared fox.'

A bull elephant, carrying ivory, appeared from the scattered scrub. It was ambling along a course that would take it across their path a hundred metres ahead. Another one, smaller, emerged some paces behind the first. Tingisha signalled for a halt. The line didn't need to be told a second time. They waited in silence, watching first the elephants, then Tingisha.

Jack sensed that the elephants knew of the group's presence as they lumbered onward towards thick vegetation on the far side of the track. 'Looks like a coupla bulls been kicked out of the herd,' Bear whispered.

'They look a bit grumpy,' Jack replied.

'Don't blame 'em.'

'They're huge!' Jack whispered.

'Well, you know what they say.'

'What?'

'The biggest elephant you'll ever see is the one you meet on foot.'

'Thanks, pal. Sometimes there's such a thing as too much information, you know that?'

Bear snorted on a stifled laugh.

The larger bull reached the grassy path where he stopped, rocking back and forth with a huge foot suspended for many seconds in a kind of dance. The group stood in hushed awe. The second bull stopped and rocked too.

'What's he doing?' Bear whispered to Jack.

'How the hell —'

The larger elephant turned towards them and, raising his tusks, gave a bellow that seemed to shake the earth. He trumpeted and lowered his head and flapped his huge ears. Dust rose about him in clouds.

Stewart shuffled backwards, staring in disbelief at the advancing elephants while his wife stood rooted to the spot, behind Tingisha's broad shoulders.

Bear said, 'Oh shit!' and Jack began to wonder how fast, or far, an elephant could run. They needed a tree they could climb and an elephant could not. The surrounding scrub sported nothing but spindly runts. Then he saw the pile of boulders almost hidden in the tall grass some thirty metres away. It would have to do.

Tingisha was trying to untangle himself from the fat Swede, who clutched desperately at his arm, his mouth moving like a goldfish out of water. Jack caught Tingisha's eye and indicated the boulders. The Maasai nodded, and pushed the Swede off the track in the direction of the rocks. He waved Bear, the blonde and the journalist to follow.

The second elephant drew alongside his larger brother and they advanced with increasing speed, bellowing, thrashing pieces from the shrubs and whipping the dust at their feet into a storm. Their trumpeting was deafening, but to Jack the most alarming sensation was the shock wave generated by their pounding feet. It rose from his boots, pulsed up his legs and thumped in his chest.

As Tingisha took the journalist's wife by the arm, she fainted, dropping like a laundry bag at his feet. He scooped her up and pushed through the clawing bushes towards the boulders. Jack followed and tripped over something in the grass. It was the shotgun. He looked from it to the elephants, now only fifty paces away and closing fast.

Bear's voice reached him above the thunder and trumpeting. 'Get the gun! Jack! Get the gun!'

He reached out but couldn't bring himself to grab it. He tried again, but recoiled as if from an electric shock. The elephants were now too close for him to reach the safety of the boulders. He clenched his teeth, the gun at his fingertips. The elephants loomed in his peripheral vision.

Bear's voice came from far away. 'Jack! The gun!'

Suddenly he knew he could do what needed to be done. His adrenaline-charged mind had slowed his world to a pace that he could handle. The elephants' trumpeting and thundering were muted, their movements now a beautifully choreographed ballet of might and grace. Each footfall raised a puff of dust but the earth-shuddering impact was gone. In its place was a muffled thud. The slow beat of a bass drum in some dirge. And his sense of smell was acute. He imagined he could smell the elephants. A recollection of a hay-strewn shelter at Taronga Park Zoo. An earthy warm smell, full of dry grass and hot steamy breath on a cold Sydney day.

There was an eternity to decide upon his next move.

He hauled himself slowly to his feet. The shotgun lay in his hands like an alien creature. It was old. He could imagine it in the hands of a great white hunter. A thing of pride and power. Now it was an ancient and unloved relic of a glorious past. A rough edge of rust ran along the barrel under his fingers. The stock was split but a remnant of lustre lingered in the redwood, the work of many hours by some forgotten hunter's gun-bearer.

It was at his shoulder.

His last thought, after the leading bull appeared above the barrel, was the chilling familiarity of the trigger release.

Click!

SWEAT ON HIS FOREHEAD.

Holding her leaping hips, one hand on the gun.

Writhing on the sand like a bitch in heat, she was killing him.

Hold back. Concentrate. Count.

So hard to control it. Hold back.

The gun, slippery in his hands.

Count them.

How many?

Click!

THE SHAPE HOVERING ABOVE HIM was in a halo of gold against the western sky. Bear's voice began to penetrate the ringing in his ears. He was asking questions. Dumb questions.

'Yeah. I'm okay,' Jack mumbled. He was on his back in the dust. 'What happened?' he said, raising himself on his elbows.

'Damn thing nearly blew your head off,' Bear answered, taking the gun from one of the others to show him. 'Look at it!'

The barrel was splayed like the petals of a lily.

Bear pulled him to his feet. Jack felt a dull ache at the back of his head when he brushed the dust and grass from his hair. 'Wow.' He looked around him. 'The elephants ... Are they ...? Did I ...?'

'Missed the lot! They just bolted,' Bear said, pointing at an impenetrable wall of scrub some two hundred metres away.

'Just plunged out of sight!' Stewart added. 'Not a sound! Not a single broken twig or branch.' He seemed very pleased with his observation and wore the relieved smile of a man who had escaped an embarrassing situation without disgracing himself.

They all had the same expression. Except Bear, who peered at Jack as though he were a bug under glass. But to the others, it had been fun. An adventure. Something to tell the folks back home.

Jack felt differently.

Tingisha loomed above them and, in the same expressionless tone, said, 'Eh, we go.'

CHAPTER 26

PEABODY'S GUIDE TO EAST AFRICA (5ᵀᴴ ED):
Alcohol was banned for black Kenyans for many years
under the British-administered Protectorate. But illicit
local whisky, called *chang'aa*, has always been available.
The alcohol is distilled from grain with various optional
additives, like roots and herbs, that supposedly add to its
strength. It is a spirit — alcoholic and dangerous —
lending truth to its other Swahili name, *machosi ya simba*,
the potent 'tears of the lion'.

There was a buzz in the air at the Cottars Camp bar. A passing
observer might have thought the six occupants were drunk —
the conversation was a little too loud, the jokes could not
possibly have been that funny, and surely such a disparate
bunch could not be close friends, sharing such extravagant
camaraderie.

They were in high spirits, but the alcohol had little to do
with it. Adrenaline was the drug feeding their exuberance.

'So, none of you got a photo!' Bear said, handing around
the drinks as the barman poured them. 'I can't believe it!'

'Well, you had a camera, Bear,' Stewart said, accepting his
gin. 'Why didn't you get one?'

'Me? 'Cause I was hiding my ass in the rocks like the rest of
you, is why.'

They howled at his joke. They slapped his back.

'Not even a picture of your friend Jack,' said Inga. 'Our hero.'

'Here's to Jack!' someone toasted, yet again.

'To Jack!' they said, raising glasses to him at the end of the bar. But he had left his bar stool and stood at the opening to the garden.

Bear collected the two drinks and eased through the convivial chatter. There was something going on that he didn't understand. Jack had been unusually quiet during the walk back to the lodge. Bear had never seen him brooding like that. When he got the chance, in a brief moment alone as they approached the lodge, he had said, 'How do you feel, buddy? You had me worried for a bit back there.' Jack had said, 'I'm okay,' and kept to his brisk stride, a half-pace ahead of Bear.

The others judged Jack's actions as a cool head under pressure. Bear knew it to be more. Much more. Before the gun barrel exploded, sending him three paces backwards into the dirt, Bear knew something had been going on inside Jack's head. It wasn't just fear. That would have been understandable. It was as though Jack would rather have faced the elephants in hand-to-hand combat than touch that gun.

Whatever it was, it had a powerful thirst. Jack was into his fourth double since they had returned to the lodge. Bear handed him his whisky. 'Here you go, buddy. How's the shoulder?'

Jack rubbed at it, shrugged. 'It's okay.'

'That's a helluva lot of whisky for a guy who doesn't trust the stuff.'

Jack ignored him, throwing his head back and taking half the whisky in a swallow. His eyes brimmed but remained fixed on the darkness of the garden beyond.

'Hey, Jack.' Bear decided to take another approach. 'Why not go get Malaika? She's missing all the fun.'

'Hmm, the Princess. No, I don't think so.'

'Sure you should! You know she'd love all this party stuff.'

Jack's face set into an impenetrable mask. 'I said, *no*. Just leave it, Bear.' He walked into the garden and slumped onto a bench seat at one of the long dining tables.

But Bear did not want to leave it. He was a man who was slow to make friends but clung tenaciously to those he found worthy of the effort. It suited Bear to be with people who were non-judgmental, good-humoured and loved a joke. Jack was all of these. What was more, he was a good colleague, a passable drinker and could handle his fists in a tight situation. Overall, Bear decided that Jack was worth the effort. He sat opposite him at the table.

Bear seldom trusted his instincts where women were concerned, but where a man's feelings were involved, he felt on safer ground. And he sensed that Jack, earlier that day, had almost revealed a part of himself that he would not want others to see. He also knew that if Jack continued to hide it from friends and loved ones, the shield was likely to not only keep them at bay, but perhaps to drive them away.

'Now you *really* got me worried,' Bear continued. 'What's goin' on?'

Jack placed his whisky glass on the table. 'That's the trouble with you, Bear.' His face was stony. 'You never know when to mind your own fucking business.'

Bear's smile retreated. The corded muscles on his thick neck tightened. He took a deep breath and allowed his shoulders to relax before he said, 'Now, let me tell you somethin', Jack. I'm in your head. I know you've got a polecat up your ass about somethin'. And I gotta tell ya, it's pissing me off! So it's okay to go for a run together, to have a few beers, to fall in a bunch of lions and to fight the bad guys back to back, but not okay to talk about stuff. Is that the way it works? Tell me, Jack, 'cause I don't wanna waste my time on no lightweight. We do stuff together, fine — we do it all.' He glared at Jack. 'You better not do this one alone.'

Jack studied Bear's expression.

'That's right, Jack. I know you. And this ain't you. So the way I figure it, we can do this two ways. I can sit drinkin' with you, pretending we're friends, but think that you're just a pain in the ass, or you can talk to me about it. Like *real* friends do.'

Jack shook his head. 'Look, I know what you're trying to do, okay?' He swirled his whisky. 'It just won't work.'

'C'mon, Jack. Try me.'

'I've just got this load of shit in my head. Better just leave it.'

'What shit, man?'

'Stuff. Stuff that happened. Stuff I can't do anything about, so I shouldn't even think about it but I do. And I thought I had it beat.'

Bear waited. The sounds of laughter drifted from the bar. Garden insects chirruped in the darkness.

'That thing I told you about ... the affair ...'

'Carla? Yeah, I remember.'

'It wasn't Carla. And it wasn't Queensland. It was O'Hara ... Hawaii.'

Bear sat quietly as Jack corrected the details of the story he'd told him at the Serengeti campsite. It was as though, now that he'd got started, he was unsure how far he wanted to go but couldn't stop. 'She was crazy. Did I tell you that? Well, I mean real crazy. The things we did. She liked the idea of danger. Risky situations for having sex. Like, one night, we were out by the pool. Nobody was around and she starts to do this little striptease in the pool cabana. Next thing, I have her up on the table. Crazy!

'It was just a mad fling. It should have stopped at that but she wanted more. The equation, she called it. Risk and consequence! She must have been some kind of fucking mathematician.

'She had a gun hidden in the sand on that last night. She was a good planner, all right. Always had something going on in her head. And this is where it gets weird. She explains how this thing is going to work — with the gun.' He gripped his glass until his knuckles went white. 'She puts a bullet in the gun. Spins it. She tells me I should do it with the gun to her head. *Count them*, she says. *Measure the risk*. Can you believe it? Apart from the stupidity of the thing, have you ever tried to do something complicated while you're having sex? I mean, Jesus, who can concentrate at a time like that?

'For the life of me ... I don't know what the hell I was doing there ... But ...' He looked at his friend, eyes glistening.

'And ...?'

'Do you understand me? What was I doing? Not thinking was what I was doing, Bear. Not thinking. Can you believe I actually began to play Russian roulette with her?' He began to laugh wildly. 'Some fucking game!'

He was silent for some time, contemplating the whisky swirling in his glass. 'I threw the gun in the sand beside her. I said something like, *You're sick*, and I left her there.

'I was about halfway to the hotel when I heard it. I knew it was a gun. Her gun. At first I thought, *Dumb bitch is trying to scare me*, but I ran back. She was ... her head ...' He took a swig of whisky. 'There was blood and brains all over the sand.'

'Oh, man ...'

'Yeah, oh man. I started back to the hotel to tell someone. I mean, she was dead, for sure, but I had to tell someone, right? Then I think, *How's this going to look?* Even if she did it to herself, what could I say? I went back to ... to her body.' He put the whisky glass on the table. 'I picked up the gun and gave it a kinda rub. Probably did it all wrong ... Then I put it back in her hand.' His eyes searched Bear's. Seeking his pity or his rebuke.

'And then?'

'And then I went back to my room. Crept back like a mangy dog.'

Bear could see Jack was trying to read his expression — awaiting his words. But for once, he could find no words. There was nothing he could offer his friend by way of solace. He could only shake his head in commiseration, painfully aware of how Jack must feel. A terrible mistake. A mistake that, apart from the tragedy at its core, makes one feel bereft by its pointless stupidity.

When Bear said nothing, Jack swept the glass from the table and swallowed his remaining whisky in one gulp. He gagged on it, coughing so violently that his face contorted and tears rolled down his cheeks. He held his face in his hands until his coughing fit abated.

Bear let his breath escape. 'Oh, man ... Oh, man.' Raising a hand towards Jack, he paused, before resting it on his shoulder. 'At least you had no part in it.'

'No part in it! Are you kidding? I could have prevented it! I should have taken that gun and thrown it into the Pacific. I should have seen she was crazy!'

'How could you have known that? If she was going to do it, she was going to do it with or without you. Was there an inquiry? The police?'

'I left for Sydney the next day. I felt like a rat leaving like that, but if they came to me about it, after running away, how would it look? And can you imagine the explanation? Who would believe anyone could be so dumb? I had to get away. It got to me. I couldn't handle it.'

'Oh, man . . .'

'For chrissake, Bear! Is that all you can say?'

'I . . .'

'Ahh, forget it!' Jack stormed off into the garden.

AS THE AFTERNOON DRIFTED INTO darkness, Malaika became concerned and decided to go to the reception area to wait for Jack's return from the *safari*. When she arrived, she was surprised to find the group seated at a large table in the dining area — Jack had said he would fetch her from the *banda* as soon as they got back.

Bear stood and came to meet her before she reached the table.

'Hello, Bear,' she said. 'How was the *safari*?'

'Great. Okay.'

She waited for more but Bear seemed content to leave it at that. 'Where's Jack?' she asked.

'He's over there.' He nodded towards the bar. Jack was alone, sipping his drink. Malaika's smile waned.

Bear shrugged at her perplexed expression. 'Beats me. We had a bit of a skirmish with a couple of bull elephants. No great drama. But Jack took a shot at 'em and the gun blew up in his hands.'

'My God! Is he all right?' She started towards the bar.

Bear caught her arm. 'He's okay. I mean, he's not hurt. But he's a bit drunk. We had a discussion. Well, an argument.'

'What about?' She tried to read his eyes.

'Oh, it's okay now. We sorted it out. But I thought you should know, he might be a bit testy.'

'What was it about?' she asked again.

'It's nothing. I just thought he needed a pep talk and he thought he didn't.'

He didn't meet her gaze. She studied him a moment then turned towards the bar, wondering at this side of Jack, one she had not seen before. *How long does it take to really know someone? Can you ever succeed?* It worried her too that Bear seemed to know more about him than she did.

Almost an hour after she had joined him at the bar, Malaika was no closer to understanding Jack's state of mind. He was off-hand, uncommunicative. Even belligerent. Seeing him like this disturbed her.

Finally she pressed him to join the others and gently tugged him towards the dinner table where the group had almost finished their meals. 'Where is der *askari*?' Raol, the blonde's husband raised his voice above the conversation. 'He must be here. He must be celebrating with us.'

'He's out there somewhere,' Stewart answered from across the table. 'I wanted to buy him a drink, but he said he couldn't. Not until he's off duty.'

'Jack, don't you think you've had enough?' Malaika whispered as he poured a large glass of red wine.

'You know, my darling, sometimes I can't say what's enough. I mean, sometimes a dozen beers will do it. Sometimes it's a bottle of scotch. But I don't want you worrying yourself, okay?'

'Jack, I *am* worried. I don't like this. This is not you.'

'Now that's where you're wrong, Malaika. This is *exactly* me.'

'No. I can't believe that. Is something worrying you? Bear said you're upset about something. Is that it?'

'Hah! Bear thinks I need help.'

'Well, we all need help sometime or other.'

'Bullshit.'

'There's nothing wrong with getting help from friends.'

'Well, I don't need it. I don't need him,' he jerked a thumb in Bear's direction, 'I don't need them,' he waved his hand around the table. 'And, my pretty princess, I 'specially don't need you.'

She was stung. Her lips parted in disbelief, waiting for him to take it back. He didn't.

'I'm going to bed.' She pushed her chair back and went quickly into the darkness.

Immediately beyond the dining area it became almost completely black. She slowed to a walk. There was only a sliver of moon, high in the sky, giving a hint of luminescence to the pebbles on the path. Occasional flashes of sheet lightning, a mute testimony to the thunderstorm hovering over the eastern horizon, added some assistance. Stopping at one of the many forks, she tried to recall which was the path to their *banda*. The fork to the right looked a little narrower. From behind her came the faint sound of music. She wondered if she should go back to the dining area but, remembering Jack's tone, her anger returned and she took the left fork without further deliberation.

Malaika smelled the heavy night air. It was rich, warm and laden with the promise of imminent rain. Jack had described it as more of a taste than a scent. He was right. She could imagine the dry savannah grasses, the stunted scrub and the thirsting trees opening every pore to draw sustenance from it. She stopped for another deep breath. This time she lifted her shoulders to fill her chest with the cleansing dew. It cleared her head. She wanted to wash away the conversation with Jack.

The path wound through a darkened patch where a clump of trees blotted out the dim light of the moon. Something scampered into the foliage. She stopped, scarcely able to breathe, in case the sound of her breath and pounding heart masked the sounds around her. She hurried forward but an exposed root made her stumble and sprawl on the soft earth.

A pair of sandalled feet blocked her path. Tingisha towered above them, a kerosene lantern dangling from his lanky arm. 'Eh, what is number of your *banda*?'

'What?' she said, scrambling to her feet.

'The number of your *banda*, madam,' he repeated in Swahili.

'Twenty-two!' she spluttered. 'Why? I know where I'm going.'

'Yes.' He led her back along the path she'd come, the lantern sending a swinging light pattern into the darkness around him. She paused a moment before following.

As the path sloped gently, endlessly, downwards towards the *banda*, a soft tropical ground mist hovered at the edge of the lantern light. An owl made a mournful call to an absent mate. Bush babies chittered and scampered above her, dropping twigs and nut husks to the ground. Finally she recognised their hut. The housekeeper had lit the kerosene lantern inside.

'You are here,' Tingisha said, stepping aside to let her onto the *banda*'s porch.

'Thank you,' she mumbled but he was gone. The kerosene lantern bobbed up the path and rounded a bend. Darkness settled softly about her.

'HEY! BIG FELLA!' JACK MET Tingisha at the edge of the dining area. Faint rumblings of thunder from out over the savannah rolled up the path, silent lightning flashes illuminating the shrubbery and reflecting from Tingisha's ebony skin.

'*Jambo, bwana.*'

'*Jambo.* Is Malaika ... the Maasai lady ... did you see her on the path just now?'

'*Ndio, bwana.* She is at the *banda.*'

'Good.' He continued down the path a few paces. 'Hey! I wanna buy you a drink later. Did a great job today. A drink.' He made a gesture of lifting a glass to his lips. 'You know, beer?'

'Yes, *bwana.*'

'Yeah ... So ... beer or ...?'

'Eh, I think beer, *bwana.*'

'Okay. Good.' He clasped his hand to his chin, frowning. 'What about scotch? Do you drink whisky?'

'Eh, no. Not *mzungu* whisky.'

'What other whisky is there?'

'We call it *machosi ya simba.*'

'What's that?'

'It means, the tears of the lion. It is *khali*.'

'*Khali*?'

'Hot. Eh, very strong.'

'Hmm ... must be. Tears of the lion, eh?' His hand went to his chin again. 'What were we saying? Oh yeah, I'll get you a box of beer. Later, okay?' He turned down the path again. 'Hey, wait a minute,' he said calling Tingisha back. 'Can you get me some of your ... *machosi ya simba*?'

Tingisha seemed to puzzle for a moment then a smile flickered at his lips. 'For *bwana*?'

'Yup!'

The smile grew. He wrapped long gangling arms around his lean frame, hugging himself, embarrassed.

'Okay. Go get your whisky. I'll be at the bar with your box of beer.'

Tingisha nodded and said, 'Eh, I take you to *banda*, *bwana*?'

Jack looked down the path and shook his head. 'Nah. Changed my mind.'

WHEN JACK HAD EXCHANGED THE box of Tuskers for the flask of Tingisha's local whisky, he returned to the dining area. The long table was empty but Jack found the remnants of the dinner party sitting at the bar. Inga was perched on a bar stool with one leg crossed over the other. Stewart, almost asleep on an elbow propped on the bar, sat on another. Bear stood between them in close conversation with Inga, who was chuckling quietly and steadying herself on his arm.

She turned to Jack. 'Oh, Jack, I'm so glad you're back. Please make him stop. He tells such naughty stories.'

Bear looked Jack up and down, 'Ah, you're back!', and gave him a punch on the arm. It was his aching shoulder but Jack grinned. There was no need to bicker with Bear. 'What stories?' he said, rubbing the shoulder.

'Naughty things about the Maasai. About the young warriors who roam the countryside seducing all the unmarried girls.'

'The golden years,' Bear added. 'Fighting, fucking and stealing cattle. Oops!'

She laughed again, giving Bear's hairy forearm a gentle slap. 'So it's a perfect bachelor's life?'

'For a few years. Then he has to knuckle down and raise cattle. And babies.'

'And become a typical boring middle-aged husband?' she asked.

'Not really typical. He can have four wives and — now here's the interesting bit.' He leaned closer to her. 'He can bed any wife whose man is not around.'

'No! What if the husband comes home?'

'Ah, now that's where the Maasai are very civilised. If he comes home and someone's spear is planted at the door, the husband finds himself another hut for the night.'

Inga giggled. 'What about the girls? Do they have fun?'

'Ah,' said Bear sadly, 'briefly. It's all over by the time they reach their early teens, sometimes younger.'

'What do you mean, *all over*?'

'That's when they're circumcised.'

'No! But that's horrible. You mean ...'

'Clitoridec ... clitoridectomy.' He stumbled over the word. 'Barbaric!'

'Maybe so. But a girl is unmarriageable ... unmarriable — how do you say it? Can't be married, without it. Or with it. If you know what I mean.'

'And with all those wonderful Maasai men around. What a waste,' Inga said, shaking her blonde head. 'They have such ... presence. Marvellous bodies. Long and graceful.' Her eyes smiled at Bear over the lip of her cocktail glass.

'Anyone for drinks?' Jack waved the gourd in the air.

'Oh, Jack! How quaint. What is it?'

'It's called *machosi* ... ah ... something. Tears of the frigging lion to you tourists. The local drop. Want some?'

'Local rotgut more like it,' Bear said, steadying the gourd in Jack's hand to take a sniff. 'It's off! You're not really going to drink it, are you?'

'Why not? I'm experiencing the real Africa. Remember?'

'You're crazy.'

'Hah! How true. But what the hell! Inga?'

'I don't think so, Jack.' Inga climbed off her bar stool. 'As a matter of fact, I'd better go. Raol, poor darling, is probably already asleep. All the excitement. Too much for him, I'm afraid.'

Bear put his glass on the bar. 'Then let me walk you there.' He turned to Jack. 'We'll have a proper drink when I get back. Okay?'

Jack gave him an exaggerated wink. 'No worrish.'

CHAPTER 27

Malaika lay on top of the bed covers in her bikini pants. The
banda held the remnants of afternoon heat, but when she had
rolled up the flaps on the fly-screened windows the murmuring
darkness beyond was intimidating. She shut and tied them.

Her book lay on her midriff as she considered Jack and his
mood. She imagined there was a time in every relationship
when reflection was needed — a time that might be thought of
as a turning point between the flush of new love and a more
endurable relationship, able to navigate the rough patches.
This was probably just such an aberration. She would sit
down quietly with him tomorrow and they would work it all
out. Whatever it was. Then he would be his usual easy-going
self.

A soft creak from the bamboo-slatted porch. A footstep.
'Jack?'

Silence.

'Jack? Is that you?'

'Peace, sister,' he said in Swahili. 'It is Tingisha. The *askari*.'

'What do you want?' She looked at the frail door latch.

'There is someone hurt.'

'Who? . . . Wait a moment.' She pulled on her jeans and a tee-shirt and stepped quickly to the doorway. Pausing a moment, she flipped up the latch and opened the door. 'What is it?' she said, a little breathless.

'We need your help, sister. There is a man injured in my *enkang*.'

'Who is it?'

'He is a Maasai. A visitor.'

She stared blankly at him, then her shoulders relaxed. 'Well, it has nothing to do with me. Speak to the manager.' She started to push the door closed.

'Please, we need help but the manager has sent our minibus to Nairobi.'

'Then send for the *daktari*, the doctor.'

'It is not possible. But you have a car.'

'No. Now please go away.' She began to close the door again.

'Wait! You are a Maasai.' This time he spoke in Maa.

'I can't help you.'

'Sister. We need your help. A man might die tonight.'

'I said, I can't help you. Now go.' She closed the door and locked it, and then listened to his footsteps leave the *banda* porch and scrunch up the path.

Only after she turned back to the bed did she realise that she had understood, and answered him, in Maa.

TINGISHA KNEW HE HAD TO ask the tall *mzungu* now. The one who gave him the beer. Even if the *morani*, Kireko, would object to having the help of a *mzungu*, it was clear that it was his only chance of getting to Isuria, and perhaps saving his life. He strode up the path as lightning added dazzling flashes to his feeble lantern.

The *mzungu* was alone at the bar with his gourd of *machosi ya simba*, staring at the wall. '*Bwana*, can you help?' Tingisha asked without proper preliminaries.

'Help?' The man turned to him but his eyes were clouded. 'What is it?'

'My friend. He is hurt. Eh, he come to my *enkang*, my village, eh, this morning.'

'I see. Hmm,' the *mzungu* said, and hiccuped loudly.

Tingisha thought he did not look well. He hurried on, 'When I see his face tonight I am more worried. His blood … eh, he has lose … he has lost much blood. I must take him to his people. It is not far.' He studied Jack more closely as the garden beyond was illuminated in a silent flash of distant lightning. '*Bwana*, do you hear me?' The *makuti* roof trapped the rumble of thunder.

The *mzungu* gave a shudder as if a chill had touched him. 'Yeah, but … No, I'm … My eyes …' He rubbed his balled fists into the sockets. 'Damn! I'd better go to bed.'

'*Bwana*, your car …'

'Oh, man,' he said, holding up the gourd and giving it a shake. 'This jungle juice is …' He thrust it into Tingisha's chest. 'Here, get this stuff away from me.' He burped loudly. 'Your lion's piss needs more bottle age.'

'Your friend. The big *bwana*. Can he help?'

'Bear? Maybe …'

'I will find him.' He knew the big *bwana* was in *banda* five.

'Only left the bar 'bout half hour ago,' the *mzungu* mumbled as he stepped down from the bar stool.

'*Ndio, bwana*.'

'Gone thataway,' he said, pointing to the opening beyond the reception desk. 'Wow.' He ran a hand across his forehead and wiped it on his shirt. 'That stuff's hot, all right.' He staggered towards the end of the bar, turned slowly, unsteady on his feet. He wagged a finger at Tingisha. 'More bottle age.'

A flash of lightning framed him at the exit to the garden. He frowned, rubbed his eyes and added, 'Definitely … more bottle …'

The end of his sentence was lost in the thunderclap.

• • •

THROUGH THE THIN WALLS OF *banda* number five Tingisha could hear the unmistakable sounds of a man and woman together. He waited, but the noises continued. After ten minutes he decided this man would not feel kindly towards a stranger's interruption tonight.

Tingisha hurried down the path after Jack. Large raindrops struck him on the face and body.

MALAIKA WAS DOZING WHEN A gentle rap on the door woke her with a start. Her book tumbled to the floor. 'Yes?'

'I am sorry.' It was the *askari* again.

'I told you, go away. I'll report you to the manager.'

'Sister, is the *mzungu* not there?' He was standing close to the door. 'I left him but a small time gone. He was unwell and was coming to his *banda*.' He was speaking in Maa again.

She stepped to the door and opened it. 'Where did you leave him?' she demanded.

'At the bar. If he is not here then he is in the bush.'

'Oh, my God.' She looked up at him. 'Where could he be?'

'There are many tracks into the bush. I can find him.' He searched her face. 'Maybe we can help each other.'

JACK STUMBLED DOWN THE PATH with a fire in his gut. Thunder rumbled and the night flashed and crackled with electricity. He was awash with sweat. It trickled down his neck, soaking his shirt. An over-inflated football sat on his shoulders where his head should have been and it resonated with each roll of thunder. No matter how much he blinked, he couldn't seem to clear his vision. From somewhere in his memory came Bear's story of Russian soldiers blinded by a binge on confiscated schnapps during the early occupation of Berlin. *Am I going blind?* It was the thought that followed him down the track, the very long track, with no familiar landmarks.

A vine grabbed his ankle and, as he hopped to unravel it, he stumbled and the ground beneath him disappeared.

Some time later, he awoke in a drowning panic. Rain poured

into his gaping mouth. He gagged and his head almost burst as the gush of bile and raw alcohol spewed out. When the throbbing subsided he put a hand gingerly to his temple. He turned his face to the rain. It felt good. He let it run into his foul-tasting mouth, then he hawked loudly and spat. It made him light-headed and nauseated again and he had to wait for the sensation to clear before dragging himself slowly to his knees.

The rain was clean. Cool.

An eerie mist hovered a few feet above the track. Or was it steam made by the rain spears on striking the hot red earth? The banana trees flickered like faulty neons on a dark street as hell's lightning glanced off their shiny wet fronds. Thunder gave a brittle *crack* as he crawled from the ditch towards the path. The red mud was slimy, making it difficult to regain his feet.

On the track at last, he made a determined effort to stand but his head spun, the ground flipped sideways and he fell flat on his back. The track, the banana trees and the whole shadowy world took a roller-coaster ride through a looping curve. Lightning flashed, burning its image into his retina, and in that instant, the percussive crash of thunder struck his chest with a frightening force. A ringing deafness followed. He had trouble catching his breath.

As his eyes began to adjust to the darkness, and the roar of the rain replaced the ringing in his ears, he tried to blink some reality into his surroundings. The night mist twirled about him, blending with the fog that filled his head. It was all mixed up. Fog and mist. He was sinking, drowning in a cloud.

Two enormous shining eyes rushed to him through the darkness. They stopped mere paces away. Another lightning bolt. Is that a white elephant? He squeezed his eyes shut. When he opened them, a tall black apparition floated from the elephant, suspended above the track by the swirling steam of hell's rainstorm. In the surreal landscape the bizarre assumed normality. The African Princess hovered above him while the enormous dazzling eyes of her obedient elephant remained fixed on her in an unblinking stare.

Black sky and jagged lightning. Silver puddles on a black track. The devil's dazzling black and white storm. Even

Malaika was a photographic study in black and white film. Negative followed by a print. A black Malaika. A thunderbolt, then a white one.

Her worried frown was highlighted under another harsh flash of lightning. Silver lines on a black canvas.

She leaned over him, water running from her face to his. He tried to say, *I love the taste of your skin*, as she shucked the water from his brow, but he was being drawn upwards.

Upwards.

Sucked through the fog into a swirling waterspout, he floated after her.

With majestic Maasai steps she led him to the side of her elephant. It opened and swallowed him whole. A tremble ran through its body as the thunder ripped through the rain.

The alleyway of banana-tree neon lights flickered once more, then went out.

MALAIKA HUNCHED OVER THE STEERING wheel, guiding rather than driving the Land Rover through the darkness. Tingisha sat beside her, making almost imperceptible gestures to guide the way. Once he stopped her a breath short of a flooded elephant wallow, now turned to a pit of quicksand by the storm. The windscreen wipers flogged rain torrents from the glass. *Swok, swok, swok.* Their metronome beat no challenge to the rage of the storm.

The downpour had continued since Tingisha had somehow managed to get Jack out of the Land Rover and onto the bed. She had been worried about him on the way back to camp. She wasn't sure if he was sick or just drunk. In the end she decided that it would probably be better for him to sleep it off, while she met her part of the arrangement and took Tingisha to his injured friend.

Small rivulets ran across their path, making it difficult to know if the car was on the road surface, such as it was, or beside it.

Swok ... swok ... swok.

It wasn't far from the camp when the headlights pierced a circle of huts. Tingisha indicated they had arrived. Malaika sat at the wheel as he strode towards the nearest hut, allowing the car door to slam behind him. It was the first Maasai *enkang* she had seen in nearly twenty years.

Swok, swok, swok. The demanding rhythm of the wipers gripped her in a maelstrom of emotions. She stared at her reflection in the wet windscreen and willed the panic to subside. Vaguely remembered faces superimposed themselves on hers. She thrust them away and cut the motor. If she was going to get this injured man to wherever he had to go, and be back before Jack awoke, she had to keep moving.

Malaika hesitated at the hut where Tingisha had entered. She was suddenly struck by the realisation that nobody knew where she was, including herself, and she was following a man she hadn't known existed a mere twelve hours ago. She swallowed hard and slipped under the cowhide door covering.

The entrance was dim, lit only by the light from the space beyond. She stooped into the main chamber where a smoky flame spluttered in a kerosene lamp set on the dirt floor. Shadows danced about the low ceiling as the lamp struggled for life. The smouldering dung in the cooking fire made her eyes water. It brought an image of herself as a child, rubbing her eyes raw in such a hut.

It took her some time to adapt to the gloom after the brilliance of the headlights.

Tingisha stood to one side. Two other men were present. One sat at the side of a bed platform where the second, a handsome young *morani*, reclined on a pile of folded cowhides.

The man on the bed slowly opened his eyes. His face was damp with sweat. He blinked at her, clearing a cloud from his eyes. They were large and had a familiar shape. She felt exposed by the fire in his gaze, as if he could see into her soul. In spite of her apprehension she was drawn a step closer.

A memory of a handsome teenage boy leapt to mind.

She took another step and gasped, '*Haki ya Mungu,*' in Swahili. 'Oh, my God,' she repeated in Maa. 'Kireko!'

'Malaika,' he said with a wan smile, then in Maa he added, 'Angel. We are empty without you.'

CHAPTER 28

PEABODY'S GUIDE TO EAST AFRICA (5ᵀᴴ ED):
The hadada ibis is a drab olive green and inhabits the lakelands and swampy areas of East Africa. It stands no more than half a metre tall, but has the most heart-breaking, penetrating call of any bird in Africa.

Beginning its call well before dawn, it sounds like a woman or child sobbing inconsolably.

The sting of morning light woke him. Jack winced as he attempted to lift his head from the pillow. His whole body ached. On the second attempt he moved more slowly. Sunshine speared through the screen door onto a pile of wet clothes — his. Malaika was not in her bunk but, strangely, her bed was already made.

He eased back his bed sheet and lowered a foot carefully to the slatted bamboo flooring. His head pounded as he sat up. Placing his other foot beside the first, he wriggled his toes. Then he leaned his weight on Malaika's bunk for a moment before lifting himself to his feet.

Walking naked to the door, he held a hand to the side of his face to shield it from the eastern sky. The morning was clear. The air had been steam-cleaned by the storm and he drank deeply of it, trying to cleanse the bitter taste in his mouth. The seemingly endless sultry days were now a distant bad memory.

But fat clouds were sucking energy from the rising heat of the Rift Valley and they towered black and menacing over the Loita Hills.

There was a muddy ring under his wristwatch band. Nine-thirty. He followed the smudge to a thin crust of dried mud at his elbow. He rubbed at it as he checked his lower body. His feet were clean, but there was more mud on his knees. The previous night began to drift back to him, and he winced with the recollection of the alcohol and his caustic behaviour.

BEAR SAUNTERED DOWN THE PATH towards Jack and Malaika's *banda*. The sun's angled rays found the remaining raindrops on diamond-studded leaf-ends. Soon the rising heat would consume them but for now they glistened amongst nodding hibiscus and frangipani.

He had enjoyed his breakfast alone at eight o'clock. Most times he preferred it. And on mornings like this, with the yellow weaverbirds darting frantically about the garden, building the best, the most perfectly constructed little love nests for the mates they hoped to seduce by them, it was icing on the cake. He was feeling quite pleased with himself. *His* cake had been iced last night by Inga, who had been an adventurous lover, playing with him, teasing out the erotic moments into an unbridled crescendo. He could hardly extract himself from her hands, her arms and her mouth for long enough to grab a condom. She had insisted he fuck her wild and wet, but he ignored it as usual. If women were slighted by his insistence, bad luck. And logical discussion was out of the question.

When he drew near the hut he called out, 'Hello? Are you guys decent?'

Jack was drying himself as he came out onto the porch. 'As good as I can be under the circumstances.'

'Man! You look ...' Bear struggled to find a simile, 'like yesterday's beef stroganoff.'

'Oh, please! Don't mention anything about food.' He wrapped the towel around his waist. 'I've never had a hangover like this. Feel like I've been beaten up by a biker gang.'

'But you'll live. We all manage in the end. Now, come on, there's a couple of us goin' to the river. Plenty of action out there after the rain, I reckon.'

'Oh, mate, I don't know about that. What's Malaika want to do?'

'Malaika? Isn't she in there?' nodding towards the *banda* door.

Jack raised an eyebrow. 'You're joking, right?'

'Well, she ain't up at the lodge,' Bear went on. 'I been sittin' there half the morning waiting for you guys.'

Jack put his hands on his knees and sank to the porch step. Her bed was made, not because she'd arisen early and made it, but because she had never slept in it. 'Oh, shit,' he said, and ran his fingers through his thick wet hair.

Bear searched for something positive to offer, but when Jack looked up, with the question written all over his face, he could only shrug and say, 'Buddy, I have *no* idea.'

JACK DRAGGED A BOOT FROM his canvas bag, which was packed but open at his feet beside the bunk bed. The pressure surged to his temples and his head throbbed. He sat back with a resigned sigh until the pain receded. The search of the lodge and its grounds had not improved his disposition. He felt terrible. He hated the depression and self-pity that came with his hangovers. But beyond the hangover, the morning's emotions were a complicated mix, including a greater than normal dose of guilt. Fragments of the previous night's conversations started to come back to mind. What had he said before Malaika left the table? *I don't need you.* He wiped a hand across his mouth and shook his head. Shit!

Taking a deep breath he laced up his boot. He was becoming depressed again. Time to take stock, he thought. Taking stock at times like this often helped him regain perspective. It can't be all that bad. Okay, the Land Rover's gone. That means she left of her own accord. That's good, right? He was not at all convinced of the logic but let it pass. So she's not hurt. Somewhere safe. He was feeling better. But why'd she leave? Simple really — she's pissed off at me. I can understand that, arsehole that I am. He stopped himself there. This was not the positive reinforcement he was trying to achieve. So I over-reacted a little with the shotgun thing. And it made me mad because I thought I had it beat. And I don't. He took another deep breath. Positive reinforcement. This was harder than usual. She's gone off on some silly little *safari* of her own. To teach me a lesson. He scratched his head. Where? How to find her? Tingisha will know! He was on duty all night.

Bear came stomping onto the porch. 'Inga's loaned us her Landcruiser,' he said, squinting through the screen door. 'By the way, where are we going?'

'We'll start at Tingisha's village.'

He picked up his bag and pulled the *banda* door closed behind him. To the east, a charcoal thunderhead plumed high above the Loita Hills; the rage at its core tossed tattered cloud fragments across the sky. The gathering storm flashed soundless lightning bolts to the bare hills. Seconds later, thunder rumbled across the brooding savannah land.

Jack brushed his hair back, put on his Akubra and pulled its wide brim down over his forehead. 'Okay, big fella, let's go.'

JACK AND BEAR FOUND TINGISHA in a pair of blue shorts and a checked long-sleeved shirt, the style made popular by country and western singers. Somehow he didn't appear as tall as he did in his *shuka* and beads.

Jack apologised for interrupting his nap and immediately started to ask him about Malaika. Yes, he told them, she had been there during the night to help an injured tribesman back to his village. He was surprised that Malaika had not already returned to Cottars.

'And nobody here went with her and the two men?' Jack asked.

'No, *bwana*.'

'And you say you've never seen these men before?'

'No. But the Maasai girl, eh ... Malaika, she know one *moran*. She know him very well. They talk. Plenty talk.'

Bear stepped in. 'Where did they go?'

'To Isuria.' He pointed down the muddy track towards Narok.

'How do we get there?' Bear asked.

'On road to Kisii, after Ewaso Ngiro, there is small *duka*. Isuria is small road near *duka*. Driving your car, eh, maybe one hour.'

They thanked him and said goodbye.

'*Kwaheri!*' he responded with a lazy wave.

Bear took the wheel and headed towards the main Narok road. Jack sat in silence. He couldn't get the sentence out of his mind. *She know him very well.*

CHAPTER 29

PEABODY'S GUIDE TO EAST AFRICA (5ᵗʜ ED):
Children are the bright moon. (Maasai proverb.)

She awoke to the suffocating smell of cow dung and the vaguely smoky taste of a cooking fire smouldering to ash. In the infinitesimal light of its last embers, she stumbled about, scattering pots and bowls and clawing at the walls. The dung powder she dislodged wafted darkly into her face. She heard herself utter a pathetic whimper and bit her lip.

On one wall she found a flap of cowhide and pushed through it into a space, narrower than the one she had fled. She moved quickly towards a hint of light, fighting her panic. As she ran her fingers around the second cowhide door, it was flung open. Noah was there. She burst past him into the faint light of scattered stars and a miserly moon and fell forward onto her knees. Her breath came from her constricted throat in rasping gasps.

Greatly embarrassed by her panic attack, she gathered herself and climbed slowly to her feet, refusing Noah's help. He mumbled something as she struggled for composure. When he repeated himself, she could still not quite catch his quietly spoken Maa, but followed him to the other side of the dim compound as he indicated.

Even in the dark of the pre-dawn, Malaika knew where she was. It was not the village so much; every *enkang* looks the same. It was the shape of the *boma*, the gate facing a shallow valley, and the creek beyond. She couldn't see the creek in the darkness, but she knew it was there. Knew that more than a trickle of water seldom troubled its smooth flat stones. One stone was shaped like a *duka*'s tabletop. A smaller one had been her chair. She and her brother had played in that creek a lifetime ago, he ignoring her while he waged bloodless battles on his friends with blocked arrows and padded spears. She had washed her dolls' tattered *kanga* dresses in its pools, all the while hoping that her big brother would notice her. Just once.

She knew this village and she knew this hut — the hut to which Noah had led her then departed. She stood alone at its entrance, fighting emotions that came rushing at her like the treacherous black wind that comes hurtling across the savannah, full of smoke and ash, and which hides a deadly grass fire at its heart.

How had she travelled back in time to this village? As the thin rays of the dawn crept across the dung-spattered compound, she looked down at her hands, her legs, her feet. No, it was not a dream. She was not seven any more.

Then she remembered the lumbering Land Rover and its slow-motion slide through the slippery bend while she spun madly on the useless steering wheel. A metallic crunch. A bright light, then darkness. Total quiet, suddenly shattered by the horror of waking in the private hell of her childhood, fighting the rapacious beast of her fear. The smell, the touch and the atmosphere had released it in that terrible darkness.

The smell would have choked her. It had invaded her nose and mouth. Maybe her brain. It had smoked out the musty memories, long buried, from hiding places deep inside. Smoked them out of a hole, as her brother had done to ant bears, so he could chase and kill them. But who would kill her memories? Who would chase away the animals in the dark holes of her mind? Who could silence the once-forgotten screams?

Her feelings were all mixed up. They immobilised her. She tried to unravel them, but each time she approached, they moved beyond the horizon of her recollection, like the dawn now lingering behind the Loita Hills, hidden in the cool green glow that would melt as the sun found its path into the sky.

Elusive emotions and missing memories. Were they memories, she wondered, or fragments of a nightmare she had almost managed to forget?

She remembered a hut, this hut, and a man standing above her mother, curling his lip. A gold tooth. She remembered him removing his belt and wrapping it around his meaty fist. And when the beatings had begun, she, Malaika, would retreat into a tiny ball in a corner of this hut, beyond that cowhide door, while her mother's cries and moans pierced her. But she could never become small enough. To become a speck then disappear. To be not there. To be somewhere, anywhere else. To be even in the African night, under the burning gaze of *simba*, the lion, and the yellow-eyed leopard. Better to have the stink of the hyena's breath on her than the smell of the smoke and the cow dung of that hut. To be gone from the inescapable horror that was her seven-year-old world.

For seventeen years she had avoided this place. She had even forgotten it existed, and now here she was, waiting. For what? Waiting for the Maa words to stop marauding through her head? The dead memories must have brought them back. Or did the Maa words wake the memories? She had refused to use them, even to herself, for all of those years since she and her mother had escaped. They had never used them in their new home on the lake. But they must have somehow endured, although they were hidden and denied.

The sound of them. The *ng* words: *ngoto, ngong, Ngai*. The *ol* words: *olchani, oltirpe*. She hated them. Her mouth could not form them. Her ears would not recognise them. Until last night. When the Maa words told of Jack's danger, she had listened to them. She had invited them in. Now they tumbled recklessly through her mind, bringing Maa memories. Bringing her back to this village, to this hut. And its terror.

Noah had left her at the door, but how could she go into that smoky space with all manner of horrors locked in its dim interior? He had said *olchani*, medicine, pointing to her forehead. Her fingers went there and found a sensitive place, crusted with blood.

Memories. Their denial had been her refuge for seventeen years. Now they rushed by, sweeping from her past like the detritus on the crest of the rainy season's first surge.

Seventeen years.

She took a step towards the entrance and stopped. Her mother had fled, naked and weeping through this doorway, dragging Malaika in her wake.

Another half-step. She could reach the cowhide covering at the entrance. If she wanted, she could touch it, or she could turn around and walk away.

Happier days began to flicker into focus. Dim and distant, but, yes, they were there. People she had loved. People who had loved her. Her mother's soothing voice and a familiar song, a lullaby. A Maasai lullaby. It reminded her that even in the darkest of those dark days, her mother's mind had refused to become the prisoner of her battered body. The lullaby, her attempt to wash away the horror of the brutal man who Malaika would not call father.

She saw her boy-man brother, playing boisterous boy-man games.

The caress of an old woman's hands, her great-grandmother, *the old one*, as she was known in the village. The hands whose magic could transform the clay of a termite's nest into a living, breathing doll. The power to clothe it by changing tattered *kanga* cloth into polka-dotted splendour. The ancient hands of her loving, fiercely protective *bibi*. Malaika remembered her great-grandmother with the Swahili word, *bibi*. When she was a small girl, she used the Maa word, *kokoo*.

The sky was shading from pink to burnished gold. She could turn around and walk back into the dawn, to Jack and her civilised life. She could put this place and its unbidden memories back where they belonged. Forgotten.

Turn around. Walk away. Forget.

Soundless cool tears trickled down her cheeks. The fear tears were finished. Now she wept for the lost memories of seventeen years. At first she felt like a pickpocket had stolen them, year by year, month by month. But she knew it was not a pickpocket, or anybody other than herself. She had simply squandered them, a piece at a time, never missing them. Not until now.

It was simple to take those memories and fold them into a smaller and smaller space until they were so small she could throw handfuls into the breeze, letting them flutter away from her life. If they were gone, they could not awaken her past. Now she knew she had depleted her life in the present to avoid confronting the days of her past. She had cheated herself of her childhood and her roots.

Inside the hut was her past. Her stolen days. The seventeen years. She couldn't walk away. Her fate had not been changed when she left Isuria, merely suspended. It could be denied no longer.

She pushed aside the covering to the inner darkness of the *olale*, the calf pen that formed the vestibule to every Maasai hut. When the covering fell closed behind her, the golden dawn was lost. Getting through the *olale* space became three formidable steps before she emerged into the living space.

On her haunches at an ember fire sat a ghostly figure gently stirring a clay pot. Her shaved head resembled a skull nodding on a stick. Malaika guessed she was female by her long red garments, which concealed her small frame like a shroud. Loose flesh sagged on upper arms as delicate as a bird's wings. The hands and fingers were fine, but moved over her cooking fire with a decisiveness that belied their fragility. She added a chip or two of herbs and a swatch of lichen to her pot.

Brittle, confident hands.

In profile, the face reminded her of a blacksmith's old leather apron. Thin, wrinkled and worn, it held the glow absorbed from years at the furnace. Deep smile lines told of a life before the crushing unkindness of age.

The old woman was humming while stirring her pot, ignoring the intruder who had so rudely entered unannounced. When she raised her gaze from her fire, a smile creased the leathery face and lit the eyes, hot coals under a thin coating of grey-black ash.

Of all people, Malaika thought, how could she have forced herself to forget this one — the maker of termite-nest clay babies? 'Kokoo! Oh, Kokoo,' she said. 'Where have I been?'

THE OLD ONE CRADLED MALAIKA'S chin in the gentle curve of one leathery hand while the other dabbed a wad of leleshwa leaves at the laceration on her ear. The aroma was vaguely familiar. Kokoo had probably administered it to her scrapes more than once during her rough-and-tumble life with her brother. But she put the thought aside. She needed all her concentration to explain to Kokoo the story of her life since leaving Isuria. It was hard to know how to put it in terms that her *kokoo* could understand. How do you describe an office building to one who'd never seen anything more substantial than the tumbledown shanties in Narok? How to relate the bustle of Nairobi to one more acquainted with the vast expanse of the Serengeti? She decided to stay with the simple version: family, home and growing up. The stories she told involving her half-sister, Ziada, whom Kokoo had never seen, seemed to occupy much of the old one's interest. She would stop Malaika throughout the telling, checking on the most trivial of details. Malaika finished with a description of the house in Mwanza with its little vegetable garden.

'The last time I saw Mama and Hamis, they were still very happy together.' Malaika's voice trailed into the final words. A heaviness settled on her and the hut felt suddenly cool. A feeling of apprehension swept over her and she shuddered involuntarily.

The old woman returned the wad of leaves to the pot on the fire hearth and took Malaika's hand in hers. Malaika felt a weight pressed into her palm. The glass prism held the warmth of Kokoo's body in it.

'Here, the sun-stone will warm your heart,' she said, trying to catch her great-granddaughter's eyes. When she did, she smiled and nodded a reassurance.

Malaika opened her fingers. A host of miniature Kokoos reflected from the prism. She turned it, fascinated by its capture of the firelight.

Malaika's story, the real story, poured from her in a breathless rush. She told her *kokoo* how she had a bitter argument with her mother and fled the taunts and unhappiness of Mwanza for Nairobi and met Jai, the boy with the most beautiful brown skin and straight nose and soft lips, and how her uncle who was not really her uncle found her alone in her corner bed and was on her before she was awake. How she froze in her worst fear — the fear of being rendered helpless. How she hated that fear more than any other and that she would for ever after fight it the most and how her love for Jai died after her uncle trapped her in her bed. And how Jai's father, the quiet wonderful doctor, had found her in the hospital broom closet and how he was careful not to frighten her further and how he put the broken pieces of her heart together and cared for her and helped her to overcome the hate and the fear. How, with patience, he helped to make her strong again and gave her confidence and gave her a job and sent her to be educated and how she never really told him how much she loved him for his kindness and patience and then suddenly he was dead. And how Jack had stumbled into her life and how things started to become easier. He ... what was it? He freed her. He liberated her from the constant vigilance she felt she needed to maintain her promise to preserve her self-respect in a male-dominated world. And when he had unwittingly released her from her cage, the cage of her own making, he had made her feel ... powerful. How, from the very beginning, he had been patient with her bad manners. How he had never treated her as one of his possessions or tried to make her into something else. And, especially, how he had restored her ability to let go. At last she could appreciate her youth and have fun, as twenty-four year olds should. And for all these things, how she so much wanted to be with him. To enjoy having him around. Perhaps she really did love him. Not like the love she had for Jai, like a child, but perhaps a real love. And she had been thinking about it a lot lately. If only she could be sure ...

The old one's wizened head nodded and her eyes twinkled an understanding through all Malaika's story, as if she knew it already.

'This *mzungu*,' Kokoo said. 'This Jack . . .'

'Yes?' Malaika said, trying to recall having said anything about Jack being white. She had been saving that information for later.

Kokoo took up the wad of leaves again and patted them to Malaika's forehead. 'This Jack . . . you are not sure of him. But when you need him, you will learn what the *mzungu* feels in his heart. Then you will know what you must do.'

'Kokoo, what do you know? What must I do?'

Ember eyes twinkled. She put the leleshwa leaves back into the clay bowl and took Malaika's hands in hers.

'Child, your mother Penina, my dear granddaughter, wanted to change all Maasai women's lives because everything in her life was so very bad. She knew she could not succeed. Instead, she tried to make you different from all other Maasai girls. She wanted you to think for yourself. In the modern way. She kept sneaking you back to school even though she suffered her husband's beatings whenever he found out.' She blinked angry tears away. 'Thank *Ngai* he was seldom in the *enkang*.'

Malaika felt her *kokoo*'s grip tighten.

'Your mother gave you a modern name. It was a disgrace. Ai-ai-ai! You should have seen them. It made your mother laugh. No Maasai had ever used a Swahili name for one of their children. And a name such as yours, why, that was even more scandalous than anything. But she wanted you to fly high and free, like a *malaika*. Like an angel.'

She paused, studying Malaika's smooth brown hands in her own wrinkled ones. When she looked into Malaika's face again, her smile melted away and she cocked her head to one side. 'Child, you are a woman of the Maasai. We carry the burden of the tribe's survival as we carry the daily burden of firewood for the *enkang* — because it has always been so. But you, child, have a destiny to fulfil. That is why *Ngai* sent you back to me.'

'I don't understand.' Kokoo's ramblings tumbled about in her head. 'What has this to do with Jack?'

'When you need him, you will know.'

'Kokoo, if you know, you must tell me.'

Her spindly
reko's head.
th detached
eld a bird.
ore. Perhaps
scrutiny she
a bird, they

extension of
his way and
r in the hut
ead, holding
uarry. With
its wings, it
hred braids.
nkled hands
s for a few
hands away

half-closed

e cloth that
edges of the
e from navel
looked like
andfuls, she
e bone and a
r beside her.
n a goat, on
torn flesh,
e would dab
returning to

ds lie on her
ith moss and
faint herbal
o bound the
cloth.

be told what is yet to be

something to do with it?'
u will know much about
about yourself.'
er on the subject of Jack.
an you tell me about my

me small items into her
me.'
lmost forgotten him.' She
sha carry him to the back
e was smiling at her, not
aware that she was with
vers down his handsome
that she had loved, even
se years ago. How could

ere is he?'
rse he must have a hut
share it with you, an
manner.' She shook her
e old ones. Of the time

andmother across the
ed after her through the
living space, Malaika
orm with Noah standing
grim countenance that
but when he lifted his
n his lips. He nodded a

began a low chant. The
wards the bed, or rather
g light of the fire. She
ike a wrinkled nymph in

long crimson garments, to stand at the bed-head
arms wove wide spirals in the space above K
Malaika glanced at Noah, who looked on w
interest. Her great-grandmother's hands now
Malaika wondered why she had not noticed it be
it was a trick of the flickering light, for on close,
thought her *kokoo*'s hands were not just holding
had *become* a bird.

The bird fluttered under the sooty ceiling, an
the old one's arms. It climbed and then angled
that, by a dip of a wing. It stirred the smoky
until it finally hovered above Kireko's lowered
its position like a hawk taking range on its
extravagant backward and forward motions of
began a slow descent to take roost on Kireko's
At that instant the bird dissolved into two wr
whose gnarled fingers slipped over Kireko's ey
moments, closing them. The old one slipped he
and moved to the side of the bed.

The whites of Kireko's eyes were slits behin
lids. His body sagged to the shape of the bed.

Kokoo sat on the bedside and removed t
swaddled Kireko's wound. She gently pressed the
ragged tear at his midriff. They met in a jagged li
to hipbone. Taking a tall gourd, she poured wh
raw mutton fat into her hand. With a few small
packed the wound cavity, then took a curve of fi
strand of sinew from her carry-bag on the flo
Threading the sinew, which might have been fro
the bone needle, she began to stitch Kireko'
trapping the mutton fat within. Occasionally sh
the wad of leaves and moss to the wound befor
her needle and sinew.

When the gash was neatly secured, she let her ha
work for some minutes before covering it again v
crushed leleshwa leaves. Malaika could smell th
aroma. Noah lifted Kireko's inert body while Kok
wad around his waist with a swathe of red and blu

She arose like bamboo straightening when the wind dies, and moved behind Kireko at the head of the bed platform. Placing her hands on his scalp, her bony fingers pointed downwards along his cheeks. Malaika watched carefully. There was a rustling sound. Vivid red and gold tail feathers appeared, draping down Kireko's neck and shoulders. The blue plumage of its wings became lost in the shape and colour of the old one's bony arms. The bird rested on Kireko's head for a few moments, testing its wings, then sprang to life, fluttering aloft, trailing flashes of iridescent blue into the smoky gloom. The bird swooped in little arcs in the hut's low confines with the old one's arms following its glinting path. Then it seemed as if she had thrust the bird into some hidden crevice in the cow-dung linings of the ceiling. The bird was gone.

Kokoo's small body appeared to shrink a little. She sighed as her scrawny arms fell stiffly to her sides. As she did so, Malaika let her own breath escape.

Kireko lazily opened his eyes and nodded thanks to his great-grandmother. Even in the dim light Malaika could see that the pain lines had left him and he had regained some of the life that she remembered. She kissed him.

'What nonsense is this, Angel?' he asked.

'It is because I love you,' she answered in faltering Maa. 'And it is not nonsense, so do not tease me. And do not call me Angel.'

She smiled and would have enjoyed continuing the banter but Kireko merely shook his head in resignation. 'Ai, ai,' he said to Noah. 'Women these days, ah?'

Malaika stepped back from the bed. 'Now, you need to rest.'

He drew himself up so that his back rested against the bolster of cowhides. 'There is no time for sitting around with the women.'

'But ...' Malaika protested, 'you can't go anywhere! You are wounded!'

'Noah and I are expected in Seyabei in the mid-afternoon.'

'Noah, Kokoo, you cannot let him go like this.' Malaika looked at them for support.

Noah said, 'You should save your caring for those who need it, Malaika. But do not worry. I have made arrangements. He will not walk far. A truck will take us to Seyabei.'

'What could be so important that you must hurry away today? You need to rest.'

'It is the business of men,' Kireko said. 'Not for you to know. Or to concern yourself.'

'Kireko must represent our *enkang* in the planning for the *eunoto*,' Noah added, a little apologetically.

Malaika sighed. 'Then at least wait here for a moment. I am going to see if one of your brave *morani* can get a message to my friends. Then I will see to your dressing before you get into the truck.'

She took another moment to study him. His fine features, his boyish grin. She had forgotten how much she loved him. A smile lingered on her lips as she departed into the *olale* space. It was so good to be back with family, with her big brother again.

Light penetrated the edges of the outside cowhide door. She stooped to pass through it and straightened into the bright morning light.

A rough hand grabbed her arm painfully tight. She gasped.

The man's face spread into a cruel grin. It revealed a single gold tooth.

PART 3

ASCENDING THE ESCARPMENT

CHAPTER 30

PEABODY'S GUIDE TO EAST AFRICA (5ᵀᴴ ED):
Getting around: there are three options. On your first visit
it is best to use a safari agent, who can add you to a group
(cheap, but limited choice of itinerary), or set up a private
safari with a tailor-made itinerary. In both cases you will
have a minibus and professional driver. Vehicles are
equipped with a roof hatch that can be opened for viewing
wildlife — very convenient when the grass is high.

Many second-time visitors choose to rent a four-wheel
drive car. Before selecting your vehicle, ask for two spare
tyres (they will probably be retreads) and check the jack.
Punctures are normal and a broken shock absorber is not
uncommon.

Public transport is not for the faint-hearted.

'I'll tell you somethin', Jack,' Bear said, manoeuvring the car
around a boulder the size of a half-buried washing machine,
'Rover knows how to make a four-wheel drive.' He made a
fist and shook it for emphasis. 'A man's four-wheel drive. Not
like this pussy. Look at this!' He slapped the tee-bar gearshift.
'What would the fucking Japanese know about four-wheel
drives? Automatic, for chrissake!' The Landcruiser plunged
into a flooded section of road. Water cascaded into the scrub.
'Give me the ol' D110 any day.'

Jack didn't respond. He had spoken no more than a few words since they'd left Tingisha's village half an hour before. Bear probably assumed it was the hangover. Maybe it was. Maybe it was boredom. The Narok to Kisii road was nothing to get excited about. The countryside was reminiscent of a lunar landscape. Even the number of animals had dwindled to the odd wildebeest and an occasional zebra. He was brooding, he decided, and he had to snap out of it. But his mind kept niggling at the mystery of Malaika's departure.

Mystery? What mystery? he thought. She had taken the spare set of keys and driven off in the Land Rover. As simple as that.

If only he had gone to the *banda* as he'd started out to do. If only he hadn't been tempted by the frigging tears of the lion.

They came upon the Land Rover on its side at a bend in the road with a camber that would cause a problem for the unwary. Jack was out of the car before Bear brought it to a stop. He leapt to the propeller shaft then onto the rear door. Kneeling on the door panel, he peered down into the cabin. 'Nothing,' he muttered. 'Here, Bear, hold the door open while I climb in.'

Bear clambered onto the front door and lifted open the rear one. Jack lowered himself down.

'The roof hatch's been opened,' Jack said. 'Must've got out through there.' He scanned around the cabin. The left-hand windows, which had taken the weight of the car when it rolled into the shallow culvert, were smashed, and the windscreen was crazed.

'What's that on the floor in front, Jack?'

Jack steadied himself with a hand on the dashboard and reached into the front compartment. It was Malaika's rain-soaked cap. He straightened up as much as possible in the confined space and looked at the hand that he had rested on the dashboard. It was sticky-red. He rubbed finger and thumb together, feeling foolish for wondering if he'd recognise Malaika's blood.

Five minutes further down the road they came upon the rusted sign, *Patel's Duka*. Following Tingisha's directions, they took the track to the right of the *duka*. It was badly rutted, overgrown and occasionally lost its way in the thorn bush. Bear was muttering something about soft suspension.

As the thorn bush cleared, a village appeared in a shallow valley across a rocky creek. Four men stood around an olive-green, canvas-covered truck. The heavy tailgate was slammed shut as the Landcruiser eased through the creek.

'Look at that,' Bear said, indicating a house on the rise above the village. 'What's it need a goddamn VHF antenna for?' He pulled up short of the truck parked at the opening of the thorn-bush entanglement that surrounded the compound.

This village was unlike Tingisha's. His had been tumbling with children. Women sat in their circle of friends and family, laughing while weaving or combing hides. A riot of calves and kids and small boys played around the *boma*'s outskirts. But this village consisted of a sullen group of men, a few goats and a handful of old women watching silently from the doorways of tattered huts. And the incongruous house on the hill — a house clearly out of place.

'*Jambo*, gentlemen,' a man in a grey pinstriped jacket said, beaming as he approached the car. Trouser legs flapped like black bunting from a belt around his generous girth.

'*Jambo*,' answered Jack for both of them.

The men standing by the truck moved off a few paces, their backward glances at odds with the effusive welcome of the man now extending his hand to Jack.

'I am Mengoru. Benjamin Mengoru. Are you lost?'

Jack shook his hand. 'Jack Morgan. This is ... um, that's Mr Hoffman over there.' Bear had wandered past the truck towards the *boma* gate. 'I'm sorry to intrude. We're looking for some people. There was a car accident up the road.'

'The UN car?'

'Yes, a Land Rover. Have you seen them?' Jack asked, feeling reassured.

'Yes, my people went out last night to assist. There was an injured man. We carried him here. Are you with the UN, Mr Morgan?'

'Yes. There was a young woman with them. Are they here?'

'Indeed there was. Is she your friend?'

'Are they here?' Jack persisted.

'Not now, no. I sent both to Nairobi in my car.'

'Is she hurt? When did she leave?'

'I think she is not hurt. Perhaps a few bruises. But she wanted to stay with the young man. He was not well. I sent them to a hospital in my Isuzu pick-up. You know you can never be —'

'When did they leave?' Jack wondered again about the so-called *young man*.

'Oh! Now let me think. It was very early this morning. About dawn when my men brought them here.'

'And do you know which hospital?'

'I asked my driver to take them to Nairobi Hospital.'

'What time was that, please?'

'Around eight.'

'Okay, thanks, Mr Mengoru. We'll be going now.'

'You are most welcome,' he said beaming.

'Bear! Let's go!'

Bear appeared from behind the truck.

'You have a silver Landcruiser!' Mengoru added, peering into the cabin. 'Very fine. I am thinking of booting my Isuzu and buying a Landcruiser. They are very good cars, I think.'

'Yes. Thanks again.'

'My pleasure.' His smile was consistent — never quite reaching his eyes.

Jack climbed into the driver's seat and revved the motor into life. Bear had barely slammed his door before Jack hit the tee-bar; the Landcruiser spewed dust as it spun around. It plunged across the stony creek and bounced onto the track through the thorn bush.

The Landcruiser did a four-wheel drift as they joined the Narok–Kisii road. It roared past Patel's. Jack calculated the travelling time to Nairobi. 'We'll go straight across the valley,' he said. 'We should be in Nairobi by four o'clock.'

'Sure, buddy. Hey, it'll be okay. She'll be fine.' Bear had to raise his voice above the roar of the motor.

When Jack made no response, he said, 'You know, that village ain't all it appears.'

'Hmm?'

'Well, for starters, they had a shit-load of ivory in the back of that truck.'

'Ivory? Are you sure?'

'Absolutely. It was covered up so as you couldn't see it from the back. But I spotted it through a gap in the canvas.'

'Jesus!'

'There's about a ton or more of the stuff in there.'

'Be worth a fortune,' Jack said indifferently. He was concentrating on dodging potholes.

'You bet! So I kept walking, you know, doin' the tourist bit around the village. They looked a mean bunch of fuckers.'

'Yeah. Glad we're out of there. I have more on my mind than Mr Benjamin Mengoru. That name ... Mengoru ... I've heard it somewhere ...'

'Him and his little private army. Hey, how about that gold tooth?' Bear guffawed. 'Wow! Anyway, he'll *need* an army these days, from what I've heard.'

He told Jack how *The Nation* had run a series of stories on Kenyan poachers and their links to Somali bandits. Under pressure to halt the slaughter, the President had appointed Richard Leakey, the son of the famous Kenyan anthropologists, to arm, train and organise the National Parks' rangers for a war on the poachers. At the outset it was just another wild-west story — gun battles in the largely lawless north-eastern provinces. But the rangers attacked with great enthusiasm and efficiency.

'The newspaper said the National Parks boys were killing more poachers than poachers were killing elephant. First time in history. Then the area along the Somali border was closed to everyone except the military. The press included. It all kinda died about seven, eight months ago.'

Bear said rumours were buzzing around the UN offices at the time. It was said that somebody well connected in the Kenyan establishment was working with the armed Somali tribesmen who controlled a stockpile of ivory and horn. The Mogadishu area was a war zone, and armed bandits were in control along the Indian Ocean coast. To the north, the

Ethiopians were skirmishing with the Eritreans, and to the west the whole continent of Africa stood in the way. Still, the Somali stockpile was somehow leaking onto the world market.

'They said there had to be a Kenyan connection. How else could the stuff get to the Asian markets? It had to come through Kenya somehow.'

It was another of Bear's long stories and Jack paid scant attention. His mind had wandered off in pursuit of his feelings about Malaika. His *real* feelings, as opposed to those he had been nurturing during the morning to preserve some of his shattered self-esteem. He was surprised at the hollowness in his gut — the sense of loss. As far as relationships were concerned, this was a new sensation. And painful.

His feelings about Malaika were always a little hazy. It was like a view through a window misted by heavy morning dew. He could see a couple making blurred, soundless gestures. The man moved towards the woman, but kept his distance. The woman was reaching out, but not necessarily to him. Things were said, but from the outside could not be heard. The figures wavered back and forth beyond the glass. They were people out of focus and out of touch. How would it end?

He was on unfamiliar ground. It seemed he was at a place where the ego and the emptiness met. At any other time, he might have been able to clinically explore the logic of the situation. But this was not it.

The irony was galling. He had come to Africa to escape. To escape Liz and his guilt. To allow some dust to settle on ... the *incident* in Hawaii — he could not bring himself to call it *the death* — and to take some steps to bring order to his chaotic life.

The first step was to get away from everyone and everything connected with his life in Australia. Second, there would be no serious commitments. No women. No complications. So no regrets when it was time to go home. Malaika just happened. But she was a temporary diversion, no added baggage there. An interesting detour in his plan. He certainly hadn't intended to fall in love with her, if that's what he thought, not that he had. Nothing like that. But how extraordinary that now, a few months later, he could feel so bereft and hurt because she had walked away from him.

Third ... Was there a third? *Of course!* Third was to avoid contact with the police at all costs — most important for settling the dust.

Bear was muttering something about the rough ride. Jack's attention had not been on the road and they had more than once thumped into huge potholes. Now the car shuddered through a long series of corrugations and began to drift sideways. He eased off the accelerator until it stabilised.

A kilometre or two of sealed road took them through Narok. Goats, children and all manner of carts contested the narrow bitumen. Jack blasted the horn but was largely ignored. He was forced to pick his way through the throng at an aggravating slow pace. On the other side of the ramshackle town, he accelerated onto the potholed road again.

He returned to his reflections on Malaika. What was the attraction anyway, he wondered. So, Malaika's attractive. So what? Okay, beautiful. And that walk. If she had no more than average looks, that walk could stop you in your tracks.

But there was another thing. She made him feel good. Not only because she was good fun, and not just for the kick that any man might feel in the company of an attractive female — it was about being half of a zebra couple. It made a statement that probably drove the racists crazy. And he would miss that movie-star feeling whenever they walked into a restaurant.

IT WAS THE HOTTEST PART of the afternoon and the Landcruiser's air-conditioning was struggling to keep up. The sun beat on the driver's side window where Jack's raised arm tried to shield him from the heat. But sweat ran down his face to be captured in the wet band of his tee-shirt collar.

As they approached the escarpment, the hot dry air of the valley rose to meet the plateau's moisture-laden atmosphere. A fluffy mist engulfed them and swirled at tree-top height, giving a welcome break from the sun.

The Landcruiser crested a ridge. The road disappeared into the escarpment a thousand feet below. Jack jabbed at the brakes.

The spectacle of the Great Rift Valley, nestling beneath low cloud cover, was like a peep under the lid of a boiling cauldron of hot colour. Far below, at the bottom of a winding drop, the road shot like a pale arrow across a landscape of pink and orange. Colours of burnished gold ran into the hazy distance before becoming warm brown on the distant escarpment.

Jack dropped into a lower gear but the lumbering vehicle still lurched suicidally close to the road edge with its eroded yawning ditch eating into the tarmac.

Grey grass stubble clung defiantly to the hard earth of the valley floor, its life all but relinquished to the dry-season sun. But here and there, in the undulations of the flat landscape, glimmering green islands had already begun to appear in response to the recent downpour.

A giraffe ambled away from the road, blinking long lashes as they rumbled past. Somehow a dozen of them had materialised, dotted across the treeless countryside. Scattered between them were small herds of other grazers. Wart hogs strutted pompously. Zebras turned their heads in mild interest, and the ubiquitous wildebeest wiggled ears and beards as they ruminated upon their cud, their brows knitted in a wildebeestian attempt at concentration.

They were fifteen minutes from the eastern escarpment, and an hour from Nairobi, when a large white shape shimmered above the road ahead. As they drew nearer, a white Range Rover loomed from the heat haze. It blocked the road at a cluster of shabby sheet-metal structures. Two khaki-clad policemen came out of a building, which had no distinguishing features other than a spindly flagpole struggling to support a faded Kenyan flag.

A man in a black suit sauntered from the far side of the Range Rover, mopping his face with a large white handkerchief as they drew to a halt.

'Good afternoon, Mr Morgan,' the man in black said, his eyes roaming the rear seat.

Jack tried to conceal his surprise. 'Good afternoon, Mr Onditi. What brings you to this beauty spot this afternoon?'

'Just a routine check, Mr Morgan.' Onditi smiled as he

continued to stroll around the car. At the passenger door he said to Bear, 'Please step out of the car, sir.'

The two police peered into the cabin and rear compartment.

Jack climbed out and joined Bear, who planted his hands into his pockets, his chin thrust forward pugnaciously.

A policeman lifted their bags from the rear luggage compartment. The other opened a rear door and pulled a tissue box and sweet wrappers from the storage pockets behind the forward seats.

Onditi began to rummage through the glove box. He took out the driver's manual, a tube of expensive face lotion and the car registration papers.

'Mr Svensson?' he said, looking from the registration papers to Bear.

'No,' Bear answered. 'Mr Svensson is a friend. He loaned us his car.'

'Really? So why did Mr Svensson loan you his car, Mr . . . ?'

'Hoffman.'

'For urgent business in Nairobi,' Jack said, folding his arms and leaning against the mudguard.

A policeman handed two pale blue UN passports to Onditi, who threw the other papers onto the front seat, except for the car registration which he folded and slipped into his coat pocket.

'And how are things in the UNDP, Mr Morgan?' he said, flicking through the *laissez-passer* pages.

'Super.'

'I almost didn't recognise you at first. And there we were on that aid project together, almost colleagues.'

'Yes, we were very close, weren't we?'

Onditi glanced at Jack and his smile thinned. With Jack's open passport tucked under one arm, he flicked through Bear's. 'You both departed Kenya on November sixth?'

Bear said, 'Yes. We drove into Tanzania. From the Masai Mara.'

'Really? Then can you explain why there is no entry stamp for Tanzania?'

'Tanzania hardly ever mans that point these days. But I think you know that. We were tourists. Just overnight.'

'Hmm. I will make some enquiries into this so-called tourist visit. And the matter of the *borrowed* car.'

His smirk, and what Jack thought to be about the clumsiest attempt at eliciting tea money, was too much. 'What's all this bullshit about, Onditi?' he said.

'I am an officer of the Kenyan government,' Onditi sniffed.

'Yeah?' Bear said. 'So what?'

'And I am temporarily assisting the police with anti-poaching checks.' His smile resumed. 'But I'm sure we can clear this up. Follow me. It will be more comfortable inside, out of the sun.'

The two uniformed men flanked them as they walked towards the police post. The office was cramped and hot. Onditi showed them towards a room at the back of the building labelled *Waiting Room*. The heavy wooden door opened into a space about four metres square with steel re-enforcing mesh on the unglazed window. Some empty soda crates, cardboard cartons and fuel tins were stacked in one corner to the side of a bare wooden bench.

Onditi was about to shut the door behind them when Jack pulled it open and grabbed a fistful of Onditi's shirt. 'Okay, arsehole, I've had enough of this. You'll tell me what this is about or I'm gonna —'

A policeman broke Jack's grip on Onditi. The other waved a handgun in his face.

'Oh, Mr Morgan!' Onditi said with a grin. 'The arrangements not to your liking? The room too cramped perhaps?'

Jack kept his jaw firmly shut, but fixed Onditi with a cold stare.

'Not like your fancy apartment where you can entertain your whores? Or should I say, Maasai whores? That's your specialty, isn't it?'

Onditi backed out, laughing. The policeman slammed the door in Jack's face.

CHAPTER 31

PEABODY'S GUIDE TO EAST AFRICA (5TH ED):
In his book, *The Maasai: Their Language and Folklore* (1905),
Sir Claude .Hollis, an expert on the Maasai, said they
would become extinct as a race if they did not undergo a
peaceful transition into the white man's world.

Given the Maasai's fierce determination to remain
isolated from the modern world, many would say that if
that transition did occur, it would effectively mean the
Maasai, as a race, were already extinct.

Malaika removed a roof panel and the golden light of mid-
afternoon splashed onto the hut's daubed wall. She sat beside
Kokoo on the bed, a squat pad of wooden slats and hides, and
struggled with the coarse ropes on the old lady's frail ankles
and wrists.

They had been bound and gagged by two of Mengoru's
thugs after the *moran* had refused to touch Kokoo. When they
returned to untie them after Bear and Jack had departed,
Malaika guessed that the Maasai had warned them about
Kokoo, because they gave her a wide berth and hurried away
after untying Malaika.

She rubbed her great-grandmother's wrists, then rubbed
some circulation into her own, recalling the mixture of fear and
anger that had consumed her as she heard Mengoru telling

plausible lies to Jack. She had seen Bear through a gap in the wall, but by the time she had crawled to the entrance covering, he had returned to the car. When they drove off, her spirits sank and her apprehension began to grow.

Malaika sensed the indignity Kokoo suffered at the hands of the young louts for she had been silent for some time. 'Kokoo,' she said, by way of a diversion, 'this morning you started to tell me about my destiny . . . '

'Yes, child.'

'Well, please continue.'

'Yes. I should.'

As a patch of sunlight crept up the wall, Kokoo told the tribe's story. She said it was important that Malaika knew it before she could understand her own role. She used a patchwork of Swahili and Maa. Even an English phrase, perhaps a throwback from some distant past, found its way into the narrative.

She started her story in the years before the *wazungu* invaded Maasailand with the iron rails, before they brought the rinderpest to the herds and the smallpox to the tribe. Mbatian, the Great *Laibon*, had recently died and his two sons had gone to war to decide the succession.

'It was Sendeyo's right by birth,' she said. 'He was the older son and should have been given the iron club of leader. But Lenana deceived his father as he lay dying. Then the terrible wars began. It was three seasons before I was born, but my mother told me of the fierce battles on the Laikipia plains. Finally, after many *moran* were dead, Sendeyo was defeated and he fled to the south.

'After some terrible years in the lands south of Kilima N'jaro fighting the *Jerumani wazungu* — the Germans, as they are called in English — Sendeyo made a truce and came home to the Ngong Hills. But he seethed for revenge and drew upon his hate to conjure powerful magic. His vengeance was skilful and cruel. It would have been easier simply to kill Lenana, but Sendeyo knew how to hate. And how to punish.'

Kokoo told how Sendeyo had put a curse on all of Lenana's descendants. The curse was unleashed only upon the birth of a second daughter to any family member.

Malaika could remember fragments of the story. She imagined they were the parts that a child would seize upon — stories of magic and murder. 'Was the curse put on all the Aiser clan?' she asked.

'No. Only our family. Lenana was your great-grandfather. I was his fourth and last wife. Our family carries Sendeyo's curse. We alone.' Naisua tugged at the long strands of her beaded necklace. 'Maybe your great-grandfather could be forgiven for his error; the wisdom was not upon him and pride led him to break our laws. If he could only have known what might follow ...' She took a deep breath. 'Lenana gave the women of our family his special gift, but, oh, the burden, the terrible burden remains.'

The memories seemed to press on Kokoo like a stone. She ran her long bony fingers down her face, drawing the skin tightly across her cheekbones. It made hollows of her eyes where two pinpoints shone like firelight deep in a cave.

'Our burden is that we must have children, but cannot conceive a second daughter. This is not just to save us, or even all the Kidongi clan. Sendeyo's curse can only be unleashed by one of our family, but it strikes widely. In our trust lies the safety of *all* the Maasai.'

Malaika began to worry that the effort of recalling the ancient stories was draining her great-grandmother of the little strength that remained. 'Kokoo, the days of the smallpox are gone. You should not worry yourself about the sins of our ancestors. These are different times.'

Kokoo began to fidget at her necklace again. She tugged the coloured sections around her neck in a red, yellow and blue procession. 'No, child, Sendeyo's curse is with us yet. Almost one hundred years have passed since the curse took its first one. I was one year old when the second daughter of Lenana's first wife was taken from him. My own son, Seggi, was foolish enough to ignore it. When his second daughter was born, he lost her and his sweet wife in a terrible storm of insects that sent the herds crashing into the village.' She placed her small clenched fists over her eyes. Shaking her head from side to side, she began to pound feebly at her

temples. 'Many died ... Oh, many died. Ai, the children ...
My people ...'

Malaika put her arm around Kokoo's shoulders. She was
trembling.

'Ai!' The old woman continued to shake her head. 'Ai, ai.'

Malaika could think of nothing to say. 'Shhh ...' she said,
patting her *kokoo*'s shoulder. 'Shhh ...'

'Lenana was wicked,' Kokoo said, 'but what can be done
now? When a raindrop falls, the ground can never give it back.'

'If Sendeyo really wanted to punish our family, why not
curse all our children? Why only the *second* daughter?'
Malaika asked, taking her *kokoo*'s hands in hers.

'Oh, Sendeyo knew how to hate. He wanted the women to
suffer most. As soon as a daughter is born, it is the end of
child-bearing — the risk thereafter is too great. The end of
child-bearing means an end to the marriage. The second-born
is the gatekeeper of the curse, but the first daughter is also
cursed.'

'How?'

'Imagine how that child will suffer when she learns of her
role.'

'Then she should not be told.'

'She must know. Otherwise how can she avoid the curse on
her daughters?' The old one dropped her head to her chest.
'Oh, our women bear the heaviest burden for those ancient
sins.'

Having led her *kokoo* into this despondent mood, Malaika
tried to lift her spirits. 'Kokoo, you say the Kidongi women
must bear the burden of the curse, but you also said we have a
special gift. What is our gift?'

'Yes. Lenana's gift.' Naisua's earrings bobbed, the silver
capturing the firelight. 'His magic could not overcome his
brother's curse — Sendeyo had learned his father's craft well.
But Lenana was shrewd.'

Kokoo told of Lenana's decree that the position of *laibon*
could pass down through the female line of the family. It had
never before been possible, but his decree meant that the
women were entitled to inherit the position, and the magic

that was its legacy. A male would only assume the role of *laibon* if his female predecessor appointed him.

'He knew that we women might be punished for the evil we carried, perhaps we would be banished from the tribe. So he changed the laws of inheritance and appointed me the first woman to be called the *laibon*. I was just a girl, even younger than you, but I led the northern tribes across the iron lines to where the British said we must go. Oh, that was so long ago … I was carrying his child, Seggi. Without a daughter to succeed me, he became the *laibon* at his elevation to elder.' Naisua slowly shook her head. 'When he was taken from me, it became my task again. But I am old. Look at me. Too old.'

She sighed. 'Your mother took you away because she could not change the Maasai world, but she did not take away your gift, the power that comes with your succession.'

'Succession?'

'Child, will you take my place as *laibon*? Will you lead our people through the terrible times that are upon us?'

Malaika tried to slip her hand from the old one's, but she held it firmly. 'Kokoo, I haven't been a Maasai since I left the village so many years ago. And Maasai magic is … is … '

'You may not know it is there. You may not feel it. But you have it.'

Malaika could see her reflection in Kokoo's eyes.

'You have it inside you, Malaika. It awaits its time.'

'When is its time?'

'When you need it most, the power will appear.'

Malaika shifted her position on the bed. 'But these are old stories, Kokoo. From a long time ago. The curse is gone.'

'No! Believe me, Sendeyo's curse is with us yet.' The sun had gone and the flames of the cooking fire glistened in the tear wells brimming in Naisua's eyes. 'The second-born … the second-born … the one called Ziada — God's gift.'

Malaika began to understand Kokoo's intense interest in her stories of Mwanza. 'Kokoo, is Ziada …? Is she the second daughter? Are you saying she is cursed?'

'Cursed? Who can say who is the cursed? Am I not cursed to have witnessed the death of my loved ones, my babies? So I weep for myself, and I weep for your sister, who is innocent of any wrong. But if she is of Mengoru's blood ... Or she may be the child of the Kunono man. Who knows how Kunono blood might change things? The spirits deny me this. But I fear she is the one because the curse is heavy upon us.'

'What do you mean?'

'There is a plague on our young people. It is a strange and terrible death.'

'What is it?'

'I have no answers. It is not the smallpox. Nor the influenza. Your *kokoo* becomes old and useless,' she said, shaking her head. 'The death comes as in the days of the famine, but of food there is enough.'

'Are you saying they can't eat?'

'They eat but grow thinner. Even gourds of blood and milk cannot fatten them. It is the young ones. Our strong young men. They come home to die. Our fine young women, some with babies. And the children, they wither like a flower plucked from the stem. And here am I ... I watch them go.'

'The slimming sickness,' Malaika said softly. The hut felt like it was about to close around her. She stood, feeling suddenly very weary, needing air to clear her head which had begun to pound with the mix of Kokoo's old fears and her own growing realisation of what was happening to the Maasai.

The air at the opened roof hatch washed her face and she closed her eyes against the bright gold of the western sky.

She wondered why she hadn't seen it before. She was an expert in rural communities, trained to identify these risks. Had others seen it? In general terms, yes. But did they understand the Maasai circumstances?

The Maasai were a special case, but no one seemed to have noticed it. Perhaps it was only the illumination of the last twenty-four hours, when she had become a Maasai again, that had enabled her to see the particular jeopardy that they faced. Her return to the community and its indomitable culture had revealed the extent of the tragedy.

She put her fingers to her temples and rubbed gently at the

soft throbbing. Through the hatch opening the sky quickly lost its gold. Ashen outcrops of cloud brooded above a blood-red horizon.

In the centuries that it took the Maasai to emerge as the most successful tribe in East Africa, rich in cattle, feared in battle, the culture had changed little. Why should it? The Maasai stamped their lifestyle on all. When they failed to defeat the white invaders, the Maasai simply ignored them. The culture remained inviolate.

In time, the other tribes flourished, adopting many of the white man's ideas. Again, the Maasai ignored them. Life would be judged in absolute terms, Maasai terms, rather than by simplistic comparisons. They cared not that sophisticated Kenyans considered them backward. They ignored the jibes about sexual promiscuity.

The tragic irony, Malaika now realised, was that the tribe's insularity, which had consigned the Maasai to a cultural, political and economic backwater and should have been their security against this invasion, was instead a monstrous trap. If the Maasai had remained cloistered within a Maasai world, they would have stayed safe. But once outsiders breached their physical isolation, once their cultural conventions came under attack, their traditions and their customs became the path to their own annihilation. Polygamy, and wife-sharing, would ensure it.

She looked at her great-grandmother, wondering how she could possibly make her understand. The old woman had lived under the care of the Great *Laibon*. He had the power — some would say, the magic — to change the world. As far as Kokoo was concerned, the world had not changed from her childhood. There was no way to explain it in terms she would understand. Only the west had the words. Only clinical scientific terms could be trusted to impart the horror of it.

Finally she began. 'We call it the slimming sickness. In the West it is called AIDS.'

CHAPTER 32

PEABODY'S GUIDE TO EAST AFRICA (5TH ED):
The Great Rift Valley of East Africa is one of the Earth's
geological features which is visible from the moon.

Jack looked at his watch again. Two-fifty. He had been pacing the floor like a penned lion for ten minutes. It soon became obvious from the long silence on the other side of the door that Onditi and the police were content to wait. He sank to the bench beside Bear, who wiped a shirtsleeve across the perspiration beading on his forehead.

A few flies made lazy zigzags in the still air near the ceiling. Jack slapped his thighs with both hands and was on his feet again. Striding to the wooden door, he banged a fist on it and shouted, 'Hey! How about something to drink back here?' He pulled a red handkerchief from his pocket, mopped his face and ran it along the back of his neck under the collar of his black tee-shirt. 'Hey!'

Still no response. He flopped beside Bear under the barred window and started drumming his fingers on his knee. Bear had closed his eyes, and was resting his head against the wall.

Ten minutes later the door opened and closed behind a young boy who came hesitantly to the centre of the room. He was carrying two 7 Ups. Jack went to the boy when it appeared that he would come no closer. He took the drinks and handed one to Bear. They were warm. Jack noticed the bottle-opener hanging from the boy's hand. He pointed at it and the boy handed it over without taking his eyes off Jack.

Jack thanked him. '*Tafadhali*,' he said, trying his best to smile. It didn't work. He popped the bottle tops.

The boy, about seven or eight, stood a safe pace away and studied Jack, who appeared to empty the bottle in a single draft. There was an inch or two left. Jack belched and held it out towards the boy, who looked unsure of his meaning. Jack nodded. The hand hesitated halfway to the bottle, then took it. With another glance at Jack, he raised it to his lips, draining it in a gulp. His eyes watered and he blinked away tears with a shy grin, then belched loudly.

Jack laughed. 'What's your name, mate?'

The boy sucked his top lip.

'Can't speak English, huh?'

'I can.' It was said so softly that Jack could barely hear it. 'I go to school,' he added with some pride.

'Okay.' Jack nodded. 'So what's your name, schoolboy?'

The boy hesitated, then said, 'Njoroge.'

'G'day, Njoroge. I'm Jack. This is Bear.'

Bear half opened an eyelid then closed it again.

'So you're helping the policemen today, huh?'

Njoroge smiled, revealing more gums than teeth. 'He pay me one shillingi.' He showed him a silver coin.

Jack dug into his jeans pocket and found a five-shilling piece. 'Okay, Njoroge, this is for you if you can help me.' He held it between thumb and finger. The boy stared at the coin. Jack guessed it was the most money he had ever been offered.

'Did you see these men arrive today?' He gestured towards the front room.

'*Ndio*,' the boy nodded.

'They came together?'

'No. The policemans, he live near here. The *mzee*, he come in morning.' He pointed east to Nairobi.

'The *mzee*? You mean the man in the dark suit?' Jack tugged at his black tee-shirt.

'*Ndio*.'

'He came from Nairobi? Good. What time did he come, Njoroge?'

'From morning.'

'Early morning?'

'*Ndio*. The sun, he was here.' He raised an arm above waist level.

'And how many cars have you seen today?'

The large brown eyes left the coin for a moment to count fingers. '*Saba*,' he said, holding up seven fingers.

'Okay, Njoroge, now listen carefully.' Jack squatted on his haunches in front of the boy. 'Do you know what an Isuzu pick-up looks like?'

'*Ndio*.'

'Now, think carefully. How many Isuzu pick-ups did you see come by today?'

The boy hesitated. 'One.' He held up a small black finger.

'Okay. And what colour was it?'

Njoroge's gaze drifted to the ceiling. 'B-b-black. He have *mbili wazungu*.' He showed two fingers.

Two white men. Jack sat back. 'Good boy, Njoroge,' he said and handed him the coin.

A policeman poked his head into the room and grunted at the boy. Njoroge scampered out and the door closed again.

'There's something weird going on here,' Jack said, turning to Bear.

'Hmm?' Bear slowly opened an eye.

Jack sat on the bench beside him. 'Something weird ...'

'Weird is right.' Bear closed the eye again.

'If Malaika wanted to give me the flick, why would she tell Tingisha where she was going?'

'What I wanna know,' Bear muttered, 'is how do you get thrown into gaol in the middle of the goddam Great Rift Valley, for chrissake.'

'And the boy was here all morning and didn't see Mengoru's pick-up. So she didn't come this way.' Jack stood, his back to Bear, his fingers rubbing his chin pensively. 'Maybe the kid made it up — took my five bob and bolted.'

'Visa irregularities ...' Bear rested his head on the wall

behind him. 'What bullshit. It's more likely to be about Mr Gold Tooth and his shit-load of ivory.'

'Or maybe that Mengoru guy was lying.' Jack took a pace towards the far wall. 'But why would he do that? To keep me from Malaika?' He searched the floorboards as if the answers were written there. 'Maybe the ivory ...?'

'Who is this Onditi guy anyway?' Bear opened his eyes. 'Holdin' us in a goddamn pressure-cooker like this ... A lousy visa. Must be more'n that. Now, if I was smuggling ivory ...'

'And what's Onditi doing here?'

'... I'd have someone down here keeping an eye out. Maybe Onditi —'

'Onditi and Mengoru!' Jack planted a fist into his palm. 'Their names were on the file in the PC's office in Kisumu! Bear, that's it! Onditi and Mengoru are in this together.'

'That's what I was gonna say.' Bear stood and poked the air between them. 'They're in this ivory poaching together and this road block is to check who goes where.'

'And Malaika must have seen the ivory. So Mengoru keeps her out of the way.' Jack began to pace, going back over the logic, testing it for holes. He was feeling better. He still didn't know the connection between Malaika and the Maasai guy she had taken to the village, but at least he knew where she was — back in Isuria. 'Wait a minute.' He stopped pacing. 'Wait a minute. How would Onditi know we know?'

'What?' Bear asked.

'How would Onditi know we know about the ivory? If we didn't know about the ivory, he wouldn't need to keep us here while they get it shipped away.' Jack searched the dirt floor again. 'It doesn't hang together.'

Bear snapped his fingers. 'The radio!'

'What?'

'The VHF radio on that weird house in Isuria.' He rubbed his hands together. 'There's a VHF station here too. All the up-country police stations have 'em.'

'So Mengoru puts in a call,' Jack added. 'No wonder that arsehole Onditi wasn't surprised to see us. He was expecting us!' He sat again and rubbed his chin. 'What if that *was* ivory you saw in that truck?'

'What do you mean, *what if*? I *told* you it was ivory. I saw it!'

'Yeah, yeah, I know. So if it really is ivory and Malaika saw it too, they might ... Jesus! We've got to get her out of there!' Jack was on his feet and pacing again.

'Meanwhile, in the local cooler ... How're we gonna manage that, buddy?'

'I don't know, but we'd better do it quick. My bet is they'll move that truck later tonight. Get it out of there before dawn. After that, the problem of Malaika goes on the agenda.'

Bear studied the corrugated-iron walls. 'Reckon I could kick these babies off their corner posts.'

Jack looked the wall up and down. 'Probably could, but they'd be all over us before we could make a hole big enough to get through.' He walked to the stack of tins and crates in the corner. There were various fuel containers, and empty soda bottles in wooden crates. He picked up a four-gallon drum and shook it. There was perhaps a cupful in it. The label said *Paraffin*.

He grabbed a cardboard carton and crushed it in the corner near the door. After dumping the empty bottles from a Coke crate, he placed it on top of the cardboard. Then he sprinkled it with kerosene. There was a drop of diesel in another container and he splashed it on too. 'That should get a bit of smoke going,' he said. 'Okay, I'll light this and then we yell like crazy. When they come in, we go out.'

Bear nodded. 'Got it.'

'Let me have your lighter, mate.'

The kerosene and cardboard caught immediately. A trickle of thick blue smoke rose from the burning diesel. Jack and Bear put their faces into the steel mesh at the window and bellowed, 'Fire! Fire! Help! Hey, out there! Fire!' They kicked the iron walls. 'Fire!'

A policeman came into view at the rear of the building, then rushed back to the front. They continued to yell, 'Help! Fire! Help!' The smoke invaded their lungs and eyes.

Jack began to gag in a coughing fit. Suddenly the smoke was sucked from the room as the door to the office swung open. They dashed to the opening. Jack planted a punch into the policeman's gut. Bear put him down with a looping fist and an elbow to the jaw.

With eyes streaming, Jack erupted from the smoke cloud and collided with the second policeman, who was blocking the exit from the office, his gun held grimly in both hands. Jack grabbed it and wrestled him to the floor. They tumbled over one another. Jack tried desperately to capture the gun-hand. It stayed just out of reach, thrashing wildly about. The policeman fought like a man with his life at stake. For a bizarre moment, as Jack pinned the gun-hand to the floor and he and the policeman were face on face, he wondered if he could make him listen to reason. After all, he only wanted to get back to the car.

Bear kicked the gun across the room. Another kick into the policeman's ribs allowed Jack to bounce to his feet. 'Let's get out of here!' he said, and led the way to the door. Bear picked up the gun at the doorway and followed.

The bright sun assaulted their eyes. It took a moment to find the Landcruiser behind a group of young Maasai men who were piling out of a dilapidated truck parked between the police lock-up and the four-wheel drive.

Jack turned to Bear. 'C'mon, big fella! The car's over here.'

It happened too quickly to shout a warning. Behind Bear, one of the policemen levelled his handgun and fired at Bear in the same motion. Bear grunted and fell to the dust, clasping at a gory hole in his trouser leg.

The policeman raised his gun towards Jack, but before either could react, Bear fired at the policeman, sending him staggering backwards into the lock-up door clutching at his chest. He slid down the doorjamb with a look of disbelief on his face.

Jack ran back to Bear, who was holding his thigh in bloody hands, staring at the small round hole in his trouser leg. The policeman remained motionless. 'Oh, shit!' Jack said, but hauled Bear to his feet and cleared a path through the Maasai, who had remained impassive observers throughout the whole drama.

It wasn't until they were ten minutes away, speeding towards Isuria, that Jack realised Onditi had not appeared during the fight. And on further reflection, he couldn't recall seeing the white Range Rover either.

CHAPTER 33

PEABODY'S GUIDE TO EAST AFRICA (5TH ED):
It is recommended that visitors to East Africa purchase appropriate medical insurance. However, check the small print. Your situation in East Africa may not be covered by some policies because travel there is considered 'a dangerous practice'.

Onditi's Range Rover bumped over the creek, crept past the entrance to the village and climbed the slope to Mengoru's house. The daily pattern of Maasai life unfolded in the valley below. A line of young warriors marched off to their *manyatta*, their long-bladed spears bobbing above their glistening braids. They passed children herding goats towards the *boma* gate. One of the older boys confronted an obstinate goat. He threw stones and sticks at it, forcing it back to the herd.

In the *enkang* a handful of old women had gathered around the stock pen, watching a woman struggle with a calf at the end of a halter. The calf had its hooves planted in the mud, refusing to budge. The other women appeared to be arguing, or shouting instructions at her.

As he pulled on the handbrake beside Mengoru's house, Malaika emerged from one of the huts below. Onditi watched her turn to help an old woman who followed through the low doorway. Malaika's blue jeans stretched tightly over her buttocks as she bent to assist her companion. He could see the curve of her hips and, when she straightened, could almost feel the fullness of her breasts.

'Ah, you're here.' Mengoru had come up behind him from the house.

'I came as soon as I had them in the lock-up.' Onditi watched as Malaika walked arm in arm with the old woman beyond the *boma* fence and out of sight. He turned to face Mengoru. 'You were right about them. Trouble.'

'More than you know. I was just now talking to the Rift Valley police inspector. Our *wazungu* friends shot and killed one of his men.'

'And the *wazungu*?'

'Gone. The inspector said they are coming this way. He wants us to help find them.'

'Escaped murderers. We can deal with them as we like.'

'Of course.' Mengoru grinned. 'I will put the men on alert.'

'So we did not need to plant the rhino horn in their car?'

'No matter, two or three low-grade pieces. And it has convinced the inspector that he is dealing with serious criminals.'

'Wonderful. What about our shipment?'

'A change of plans. I have sent for the truck. You will take the shipment to Muhoro. Make sure our Arab friends are satisfied. I will stay here in case the *wazungu* return.'

'As you wish.' Onditi turned his attention back to the village to conceal his smile. At last — his chance to deal directly with the Arabs.

Malaika and the old one were climbing the far slope. 'What about her?' he said, jerking his head in Malaika's direction.

'What? Hmm, yes. The bitch refuses to obey me. There is no chance of a wedding.'

'And what about her silence?'

'Hmm, yes. You are right — a bigger problem.'

'Ah, daughters these days ... so difficult for a father.'

'Difficult? Pah! It is impossible! They do as they wish. Running around like whores. No control ...'

'No respect.'

'Exactly! Whores with no respect for a man. And the Kidongi — oh, they are the worst. They have a woman for their *laibon*! A woman for a leader!'

'Disgraceful.'

'It is surely a disgrace! Now, if I were the *laibon*, if I were leader here, there would be no such nonsense. Women would behave.'

'Keep them in their place.'

'I would keep them in their place. Whores. And that old crow — she would be gone. I would see to her. Just like her dullard son. Ah, but these young *moran* — they worship her.' He spat into the dirt. 'The women in this village have always been against me, you know.'

'You could be leader.'

'I could lead all the Maasai! Votes in the regional elections ...' He began to pace the length of the car.

'The Party would take some notice of you then.'

'The Party would take some notice of old Mengoru then,' he said, pleased with his idea.

'If it wasn't for the women ...'

'The women! Whores! Good for nothing ... When the old witch is gone, like that wife of mine ... Ah! To hell with her!'

'So, it is only that one down there ...'

'It is just that disrespectful bitch of a daughter ...'

'You should deal with her.'

'I know what I will do. I will deal with her. She must be silenced.' Mengoru's eyes were darting to left and right as he paced.

Onditi moved into his path to get his attention. 'My friend, may I make a suggestion?'

Mengoru, lost in his own thoughts, said nothing.

'If I might be so forward ... why risk trouble with your *moran*? I mean, you don't want trouble in the village. Why not, how should I say it, move the problem? Why not *export* the problem?'

Mengoru cocked an eyebrow. 'What are you saying?'

Onditi couldn't proceed under Mengoru's intense gaze. He took a pace away. With his back to him he continued, 'Our

Arab friends in Entebbe are known to appreciate young black girls. They say they have an appetite for them.' He glanced back at Mengoru whose eyes told nothing of his thoughts. 'Well, so I have heard,' Onditi went on. 'Now, if you were to offer them a pretty gift, they would say you are a generous business partner. Very gracious. A Big Man. A leader of men.' Onditi pressed on, anxious now to draw it to a close. 'And second, you would remove the problem of your talkative young daughter.'

Onditi turned to face Mengoru. For a moment he was afraid that he had overstepped the mark as Mengoru's expression remained blank. It was as if he were struck dumb. Offended. It was, after all, an outrageous suggestion to make to a father.

Then Mengoru nodded. The nod was so slight it might have been missed. He raised an eyebrow a fraction. Onditi held his breath.

A look of begrudging approval came to Mengoru's eyes, and a smile spread across his crooked mouth. He began to chuckle. It was low in his belly at first. It wobbled there, then grew to a laugh. He slapped Onditi on the shoulder. Now he could not hold the laughter back. The more he laughed, the harder he slapped the shoulder. His face contorted with delight and he began to choke and gag with it.

'Hah! Hah! Hah!' he bellowed, gasping for breath. 'Hah! Hah! Hah! Yes! Of course. My friend, it is good. Very good.' His tears streamed down his face. 'A gift. And you will tell them from me, from Mengoru, not to spare her. Use her well. Hah! Hah! Tell them to use her well!'

MALAIKA LED KOKOO TO THE shade of a huge baobab on the outskirts of the *enkang*. She could hear Mengoru's laughter coming from the house on the hill above. They moved behind the thick trunk to be out of its sight. The armed guard, who had followed them all day, squatted on his haunches in the shade of a shrub, twenty paces away. He picked at a blade of dry grass and pretended to ignore them.

Malaika took Kokoo's frail arm to help her down to a seat on one of the huge roots that ran from the base of the bottle-shaped trunk. The old woman's wheezing came from deep in her chest. She was almost gasping for breath, but gave Malaika a wan smile and patted her hand as she settled herself.

Shortly after noon they had been to visit Kireko, who had moved himself to the *moran*'s *manyatta*. He would not stay in the women's quarters, as he called the *enkang*, any longer than necessary. He had been about to leave for the nearby town of Seyabei for the meeting of his fellow *eunoto* initiates and was determined not to postpone it. But it had been clear that he was on the mend, which briefly cheered her great-grandmother. Malaika had hoped that Kireko's recovery and the blue sky and gentle breeze would wash away Kokoo's depression. But looking at her now, struggling to catch her breath, she was alarmed by the old woman's deterioration in the few hours since the day had begun. It was clear that her anguish was taking a heavy toll.

She seemed to be obsessed with Ziada, insisting that Malaika's half-sister was in mortal danger. Malaika had tried to steer the conversation into light-hearted matters, anything but Ziada. Finally she relented, thinking it wiser to let her talk it out.

'The wide golden waters come again to my dreams after all these years. It was when you were a child that I last saw it. When you fled with your poor mama.' Her voice trailed off.

Malaika patted her hand. 'It's Lake Victoria, Kokoo. And I told you — Mama and Ziada are still there. With Hamis. They are happy.'

'But I cannot go to this Lake Victoria to find your sister. I see her suffering.'

'Suffering?'

'Yes, child. There is evil there. The spirits send messages. What can I do but listen? An old woman, useless and losing her powers.' She sighed.

'Kokoo, you worry yourself for nothing. Ziada is fine.'

'You have seen her?'

'Well, not for a few years.' Malaika didn't want to admit that she had never returned. 'When the border was closed it was difficult. And then I went to college and, well ...' She felt saddened by her deception. Like so many other things in her life that she had wanted to change, she had never plucked up the courage to go home again. It was easier to believe she had been too busy. In hindsight, she may have blocked out her family as she had blocked out the other memories from her past. But she didn't want to discuss it just now. 'Please, Kokoo, there is no need to worry.'

'Malaika ... child. Look at me.' Naisua grasped Malaika's hands. 'I am old. These bones are old. They need their peace. The people in our village, they say, why is this old one still with us? Ah? Well, I know they think it. And why not? Look at me. What can this old body do? I ask you. Can I even take myself to this place of the wide waters? No.' She squeezed Malaika's hands and tilted her head to one side. 'I have lived too long, Malaika. And I want to die. Oh, you are so young. Can you understand? It is time. But my soul can find no peace unless I can find the answers to the curse.'

Malaika saw the agony in her great-grandmother's eyes, but what could be done to convince the old woman that the cause was lost? She didn't seem to understand. With or without someone to carry on the duties of *laibon*, the pandemic would continue to run its course. Yes, the Maasai would suffer it like no other. And yes, they needed help. But it didn't change a thing. The Maasai's cultural legacy would see infection rates skyrocket.

'Oh, if only I could see this young one — your Ziada. Somehow she holds the answer. She has the key to break Sendeyo's terrible curse. I *must* find her.'

'I will bring her to you, Kokoo.' If this simple matter could give her great-grandmother peace, it was the least she could offer, she thought.

The old woman brought her hands together at her lips. 'But it will be difficult. It is far. And the great golden waters surround her. I see a small place between the high rocks. Many people. It is a very unhappy place. Evil dwells there.'

Malaika thought of her mother's little house set in a vegetable garden in Mwanza, amid a crush of squatters' huts and rows of identical concrete-block houses. It was hardly an evil island in a golden sea. 'I will bring her, Kokoo.' She was pleased to have found something that gave relief to her distress.

Kokoo's eyes brightened. Malaika nodded. 'I promise.'

'Look at this, Onditi!' It was Mengoru who had walked down from the house above. 'A family reunion!'

Her father's voice could still alarm her after all these years. She glanced over her shoulder in spite of her resolve to be strong in his presence. James Onditi! She turned back quickly. How could *he* be here? With her father? In her village. He obviously knew her father well, and must now know everything about her too.

His eyes were on her, she felt sure, enjoying her mortification. Seeing him standing there with her father, she suddenly realised why she had always disliked him. His crude sexual harassment and his pig-headed arrogance were reason enough, but until now she had not realised that he reminded her of her father. He displayed the same ruthless use of power, but in Onditi she sensed a greater danger. Onditi knew how to exercise it with subtlety and cunning, working on hidden fears. Finding him with her father was her worst nightmare. Between them she was afraid they would try to control her body and her mind.

Malaika had not seen her father since around noon, when he had come into her hut to gloat at how he had outsmarted her white friends. He had looked smug, rocking on his heels in his polished black shoes like some puffed-up overlord.

'You don't seem pleased to see me, my love,' Onditi said, his smile cold and remote.

She remained silent and bit her lip. She glanced at Kokoo who had her chin up and was staring solemnly at the hills above the village.

'Or are you feeling guilty about all the times you were rude to me?'

'Go to hell, Onditi,' Malaika said with more conviction than she felt. Pretending to search for a thread on the hem of her jeans, she avoided the sight of him.

'My goodness, Mengoru,' Onditi went on in mock surprise. 'Your daughter is lacking in respect.'

'Hah!' said Mengoru. 'Daughter, is it? I have no daughter. Only a runaway whore.'

'She needs a good man to teach her a lesson in manners.'

Mengoru chuckled. 'I have a few friends who would be happy to teach her how to behave.'

'But you will need to call in the circumciser first, my friend.'

Mengoru laughed loudly. 'Yes! Oh yes. We haven't seen a good circumcision for some time!' Malaika felt something from the past clutch at her heart. She shot a glance at him. The manic laughter, then silence. The curled lip as he brooded and planned his punishment. Then the violent explosion of fists, belt and boots. Her fingers froze on the thread at the hem of her jeans.

'She is needed for this one.' Onditi jabbed a thumb in Malaika's direction. 'She is far too proud.' His jaw was clenched, clipping his words. 'She wouldn't be so proud after a little chop here and there.'

'Yes, too proud.' Mengoru's malevolent smile vanished. 'But she will learn her lesson soon enough. Now you,' he thrust a finger at Malaika, 'take the old witch back. And then you will go with Onditi.'

CHAPTER 34

PEABODY'S GUIDE TO EAST AFRICA (5TH ED):
You may find it useful to know about the Flying Doctors
Service, operated by the African Medical Research
Foundation (AMREF). The insurance they provide is
inexpensive and will cover your aeromedical evacuation to
a hospital in case of emergency.

There was perhaps an hour of daylight remaining when Jack
pushed the Landcruiser into some thick scrub at the side of the
Narok–Kisii road. It would be secure there against a casual
glance from passing cars, and since they were about half a
kilometre from Patel's *duka*, passers-by would not be a
problem.

The handbrake clunked on. He cut the motor before turning
to Bear. 'How's it going, mate?'

Bear looked down at his bloodied thigh. 'Yeah, okay, I
guess. It's stopped bleeding since I been sittin'.'

'Is the bandage okay? Not too tight?'

'No, it's fine. What's the plan?'

'The plan? Right. The plan. Well, I take a bush walk
through there to the village. Can't be more than ten minutes
away. I wait for a chance to grab Malaika. Then we get you to
a doctor to have you patched up.'

Bear sniffed a chuckle.

'What's funny?' Jack said, beginning to smile with him.

'I can just see the sick leave form sittin' on the boss's desk. He'll be thinking I'm jerkin' him around again.'

Jack smiled. He had to agree the whole thing was bizarre. Two days ago they'd been on a brief, relaxing *safari*. Now it was more than a sick leave form on the boss's desk. A cop was dead, he was about to take on an army of ivory poachers, and his friend was nursing a bullet wound. While they had spoken only briefly about the shooting on the drive back to Isuria, they both agreed it looked bad. No witnesses. Their word against the police.

Jack put aside what the future might hold and tried to recall the layout of the village. He hadn't taken much notice of it at the time. Was there enough cover to get close to it during daylight?

He took a sip of water and passed the bottle to Bear. 'I'll probably have to wait near the village until dark. Will you be okay?'

'Sure. But it's gonna be hot until the sun drops. Better open that back window behind me, buddy. Get some air coming through here.'

Jack climbed out and carefully closed the driver's door. Going around to Bear's side, he opened the rear passenger door, wound down the window, and closed the door again with a click.

'Okay, mate,' Jack whispered. 'Hang in there.' He reached through the window and patted Bear on his balding head before disappearing into the bush.

Although the undergrowth was patchy, he could seldom see more than thirty metres ahead. Every footfall on dry twigs seemed deafening. His scalp tingled. More than once he became tangled in thorn bush as he watched his feet rather than his path.

At the track that led to the village, he crouched for a few minutes before being sure it was clear, then followed its gentle slope. The grass and small shrubs were flattened along one side. Heavy tyre marks were imprinted in the soft damp soil.

Suddenly he caught a glimpse of the creek. It startled him —

he had thought it was further away. The scattered thorn bush stopped twenty paces short of the creek, and more clear ground lay beyond it. Getting inside the village unseen would be impossible before dark.

He squatted behind a waxy-leafed shrub to the side of the track and glanced at his watch. The sky was still bright in the west. Patience was not one of his virtues.

There was little activity in the circle of village huts. A few old people moved aimlessly about. Four calves nosed handfuls of grass that a woman threw into their pen.

The Range Rover rumbled down from the house to where two armed men stood at the *boma* gate, smoking and talking. Onditi climbed out and took a cigarette from one of the guards, who rested his rifle against a wheel to light it for him. There was no sign of Malaika and the light was fading fast. Jack thought he had maybe twenty or thirty minutes at most. He worried about finding her in the darkness.

His knee was becoming numb. He moved into a more comfortable position then felt something crawling up his leg. Lifting up his trouser, he flicked a scorpion away.

Malaika's white tee-shirt was unmistakable. She made her way across the compound with an old woman tottering on her arm. He felt an urge to rush to her, to sweep her up and carry her away. Instead, he peeped above the bush for a better view.

A low growl came from behind. He turned his ear towards it, but it was soon gone on the breeze.

Back at the village, Malaika led the old woman into a hut near the gate.

The growl returned, louder this time. And closer. Again it wafted away, lost within the rustle of wind through brittle vegetation.

Jack brushed some stones aside and sat behind his bush to await the night.

The village was completely surrounded by the thorn bush fence. It was six feet high and about as deep. The only opening faced the creek. He noted some good-sized boulders that would serve as a cover while crossing the water to the fence opening.

A crunch of stones and the low throb of a diesel came from behind him. A truck rumbled past. He rolled into the waxy shrub, wondering if he had been seen. The truck lurched across the creek and stopped at the *boma* entrance. Shouted conversation and laughter followed as Mengoru's guards gathered around it.

Mengoru came down the hill and immediately grunted some orders. The men began to move ivory into the truck from one of the huts. Before long their shirts were dark with perspiration. Onditi stood beside Mengoru, his hands stuffed into his trouser pockets, watching the work.

The village had faded into the brief twilight before all the tusks were secured. Jack, who had lost interest in the loading, just sat awaiting the end of activities, and the night, before making his move. A crash of the truck door brought his attention back. A few muttered words drifted across the creek to him, then another door slammed.

The truck throbbed into life. Headlights speared into the foliage above Jack's head. He flattened himself on the hard damp earth as the truck rolled past. The men at the village gate laughed and joked until the truck was out of sight and hearing.

Jack looked to the purple sky. A pale half moon was rising. He would wait for the darkness to settle on the village.

BEAR HOFFMAN WONDERED IF, IN all of his fifty-four years, a woman could have inspired him to do what Jack was doing. Would he have followed her halfway across Kenya, break out of gaol, and attempt a rescue from a bunch of armed ivory poachers? He thought about it, then decided he probably would. Not because of the woman necessarily, but he *did* enjoy a good fight. That's why I'm sitting here with a bullet in my leg, he thought ruefully.

He looked at the bandage. The moonlight didn't reveal much, but he noticed a patch of blood had leaked onto Inga's upholstery. He rubbed at it. The smear spread across the material. He sighed.

He checked his watch. Jack had been gone over an hour. He

wondered if he was okay. He hated not being able to be down there with him, helping out.

What a different person Jack was, these days. Bear couldn't believe he was the same guy he had met seven or eight months ago. *No way!* He was so cool back then. Nothing was going to invade his carefully guarded isolation. But there he was, down in the village risking his balls for a woman.

Bear wondered why he, a man who'd had more women than a rock-band lead singer, couldn't feel that way any more. Too old? he asked himself. No. It just ain't the same since Violet. What's the point?

Bear was adept at gathering all the parts of a person and putting them together. Like a jigsaw — a piece at a time. He didn't believe it was cynical or calculating. It helps me get to know them better, is all, he reasoned with himself. At the outset he couldn't unravel Jack at all, although he had put in some of his best work on him. How does one man ever get to know what goes on inside another man's head, unless there's a chink in the armour?

That's when Malaika came along. Without her, Bear may have never seen the real Jack. He could have remained an enigma. Bear would have always found Jack's company enjoyable. He was Bear's kind of man. But as he opened up, Bear discovered a likable human being. Jack's early cynicism of the UN changed. Although never what the New York bureaucrats would call a career field operative, he put in some hard work on his projects, often cutting through UN red tape and sticking his neck out in the process. He became more laid-back, not so easily riled — more likely to laugh at a setback than become angry and frustrated with it. He had started to let his feelings rise to the surface.

Bear felt the pain when Jack confessed his involvement in the death in Hawaii, but he felt sure Jack would learn to live with it. In time.

His worry about being implicated was unfounded. Bear would tell him he had nothing to worry about. Forget the fingerprints — even if Jack had left some on the gun. Position of the barrel. Entry angle. Burns. Any coroner worth his salt would conclude suicide.

A breeze stirred the bush that surrounded him in dark silence. The deep quiet had not been broken since the truck rolled up the track behind him, about a half hour ago, and headed west.

There was just one niggling item remaining about Jack. He seemed to be in denial about his feelings for Malaika. There was no doubt in Bear's mind that Jack was deeply in love. He'd been there often enough to recognise the symptoms. But Jack appeared to have switched off that side of his brain. The woman in Honolulu really screwed him up, Bear thought. She definitely had a death wish. Jack seemed intent on taking the blame. Maybe it was a little more than that. Sometimes a man can get a glimpse of a part of himself he didn't know existed. It can scare the bejesus out of you, he thought.

Bear felt sure that in recognising his need to explore a wider world before it was too late, Jack had done Liz and himself a big favour. Better to face the unpalatable fact that he needed more from life than Liz could give, than to let the relationship suffer a slow and painful death through the years of regret.

Jack seemed to have the tragedy of O'Hara's death all mixed up with his guilt about breaking Liz's heart. He needed to separate the two and deal with each in its own manner. Until he could open up in that way, particularly to Malaika, his feelings were going to be locked away as tight as a drum.

A rustling sound in the bush behind the car distracted him. He looked through the rear window. Nothing. Probably a couple of dik diks rooting around.

He decided he needed a long quiet chat with Jack when they got back to Nairobi. He could see his problem. Malaika was so exotic, so far out of this Aussie boy's traditional comfort zone, he was probably afraid it might be some kind of vacation romance. The Disneyland Syndrome as Bear liked to describe it. Great to visit, but could you live there? In other words, would she be so lovable, exciting, desirable, or whatever, if she were white? As far as Bear was concerned the answer was, who cares? In his case, the answer had come too late. Only after she was gone had he realised he'd loved Violet for who she was, rather than for how she appeared. Jack, he'd say, Malaika's black. That's a fact. Just take all that exotica as a bonus. The question is, do you love her? Simple as that. That's what he'd say: Jack, do you love her?

Sitting in the darkened cabin, Bear grunted in approval. It was a good plan. He wished them luck. Everybody deserved a lucky break once in a while, and Bear had to admit that, over the years, he had enjoyed his fair share of it. Sure, there'd been some setbacks in his life. Losing his father before he knew him, for one. Being booted out of home into the hands of boarding school teachers at age eight. It was tough at times. Losing Violet ... But he had made the best of the cards dealt to him. He was lucky that his mother finally got him to the USA. Lucky that the education he'd despised ended up getting him a good job — one that allowed him to travel. Of all the things he had done right, taking a risk with Africa was way up there with the best.

He tilted his seat back and laid his head on the rest. The stirring of a night breeze through the window wafted the wispy strands of grey hair across his balding head. He'd always had trouble keeping the damn things in place. He was for ever plastering them down. *The hell with it.* He closed his eyes.

It was good to be in Africa.

THE MOONLIGHT WAS SUBDUED BY a thin film of cloud. Jack scampered from boulder to boulder across the creek until he reached the *boma* fence. It gave scant cover but he kept close to it; there was no other option.

He didn't know what to expect of an African village after dark, but this one was quiet. The faint sounds of music and laughter drifted on the breeze from Mengoru's house on the hill. When the breeze changed it was gone, and the village held an eerie silence.

He was in luck. The guards' voices came from the other side of the Range Rover, which was now standing within the opening in the *boma* fence. He crept towards it, keeping low

373

to the ground. He peered under the car, finding the feet of three men on the other side.

He slipped into the hut that Malaika had entered earlier in the evening. Inside the smoke-filled vestibule he took a deep breath and peeped into the larger chamber. An old woman, a very old woman, sat cross-legged across from a flickering fire. He could see her clearly in the firelight and decided she was female only because of her size, which was that of a child. But no child had eyes like these — they fairly burned in her wrinkled face. And with some surprise, Jack found she was studying him. Not just looking *at* him, but also looking *into* him. She might have found his deepest secrets if he had held her gaze, but he shrugged it off. The adrenaline was doing strange things to his imagination.

He took a tentative step towards the fire. She accepted his entrance with equanimity. The fingers of a small fragile hand gestured to a squat, three-legged stool opposite her. When he sat, he felt awkward. His knees were as high as his shoulders, whereas she seemed to be contained within the gentle folds of her red cotton gown. She wore an unruffled smile, as if she had been expecting him. Maybe Malaika had told her he would come.

He wondered where to begin. His instinct was to assume she knew everything. 'Umm ...' he began in a whisper, 'where is she?'

The old woman shook her head. 'Gone.'

'Gone! Gone where?'

'They say Muhoro.' It appeared the effort it took to reply exhausted her. She struggled to keep her head erect.

'Muhoro ... Muhoro ...' He had arrived in the small fishing village when the sun was setting over the lake. Three women carrying firewood had cast the longest shadows he had ever seen — three endless stripes that ran across the road, up the gentle slopes of waving yellow grass, and out of sight. He could remember little else about the place.

'I do not know this Muhoro,' the old woman said.

'Lake Victoria,' he said, remembering he had gone to Muhoro mainly to kill some time. But he had been curious about Onditi's name appearing with it on a file in the Provincial Commissioner's office in Kisumu. They would obviously load the ivory there and ship it, and Malaika, out of Kenya. To Tanzania? Uganda?

'What time did she leave?' he asked.

She cocked her head and turned a slender hand upward to show she did not understand.

'Malaika ...' he touched his watch, 'go?'

She nodded, raising a finger. 'One.'

'One hour. Damn! She must have been on that truck.'

She nodded. 'Gone. Truck.'

From his hazy recollection of the map of Kenya, the lake was about a hundred and fifty kilometres west. Three hours for a truck on those roads. The Landcruiser might do it in two. It would take time to load the ivory at Muhoro wharf. He might just make it.

He thanked her, then went to the main doorway and peeped around the cowhide covering. The men were out of sight but their voices came from the front of the car. He could not get out the way he had come in.

'The gate,' he whispered, back at the fireside. 'No go.'

She nodded and he helped her struggle to her feet. She weighed nothing in his gentle grip.

'Come.' She led him outside and to the rear of the hut. There was a small hole in the *boma* wall. The village children probably used it. She watched him drop to his belly to slide through, but he became stuck halfway. Reaching over his shoulder, he tried to get to the thorn that had snagged his shirt. It was out of reach. He rolled to each side but remained caught. The *boma* shook with each movement. The old woman poked his shirt with a long stick and it came loose. He crawled from the fence and hurried towards the creek.

The meagre cover of bushes ended short of the creek's edge. He stopped at the last of them, waiting for his eyes to become accustomed to the darkness. The next fifty paces, across the stony creek bed to the thicket, were without cover. Even in the darkness he knew he could be seen if the guard on the gate happened to look. He would have to wait again.

For fifteen minutes he waited impatiently for the guards to move away. Then two men came running down the track. He presumed they were Mengoru's men as there was a loud exchange of abrupt words before all four hurried into the village.

Jack scuttled across the creek. In the relative safety of the scrub, he increased his pace. From the village behind him came voices raised in excitement. Thorns clutched and tore at him as he ran.

When he burst onto the Kisii road, the Landcruiser was twenty paces away. Jack went quickly to it. Bear was silhouetted against the sky through the rear window. It didn't look right — his head resting at an odd angle, resting against the window.

Jack jerked the door open. Bear's body crumpled heavily to the ground. Face down. Motionless.

Jack dropped to one knee and rolled the body over. Glazed, sightless eyes reflected the cabin light. A slim bone handle and the start of an evil narrow blade protruded from the soft indent above the collarbone.

The sound of boots hitting the gravel road intruded. Four men rushed towards him from the head of the track.

He stepped over Bear's body. It seemed wrong to leave him there. A shot whined off the door rim above his head. Jack ran to the driver's side and jumped in.

The motor roared and the vehicle leapt and crashed through the roadside bush. Jack hit the accelerator and spun the car in a tight U-turn. He lined up the men running down the road at him. They dived into the bush. The Landcruiser swerved at them, spraying gravel as it raced past. An explosion of glass shards hit him as the rear window shattered.

Dust, and the night, concealed him at last.

JACK SAT IN THE DARKNESS, staring into the night. Ahead, the hills formed a gloomy barrier against a black and brooding sky. Periodic flashes of silent lightning gave the hills their shape, a high wall between where he sat in the silent vehicle, and Lake Victoria where he must soon be if he was to reach Malaika in time.

Behind him, a dead man. A dead friend — his body abandoned by the side of the road.

There was no choice. Going back would not undo Bear's death. And against the poachers, revenge, no matter how attractive, would be another folly. One more to add to his growing list.

He felt he had twice betrayed Bear. In the first place, by getting them into the situation that led to his murder, and then in death, by leaving his body behind.

Jack lowered his head to the steering wheel and closed his eyes. Memories came back. Bear wrestling in the mud with the four thugs on the Hash run. Another, just two days ago: Bear laughing after Jack fell off the Land Rover into a ring of Masai Mara lions.

Tears are poor substitutes for time. It's time that is needed to farewell a friend. To grieve. And Jack had none to spare.

CHAPTER 35

PEABODY'S GUIDE TO EAST AFRICA (5ᵗʰ ED):
The quest to find the source of the Nile grew to become a scientific obsession throughout the late eighteenth and early nineteenth centuries.

Many explorers tried to reach the source by following the river upstream. They invariably met disaster because of the hostile terrain and the even more hostile inhabitants of its upper reaches.

Jack bounced the Landcruiser over the ragged start to the bitumen at Ewaso Ngiro — little more than a small huddle of squalid dwellings. Lanterns flung yellow shafts through shutters propped open to the evening air. Some townspeople sat outdoors, vainly seeking relief from the heat that hung about their rusted sheet-metal homes like an unwanted guest.

A white goat was trapped in the high beam. It darted left, then right. Jack swerved onto the verge at a bus station. The four-wheel drive spewed a muddy-water cascade into the empty bus shelter, leapt back onto the bitumen, and moments later disappeared onto the dirt road at the town's outskirts.

The road took a swing to the south and began to climb a long slope. According to Inga's useless road map, the bend and the hill did not exist. Jack had already taken one wrong turn, costing him several precious minutes.

He slammed on the brakes. *Doinya Loongarya Escarpment,* the map said. He snapped off the light and continued the climb, hoping that the truck had taken the same route. It would slow them down. He guessed he would be about thirty minutes behind them by the time he reached Muhoro.

At the top of the escarpment he sighed with relief when the road headed northwest in the direction of Lake Victoria. For the next half hour there was an undulating but downward gradient. At last he felt he was making good time.

The waters of Lake Victoria appeared as he crested the last granite ridge. Under the light of the moon, the lake was like silver hammered into a slab of gunmetal. It ran to a dark horizon far away.

Below, Muhoro waxed and waned as the moonlight danced through clouds racing in from the west on a stiff warm breeze. The town was a smattering of modest houses surrounded by the usual array of squatters' shacks. The wharf, a long grey finger pointing towards the oncoming storm, sprang from a collection of warehouses — the mistreated remnants of a once-healthy lake trade.

Lightning fractured the western sky. It sent jagged lines to strike the lake somewhere over the horizon, perhaps in Uganda. Beyond the shelter of the wharf, whitecaps pitted the water's surface. The breeze was moody, uncertain of itself amid the encircling granite monoliths. It came in warm breaths through the open car window.

Pencils of light moved between a boat and a bulky shape at the wharf's end. They were already unloading the truck.

Jack turned off the headlights and drove down the hill. The houses that lined his path, in fact, the whole town, seemed to have battened down against the oncoming storm. Papers and debris whirled above deserted streets.

A single mangy dog lay in the shelter of a tumbledown warehouse where he parked the vehicle. As he made his way towards the wharf, four flashlights moved between the truck and the boat moored at its furthest end. But before he reached the barrier, where an old guardhouse stood, they had disappeared.

379

The moon made one of its infrequent forays from behind the dashing clouds, revealing the boat to be a fishing trawler with a tall wheelhouse and a high bow. The stern was set low for hauling nets aboard. Aft of the wheelhouse was planted a derrick holding a robust boom.

The truck started with a growl then moved down the wharf towards the shore. Jack hid in the remains of the guardhouse, which was missing most of one wall, the door and roof. He peered through a gap in the lining boards as the truck rolled past. In the cabin were the driver and another, meaning two men remained aboard the boat.

Before the truck's rumble had faded in the distance, another motor spluttered to life at the end of the wharf. The fishing boat was moving off its lines.

There had been no sign of Malaika, and now he began to wonder if she was in fact on board. After all, he only had Kokoo's guess that they had brought her here. She might have been dumped along the way. It was a thought he would not contemplate for more than a moment. She just had to be on that boat. He mustered his courage and, ignoring all caution, sprinted down the wharf towards the departing trawler.

By the time he reached the berth, lungs bursting, the fishing boat was rounding into the heavy chop. It floundered momentarily as the screw broke the surface. The motor snarled in protest. But it was a boat built for such capricious behaviour and would not be fussed by the lake's mischief for long. It soon settled into the swell and the motor dropped to a workmanlike warble.

Jack ran towards the shore, hoping to find another boat.

A large coil of rope was flung over the railing ahead of him, and a man in a glistening wet cape with a bundle of nets over his shoulder appeared from the water below. When Jack bounded up to him, his jaw dropped open and he nearly lost his grip on the rail.

Jack clambered down to the lightweight wooden dinghy before the fisherman could give voice to his outrage. In another moment he had pulled the outboard into life and was heading into the wind.

Waves broke over the bow, drenching him and threatening to swamp the boat. It worsened as he rounded the end of the wharf. The dinghy bucked and tossed in the chop and the skills of his boyhood boating experiences on Broken Bay returned. He trimmed the throttle to avoid flipping off the wave crests, and took his bearings.

He felt as if he had been staring into the storm-darkened night for hours, searching the rain for the trawler's lights. In fact, it was no more than fifteen minutes. But his perception of time was distorted by the utter loneliness of the lake, and by the black despair of failure. He thrust the idea aside. Self-pity was an indulgence he could ill afford out there. But thoughts of Malaika continued to intrude upon his mind, making him sick with the desolation of losing her. He would find her. He must.

The fishing trawler had headed west into the wind. He had no idea if the dinghy could overhaul a trawler under those conditions. Jack held as much throttle as the wind would allow him and ran into the teeth of the storm.

Perhaps the trawler ran no lights? He shut the motor down. The dinghy wallowed in the chop. Rain, driven on the strong westerly, beat savagely into his face. Between the thunder and the slapping waves he imagined he heard the faint throb of a diesel motor, dead ahead. It was immediately ripped away by the wind.

The dinghy shipped water at an alarming rate and its pitching threatened to throw him overboard as he made a pull at the starter cord. It caught first time. He throttled up, lifting the bow into the wind again. His heart leapt as a whiff of diesel fumes came on the bow spray. Ploughing through the waves, the rain stinging his eyes, he peered into the blackness. A flash of lightning exposed the trawler's wheelhouse rising on the swell. He pointed the dinghy towards it and gave as much throttle as he dared. Timing his approach was tricky. At times the trawler's stern soared high above the dinghy, threatening to crush it, and him. He took his chance during a lull in the waves, dashed in and tied his line to the bulwark towards the walloping stern, leaving a long mooring line to keep the dinghy at a safe distance.

Using the bulwark as cover he paused to catch his breath and to steel himself for the next, most dangerous step. He concluded that the storm would occupy all of the two men's time, and felt confident he had not been seen. As his head came above the railing, a grappling hook slashed from the darkness. He ducked and it tangled in the boom rigging. The man wielding it cursed and ripped it free, tearing the derrick line loose as he did so. The boom fell to head height before the line tangled in the topmost pulley.

Jack had an instant to respond. He leapt the railing as the man staggered back, cocking the hook for another swipe. Jack launched himself low, driving hard with his legs as his football coach had taught him, and caught the man in the midriff, forcing the breath out of his lungs with a rush. He dropped the grappling hook and tried to lock Jack in a bear hug. But Jack had the momentum and drove him backwards. The man threw an arm back, but too late — his head struck the wheelhouse steps with a thud, and he lay where he fell.

The motor's steady beat dropped as Jack regained his feet. The change in impetus sent him stumbling across the deck and almost overboard. When he regained his balance he headed to the wheelhouse. A flash of lightning revealed Onditi at its steps, gun in hand and a grin on his face.

Jack backed off, wiping the rain from his eyes. Behind him the boom thrashed at its loosened lines. The boat, drifting at the mercy of the wind, began to pitch and roll. Jack had trouble keeping his balance, the deck rose and fell under him, but his mind was totally focused on the gun.

Onditi clutched the handrail on the steps to steady himself. Jack wondered why he had not already used the gun, but now that he could see his expression, he realised that Onditi was enjoying the moment.

Malaika flung herself at Onditi from the wheelhouse. Her arms were tied at the wrists, but she threw them over his neck and wrapped her legs around his waist. Onditi swung her like a rag doll on a string, keeping Jack in his gun-sights as he tried to dislodge her.

The boat pitched, throwing Jack backwards over a pile of nets, as a bullet twanged into the rigging.

Onditi shrugged Malaika's arms from over his neck and, with a vicious backhand swipe, sent her reeling across the deck into the starboard railing. She balanced for a long moment, unable to grasp the rail with her tied hands. Her feet went from under her and she flipped backwards, over the side.

Jack rushed to her but Onditi fired again, splintering the woodwork at his feet.

The boat's bow swung to leeward, tilting the trawler savagely broadside to the thrashing storm. The boom snapped to a stop on its starboard swing, tearing loose its remaining line, then catapulted through a 180-degree swing to port.

Onditi had no warning of it. He had crossed the deck to brace against the port railing for better aim, the gun in both hands. The boom hit him with the crack of a rifle shot, pitching him into the turbulent water.

Jack dashed to the starboard side. 'Malaika!' he yelled into the wind. 'Malaika!'

He dived overboard. The waves beat him down as he fought to see above them in the gloom.

'Malaika!'

'Jack.'

It was a feeble call from the direction of the trawler.

'Malaika!' She clung to the dinghy, still tied on its long mooring. He swam towards it with as much power as he could muster, but the idling diesel continued to carry the boat inexorably away. It bobbed and tossed in the wind and waves, but its forward momentum was more than Jack could match.

He struggled on. For a time, as each wave lifted him on its crest, he could see the trawler bobbing away in its ungainly waltz. Soon it was gone. And the dinghy with it. Determination kept him going, fighting the storm with each stroke, but his feet became heavy. They pulled him down.

Jack! How many times have I told you to watch that bloody rip? His father was red in the face, having raced through the surf to pull his six-year-old son from the water. *It'll bloody well drown you some day. My word it will!* His father never told a lie. Death by drowning had been Jack's enduring childhood nightmare.

'Jack!' Malaika was above him in the dinghy.

He grabbed her arm but she had no strength to pull him up. He threw a leg over the side and tried to haul himself free of the water.

Onditi burst from below the dinghy, eyes wide in his swollen face. He grabbed at Jack, but sank immediately. Jack's ankle became locked in a grip of iron. He thrashed his free arm at the water, but there was nothing to fight. Onditi was below him, a dead weight dragging him down. With his last reserve of energy, Jack kicked and twisted, but Onditi's hand on his ankle was a vice. His own grip on the dinghy began to slip.

Malaika clung ferociously to his wrist, but when his fingers slipped off she could hold him no longer. He disappeared into the inky water.

In total darkness, Jack grabbed at the dead hand on his ankle. His lungs were bursting as he prised the fingers loose, one by one. Finally, he was free. Kicking furiously, his return to the surface took for ever. On his first breath he sucked in a whoop of air and lake water. He gagged and choked, but with Malaika's help clambered into the dinghy.

They lay exhausted in the bottom of the boat. Jack leaned his head over the side, coughed and vomited.

The dinghy was tossing violently. Jack clambered towards the stern where an alarming amount of water collected with the transfer of his weight. He fumbled with the fuel primer.

First pull. The motor coughed and stopped. The waves threw them from side to side.

Jack gave another pull.

Another wave buffeted them broadside, sending the dinghy into wild pendulum swings while they both held the sides, trying to steady it again.

He adjusted the throttle. Third pull. A promising stutter, then silence.

He pumped the fuel line. A touch more throttle. He looked over his shoulder at Malaika. She was clutching the side of the dinghy with both hands. He showed her his crossed fingers then pulled the starter cord again. The outboard roared to life. He throttled back a little then engaged the gear. The dinghy lurched forward.

Jack swung it downwind and ran full throttle ahead of the storm. The waves boiled in their wake, threatening to run them down from astern.

CHAPTER 36

PEABODY'S GUIDE TO EAST AFRICA (5TH ED):
Except for in Nairobi and Mombasa, tap water is not safe.
Use water boiled for ten minutes, bleach-chlorated water
(two drops per litre of pure sodium hypochlorite devoid
of detergents or perfumes), chemically purified water, or
bottled drinks. In hotels and lodges you will be provided
with bottles or flasks of mineral water.

The Landcruiser rippled across the railway lines at Musoma.
There were a dozen rusted tracks snaking through and beyond
the crossing, but Malaika saw not a single train, truck or
carriage in either direction.

Musoma was one of the larger towns on the Tanzanian
shores of Lake Victoria. In school she had learned of the time
when the lake was the principal means of trade and Musoma
rivalled Mwanza in its shipping tonnage to Kenya and
Uganda. By the time she left school, lake trade had died and
the rivalry was limited to the football field where, again,
Mwanza won.

The storm had blown east during their drive down the
coast. By the time they reached Musoma, the town was
peaceful and had long since retired to its bed. They found the
Railway Hotel a block from the station.

When the manager arrived, rubbing his eyes and holding a

lantern, he took some details from Malaika in Swahili and handed her the keys. Only then did he seem to notice their dishevelled appearance. Malaika folded her arms across her tee-shirt, still wet from the lake. Jack's sneakers squelched on the polished timber floors. At the door to their room, he gave Jack one more look before he bid them good night.

Jack flicked the room switch. Nothing happened.

'He said the town supply is sometimes off at this time,' Malaika said. 'There's candles and matches on the bedside table.'

The candlelight revealed a pleasant room, small but tidy. The manager had said it was a *superior* room. One of just two with *en suite* facilities. The big bed had clean white sheets and two towels on it. Malaika took a deep breath and then let it go, dropping her shoulders for what she felt was the first time in days. Jack sighed too. They stood awkwardly, looking at each other's wet hair and muddy clothes.

Malaika had suggested Musoma as it was across the border in Tanzania and avoided retracing any part of their journey towards Isuria. Their dash through the night had been crowded with many thoughts. Apart from an occasional word to get Malaika's help from the map, they drove in silence. At the border it had been tense. Jack tried to convince the official that they had lost their papers in a nasty river crossing. A small bribe finally clinched it.

Malaika closed the door. Jack took a step forward and hesitated, but she held out her hand to him and they hugged, one damp body against another. She buried her face in the nape of his neck. There was the reassuring presence of him again. Strong, hard, safe. With his body pressed against hers, she felt his chest rise with a heavy sigh. 'I thought I'd lost you,' he said.

There were two ways his words could be taken. Perhaps he meant both.

'Are you okay?' he asked, holding her away from him and frowning a little as he looked for an answer in her eyes.

It was the question she had not dared contemplate in the twenty-four hours since she had awoken in Isuria. Had she done so, she might have lost her nerve and admitted, no, she was not okay. She was afraid. Desperately afraid. Afraid of the physical danger and afraid of losing the self-esteem that men like her uncle in Nairobi had taken from her, and men like Onditi and her father would take again if she lost the battle of wills. She had fought long and hard to redeem it. She would die if she lost it again.

But now, in the cosy candlelit room, with the clean sheets, the prospect of a hot shower and Jack holding her, she permitted herself the luxury of thinking about herself, of answering the question, am I okay?

He had hurt her with his words at Cottars, but in those few seconds, an unguarded moment, with Jack looking so contrite and worried, she could weep with the wonderful feeling of relief. 'Yes, Jack. I'm ... okay.' She wiped her eyes hard.

'You're allowed to cry if you want,' he whispered.

'Oh, Jack,' she said, throwing her arms around him again. 'Hold me.'

He took her in his arms, pressed her to his body and held her there. Held her while she clung to his shoulders and buried her face in his chest, smelling the maleness of him, the strength it implied.

'Bear's gone,' he said simply. He told her about how they had escaped the police at Onditi's checkpoint in the Great Rift Valley; how he'd left Bear in the car while he crept into the village to find her. He struggled with the description of Bear dead, stabbed through the neck. 'Oh, no. No,' she said, releasing him to study his eyes. She ached at Bear's death and hurt the more to see Jack so distressed, so desolate, and pressed her face to his shoulder, holding him tight to squeeze the pain away.

'One of the police at the lock-up got shot.'

'What?'

'It was all so crazy. He shot Bear, then Bear ... a reflex action. I think the cop's dead.' He ran his hands through his wet hair. 'It shouldn't have happened. We knew it was some kind of trumped-up charge. About a stupid visa of all things. But we ... I was so desperate to get out of there. I was afraid you were ... I mean, I was afraid you might be ...' She could feel his heart thumping against her cheek.

'I can't believe he's gone,' he whispered. 'I always thought of him as being indestructible somehow. That's what he was ... indestructible.' His chest rose and fell. 'It shouldn't have happened.' He shook his head. 'It just should not have happened.'

AFTER HER BATH MALAIKA FELT more relaxed and fell asleep while Jack was having his shower.

She awoke slowly. The nub of the candle on the bedside table guttered in its saucer of molten wax. Jack was towelling himself dry. His hard body seemed familiar and reassuring. He put down his towel and sat on the side of the bed, watching her as she rubbed the sleep from her eyes.

She sat up and he put an arm over her shoulder and drew her to him.

'I was only going to be gone for an hour or so,' she said. 'But the rain ... Then the car ran off the road.' There were so many mixed-up thoughts. 'My brother, Kireko. I couldn't believe finding him after all these years. He was injured and I had to take him home ... to my ... to the village. Isuria. I met my great-grandmother again. It's been so long, I had forgotten them.'

The story from her last glimpse of Jack, unconscious on the bed at Cottars, came in disjointed detail. In truth, she told him only of the events, not the reality. She said nothing of her emotional re-awakening. Nothing of how she had blocked the links with the Maasai part of herself. She held it back, including the horrible truth that Mengoru was her father, without wondering why she did so. In a quieter moment she would examine it — would ask herself why she couldn't reveal it to Jack. At a better time she would tell him all.

'Jack ... ?'

'Yes?' His answer echoed softly in her head as she lay with her ear on his chest.

'What happened to you that night at Cottars? You were like ... You were like a different person.'

'Yes. I know. I'm sorry. But you're right, I *was*. Someone I don't like very much.'

He had already told her pieces of his life. Of his parents and where he lived. He had even told her, with a little persuasion, about Liz.

'Malaika, there's something I've been wanting to tell you. When I left Australia, it wasn't just because I wanted a job with the UN. I was ... Well, it was ... There was an accident ...'

'An accident?'

'No, not an accident. I mean ... I made a terrible mistake. I got involved with a woman. An affair. I didn't mean it to go so far. But it did. And, well, Liz found out. And that was it. We broke up.'

'You never told me how it ended with Liz. Did you try to work it out?'

'No. Yes. We talked, but she was mad as hell. It was all my fault. I can't blame her.'

'But if you were sorry about it, couldn't she forgive you?'

'It was complicated. Look, I don't want to talk about that now. Do you mind? It's over. It was for the best. Let's talk about what we have to do next.'

She said nothing, wondering if *wazungu* relationships were different. If they felt love the same way Africans did.

'Tomorrow I'm going to call old Bhatra. They have to do something about Bear. And then we can get out of here.'

'Jack ...'

'Huh?'

'I can't go to Nairobi.'

'Are you worried about Mengoru's friends? Okay, we can go to Dar —'

'Jack ... I can't go to Dar-es-Salaam either.'

'No?'

'I have to go to Mwanza.'

'Mwanza? What's at Mwanza? Malaika, we need to be in a city. With communications. We're in some kind of shit here. I mean, the police and —'

'I have to go to Mwanza.'

'Princess ...'

'Don't . . . Please don't call me Princess.'

'Okay.' He took a deep breath. 'Malaika. Why Mwanza?'

'I've been thinking about . . . well, thinking about me. And my family. Kokoo. Everyone.' She turned towards him; the flutter of candlelight etched his profile against the darkness. 'I've got to find my sister.'

'Your sister? I didn't even know you had a sister.'

'Half-sister. Anyway, she's in trouble.'

'What kind of trouble?'

'I don't know. Kokoo has this . . . It's hard to explain. I just have to do it for Kokoo, if not for Ziada.'

'Malaika, look, I don't know what to do. I can't think.' He moved to the edge of the bed. 'Of all the things I want to do, need to do, it's not driving way across East Africa to find your long-lost sister. Why now? I keep seeing Bear dead on the side of the fucking road, and I want to go back there. Bring him home. I want to get those bastards who killed him. But I can't. Not while those thugs are around. Not until the authorities get behind us. I want . . . I want it to be like it was. When it was . . . fun.'

'Jack, you can't understand. But Kokoo has had this . . . this vision. Something bad is going to happen. My sister is somehow in danger.'

'What do you mean?'

'Oh, I don't know. Some kind of tribal thing from years ago. Spiritual things. Magic.'

'Magic!'

'But to Kokoo it's real . . . and I promised.'

'Magic and family feuds! Malaika, for chrissake! Bear's dead and we may be too. How can you be worried about silly things like that?'

'They are not silly things. They're important to me now. Important to my whole family. The clan. You may not believe it. Even me, I don't believe it. But Kokoo believes it, and I promised I'd help.'

She pushed the sheet aside and swung her feet to the floor. 'Don't worry. I'll find her myself.'

'Oh, yeah! Sure you will! It must be easy to catch a taxi to Mwanza. To look up missing persons.'

She grabbed her towel and wrapped it around her. She realised he was right but tried to hide her dismay.

'Oh, shit!' he said. 'I'm sorry. Let me think this through, will you? I mean, just let me think a bit, huh?'

He went into the bathroom and shut the door. When he came out he was patting his face dry with a towel. He shrugged. 'Okay.'

She sighed and brought her hands to her temples, gently massaging the pressure she felt there. Mumbling her thanks, she was immediately aware of its miserly expression of her gratitude.

'Jack,' she said, reaching for his hand, 'I know you are hurting. For Bear. And this must all seem so strange to you. It's just ... well, I've been denying every part of my — what do you call it? *Roots?* — these past years, and now I have a chance to do something to make up for all the lost time. I feel I owe my family something. Kokoo hasn't long to live, and if this one small thing can make her rest in peace, I've got to do it.' She planted a kiss on his cheek. 'I really appreciate this. All of it.'

'Well,' he said, flustered by her contrite manner, 'we'll go to Mwanza and make sure your sister is okay. But!' he cautioned with his forefinger, 'I still think it's crazy.'

'There's just one more thing.'

'Hmm?' he said, taking her in his arms.

'We have to take her back to Isuria too.'

'Holy ... !'

CHAPTER 37

PEABODY'S GUIDE TO EAST AFRICA (5ᵀᴴ ED): Nairobi's climate is said by many to be Africa's finest. The high Athi Plains enjoy dry equatorial heat by day and mild, often cool nights.

During the period 1960 to 1980, the city emerged as the preferred regional headquarters site of many multinational companies. Development money flowed into the newly independent nation. Sporting clubs, hotels and nightclubs sprang up, reflecting the cosmopolitan nature of the well-heeled expatriate residents.

Restaurants offering Korean, Arabic, Cantonese, Japanese and all major European cuisines are to be found in the city and the classy western suburbs.

The road to Mwanza airport was as busy as Malaika remembered it. A gaudy *matatu* roared past the Landcruiser. On the back panel was a gruesome picture of a skeleton. The message *Death Without Glory* dripped blood from its letters. The *konda* hung out the door, gyrating to distorted rap music roaring from the tape player. '*Pansiansi! Pansiansi!*' he yelled above the din. '*Twende! Twende!*' The *matatu* splashed through a set of potholes and the cabin leapt and bounced.

They had stopped briefly in Mwanza's small town centre to change soggy dollars Jack had miraculously produced from a pouch in his belt. Then, each with a new set of clothes, they checked into the only sizable hotel in town — the New Mwanza. Jack had wondered aloud at the aptness of the adjective but Malaika hushed him. They were already the centre of much speculation by the gawking hotel staff.

'*Pansiansi! Pansiansi!*' the *konda* yelled again.

Malaika remembered the neighbourhood well. It hadn't changed much. Maybe a tree lost here and there, a few more ramshackle *dukas* plying food and utensils beside the road. The bus stop was there. Fifty yards further on was her mother's house. It needed painting, but was otherwise the same little concrete-block house from her childhood. Hamis had still not added the gate and picket fence he had promised.

An elderly woman stood in the front garden, one hand on her hip and a hoe in the other. She was staring at the lines of beans, *sikuma weeki* and maize. Strips of cotton, torn from an old dress or shirt, flapped on strings suspended over the vegetable rows.

Malaika pointed to a place where Jack could stop. The closing car door was lost in the cacophony of traffic noise. The woman in the garden paid no heed as Malaika stepped out, but placed both hands on her hips and stretched her back. The mannerism was familiar.

Malaika needed time to adapt to the concept of her mother with the shape and posture of middle age. Her shoulders were beginning to slope, and her back curved inwards before it met her well-rounded buttocks. She was not fat, but her waist was wider than Malaika remembered it. Her hair, still black, had none of the lustre of ten years ago and was pulled back with a red scarf. There were some traces of her mother as a younger woman. Her upright stance still gave her head the familiar defiant set. The elegant nose. Sad, soft eyes.

The woman turned away towards the house. She almost shuffled up the path. The confidence of earlier years was gone. She looked ... crushed.

Malaika stepped forward, now afraid. Afraid of what, she could not say. Tears were welling in her eyes as she stumbled over the word, 'Ma ... ?'

The woman didn't seem to hear, treading wearily towards the house. At the porch step, she glanced back to the road. She had been far away with her own thoughts and she looked surprised to see someone standing in her garden.

'Mama,' Malaika repeated.

Penina's hands went to her cheeks, then covered her mouth as if to halt a cry. She took a quick step towards Malaika then came to an abrupt halt. She stared in disbelief. Tears came to her eyes and streamed down her face. She made no attempt to stop them.

Malaika held her hand out. 'Mama?'

Her mother rushed to her. 'Malaika! Oh, Malaika!' She threw her arms around her daughter's shoulders. 'Praise God! Oh, praise God. You are here!'

Malaika hugged her, forgetting her fear, her prepared speech. Forgetting the apologies for being a headstrong foolish daughter. How many years had it been since she last wanted to be held in her mother's arms?

They hugged, broke apart to look at one another, and hugged again.

Malaika thought that her mother must have shrunk. She was no more than shoulder-height. Her arms were thinner and her elbows protruded in pointy ends. Her cheekbones were more prominent these days, and there were hollows under her eyes.

'Ma,' was all Malaika was able to say. It had been so long. Malaika was still a growing girl when she had left home and a void seemed to have filled the years since.

Through her tears Malaika found Jack on the other side of the row of beans and maize. He was nodding, a pleased expression on his face. Malaika gently broke her mother's embrace. 'Mama,' she said, then sniffed and rubbed her eyes with the cuff of her shirt. 'Mama ... this is Jack.'

With her daughter's use of the English words, Penina gave Malaika a puzzled look, but followed her nod towards the vegetable garden.

Jack smiled at her over the line of flapping cotton strips. 'G'day.'

Penina said, *'Haki ya Mungu!'* Then resorted to her own limited store of English, 'My God!'

PENINA'S CHATTER, AN INTERMINABLE RENDITION of Mwanza minutiae about the nine years since Malaika left home, consumed an hour. Malaika felt sorry for Jack who sat, numb with boredom, watching lake flies beat tirelessly at the glass shutters in the hot little sitting room on the airport road. At times she would translate for his benefit, but he eventually eased his sticky shirt off the vinyl seat and said he would stretch his legs in the garden.

When Malaika made an attempt to change the subject to Ziada, her mother put it aside while she finished yet another of her stories. On the second and third try, Malaika's unease grew.

'Where is Ziada?' Malaika asked in the hiatus as her mother brought tea from the kitchen.

'Oh, look. I spilled some sugar.' Penina sat at the low table and fussed with a cotton towel, lifting the sugar bowl and milk, sweeping the spilled grains onto her saucer.

'Ma, Ziada. Why isn't she here?'

Penina set the cup on the table. She folded the towel into a neat square and patted it flat on her knee. 'She's gone,' she said in a small voice.

It took time for the story to be told but Penina did not equivocate further. It was as if, having lifted the lid of her basket of sadness, she would not stop until it was scattered around them, to be picked over like second-hand goods in a market.

Ziada had left home more than a year before, leaving no clue as to why or where she was going. She had taken a few clothes and not much else. She was sixteen, about the same age as Malaika when she left her mother's house nine years ago. It gave Malaika a twinge of guilt, remembering that she had promised to come back for her sister when she had made her way.

'So there was no argument, no discussion? She just disappeared?'

'*Haki ya Mungu*, I swear to God, gone! Like that. And not a word to her mother. Not a message to put my poor heart at ease.'

'Did the teachers suspect anything was going on?'

'She had not been to school too often. She had been sick. A long spell of the influenza. Some funny pains.'

'What about her friends? Did you ask them if they had seen her?'

'Yes. More than once. At first I thought they were lying to me, that they knew where she was hiding. But in the end I had to believe.' She dropped her face into her hands. 'Oh, my baby. Where is she?'

Malaika patted her arm but could find no words of hope. A year was too long for it to be teenage moodiness.

'She was not a bad girl, you know? She was just . . . itchy.'

'Itchy?' Malaika said. 'What do you mean?'

'Unsettled. Always moving. Always looking for the next thing.'

'Kids are like that, Ma.'

'Oh, but Ziada, she had that itch and it wouldn't let her stop. Until she had done everything.' She smiled into her cup. 'Do you remember when she was learning to walk? Soon she was running. And falling. My, my, my. How many times did I find her out near the road? Even then, so tiny, she was running away.' Penina grew quiet again. When she continued there was a note of bitterness in her voice. 'If her father had been here it would not have happened. A girl needs a father to stop her running around.'

'But with him working all over Tanzania . . . '

'That is only in these past months. Even when he was in the tool shop here in Mwanza, he was not at home.'

'What do you mean?'

Penina smiled at her. 'It is good that you have a *mzungu*. I hear they do not run around like our African men do.'

'Hamis?' Malaika thought about the gentle man who had been her personal protective giant during her childhood. Through her child's eyes she had seen nothing but devoted husband. 'Oh, Mama,' she said. 'I'm so sorry.'

It was hard to believe he would be running around with other women. And the risks! It was impossible — surely one's mother could never get AIDS! But the statistics would deny that. As the old Ethiopian doctor at her clinic would say: *A partner who strays walks amongst the tombstones of the dead.*

She tried to summon her courage to launch into her 'safe sex' lecture with her mother. She couldn't. Even when playing the role of dispassionate health worker it was never easy to point out the horrible possibilities. But with her mother ... She just could not do it.

'I'm ... I'm sorry,' she mumbled again.

'It is Ziada I am sorry for,' her mother said. 'Why should a girl suffer because her father is not where he should be? He did not even come to Dar-es-Salaam with me.'

'You went to Dar?'

'Yes. Looking for your sister. Her teacher thought she might have gone to stay with her girlfriend. The friend went to Dar-es-Salaam.'

'When was that?'

'When she was gone but a month. Three full days on that train I sat.'

Malaika remembered how awed her mother used to be of someone who made the journey to the coast by train. *Five hundred miles!* she would say, as if it were to the moon.

'I found her friend, as the teacher said — at her cousin's house. She did not tell me that the cousin had a boyfriend there.' She shook her head in disbelief. 'But they knew nothing of Ziada.'

Malaika tried to imagine Ziada, a girl she recalled as no more than a child, having a friend who lived with a boy in faraway Dar. 'Did Ziada have a boyfriend?' she asked.

'Oh, she was always interested in boys. She started getting her flow at age eleven. Like you. By twelve she had a boyfriend — Moses, the son of the school caretaker. Do you remember him? The house on the corner, opposite the school? Well, I got so cross about that, but she would sneak away and see him. An itch, she had.'

'Where is this Moses now?'

'Oh, Ziada did not stay with Moses for long. *Haki ya Mungu!* I thought Moses was bad. That's when she wanted Freddie.'

'Who's Freddie?'

'A *konda* boy.'

'A *konda*? How old was this boy?'

'Ziada was thirteen when she met him. He was much older. Maybe six or seven years older. Those *konda* boys are too smart. Too clever.' Penina took the cups to the washbasin on the bench under the kitchen window. She continued the conversation through the door to the sitting room. 'They are always chasing the girls. They like the younger ones. Working on the *matatus*, girls are too easy for them.'

'Do you know him, Ma?' Malaika joined her in the kitchen.

Penina scrubbed vigorously at the cups. 'Freddie! He was too old for Ziada. I told her, Too clever these *konda* boys. She did not listen. She never did.'

'Mama, can you tell me where I can find him?'

She put down the cup. 'He goes to the *duka* near the bus stop. I see him there from time to time. When he has finished on the *matatu* in the afternoons.' Penina wiped her hands on her apron and leaned against the bench with a sigh. 'Oh, your sister is not a bad girl. But she just did not listen. What could I do? Her friends are the same. Running around.' She took Malaika's hands in hers. 'You were not like that, Malaika. You kept to yourself. I know you were unhappy here and maybe I was too harsh with you —'

'Mama —'

'No, it is true. I was so afraid ... I did not know how to raise a child in a big town like this, and I made mistakes.'

'Mama, we both made mistakes. It's over.'

'Yes, it is over. And it is so good to see you here. We should not talk about the past. It is done.'

'Yes, Mama, it is done.' Malaika retrieved the small *chondo* she used as a handbag from the sofa in the sitting room. 'Jack and I will be in the New Mwanza. This afternoon I am going to see if I can find Freddie. I'll maybe see you tomorrow, Mama.'

Penina frowned. 'Please be careful. I don't know this Freddie. But those *konda* boys ... ' She shook her head.

Malaika hugged her mother at the front door. 'I'll be careful, Mama.'

Jack joined her at the vegetable patch and waved goodbye. '*Kwaheri*,' they said to each other.

Her mother stood on the doorstep, her hands pressing into the small of her back, nodding and smiling at her — an average middle-aged mother, just like any other. Malaika wished she knew none of the statistics. It was too difficult to deny them. It was so unfair. People's mothers just can't get AIDS! Next time she would talk it over with her.

She waved and walked with Jack to the Landcruiser.

'I'M SORRY, MR MORGAN — THE lines are still busy to Nairobi. Can I call you when they get clear?'

Jack swallowed his anger, he had been waiting around the reception desk of the New Mwanza Hotel for an hour. 'I suppose so. I'll be upstairs.' He grabbed a newspaper and climbed the stairs to the dining room and bar where he found a table on the veranda overlooking the street.

The delay in getting his call through to Bhatra did nothing to allay his anxiety at being stuck in Mwanza while Malaika looked for her sister. He could understand her concerns but the girl was seventeen. If teenagers in Africa were anything like they were in Australia, or anywhere else he could think of for that matter, she had probably run off with a boyfriend. From what Malaika had said, she was probably also trying to escape her mother's harassment and fretting about the family curse.

Magic and family feuds! he thought, wondering how long it would take Malaika to realise it would be impossible to find the girl if she didn't want to be found.

His anxiety came from his enforced idleness at a time when his mind was full of the urgency to do something about Bear's death. It made him sick to think that Bear's body was out there in the bush, that his murder was probably unacknowledged, and his murderers running scot-free.

He was anxious, too, about the police. Leaving aside Onditi, whose body might never be found, having lost one of their own would surely motivate them to search for Jack. The redeeming feature was that even if they knew he was in

Tanzania, it would take weeks to get an order against him. He and Malaika would be gone by then.

The same could not be said about Mengoru. The Tanzanian border would not inhibit his revenge once he discovered his plans for Malaika were lost, and probably his ivory too. Jack felt reasonably sure that he and Malaika would be safe from him, so long as he remained ignorant of their whereabouts.

All these tumbling thoughts made him agitated yet again. He stood and walked to the railing. A waiter passed and he ordered a beer.

Malaika had gone shopping for some local clothes. 'So I don't look like such a tourist when I go to talk to Freddie,' she had said. From his vantage point at the veranda rail he could see the whole street. A group of schoolchildren alighted from a bus, dragging their feet as schoolchildren do when in no hurry. A fruit vendor pedalled past on the opposite side, ringing the bell on his three-wheeled cart and calling his wares. A following truck driver began to toot and his turn-boy hurled abuse at the vendor from the top of a mountain of bulging hessian bags.

Two white men entered the dining room wearing *de rigueur* business attire — pale slacks, short-sleeved business shirt and tie. They sat at a nearby table and chatted as they looked over the lunch menu.

One o'clock. Malaika had said she would be gone all morning but hoped to be back by midday. The waiter appeared with the bottle of Safari. Jack signed and took it to his table.

Another bus drew up opposite. Malaika stepped lightly down and crossed the road to the hotel, brown paper carry-bags in each hand. A moment later she appeared at the head of the stairs.

The white men at the next table watched her cross the dining room to stop at Jack's table, where she dropped her shopping bags and put a hand on his cheek before taking her seat opposite.

Jack looked pointedly at the businessmen. They returned to their menus.

'I see your shopping was successful.'

'Yes. I got a few things for you too. What do you think?' she said, looking down at her new jeans and simple cotton top. 'It's not the kind of thing I would usually buy, but it will help me ... what's the word ... blend in?'

'You look great. As usual.' He doubted she could ever fade into a crowd. She just wasn't built that way. 'What time do we leave to find your man?'

'I think I had better go soon.'

'I'll take you.'

'I don't think that would be a good idea for the blending-in. This is Mwanza. Zebras are rare.'

'I've noticed. So have a few others,' he said, glancing at the two businessmen.

'My American friends, you remember the ones I told you about? The ones who came to our Nairobi office? Well, they said it depends on where you are in the world. In London and Paris, zebras hardly rate a second look. In parts of the US, they are a bit of a curiosity. In Nairobi — well, you've seen them in restaurants and such ...'

'I have.'

'But in Mwanza ...'

'Slack-jawed amazement would be my guess.'

'Right.'

'So at least take the car.'

'Mr Morgan? Mr Morgan?' The barman's call carried to the veranda.

'Here!'

'Telephone, sir.'

'There's my call to the office. I'd better take it. Here's the car keys.'

'No, it's too much. If it was a little old sedan, maybe. You take your call. I'll take the bus. See you later.'

'Okay. Bye.' He tucked the newspaper under his arm and followed her as far as the bar where she skipped down the stairs to the lobby.

The barman handed him the phone. 'Please hold while I connect you to Nairobi,' the voice on the telephone said.

After a few moments drumming his fingers on the bar, Jack

assumed it would be another long delay and flipped open the newspaper. A small news item caught his eye.

Nakuru. Sunday.

A policeman was shot in an incident involving two foreigners at a checkpoint in the Rift Valley around midday. The foreigners were believed to be involved in smuggling rhino horn from Somalia. They escaped in a stolen Landcruiser.

'Putting you through to Mwanza,' said the operator.

'Hello?' It was Bhatra.

Jack's mind began to race.

'Hello?' Bhatra repeated.

He thought about hanging up. 'Oh, Bhatra? It's Jack Morgan. Can you hear me?'

'Mr Morgan. Yes, I hear you.'

'Look, there are a few things you need to know.'

'I'm sure. We've had a visit from an inspector of police. Inspector Achieng.'

'I saw the item in today's paper —'

'He was looking for you and Mr Hoffman.'

'That's what I want to tell you. Bear —'

'Mr Morgan, this does not look at all good for the UN. Is Mr Hoffman with you? Where is the Land Rover? And what is this about the rhino horn in your car?'

'I don't know what you're talking about.'

'There was a quantity of rhino horn found in your car.'

'There was no horn in that car before we got to the police station.'

'Not according to Inspector Achieng's sources. They said it was seen in your car earlier that day.'

'Seen by who?'

'By a Mr Mengoru. I spoke to him less than an hour ago —'

'Mengoru!'

'He's coming to see me later. Apparently a highly regarded Party member. He also said that you and Mr Hoffman had a violent exchange. Threats were made. Is Mr Hoffman with you?'

Jack clasped his forehead in his hand.

'Mr Morgan, where are you staying in Mwanza?'

Jack hung up.

CHAPTER 38

PEABODY'S GUIDE TO EAST AFRICA (5TH ED):
In 1858, John Speke set out from Zanzibar on Africa's east
coast and marched into central Africa. When he arrived at
the little village of Mwanza, an enormous body of water
spread before him.

Instinct told him the lake was the source of the Nile,
and he named it Victoria, after his queen.

The bus ride through Saba Saba to her mother's house was a
ride through her childhood. Her school days and all their
horrors, perceived and real, came back.

The bus was not well patronised; people preferred the
cheaper, faster trips in the *matatus*. Although she was dressed
in her local clothes, Malaika felt the people on the bus were
studying her. Maybe they, like her, felt she was out of place.

The *duka* at the bus stop was typical, selling snacks, drinks
and a few essential canned goods. She was told that Freddie
was not there, but Malaika found a young boy who said he
could find him. He ran off with Malaika's ten-shilling note in
his pocket.

Malaika bought a Coke and settled on one of the packing-
case stools, wondering if she would see Freddie, the boy or her
ten bob again. She decided to wait until she had finished her
drink before declaring the investment lost.

The Coke was only half empty when the boy reappeared, grinning. A tall young man ambled along behind him.

Freddie was a couple of years younger than Malaika and certainly looked like a *konda*. His stride was set to a rhythm that only he could hear. It was more of a bop than a walk, as if accompanied by the music now heard on almost every *matatu* in town. His feet moved with one beat while his head and body to another. He wore a red, yellow and black knitted beanie, loose enough to accommodate the Afro hairstyle. His shirt was open to the navel, revealing a foppish imitation gold chain and pendant. Jeans were low on the hip and fashionably frayed. There was a wisp of growth on his chin. He wore no socks and his ankle-high sneakers were unlaced.

As he drew closer, he slowed to a shuffle and his grin spread. He chewed gum with an exaggerated action, occasionally blowing a bubble, then lassoing it with his tongue, dragging it back to his mouth and repeating the sequence.

Malaika took a sip of her Coke as Freddie sashayed up to her table. '*Sasa?*' he asked. It was the rhetorical question: So, what's up? He slipped his hands into the hip pockets of his tight jeans, thrusting his pelvis forward. He flicked his knee to his secret beat.

'Are you Freddie?'

'So who wants to know, baby doll?' His eyes ran down her body to her sandals then up again, lingering on her breasts. He spiked his Swahili with trendy English words. He blew another bubble of gum.

'I'm looking for a friend of mine,' she said, trying to ignore his leer.

'That's cool. I'm looking for a friend too.'

'Someone said you might know where she is.'

'Uh huh.' He sat on the opposite stool, his knee jigging non-stop to the hidden beat. '504s?' he said, looking under the table.

'What?'

'The Levis, 504s?'

'Um, no ... they're local.'

'Look like 504s. You should wear 504s. A body like yours ...'

'So anyway, her name is Ziada.'

He stopped chewing. The pause was barely noticeable. His grin returned and his open-mouthed chewing resumed. 'Blaaaah, blaa-blaa ...' he sang and slapped a drumbeat accompaniment on his knees.

'Do you know her?'

He laughed. 'Baby, I know a lot of chicks. Blaaaah, blaa-blaa ...'

'Yes, I'm sure, but a friend told me you went together ...'

'Another friend? Baby, you got more friends than Freddie! And you're just new in town. Maybe Freddie should be your new friend, huh?'

Malaika swallowed the reply she wanted to give. Instead she said, 'Look, Freddie, I'm sure you have many girlfriends already. Ziada went missing about a year ago and you were her boyfriend at the time and —'

'Hey! Hey! Freddie has a lot of girls. But no girlfriends. I run loose, baby. I'm loose.'

'Okay, okay. But have you seen her? Do you know where she is?'

He stood and thrust his hands into his hip pockets again. 'I don't know anything about it.' He turned to leave.

Malaika leapt to her feet. 'Freddie!' The table rocked and her Coke toppled. It rolled to the edge and dropped into the dirt. 'Freddie, I'm Ziada's sister. I must find her! Her old grandmother is dying and ...' She trailed off, seeing his expression.

Freddie was chuckling at her. He scratched his head through the baggy beanie and dropped his gaze to the Coke bottle under the table. 'Ziada ...?'

'Yes, Ziada.' She held her breath.

'She's gone, huh?' He bent to retrieve the bottle.

'Yes. We've looked everywhere. More than a year.'

Freddie put the Coke bottle on the tabletop with a bang. Malaika stepped back, startled.

He began to chew in earnest again. 'You think she's so different to other kids? Kids go missing. Most people don't care. You should maybe forget her.'

'No! I will not. I can't ... I have to find her. Won't you please help?'

'You aren't listening, baby doll. I said, kids go missing. What's so special about your Ziada anyway?'

Malaika searched for something glib that might appeal to him. She was afraid to risk any of them. Instead, she resorted to the truth. 'I don't know if she's special. She's my sister. That's all.'

Freddie's smile was contemptuous. He slowly shook his head and turned his back on her. Malaika caught a look in his eye that denied his confident veneer. Maybe he let it escape thinking it was safe as he walked away. On instinct she said, 'She may not be special. She's probably just like the rest of us. Afraid. These times teach us to be afraid, don't they, Freddie? This slimming sickness is everywhere, isn't it? But it's all right. Being afraid is okay. If we can help each other.'

He turned and walked slowly back to her, his smile gone. He leaned into her face. She held her ground as he snatched the Coke bottle from the table behind her. He peered at it as if looking for flaws in a diamond.

'Leper's Island,' he said, studying the bottle.

'What?' she whispered.

'Leper's Island.' He dropped the bottle in the dirt at her feet. 'Kids go there,' he said, and bee-bopped his way down the road.

MALAIKA SAT ON THE BEDSIDE chair and reread the newspaper item. 'But there's nothing to say you are a suspect in the shooting.'

'No, but with no witnesses ... it's my word against theirs. And there's Bear's death. When — if — they find the body, they might try to pin that one on me too.'

'No! That's impossible.'

'Mengoru's in on this. He says Bear and I had a huge fight.'

'Mengoru!'

'That's right. He's been in touch with the police. And Bhatra. By now they're probably all aware we're in Mwanza. We have to get out of here. Now.'

'Yes. But he doesn't know where we are. Does he?'

'It won't take him long to find that the New Mwanza is about the only tourist hotel in town.'

Malaika began to pace the length of their room. 'We've got a day to spare.'

'What do you mean? We can't hang around here waiting for him. Let's just split.'

'Jack. I know where Ziada is.' She sat on the bed beside him. 'We can go first thing in the morning. And I promise, if she's not there we can go. Anywhere you want to.'

It was Jack's turn to pace. It would take Mengoru twenty-four hours to reach Mwanza. If they immediately checked out of the hotel, which was an obvious trap, it should be okay.

Malaika sensed him wavering. 'Just this one trip.'

'Where to?'

'Leper's Island.'

'WHAT IS IT ABOUT THIS Leper's Island?' Jack stepped from the fishing boat to the wharf and held out a hand for Malaika. She stepped down and they continued along the row of moored vessels.

'Maybe it's because it's remote.'

'Hmm, I get the feeling that any of these guys would happily take us to Uganda and back — for a price.' He looked to the northwest. The sky over Uganda was clear but a band of cloud to the east threatened to block the morning sun. 'One mention of Leper's Island and zip! Forget it!'

'Maybe we need to try some of the smaller boats?'

They walked along the wharf, past many of the larger vessels they had already tried. 'Here's one. Let me try this time.'

She came back ten minutes later. 'He'll take us!'

LEPER'S ISLAND APPEARED ON THE horizon just an hour later. The narrow boat was built for speed — a useful attribute on a lake notorious for sudden violent squalls. It fairly flew along, its long sleek nose bobbing on an insignificant swell. Jack and Malaika rested in the shade of the fly cover, while the owner sat amidships with one hand on the wheel.

The island was a massive granite boulder with a skirt of greenery running about a quarter of a mile inland from the water line. A few fishing dinghies were anchored around the island. A solitary fisherman sat in each. All eyes followed their arrival.

Huts began to appear amongst the palm trees as they drew nearer.

At the jetty, Malaika was in animated conversation with the boat owner. 'He won't come on shore with us,' she explained. 'He wants to sit on the lake until it's time to go.'

'Just so long as he knows I'm not paying until we get back.'

'I don't think that will make much difference. He says he will wait for just two hours. In two hours he will leave. He is afraid of the lake after dark.'

Jack looked at the rocky foreshore, littered with cardboard and plastic rubbish. 'Do you think the Holiday Inn people have built here yet?'

'And he says that if a storm comes up, we have to run back or he will leave without us.'

'This guy runs a tight ship. Do we have time to search everywhere in two hours?'

Malaika could see about twenty huts, but imagined there were many more scattered about the island. 'Let's go,' she said.

CHAPTER 39

PEABODY'S GUIDE TO EAST AFRICA (5ᵀᴴ ED):
The demise of the East African Community, consisting
of Uganda, Tanzania and Kenya, drove many shipping
companies on Lake Victoria to the wall in the 1970s.

The commercial lake traffic is now very much reduced,
causing the closure of many wharves and forcing the
smaller island communities to abandon their offshore
villages.

The jetty was not long. Missing planks, and planks so rotten
that a foot could fall through, made the going slow. The far
end, where they alighted, was the best part of it. The closer to
shore they walked, the worse it became. The last few paces
were on a single beam; the other beam, and all the planks,
were gone. Malaika suspected that the jetty had been
progressively cannibalised for building materials.

In a direct line from the jetty were the remains of what
would have once been a large timber building. The roof had
been stripped, as had most of the timber lining boards.
The most substantial reminder of the structure was a stone
fireplace. Even that had been partially removed, along with
most of the stone chimney.

'This must have been the hospital,' Malaika said, as she and
Jack passed.

'Hospital? Why would they have a hospital way out here?'

'For the lepers.'

'Lepers? You mean it was a leper colony?'

'Of course. Years ago. The boat owner said they closed it after independence.'

There was not an unruly schoolchild in Mwanza who had not, at some time, been threatened with banishment to Leper's Island — the abode of ghosts and black magic. Malaika did not know what to make of the remainder of the boatman's story — that the island had become a hideout for escaped convicts and smugglers. She decided not to mention it to Jack.

At the rear of the old hospital was the first of a string of huts. They were constructed — if that was the appropriate term — of various materials, mostly flotsam. The inhabitants, one or two per hut, were in a terrible state. Malaika felt guilty about staring into their squalid shanties without so much as a word. But most were too weak, or too despondent, to notice.

'What is this place?' Jack whispered. 'What is wrong with these people, Malaika? Is it some kind of epidemic?'

Malaika had noticed it too. Coughing fits. Excessive sweating. Weeping sores on malnourished bodies. There wasn't a healthy person in sight. 'Not an epidemic. My guess is it's what the western doctors call opportunistic diseases — those that attack when the body can't fight back. Tuberculosis. Malaria.' She glanced around her. 'I think these people have AIDS.'

Jack looked back at the huts they had passed, then ahead to the others. 'How do they live?'

'I guess people make trades ...'

'What have they got to trade?'

A girl, probably a teenager, but so thin as to have no shape or features in her face, watched them from the door of her hut. 'Sometimes it's better not to know.' There was nothing behind the girl's eyes. No curiosity at their passing. No hope.

Malaika searched the wretched faces as they walked. Despair and hopelessness appeared in every expression. No one spoke. At best, they would receive a mildly curious glance from one who was perhaps in slightly better health. There was an eerie silence to the place, like a walk through a cemetery, with scattered shanties instead of tombstones. And where the corpses were yet to have the pennies placed on their eyes.

Jack was searching faces too. 'Hey, Malaika. I've been looking at all these people, but I don't know what —'

'Oh! Neither do I!'

'What?'

She had just realised with a shock that she had been looking for the face of an eight-year-old girl. 'I don't know what she looks like either. Oh, God!' Her shoulders slumped at the knowledge of how foolish she'd been. How would she recognise her seventeen-year-old sister after all this time? 'How could I be so dumb? I just didn't think.'

'No photo of her?'

'Nothing. I should have checked with Mama.'

'Well ...'

'Maybe she'll recognise me!'

'Yeah, that's it. Maybe she'll recognise you.'

'I was nearly grown when I left home. I don't think I've changed much.'

'She's sure to remember her big sister.'

'Yes.' She searched Jack's face for reassurance. 'I ... I hope so ... Oh, Jack. I've brought you here for nothing!'

'C'mon. Let's not give up yet. There's still time.'

At the boundary between the vegetation and where the bare sloping rock began to rise towards a sheer granite cliff, they stopped. It gave them a view over the whole settlement below.

Jack looked at his watch. 'We've been here nearly an hour. There's more huts along there,' he said, pointing to a pocket of three huts clinging resolutely to a crevice in the rock.

'But we haven't seen all of them back there along the beach,' Malaika said.

Jack shrugged. 'Beats me. Which way?'

'Let's check these three. Then we'll go down to the shore and check those along the beach.'

The huts on the rockface, pieces of rusted roofing iron propped up by a tree branch, were even more decrepit than the others; the occupants, more wretched.

At the last of the three huts, only a pair of feet was visible. Malaika thrust her head in. She had become accustomed to invading privacy. Nobody seemed to care. The face that stared at her from vacant sockets was a grotesque caricature of a human. The lips were almost dissolved into putrescent blobs. Skin hung from the cheeks like mouldy dough. Protruding from swollen gums were teeth that made the whole face look like a monstrous mask.

The stench assaulted her. In the hot, airless confines of the hut she almost gagged and felt instantly weak, too weak to push herself away from the body. Then it moved. The body flung an arm across her shoulder. It grabbed her hair. She screamed.

Jack pulled her from the opening and helped her to her feet. Malaika pushed him away and vomited. Jack held her shoulders until she stopped heaving. Her eyes were streaming and she spluttered and coughed. She looked back at the hut. The feet were motionless.

She wiped her mouth and brow with Jack's offered handkerchief. 'Oh ...! Oh ... Jack! That poor ... person.' She shuddered. 'I can't believe it. What kind of place is this? How can ... Where a person can't even die with any shred of dignity?'

'There ... there ...' Jack said, patting her and holding her firmly. 'Take a big breath.'

She slowly disengaged herself from his arms. 'Come on. We'd better keep going.' She took his hand as they climbed down the rocky slope to the line of greenery.

At the first of the huts near the beach, Malaika was relieved to see that the female occupant lay outside the shelter. The close confines of the previous hut had stolen her nerve. Two other women sat with her. One was fanning her with a frond.

Malaika squeezed Jack's hand, then moved closer. The woman's mouth was drawn into pain lines. She was almost panting, rather than breathing. Malaika sighed. How would she know if she was looking at her sister? This woman could be seventeen or sixty. She decided that the search was a total waste of time.

Malaika was about to retreat. Then she noticed the necklace on the person fanning the frond. It was a malachite stone, the size of a green pea. It lay between three red trade beads strung on a piece of fishing line.

She glared at the wearer, at first suspecting that the necklace she had given her sister before leaving Mwanza had been stolen. But was it possible ... 'Ziada?'

The young woman made no response, but Malaika searched the eyes — a little dreamy, like when Ziada was a child.

'Ziada? It is Malaika.'

The girl slowly focused on her. Her mouth opened and closed. She mouthed the word, Malaika.

Malaika might have been looking at a sleepwalker staring at the moon. Oh, Ziada, she thought. Look at you. Your face — it's so thin. And your hair ... a pile of knots. Then she noticed her skin. It was discoloured and she had a line of small lesions from her wrists to her elbows. And there were others on her neck and cheek. Oh, my God ... Oh, my God.

'Ziada. Oh, my *kidogo*,' she said, using the nickname from their childhood.

'Malaika ...' she whispered in reply.

'Jack! It's her! It's Ziada. I've found her!'

She turned back to her sister, taking her in her arms, but she had to break the hug when Ziada began to cough uncontrollably. As it passed, Malaika took her hand. 'Ziada ... listen to me. We're going to take you away from here.'

'Away?'

'Yes, back home.'

'Home? No!' She pulled her hand away. 'No! No!'

'Ziada, listen. This is not the place for you. This is not good. We have a boat.' She indicated Jack who had stepped closer to the shack. 'See, we are taking you home. To Mama.'

'I will not go home. I cannot bear it.' She fought Malaika's hands away from her. 'I will not go home.' She was becoming distressed and tearful.

'Ziada, shh. Shh. We can get help for you. This place is not good for you.'

Ziada began coughing again. When she had it under control, she took a moment more to gather her strength. She sat straight and fixed Malakia with a look of determination in spite of her frail condition. 'Malaika,' she said, tears filling her eyes, 'I'd rather die here than go back to Mwanza.'

'But why, Ziada? Why?'

'Look at me.' She lifted her arms.

Malaika looked again at her sister's carcinomas. She could think of nothing to say.

'You see? You do not understand. And you could never understand unless you see the looks. The pity. No, not pity — disgust! The eyes they give you, knowing that you have it. They fear you.' She showed her arms again to emphasise it. 'They cross the street to avoid seeing you. When your friends just want you away from them, out of their town, you will know what it is like to have this.' Her tears spilled down her cheeks. 'They want you dead.'

'Oh, no, Ziada . . . Oh, no.'

'Until you have felt the shame, do *not* tell me this is not a good place for me. There *is* no good place for me.' She dropped her voice, which had become angry. 'Malaika, you . . . everyone out there . . . cannot know.'

'I want to help you.'

Malaika felt she had almost convinced her sister, but Ziada said, 'Just leave me. We are mostly the same here. There is no need to hide our face. We know each other. We understand what is coming.'

'Ziada, listen, we can go somewhere else! We don't have to go to Mwanza. We could go to . . . to Nairobi!'

'Nairobi?'

'Yes! To Nairobi. I can take you. You can stay with me. You always wanted to go to Nairobi, didn't you? Remember? When you were a little girl. You wanted to run away with me.'

Ziada was silent.

'Nobody knows you there. We will be together. I will look after you. There is medicine . . .'

'Nairobi?'

'Yes, something can be done.' She began to take heart at Ziada's silence.

Ziada turned to the others in the shack. They showed no interest.

'Malaika?' It was Jack. He pointed to his watch.

'Ziada, *kidogo*. We have a boat waiting. But he must leave soon. We must hurry.'

Ziada wavered.

'Come with me to Nairobi, sister.'

'Are you a doctor yet?' A smile crept to her lips.

Malaika sighed, tears of relief came to her eyes. 'Not quite.' She helped her sister to her feet and hugged her. 'Come.'

JACK SQUATTED IN THE BOW of the fishing boat and peered into the gloom of the Mwanza wharf. Behind the boatman at the helm sat Malaika and Ziada, huddled together to avoid the spume.

'Okay! Go! Go!' Jack called back to the helm.

The fisherman turned the wheel and the sleek fishing vessel responded immediately, banking in a tight curve and roaring away to the headland protruding beyond Bismarck's Rock. Jack scuttled to join Malaika at the stern.

'Did you see him?' Malaika wore a worried frown.

'I'm not sure. There was a big guy and a couple of others hanging around the hut near the shore. Better to be safe.'

'I'm glad we hid the car away from the wharf.'

'I would have liked to be absolutely sure it was him. But it's too dark now.'

'What will we do?'

'I still think we should make a dash to Isuria. If it was Mengoru and his friends, they are going to spend time here looking for us. We can get in and out of the village before they return.'

The boatman eased off the throttle and nosed the bow onto the sandy beach.

Ziada looked drained and exhausted but mustered a smile as Malaika helped her to her feet.

CHAPTER 40

PEABODY'S GUIDE TO EAST AFRICA (5ᵀᴴ ED):
Kenya: Population: 21.4 million. Literacy: 69.4% (Male
75.7%, Female 63.3%).

There are 42 tribal groups in Kenya. English is the
official language, while Kiswahili (Swahili) is the national
language.

They crept through long moon shadows.

Jack held Malaika's hand. He could see by her backward
glances that she was anxious about Ziada. But they had no
choice. If Mengoru and his men were in the village, Ziada's
incessant coughing would expose them. He finally convinced
Malaika to leave her in the car until they had confirmed it was
safe to take her to Kokoo.

They knelt behind a bush when the *boma* came into view
across the creek. The cattle and goats were already in their
night pens and an enormous fire burned untended in the
enkang's small enclosure. Within the village, nothing stirred.

'Jack,' Malaika whispered, 'it looks strange to me.'

'Maybe they're all out to dinner,' he answered.

'No, I mean there's no —'

He squeezed her hand. 'Bad joke. Bad timing,' he said with
a smile. 'It's just that you look so tense.'

She turned to him, letting her small frown dissolve into a smile. 'Yes ... I suppose I am a bit uneasy.'

The smile was unconvincing, even self-conscious, but like many of her intimate gestures, it opened her soul to him. She looked so vulnerable he was profoundly grateful she could trust him with it.

A blink took the mist from her anxious eyes. He knew that if he could capture that image, then at any time he needed reminding of her beauty, to remember how much he loved her, it would be that face he would recall.

She inclined her head to show her bewilderment at his gaze. He kissed her. A gentle touch of lips to lips. 'It'll be okay,' he said. 'You stay here if you wish. I'll go in first to check.'

She looked to the village and nodded her understanding. She was silent before turning back to him, her expression that of a gazelle caught in the hypnotic stare of a lion. 'No. I have to do it.' She tried to smile again. 'Thanks, anyway.'

Jack wanted to hold her, to rescue her from her nightmare, but a brittle crack from the village distracted him. A bone-dry timber had exploded in the fire, despatching a contingent of sparks into the violet sky. The reality of the village returned to their thoughts.

'What does it mean?' she asked.

'Someone must have lit that fire, but otherwise ... awfully quiet.'

'Yes. Strange.'

'His car's not here. So I guess it was Mengoru on the Mwanza wharf, after all. This is our best chance.'

They stood and picked through the thorn bush into the clearing. She let him take her hand in the stony creek bed. Beyond the *boma* opening the fire crackled and roared, casting dancing shadows against the hut. Pink eyes shone from the cattle pens.

Malaika led the way into Kokoo's hut.

'Kokoo?' Malaika called softly. 'Kokoo?' No firelight eased the intense blackness.

Jack fumbled in his pocket and found Bear's lighter. It seemed a lifetime since he'd taken it to light the fire at the police lock-up. The feeble flame filled the small hut. There was no sign of Kokoo. Even her bed cover was rolled up. The paraphernalia of her simple kitchen was gone. Jack lit the lamp on the wall above the bed.

Malaika felt the stones at the cooking fire. 'Cold,' she said, as if to herself. Then she looked up at Jack, the truth of it crystallising.

'Maybe she's gone to another village. For a visit.' As soon as he said it, he knew how lame it must have sounded. The old woman could hardly make it to the other side of the compound. 'Or maybe she's in another hut somewhere,' he added quickly.

Malaika stood and looked at Kokoo's bed platform, bare and cold. She slowly shook her head. 'Grass clumps on her bed-head. It's a sign of peace. Or of passing.'

Jack came up behind her and, gently placing his hands on her shoulders, held her firmly to him.

'She's gone,' she whispered.

He kissed the back of her head, feeling the sigh leave her body. Her shoulders dropped and he waited.

The lamp fluttered beside the bed.

He could feel the power of her swallowed sobs. Her shoulders tightened with the convulsions that racked her body. She trembled with the effort, but fought them, keeping them captured inside.

When her breathing calmed, she leaned against him, as if exhausted and needing his body for support.

'What do you want to do?' he whispered at last.

'We'd better go.'

Jack stooped under the cowhide door covering, but black trouser legs and a pair of dusty black shoes blocked his way. An explosion of light erupted in his head, eliminating all else.

HE WAS CAUGHT IN ONE of those frustrating dreams where he was rendered utterly powerless. Even lifting his head became a challenge requiring more strength than he could muster. From experience he knew his only escape was to force himself awake, but this time it didn't work — the dream pinned him down.

He fought it. Penetrating yellow light stabbed his eyes through closed lids. The air roared and crackled around him, hot against his face.

Beyond the dream, he sensed something terrible was happening. He forced his eyes to open a chink and saw Malaika being pulled from the hut by her hair. She made a faint cry — his name. A plea for help.

The night's golden light hissed and crackled at him. He struggled to get to his feet but the ground held him while the black hole of unconsciousness sucked him down again.

AWARENESS RETURNED IN PATCHES, LIKE cameo scenes in a silent movie. In one he was being dragged across the dirt to a place near the fire. Then in another, he saw Malaika struggling with a large man in black, who tore her blouse and struck her across the face.

He grasped at things tangible to clear his head — the soft dust pressing into his cheek, the warmth of the fire on his face, dancing shadows on daubed walls. Sounds. The pop and crackle of the fire, an angry voice — the language foreign, but strangely familiar. A man's thick black silhouette stood before the fire, his shadow gyrating under the influence of the leaping flames.

Jack lifted his head. Malaika was sitting on her heels to his side, just out of reach. A trickle of blood ran from the corner of her mouth. She appeared dazed — her head was lowered, her dull eyes were on the dirt and made no acknowledgment of his stirring. 'Malaika?' His voice came in a grating whisper.

'Ah! The *mzungu* wakes,' Mengoru slurred. He held a gun in one hand and a gourd in the other.

Jack struggled to get his body to a sitting position. His head throbbed with the effort.

'*Mister* Morgan. *Karibu*. Welcome to our party.' Mengoru raised the gourd in mock salute. 'We have started without you. So sorry. Hah, hah. A little drink?' He held the flask towards Jack then clutched it back to his chest. 'Oh! I forgot. *Chang'aa* is not for the *wazungu*. Oh no!' As he raised the gourd to his mouth he took a stumbling step backwards towards the fire.

Jack took the chance to study Malaika. Her blouse was torn, exposing one breast. Braids dislodged from her hair clasp fell like soft black cords down each side of her face. 'Malaika, are you okay?' he whispered.

Her head turned towards him and her gaze followed. He could not recognise her eyes. She was a Dante character — her soul on the brink of hell. Jack's breath caught in his throat.

Mengoru yelled, 'No! No talking!' He waved the gun towards them. 'No talking. Talking to whores ... not allowed ... because ...' He began to mumble, his gaze roaming the ground between them. 'Because a wife ...' He took another gulp from the gourd. 'You and the ... and the blacksmith! The Kunono man!'

Jack struggled to clear his head. Mengoru, in his mad imaginings, had mistaken Malaika for his wife.

'No more running away. Hear me, woman?' he growled. 'You will never leave this village again. You shamed me. Shamed me before the whole village. Never leave this village again. You hear me?' His bloated face broke into an ugly leer. 'Not yet ...' A drop of spittle dribbled from the corner of his mouth. 'Not yet, my sweet wife.'

'You! *Mzungu*. Sit!' He made a threatening gesture with the gun.

'My sweet wife ...' he repeated, swaying as he brought the gourd to his mouth. When he lowered it there were tears in his eyes. His voice was almost a whisper. 'Sweet Penina ... Why did you leave? Why, my sweet?' It was almost a loving lament. 'You know I ... why, I cherished you.' He wiped at his eyes with the cuff of his jacket.

His lip curled into a grimace. 'Cherished you! Hah!' His menace grew. 'You didn't care for me. You and the ... and the blacksmith! You whore! Time to settle it with you ...' He pointed the gun unsteadily at Malaika.

Jack made an attempt to get to his feet but Mengoru moved quickly, giving him a savage kick in the ribs. He collapsed, gasping for breath.

'I said, *Sit!*' Mengoru bellowed. 'Hah! Look at him. Weak! *Mzungu* men are all weak. Look at me!' He staggered as he lifted the gourd high. '*Chang'aa* ... A black man's drink. A strong man's drink.' He held the flask at arm's length, then raised it with two hands like a chalice of communion wine. It splashed into his mouth, the trickle of clear fluid reflecting the firelight.

'You *wazungu* think you own Africa. Well, I tell you something. *I* own Africa. I do what I want. I drink the *machosi ya simba*. I take a woman. Even this whore,' he said, pointing the gourd at Malaika. 'No more running. You see this gun, woman?' He pointed it in her direction. 'Ah? You see this?' His voice rose to a shriek.

Jack felt he must act soon, but in spite of Mengoru's obvious intoxication, the alcohol had not dimmed his awareness or agility. He made another tentative move to launch an attack, but froze when Mengoru turned to him.

'And you, *mzungu*. Do you see this?' He raised the gourd at him, taunting him with a leer. '*Chang'aa*. Man's drink. You know what it is? Huh? Do you? Stupid *mzungu*. *Machosi ya simba*. Swahili. You speak Swahili?' he spluttered. 'No — 'course not. *Machosi ya simba*. The tears of the lion. You know that, huh?' He threw his arms wide, the gun in one hand, the flask in the other. 'Tears of the lion.' He frowned at the gourd. 'My power.' He poured the gourd towards his mouth. The liquor ran down his elbow, drenching his trousers. 'Ha! Ha! Ha!' he bellowed, looking down at his wet shoes. 'The tears have fallen!'

The smell of spirits wafted to Jack on the still night air.

'Fallen! Ha! Ha!' Mengoru's laughter dwindled away. He coughed and his eyes moved back to Malaika. 'Strong like the lion.' It was a growl. 'No one can stop Mengoru. No one!' He thumped his chest. 'The Big Man of the Maasai.'

His face screwed into a look of disgust. 'The Maasai! What fools! What stupid fools I have around me. Fools who know nothing of money. Just stupid cattle. Pah! Cattle. Who wants cattle? Money is what I want. One day ... Don't you look at me like that! You whore! I know you. Spoil it, won't you? Again. You spoil everything I ever ... have ever tried to do. No respect!' he bellowed, jerking the gun towards Malaika.

Jack seized his chance, lunging at Mengoru. Before he could claim him, Mengoru caught him high on the cheekbone with his gun hand, knocking him back to the dirt. Stunned, Jack saw rather than heard Malaika scream *No!* at Mengoru, who was waving the gun unsteadily in Jack's direction, his eyes bulging and his mouth contorted into soundless ravings.

A log collapsed into the fire's white-hot centre, sending silent spark-clouds skywards. An instant before the flash leapt from the barrel with a muffled roar, Jack rolled to one side. The bullet puffed the dust beside him.

Malaika rushed Mengoru, trying to pin his gun arm, but he parried her feeble efforts, pushing her back to the ground with a snarl. He took a gulp of liquor before haphazardly firing a second shot at Jack. It went high.

Mengoru flung the gourd into the fire where it exploded, sending flames spiralling into the night. He smiled over his shoulder at his handiwork and wiped a sleeve across his mouth. When he turned back to level the gun in a two-handed grip, it was in Malaika's direction.

A sudden wind rushed from the darkness beyond the clearing. It tore at the flames and spun a vortex of hot air and ash around Mengoru standing unsteadily at its centre, gun-hand raised. He was distracted for a moment, but with a curse he dismissed the swirling force tugging at his trouser legs and redirected his attention to Malaika.

The wind leapt in intensity, howling and hissing in the night. It seemed to suck every molecule of dust and debris into its core. The air crackled with an invisible energy, like in the instant before a lightning strike when body hair on arms and legs prickles, and a crawling sensation invades the skin. Jack struggled to find the air to fill his lungs.

A flash of colour flew from the darkness, catching Mengoru's eye.

Jack saw it too — a red shape flying swiftly out of the gloom. At first he thought it was human — a diminutive figure in a long red robe and cowl. But a wild shriek, like that of an avenging eagle, filled the darkness. The shape flew through the fire, drawing flames with it.

Mengoru unleashed a terrified cry. He tried to fend it off, but the flames leaping from the red robes were upon him.

They engulfed him, sending him stumbling back and forth in a panic, his spirit-soaked clothing erupting in a fireball.

With an arm sheltering his face from the heat, Jack watched Mengoru grapple with the shape. It seemed to embrace him. He staggered backwards towards the fire, fighting it, cursing, then screaming for God's mercy.

In the last moments, teetering on the edge, he reached a hand to Malaika. A firestorm of ash sparks and flames roared skywards as he fell backwards into the inferno.

THE NIGHT SKY LOOKED THE same. The stars were as bright and as big as they were in the sky above Isuria, but Kireko saw them differently. Here in Laikipia, he knew this sky had been his father's night coverlet as a child. It had covered his grandfather, Lenana, who was the son of the Great *Laibon*, Mbatian. Mbatian was the son of Supeet, who was the son of Kipepete who was the son of Parinyombi . . . '

Kireko recited the litany of his tribe back to Ole Mweiya, who came down from heaven and was found by the Aiser, Kireko's own clan. He then anointed the Aiser as the guardians, the defenders, of the Maasai way.

Under these stars, Lenana, in a misguided endeavour to maintain peace, had made a pact with the British invaders. The Maasai would leave this land of their ancestors so that the whites could farm it and build a railway. In return, the Maasai would be allowed to keep the land of the southern Rift Valley for so long as the Maasai existed as a people. For ever. That was what his *kokoo* had told him since he was a child at her hearth.

Now she was gone. Buried here in Laikipia, as was her wish.

He wondered if perhaps the Maasai were dying too, but were unaware of it. So much was changing. The treaty was never observed. Contrary to its terms, the Maasai had lost much land, even sacred Mount Kinangop, where for generations they had conducted important tribal ceremonies. Kinangop was where Kireko and his age-set brothers should have been holding their graduation ceremony into the ranks of the elders, their *eunoto*, next month. Against the treaty their land was seeping away: to the *wazungu* for their *safari* camps; to the government for their game reserves; to the Kikuyu for their farms.

Now that Kokoo was gone, who would be the soul and the spirit of the Maasai? Who would take over the position of *laibon*? Of the Kidongi clan, the traditional holders of the title of *laibon*, only he and his sisters remained.

Kireko did not want any of it. He had no heart for the tasks of an elder; no patience to sit with the old people to discuss boring matters of protocol, bride-price and the holding of ceremonies; no desire to leave the hunt and the raid.

Many of his age-set brothers had already deserted the ranks of the *moran*. Some were now in the cities, doing Kireko knew not what. But their sons would never know the thrill of the lion hunt. Would never feel the power that a solid spear and a well-crafted shield could give a man. Never know the overwhelming joy of the endless sun-bleached savannah, running unhindered to a distant horizon, where a man's cattle could grow fat and contented.

And even the young women became unhappy at home. The men in the cities had money that could buy them city things. They would not need to tend goats and carry firewood all day or spend the twilight hours of their lives weaving and beading. There were men in the cities who would take a Maasai bride and suffer the taunts from marrying into such a primitive tribe. But the women would lose their tradition. What would become of their children, he wondered. They would be Kikuyu, or Turkana, or Kalenjin, or whatever was the tribe of their husband.

Sometimes he felt the burden of being a true Maasai was too much. He was for ever fighting to keep Maasai traditions alive. It wore him down, like a man whose task it was to carry a heavy stone all the days of his life.

Without a *laibon*, who would carry forward the Maasai stories? Of how thunder and lightning were made? Of Maasinta, the first of the Maasai, the original man? Who would see that the boys learned how to become a *moran*? Who would defend the old ways?

He sighed and took his eyes from the mound of soft new earth and searched the sky again. His *kokoo* had for some years desired the peace of death, so why was his heart troubled?

Something had been left undone. He could not resist it any longer. The message was clear.

It was not the Laikipia sky that gave him the strange feelings. Kokoo had prepared him for this moment, and it was she who told him what must be done. But it would be a burden. A painful burden. He needed the magic of Kokoo yet again.

At his call, the *motonyi* bird swooped out of the night, covering his eyes with its brilliant plumage.

CHAPTER 41

PEABODY'S GUIDE TO EAST AFRICA (5ᵀᴴ ED):
Never forget to take your own water on your game drives.

Ziada was on the pallet to one side of Kokoo's kitchen. She had fallen asleep almost the moment they had helped her inside the hut, but it was a troubled sleep, occasionally punctuated by a lacerating cough.

Jack nursed Malaika's head in his lap, bathing her bruised face in the light of the fire he had rekindled in the hearth.

'How do you feel, Princess? I mean ...'

She slowly opened her eyes. 'Tired.' She raised a hand and caressed his cheek. 'And Princess is okay. It goes way back, doesn't it?'

He nodded, his eyes smiling in the lamplight.

Their meeting at Carnivore was becoming a distant memory to Malaika. Even the few days since Cottars Camp — the period she now considered to be the last days of her previous existence — appeared more like months ago.

She was more than tired. She felt numbed. Since Cottars Camp she had found a forgotten family, been reunited with her community, and had experienced a rebirthing by once again becoming a Maasai — the crucial missing part of her psyche. She had escaped kidnapping and murder, and had witnessed more violent deaths than she could have imagined.

But in the back of her mind was an unsettling sense of guilt. It had lurked there for years, hiding behind the camouflage of her personal problems like finding a place to live, a job, getting an education. Dealing with people like Onditi. There were many excuses and ways to avoid confronting her neglect of Mama, of denying her eight-year-old sister's dream of an escape to Nairobi. Of turning her mind from Kokoo. Even her lovable, irascible brother, Kireko, deserved to be remembered. To be missed. She supposed the guilt had always been there, buried like so much else under a mountain of indulgent self-pity.

And there was Jack, his unstinting presence and his strength unchanged. She had accepted all of his help, to the point of risking his own life and the lives of others. In return she had offered not a single clue to her sudden urge to become involved in historical family turmoil. In truth, her obsession had been unknown even to herself until this last day or so.

She took his hand, put aside the damp cloth he held to her forehead, and sat up. 'I'm so sorry, Jack.'

'Sorry? What do you mean?'

'I'm sorry for putting you through all this. Risking your life. I'm sorry about Bear's death —'

'Hey. It's okay . . . It's okay.'

'But I never knew the cost . . . When we started out —'

'Malaika, Bear's death was not your fault.'

'Maybe. But instead of stopping it there, instead of taking time to grieve, to go to the police, I dragged you all over Tanzania, chasing superstitions. If we had gone to the police then, maybe you wouldn't have to run away. You were right. It was silly. Even me, I had trouble understanding it. Now I do. But it doesn't take away from what you've done.'

He patted her hand, kissed her forehead.

'You see, in these last few days I've come full circle. This is the hut where I was born. When my mother took me away from here, I shut it out. Bad memories. So bad I couldn't bear them. So I blocked them all. Even the good ones. It was Mengoru. He terrified us. My mother, my *kokoo* and I.' She paused. 'Mengoru is, was, my father.'

She shot a glance at Jack, expecting a look of horror, but instead found sadness in his eyes.

'The cruellest father imaginable. Am I a bad person, Jack? Because I can't feel sorry for him. I should feel a loss, but there's nothing there. He terrorised me. It seemed to go on and on. Every day ... for as long as I can remember. I'm sorry that a man has died. But I can't be sorry for losing my father and —'

Jack squeezed her hand. 'Ssh,' he whispered.

She took a deep breath and continued in a calmer voice. 'Wanting to forget is one thing. But I did more than that. I closed the door on my whole life. All the memories were gone. I even forgot my language, and the old stories. I forgot my *kokoo*, and that was the worst. I had no soul. Can you understand, Jack?'

'I ... I think so.'

'A Maasai is only a Maasai so long as she, or he, stays part of the Maasai world. That doesn't mean you have to live in a Maasai village, but there's our culture and the special feeling we have about the land. The myths and the songs. And yes, the magic. When you turn your back on those things, the Maasai part begins to die. But I wanted out of my Maasai life. I tried to become someone else. In the end I was nothing. Just plain *khali* — angry.' She lowered her face into her hands. 'Oh, God,' she sighed. 'There's been such a terrible price.'

'You weren't to know the price when we began. It just went wrong. You can't blame yourself for all that.' He took her hand, lifting her face to him. 'And you saved your sister from that hell hole. Surely that counts for something.'

'Yes. It does. But it's not enough. I have to do more. First, I'll find a place for Ziada. AmericAid has connections with hospitals in Nairobi.'

'Yes ... Nairobi ...'

She brought her other hand to his, trying to read his thoughts. He had not mentioned his plans other than to get out of Kenya — to go to Dar-es-Salaam. 'She feels she can't go home. She's probably right.' Ziada was asleep at last. 'I can't believe there's so much ... prejudice? Yes, prejudice. It's not like us.'

'It's like Bear said — AIDS frightens people. They're like the lepers in the old days.'

'But we Africans think of each other as brother and sister. We help one another. But this is ... terrible. There's no pity. No —'

'It takes a long time to change people's fears.'

'It's wrong.' She shook her head slowly. 'Then, after I've found a place for Ziada, I'm going to do something about the way people treat others with AIDS. The charities try hard, but maybe they don't see what's going on.'

'I guess money is always the problem. Or lack of it.'

'Yes, they need money to do what they do. But maybe it doesn't go to the right places. People think the Maasai's problem is alcohol — the *chang'aa*. They say if they didn't spend all their money on the *machosi ya simba* they would be a lot better off. Everyone's an expert. Stop the tears of the lion and you will stop the tears of the Maasai. Nobody really knows. They get the symptoms confused with the cause. The tears of the Maasai are here.' She nodded towards the sleeping Ziada. 'AIDS is our sickness. HIV brings our tears.'

'Maybe the government and agencies are more accustomed to big projects. Big budgets.'

'Maybe. But they need to understand how these poor people suffer in the villages. Maybe some of the money should go there.' As she said it, she realised she had been guilty too. Working in an aid agency, worrying about budgets and approvals, she seldom saw the private hell in the villages. Maybe she had assumed the West's more tolerant view was miraculously transferred along with their money and their technology. Her failing, she suspected, was due to her isolation from her African community. She'd had no first-hand experience of how the disease affected family, friends, neighbours. It was efficient to adopt a western system to combat a massive problem such as AIDS — but in Africa's case, it needed to be softened. Institutionalised aid did not suit Africa, with its poor understanding of how the disease has spread, and a lack of compassion.

'Governments always think throwing money at a problem will fix it,' Jack said.

'Governments don't talk about things like love. There are no education programmes on AIDS. Or any counselling for victims or their families. What we need is someone in the villages, where the AIDS sufferers live.'

As she began to build on the idea she became more confident of its merit. It was a good idea, a proposal that agencies like AmericAid might support. Her passion rose with the telling — one thought leading to another. She could see a pilot study in Maasailand, and similar programmes with other tribes.

Deep inside, she could not deny that her guilt was a motivator — this was a way to forgive herself for her past sins of omission. It would be her contribution: a payback.

In her excitement, she had failed to notice Jack's increasing withdrawal. He had begun by offering encouraging comments, and then fell to nodding agreement as he stared into the fire, its patterns playing on a lingering remnant of his smile. She hadn't meant to exclude him, but it would be shamefully presumptive of her to find a place for him in her plans until he expressed some desire to be a part of them. He could have at least asked where he fitted in. If he was ever going to say something about their future, surely this was that time.

But he remained silent.

Her hand was still clutched in his. She ran her fingers over the large smooth knuckles and the tendons that snaked up his arm to merge with tight muscles under the soft fuzz of golden hair. His arms were familiar and reassuring. They were arms to love.

CHAPTER 42

PEABODY'S GUIDE TO EAST AFRICA (5TH ED):
The hypothesis called 'Mitochondrial Eve' states that modern humans have their origin in a small African population that lived 200,000 years ago, and of which only one maternal lineage survived.

Hence, all of us are descendants of a single common 'Eve', whose inheritance is still found in our mitochondrial DNA, the genetic sequences which only the mother transmits to all her progeny.

If Jack concentrated long enough, he could detect individual insect sounds within the cacophony surrounding them. When he let his mind wander out over the languid Mara River, the sounds again fused into the familiar background hum of a hot Kenyan afternoon with the sun sliding at snail's pace towards the horizon.

The Dar-es-Salaam bus was due at the border bus station at 5 p.m., about a thirty-minute drive away. Until then, Jack wanted to avoid any unnecessary exposure to either the police or Mengoru's people, so they had pulled off the dirt road and found a shaded place above the river to wait.

Beside him in the Landcruiser, Malaika rested her head on his shoulder. She had not slept well. Ziada, who had probably had a better night's sleep than either of them, had grown bored after half an hour and had walked the few yards to the river's side where she sat on a rock, flicking pebbles into the water.

There were no animals to be seen out on the shimmering Mara plains. Jack again saw within its boundless expanse a similarity to the Australian outback. This time there was no tug of the homeland. With his part in an international incident involving both police and the United Nations, Australia was not a haven, any more than Kenya was. Now he was unsure where *home* was. The thought of leaving Malaika behind tortured him. He had hoped to find evidence of similar feeling within her. But it appeared she had already moved on to her next project. Given recent circumstances, he understood her need to get involved in AIDS work. If it were possible for him to be altruistic, he could have applauded it. AIDS had to be tackled at all levels. The main battle needed massive foreign aid, but there was a place for ordinary folk, people like Malaika, who could help to overcome ignorance and prejudice. However, this was not what he wanted to hear. He wanted to hear how they could continue to be with each other. She had not once mentioned him in her whole plan. At least she had been honest.

'What are you thinking?' she said.

Her voice took him by surprise. 'Thinking? Oh, not a lot.' He felt a twinge of conscience. Perhaps it didn't matter so much now, but he needed to get it off his chest. 'No, that's not right.' As she sat up, he took her hand. 'I've been thinking ... I should be honest too. I need to tell you what happened in Hawaii.'

'The affair? You already told me.'

'Yes, but not the whole story. It was ... it was a lot worse.'

She was silent so he continued quickly, afraid of losing his nerve. It was never going to be easy. 'The woman I had the affair with ... well, she was, she invented these situations where we would take risks, a dare. Do you understand, dare?'

She nodded.

Now he wondered how to describe their games without going into the sordid details.

'Jack. Let me ask you something. You made a mistake?'

'A big mistake,' he said, nodding.

'And you're sorry?'

'Yes.'

'Then that's all I need to hear.'

'You know, Malaika, with anyone else I would take that reprieve and run a mile. But with you I just can't leave it at that. I hope we have something worthwhile between us. I really do. So I need to get this off my chest. I've never been good at communicating my feelings. That was one of the problems between Liz and me — I bottle things up. The night in Hawaii might be behind me, but I can't close it until I tell you about it.'

'Is it bad?'

'You'll have to be the judge of that.'

'Then tell me quickly.'

'I don't think I need to go into all the ... you know, details, but one of the games involved a gun.' He watched her expression carefully as he went on to explain the game of Russian roulette. 'The really dumb thing was, I actually began to play this ... this game! I know, it was stupid and I can't really explain what drove me to do it, but I ... I pulled the trigger. I pulled it three times before I finally came to my senses. Then I walked away.'

Malaika pressed his hand.

'That's not all. I didn't realise, maybe I was too damn selfish to even think about it — I didn't realise she needed help.' He swallowed hard. 'Not five minutes later she used the gun to kill herself.'

'Why?'

'I have no idea. I hardly knew her. That must seem a bit strange, but ... well, that's how it was between us ... '

'You had no idea why she did this?'

'No. That's another reason I felt bad. A person shouldn't just die like that. For nothing. Later on I read — in the *Honolulu Star* — that she was a call girl, known to the LA police. No ties. No family.' He ran his hands through his hair. 'The thought that I could have got into such a desperate situation drove me crazy for a long time. I began to doubt my sanity. It made me examine every decision I'd ever made.'

'Was it the reason you and Liz broke up?'

'Yes. It wasn't the affair that finished us, although I was disgusted with what I'd done. All of a sudden I was dissatisfied with my life, my job, and I began to doubt what Liz and I had planned. It changed me in a way I still don't understand. I just knew I couldn't settle down with Liz.'

'And now?'

'Now I think I'm getting over it. I still have some guilt there. It was hell not being able to tell the people close to me.'

'I meant, how do you feel about your life now?'

'Now I'm ... Until a few days ago, I felt at home.'

'I'm glad. And I'm glad you wanted to talk to me about it.'

'You most of all. Malaika, you're the most important person in my life.'

She looked into his eyes. He thought he could read something in her expression. 'Jack, what are we going to do?' she said.

There was so much in his head, things he wanted to say; they built up, making it difficult for him to speak. The weight of the moment prevailed. 'Malaika, I have to get away.'

'I know. The police ... But what then?'

'I ... Malaika, come with me. Come to Dar with me.'

'Jack, I can't! Ziada ...'

'I know. But after Nairobi. Come to me.'

'In Dar?'

'Yes, in Dar. For a few days. I was thinking maybe South Africa.'

'South Africa! Why?'

'It's safe. Nobody deals with South Africa these days. I couldn't be found there. I could get a job. You could ...' The absurdity dawned.

She sighed. 'Of all the places where a couple of zebras could live, I can't think of a worse one.'

He shook his head at his own foolishness. 'Of course.' Again he searched for an answer in her eyes.

Her brow furrowed and her eyes filled to brimming. 'Jack ... I can't.' Her reaching hand paused midway to him before falling, defeated, into her lap. 'I just ... can't.'

MALAIKA STOOD IN THE GOLD of afternoon light, watching Jack disappear in the crowd near the ticket sellers. The border bus stop was the usual riot of disorganisation. The long-distance Tanzanian and Kenyan buses that congregated at the border checkpoint around dusk each day fought for road space with the smaller feeder services and *matatus*.

The Landcruiser keys lay cold in her hand. She stared at them, feeling as she had when driving down the muddy road to Isuria just days ago — sliding slightly out of control and at a speed she knew was dangerous. She needed to steer things back on track. To find the brake while she got things into perspective. To think.

She was glad Jack had told her about his past. Somehow she loved him all the more for his mistakes. He seemed more vulnerable and therefore more human than before. She was also relieved to find that making big mistakes was not her exclusive realm.

Accepting he must get out of Kenya, that his life may be at stake, was okay. But would she ever see him again? They hadn't really discussed it. They had circled it, stalked it. They had made tentative swipes at it. But when an attack on the matter appeared imminent, one or the other had shied away.

She regretted not taking the chance earlier that day, by the river, to tell him how she felt about him. It was a strange sensation. Here was a man who respected her. He even accepted her mistakes and shared his most private thoughts with her. As equals. For a long time, she now realised, she had been expecting him to revert to something like the male African stereotype — chauvinistic and unfaithful. In his own quiet way, Jack had proved her wrong.

She must tell him before he climbed into the bus. She began to rehearse it. *Jack, I love you. I'm sorry it's taken me so long to tell you. But I do. I love the way you make me feel. I love the way you love me. I understand we could have problems —*

people can be cruel. But so far we've made it work. Somewhere in the world is a place where zebras can be happy.

The bus to Dar-es-Salaam breathed fumes into the crowd as it shuddered and throbbed with the irregular grumble of its ancient diesel motor. It was nearly an hour late and, although the driver would be eager to leave before dark, he was unlikely to do so without cramming as many paying customers on board as possible. Most of these were with Jack, scrambling for tickets.

She began to doubt her plan. Was it wise to tell him she loved him as he was leaving? What could he do — jump from the bus? And then? It was blackmail. No, she couldn't do that to him. It was up to Jack. It must come from his lips.

Malaika looked beyond the dust cloud into the western sky. In a little while it would be dark.

Between the rows of buses, behind the clutter of travellers, bags and assorted vehicles, a lone figure emerged from the latest arrival — a *matatu*, belching smoke and rock music into the pandemonium.

It was a familiar shape, although the cloud of golden dust surrounding him made the man impossible to recognise. He held a spear and a shield. Long gangling legs carried him above rather than through the crowd. People glanced up at him as he swaggered past. He continued towards her until, stopping within touching distance, he said, '*Sopa*, Angel.' He gave her a languorous smirk.

'*Hepa*, my brother,' she managed to reply in Maa, remembering her Maasai manners at the last moment.

Neither spoke for some time. Malaika was caught in her amazement at again finding Kireko in such odd circumstances. Meanwhile her brother appeared slightly amused at her uncommon silence.

She wanted to hug him but dared not. Finally, with typical Maasai understatement that she knew would please her brother, she said, 'You are far from your *enkang*.'

'I am.'

'What is your journey?'

'To Mwanza. You have heard about Kokoo?'

'Yes. The people of the *enkang* were returning as we left at noon today.'

'She was at the heart of my life.'

'Yes.' She felt awkward discussing her great-grandmother in the midst of such an irreverent scene. 'How is your wound?' She wanted to inspect the dressing but knew it would embarrass him.

He nodded in dismissal.

'Did you say Mwanza?' she asked. 'To see Mama?'

'And to make peace.'

'And then?'

'To return to Maasailand, as *laibon*. Kokoo said I must.'

Malaika nodded, surprised at the strength of his resolve. It was quite unlike the immature response she might have received from him just a few days ago. Then again, she had probably changed a lot in the same time.

Jack joined them as the Dar-es-Salaam bus gave an impatient blast on its horn.

'Jack, this is my brother, Kireko.'

Jack appraised the tall man. 'G'day.'

After a pause, Kireko took his extended hand, African-style. He remained solemn, studying Jack for the brief time it took them to grip palms, clasp thumbs, then palms again.

Jack turned to Malaika. His sad smile failed to conceal an agony of doubt behind his eyes. Without a word he pulled her to him. His embrace squeezed the breath from her but she clung to him ferociously. When he released her, he explored her face as if he had never set eyes on her before. As if he were trying to recognise her. Or to remember her.

'I'll try to ...' he started.

'Where will you ...' she said simultaneously.

'What?'

'Did you say you'd ...?'

'... a hotel. But ...'

'What?'

'Malaika.' His fingers gripped her upper arms.

'Yes?'

The bus grunted with the release of the air brakes.

'There was so much I wanted to say.'

An indisputable blast from the bus signalled the driver's intentions. It moved forward with a half-dozen travellers still clambering aboard.

'You must go,' she said, letting her hand linger on his cheek. 'You'll miss it.'

Jack tore his eyes from her. The bus jerked forward, the brakes groaning as they released.

'Go!' she repeated, giving him a gentle push.

He hesitated, and then jumped aboard, struggling to find a grip on the step. 'Take care!' he shouted and slung his bag over a shoulder to give her a wave. He mouthed silent words. She tried to make out *I love you* in them. Perhaps they were there. Perhaps they were only there because she so desperately wanted them to be there.

The bus swayed and groaned onto the road and Jack was lost from sight.

'This man,' Kireko said, nodding in the direction of the disappearing bus, 'he cares for you, sister.'

'Do you think so?'

'It is in his eyes.'

The bus was gone now, smothered by dust clouds from the following flotilla of vehicles, each trying to beat the sunset.

'Where is his friend?' Kireko asked as the roar of motors died away.

'His friend? What do you mean?'

'The big one with hair of red and grey.'

'Bear? How do you know about him?'

'I saw them at the police station in Seyabei. His friend shot the policeman.'

'You saw it? You saw the shooting? Kireko! You're his witness. A witness!'

Kireko raised his eyebrows at the unfamiliar English word. Malaika explained it in Maa. 'You saw Bear shoot the policeman. You saw it.'

'Is that not what I said, sister?'

His expression made her laugh. The news delighted her. Jack could fight his case.

Abruptly her laughter stopped. He was gone. In the haste and confusion she could hardly recall their last conversation. Maybe he had said he would call her from Dar. She had not paid attention. She was more interested in what she had wanted to say, but in the end had no time to say it.

Would he call? Could she tell him she loved him over a thousand-mile telephone line? Would she have the chance to tell him that her long-lost brother held the key to his return to Nairobi?

And if he knew, would he come?

CHAPTER 43

PEABODY'S GUIDE TO EAST AFRICA (5ᵀᴴ ED): Getting there from Australia: Qantas runs regular flights to Harare from Sydney via Perth. Connections to Nairobi, Dar-es-Salaam and Entebbe are provided by regional airlines such as Kenya Airways and Air Zimbabwe. Onward travel to provincial cities, such as Mwanza and Kisumu, should be arranged via the respective domestic operators.

David Shakombo swung AmericAid's Peugeot station wagon out of Peponi Nursing Centre into the traffic stream headed towards town. Waiyaki Way was its usual rainy morning disaster as cars converged on Westlands Shopping Centre.

David was a competent driver and Malaika watched the passing array of shoppers in silence.

'The newspapers are still saying there's no news on Mr Onditi,' he said.

'Yes.'

'I feel bad for saying those nasty things about him, you know?'

'Well, he was a nasty man. You weren't to know.'

'No. Only God knows these things.'

He gave a *matatu* a toot and went on with more mundane topics. She wasn't particularly interested in office politics and an occasional *Hmm* from her was sufficient for him to continue unabated.

Her boss, Joe Kibera, had pulled some strings to get Ziada's admission approved. It had taken Malaika three weeks more to get her to agree to go. Overall, it had gone as well as she could expect. One of the nurses took them for a familiarisation tour. Ziada had crept around the communal areas and the room she would share with three others. Malaika had sighed with relief when she made a reluctant nod of acceptance.

She thought it unlikely that her sister would be seeing the city any time soon, as she remained very self-conscious about her condition. But the centre would monitor her medication and help her to regain her strength for the long fight ahead. Later, there would be opportunities to rejoin the community, to work and to build a life as normal as her sickness would permit.

With her mind now at rest over Ziada, Malaika would redouble her efforts to find Jack. She didn't know Dar-es-Salaam and had no idea where he might stay.

She had begun calling hotels a day after she arrived back in Nairobi, tired to the point of exhaustion by the overnight drive from the border. Many attempts were needed before a connection could be made. Then the lines went down for nine days. Following the eventual repairs, the network backlog made it impossible to make a call from the office, so she had spent every spare hour at the international exchange, pleading with the operator to try her call one more time. When her bribes were successful, the apathy of the Dar-es-Salaam hotel receptionists was the next problem. After four weeks she had succeeded in contacting just seven hotels — with no luck.

Last Tuesday, when a phone call arrived for her at AmericAid's office, the receptionist accidentally dropped the call without recording the caller's details. Malaika nearly took his head off for his incompetence. When she calmed down she reminded him of proper office procedures. However, from his description of the 'funny *mzungu* accent', she felt sure it was Jack.

An ache developed in her chest when she thought of him,

alone in Dar, perhaps construing her continuing silence as indifference. She needed to tell him she loved him. More urgently, he had to know that Kireko was the witness he needed to clear his name in the police killing. More than once she found herself planning a dash to Dar. According to Sandra, Kenya Airways made daily flights at 2 p.m.

She wondered what her chances were of finding him in a city of some two million people. Indeed, she had no idea if he was still in Dar. As far as she could remember, he had planned to stay only a few days before flying to Jo'burg. Air Tanzania did not fly to South Africa, but Sandra said air charter companies were making a packet from businessmen and well-heeled tourists by skirting the ban.

'Malaika?'

'Hmm?'

David was looking at her with a puzzled grin. 'I said, do you want to get out here while I go to park the car?'

'Oh!' They were in Moi Avenue outside the office. 'Yes ... Sorry, David, I was thinking about something.' She climbed out of the car and entered the building, nodding to the young US Marine on guard duty at the entrance.

'Oh, Miss Kidongi!' The receptionist stopped her as she was about to go through into her office. 'I had a long-distance phone call for you just now.'

'Who was it?'

'From Dar-es-Salaam.'

'Who was calling?'

'He did not say.'

She glared at him.

'Truly. I asked him, "Who is calling please, sir?". And he did not say.'

'A phone number?'

'Nothing. But I heard the operator say Palm Beach Hotel,' he added sheepishly. 'I'm sorry, Miss Kidongi. Perhaps he will call back or ... '

She did not see the remorse on the boy's face but muttered, 'It's all right, Henry,' as she scrambled through the contents of her handbag. She found her ID card and sighed with relief.

Henry brightened at her smile. 'Oh, and Miss Kidongi, Mr Kibera would like to see you as soon as possible.' But she was at the door. 'Miss Kidongi?'

His voice followed faintly down the corridor behind her. 'Miss Kidongi?'

On Moi Avenue she jumped into a taxi. 'Airport,' she said.

THE WINE WAS CRISP AND cold. Pineapple and ripe pear flavours and a lingering hint of oak on the palette. Or so it said on the bottle label.

A wing tip dipped as the pilot made a fractional correction to his course. The darkened cabin thrummed to a change of beat until the jets settled back to their monotonous thirty-five-thousand-foot hum.

According to the route map displayed on the in-flight entertainment screen, they were over the Australian red centre. The acrylic window obscured the boundary between vast empty land and limitless sky. Pinpoints of starlight dwindled towards the horizon, finally disappearing where the black featureless mass of the outback lay. Not a glimmer of light appeared below them. The route map said an hour and twenty minutes to Sydney.

He shook the last drops of chardonnay into his plastic glass.

The stewardess was nowhere in sight. People were asleep in their tilted seats, heads slumped in uncomfortable positions. The lucky few, alone in the centre row, were lying at full stretch, pillowed and tucked up.

He pressed the call button. A faraway *ding* came from the rear of the cabin.

The wine label read *Rosemount Chardonnay. 1989.* The new vintage.

How's the chardonnay?

Hmm, not bad.

Rosemount. A friend of mine in the Australian High Commission gets it for me. There's no Aussie wines on the UN's duty-free list.

It's tough in the tropics.

It has its moments.

Yes, the tropics had been tough, but not in the way he had expected. When a similar jumbo flew him to Africa, some nine months ago, he'd had a simple plan. Be cool, keep the head low, and avoid commitments and complications. The long boring month in Dar-es-Salaam had given him time to reflect upon it. He had failed in all respects.

There was little else to do in Dar other than think. And wait. Waiting for his fake travel papers to come. Waiting for confirmation from the charter company. Waiting for the hotel's daily power outage to end so they could chill the beer. He hated waiting. Dar-es-Salaam was hot. It was boring. And worst of all, it was not Nairobi.

He remembered the view from the balcony of his apartment on Nairobi Hill. Uhuru Park spreading before him, the Kenyatta Centre dominating the skyline. The Intercontinental Hotel.

Nice dress.

Thank you.

White suits you.

She had been wearing white at the bus stop the evening they parted. A white tee-shirt and blue jeans.

'Be careful,' was all he could think to say from the bus.

'I will,' she had shouted back.

Oh, he could have said more, but *Be careful* was all he could trust himself to say at the time. Things were happening too fast. He was a fugitive. If he went to the police there would be a trial. *Trial?* Who was he kidding? He would be lucky to live long enough to get to the police station. Mengoru's backers would make sure of that. No nosy *mzungu* would be allowed to put the finger on their ivory business in court.

He wondered again whether, if he had told her he loved her, she would have changed her mind and come to him in Dar.

After he'd realised he was in love, there were a number of opportunities to tell her. In Musoma at the Railway Hotel, for instance, when he knew he must be in love for agreeing to take part in such a crazy excursion. Or that last night in Kokoo's hut when his heart ached at her despair.

But he couldn't say it standing beside the bus in the red light of dusk, trucks roaring past, dust clouds whirling about them. The press of the crowd and the toot of horns. There were officials everywhere, checking travel papers, stamping passports.

Who was he kidding? How hard could it be? *I love you.* It was a simple statement. It was so easy to get perspective on it now, sitting in a jumbo, where the altitude and alcohol fashioned scintillating logic.

During the days he'd waited for the charter company to get his entry permit to South Africa, he'd had time to regret his inaction. Of course there were many responses she may have made. But he hadn't told her.

He had planned to do so as he returned, ticket in hand, to where she waited for him at the bus. But instead of saying, *Malaika, I love you. Whatever happens, I love you. And I want us to be together always*, he made some inane comment to her brother while the passengers bustled about them, with bundles and bags, pushing and shoving.

'Go,' she had said, searching his face for the words unspoken.

Then she had put her cool hand on his cheek — her *kiss*.

'Can I help you, sir?' The flight attendant was at his seat.

'Another chardonnay, please.'

'I'm sorry, sir, that was the last of the Rosemount Chardonnay.' She extinguished the call lamp on the overhead console.

'What else do you have?'

'Would you like a Koonunga Hill Shiraz?'

'Yeah. Why not.'

'I'll just take those for you, shall I?' She gathered the empty bottles and glided down the darkened aisle towards the galley.

Malaika was constantly on his mind. Even when he was boarding his mid-afternoon flight in Dar, he had sensed her presence while watching a Kenya Airways plane arrive from Nairobi. It had taxied to a stop beside his aircraft. He felt compelled to watch until the passengers were on the tarmac. But his final boarding call arrested his attention. By the time he was through the gate and onto the tarmac, the Nairobi Airbus was being refuelled and cleaned. It bothered him to miss them disembark, but he dismissed it as just another sentimental notion.

Right now Malaika would probably be getting her AIDS work started. She had said she'd target the Maasai first, but similar clinics would be needed for other tribal groups. Each tribe had their particular cultural and social barriers to be tackled. Who knew if her plan would succeed? Simply overcoming the prejudice could take a lifetime. Education on safe sex was not going to be easy either. How did you change the African male's attitude to his women? But until the billions began to roll in, Malaika's plan was a good start to turn the tables. To beat the curse.

What did a boy from the Australian bush know about African curses? About magic? Something had happened that night in Isuria that even two knocks on the head could not explain. When the blanket blew across the fire, just before it hit Mengoru, setting him alight, he thought he saw the old woman's eyes within the folds of the material. She had such distinctive eyes. A trick of the light, perhaps.

Malaika was sure it was her great-grandmother. She had later found a handful of orange and blue beads near the fire, but Jack reasoned they could have been there for days. Could have belonged to anyone. She might never have been convinced without the return of the villagers from Kokoo's funeral. They had taken her body to where she was born, somewhere up north. Malaika didn't know what to think then.

That made two of them. He didn't want to mention it to Malaika because he wasn't sure of the relevance. And it wouldn't have helped her condition to make too much of it. But on his return from the creek on the morning following Mengoru's death, he saw a glint of light in the remains of the fire. It reflected the dawn in a rainbow of colours. When he kicked aside the ashes he found a glass prism. It was still warm.

The prism was in his pocket when he arrived in Dar-es-Salaam. In some curious way it was a comfort during the time he spent holed up in his hotel room. He set it on the windowsill, where it caught every speck of light, whether sunlight or moonlight, and splashed it on the walls in a kaleidoscope of colour.

Late one afternoon, while he was staring at the place where the rainbows were formed, he had a wonderful insight. He suddenly knew what he must do. In the days following, he refined it, tested it. He wanted it to work so badly he didn't trust his thinking, afraid he would overlook a hidden trap.

Sometimes, when the airless hotel room lay hot upon him, denying him sleep, Malaika would come. She would appear in the prism's rainbow on the wall. The copper of her skin; her long braids with the malachite clasp. When clouds teased the moonbeams on the prism, she would prowl majestically across the room, letting her blood-red garment flutter to the floor. The hint of almond about her eyes; the all-over, smooth caramel colour from ankles to nape; the black aureoles of her firm breasts teasing him, just out of reach of his fingertips; her smile — a peep of the moon on a cloudy night.

If he had shown her the prism by the river that last afternoon, if its revelation had come then rather than in Dar, he would have had a plan. He could have explained how he wanted to be with her for ever — hell, he almost did when she gave him her secret kiss at the bus station — but first he had to get back to Australia.

She went to Nairobi with Ziada. He went to Dar-es-Salaam and waited.

The more he thought about it, the better it seemed. He would tell the story of the dead policeman — witness or no witness. He would return to Kenya through the diplomatic route, perhaps under the auspices of Interpol. It would help to avoid any 'accidents' the ivory poachers might try to arrange. It was his best chance to clear his name, and to find Bear's murderers. It was his only chance to see Malaika again.

With his new plan he needed another set of papers, which seemed to take for ever. Well, the best part of a month — but it seemed for ever. Endless warm Safari beers, antiquated telex messages to Sydney and Canberra. The delay was a blessing in disguise. If not for his enforced stay in Dar-es-Salaam, with only warm beer and the prism for company, he might not have decided to return to Sydney rather than disappearing into the pariah state of South Africa.

He tried to ring Malaika. For days the lines were down. He was disconnected at the other end on his only successful attempt. Then there was a problem with the Nairobi exchange.

The morning before his flight home, he finally got another call through to AmericAid. She was not in the office.

'Would you like to leave a message, sir?' the helpful voice had asked.

'Yes, please tell Miss Kidongi that ... that ... No. Never mind.'

There would be time to say the things unsaid when he returned. A telephone made for imperfect communication. He wanted it to be right when he asked her to marry him.

Jack, can zebras ever be happy?

The answer was yes. *Absolutely* yes! The real question was, where can zebras find acceptance as people, as lovers, beyond the prejudices of race? That was not so easy. There would always be the few who would stare and make judgments. But Kenyans were more accepting than many. And Nairobi had been good for them at times. There was probably still a job for him in the UN, when all the legal matters were sorted.

Yes, Nairobi had been good to him.

Hey, lady! What's your problem?

I don't have a problem.

Who the hell do you think you are anyway?

Me? An African Princess.

Well, I wouldn't care if you were the Queen of friggin' Sheba.

Well, bad luck. I'm Maasai.

She'd said she was going to start her clinic in some place called Laikipia — the Maasai homeland. It was where her family's curse, Sendeyo's curse, started. Jack imagined a place of windswept isolation. Bear would probably know it well.

Tell me again why we're camping?

To experience Africa.

I see. Can't we experience it in the Seronera Lodge?

No.

In the distance he could see the lights of Sydney beyond the blue-black mass of the Great Dividing Range. Jack felt good about his decision to live in Africa. It was the right one for him. For them. What was it Bear had said? *Watch it, buddy, Africa'll grow on you. It's outlasted three wives.*

He wondered if they would ever find Bear's body. Mengoru's men had probably buried him deep in the bush, miles from anywhere.

Or maybe, like a Maasai warrior, they left his body in the open, under the stars, to be taken by the predators of the African night.

Jack smiled. Bear would have liked that.

AUTHOR'S NOTE

The short extracts from Kenyatta's inaugural speech as Prime Minister of Kenya were sourced from *Harambee — The Speeches of Jomo Kenyatta*, Oxford University Press, Nairobi, 1964.

The other characters portrayed in *Tears of the Maasai* are fictitious with the exception of the *laibons* (*oloiboni*), Mbatian, Lenana, Sendeyo and Seggi, who are important historical figures. The author has taken many liberties in depicting the events of their lives.

The conflict between the brothers Lenana and Sendeyo originally came from Maasai oral history. In researching these stories and in interviews with various members of the Maasai tribe, the author found two different opinions regarding which brother was the true successor to Mbatian. The interpretation adopted in *Tears of the Maasai* is arbitrary, and the actions attributed to the brothers are purely for dramatic effect.

The life and behaviour of Lenana's son, Seggi, is a total fabrication. It should not in any way be taken as a reflection upon the real character.

The author recognises the high esteem that the title of *laibon* holds within Maasai culture, particularly the historical positions depicted in *Tears of the Maasai*. No disrespect was intended to any person living or dead, nor was the telling of this story meant to harm the reputation of these important Maasai leaders.

ACKNOWLEDGMENTS

It has taken a long time, thirty years in fact, to reach this point. Remembering the people who have helped get me here is something of a challenge.

There are those who have unwittingly contributed by being part of events that were pivotal to my decision to at least begin to write.

I remember a cycling tour through Provence with a friend in 1998. The weather was unkind, but, as it has for eons, the mistral sharpened the resolve — in this case, it was to do something about that story I always wanted to tell.

Joy Atkin invited me to join an informal group sharing a common and chronic urge to write. In this company I received the critical appraisal and encouragement needed to sustain me through the months, the years, of self-doubt.

The group morphed over time but thanks go to all involved. The special few who persisted through the countless rewrites and remained supportive during the whole painful process must be mentioned individually.

James Hudson persisted through chapter after chapter and then did it all again in appraising the final manuscript. He was always honest and would often plant the seed of an idea to bring the story to life.

Linda DeVitre, while raising a family and managing the daily crises that go with the job, could still find the time to critique *Tears of the Maasai*.

Our gracious host, and a gentleman of the old school, Keith Youman, not only made us feel at home, but was our literary referee. Not a syntax error or illegal change of tense escaped him.

The feedback from James, Linda and Keith was all the more valuable as it came from writers I greatly respect.

Although not part of the group, I am blessed with two great supporters and diligent readers of drafts and 'finished' manuscripts. I pity, and thank them. They are my daughter-in-law, Sophie Avgoulis, with a nascent writing talent which I am sure will soon emerge, and my darling Rosalind Williams, who has been my strength and a continuing source of encouragement.

FRANK COATES